I0685074

First Published in Great Britain by Amazon.com via Create Space in 2014
Copyright © 2014 by C. E. Sundstrom
Excerpt from Grave Misgivings *Phoenix*
Copyright © 2014 by C. E. Sundstrom

The moral right of the author has been asserted.

All characters and events in this publication, other than those clearly in the public domain, are fictitious and any resemblance to real persons, living or dead, is purely coincidental.

All rights reserved.
No part of this publication may be reproduced, stored in a retrieval system, or transmitted, in any form, or by any means, without the prior written permission of C. E. Sundstrom, nor be otherwise circulated in any form of binding or cover other than that in which it is published and without a similar condition including this condition being imposed on the subsequent purchaser.

ISBN 978-0-9924741-0-2

Printed and bound by Amazon.com via Create Space

Follow on Twitter @ cesundstrom
Follow on Facebook @ http://www.facebook.com/cesundstrom
Website http://cesundstrom.com/

Cover Concept & Design by Lacey O'Connor.
www.laceyoconnor.com

Grave Misgivings

Awakenings

By C. E. Sundstrom

For Joy

Thanks for all your love, support and patience.

Sorry about the weeds.

Much thanks to everyone for their support, proof reading and honest appraisals.

Michelle Daniel

Lisa Kyllo

Melanie Pearce

Christine Stonehouse

Len Sundstrom

Margaret Sundstrom

In Memory of My Mother

Margaret Rose Sundstrom

1937-2014

"Hope is a waking dream"

Aristotle

Prologue

Sunday, February 12th, 2006.
11.35 A. M.
Kinglake, Victoria, Australia.

"Monsters!" I say absentmindedly as I peer over the top of my dog-eared novel, distracted from my fantasy world by the chatter coming from my geriatric box television. It had always been my intention to upgrade my T.V to something created this century though when push came to shove, I just couldn't bear to retire old faithful and its unique milky pink picture quality. My television has character, which is undeniable. Unfortunately that is its sole redeeming feature.

"Yes, Michael. Many children of pre kinder age show a propensity to make up stories about Monsters," Carmen Montague, T.V psychologist extraordinaire says determinedly as her shimmering tangerine dress sends my head dizzy with some sort of mild epileptic fit.

"Really," Doug Sullivan says as he tries unsuccessfully to display some interest in the topic he has been blessed with today. He can't help but wonder if a subject such as this is the reason why he decided to take up journalism in the first place. Surely there has to be a more relevant topic for his talents to cling to than this drivel. "Does the research show why this would be the case? Is it simply a matter of growing minds letting their imagination run wild?"

"You would think that would somehow be the case," Carmen continues as she leans forward, trying to add an air of anticipation before she releases her no doubt extraordinary insight into the inner mechanism of a toddler's brain. "However, the latest research from Cambridge shows something more deliberate is taking place."

"How so?" Doug drawls as he too leans forward, as if they are about to exchange some form of massive secret, keeping the rest of the world ignorantly in the dark.

"Well, the latest results are somewhat anecdotal at this point but the researchers are already making some surprising findings."

That's code for this is interesting hearsay, I guess.

Carmen continues, "They have discovered that there seems to be a direct correlation between children inventing imaginary monsters and a child's desperate need to feel loved."

"So to clarify this for the viewers out there," Doug says with a cheery grin of disdain towards the camera, "you are saying that young children invent monsters in order to gain some attention when they are feeling lonely or neglected?"

Carmen nods, "That is a little over simplistic but generally speaking you are correct in your assertion. Young children invent monsters as a devious and deliberate way to manipulate parents into spending some time with them………"

My mind begins to drift as their words become unintelligible. Their conversation becomes white noise as I ponder this last statement. I say to myself, "Is that what I did? Was I just seeking attention as a child?"

It makes sense to me now that I am an adult, though there is nothing sensible about imaginary monsters.

"Julie!" I hear a familiar voice call out to me. I pause, considering the validity of what my ears have heard. The notion that he is here is too crazy to even contemplate.

I stare blankly outwards into the room as the weathered novel slips through my careless fingers. A fog descends, blanketing the room. Eventually it becomes disturbed by an unseen breeze. To my surprise the décor has changed. All my furniture is gone, replaced by a single bed covered in all manner of soft toys. As I watch I see a tiny hand reach out from under the bed and snatch a black and white striped bunny with oversized frayed ears, down to the floor and under the bed.

Flopsy! How I loved that bunny to death. He got me through such tough………...what the hell!

I shake my head as I realize I am standing like a ghost in my childhood bedroom, bright pink floral walls and all. I must have been about four or five years old, judging by the toys and décor. I watch, like a ghost as I consider the fanciful notion that it must be a younger version of me under the bed. I recall how that bed had been my fortress, offering me protection from the monsters that would hound me mercilessly back then. Flopsy and I spent many an hour hiding from the creatures of my darkened imagination.

I have little time to consider the insanity of the transformation in front of me. I remain transfixed by the memories held in the relics of this room, relics which are all now well lost to the ravages of time. Even Flopsy has gone to wherever soft toys go when children grow too old to play with them anymore. Two questions scream out in my brain; why have I travelled back in time to this moment? Why am I here?

As if by magic, some semblance of an answer mysteriously appears as my bedroom door opens and a familiar face peers inside. He glances in my general direction as a smile forms on his face. I gasp as I catch my breath.

Dad!

My father's attention drifts from me as if he cannot see that I am in the room. He makes his way to the single bed and gently sits down. As he does so, a leg clad in white stockings is pulled to safety under the bed.

"Hey Cupcake," he says as he stares absentmindedly at the callouses on his hands. There is no reply from underneath the bed, just the rustling of a younger version of me as I no doubt fortify my barricade of soft toys around me. My father tries again, "Hey, you're gonna miss it Cupcake. This is a special night."

"What's so special about it?" I ask from under the bed. It surprises me just how squeaky my voice is at this age. It is amazing the little things you forget as time marches on.

My father smiles, "Well, it's hard to explain exactly. Why don't you come out and see for yourself?"

"No!" I sob firmly. "I can't."

I stand and walk towards my father. I stop right in front of him, though he fails to acknowledge my presence. I reach out to touch his hand and am shocked that my fingers pass right through his. I sigh as I regain my faculties and shake my head, "I guess this is just a daydream after all. Hell, it seems so real, though."

I flop onto the floor, resigned to simply enjoy the wonderful daydream for as long as it lasts. I had forgotten just how wonderful, caring and patient my father was. It was such a short time that he was involved in my life. I must have been around nine when he left without trace. Where did he go? I don't remember. My mother just said he wouldn't be back again. He either left mother for someone else or he passed away suddenly and, for whatever reason, she felt the need to shield us from this trauma because of our tender age. I suspect the latter is most likely for he hasn't tried to contact me in my adult life. Though there is always an element of doubt in these things, for I have searched for him on several occasions without success. There must be some record somewhere if he has passed away. There just has to be.

"C'mon Cupcake," Dad cajoles. "The stars are shootin' across the sky tonight, lighting up the world in a fireworks show you may never see again. This is something to behold Cupcake, something you may never see again."

"I don't wanna see 'em!" I squeak. "It is a trick just to get me to come out. I am safe here. I want to stay here."

I glance out the window through the flimsy lace curtains. I see a comet fly through the sky, bright blue tail of flame before it suddenly evaporates and is gone. My father stands and walks the short distance to the window. I follow. He moves the curtain aside as he calls out to me, "C'mon Cupcake. This is incredible. You can see them as clear as anything from here. You don't want to miss this."

"I don't care. I'm scared to come out. They are still here," I offer from my hiding place.

I stare out the window as I reach for my father's hand once more without success. I stare in wonderment at the scene before me. A comet streams across the sky to our left. This one is closely followed by another.

"I don't remember this night," I say to myself. "Why don't I remember this? This was surely one of the precious memories I would hold onto. Why would I forget this? Why?"

"C'mon Cupcake, come out from under the bed. The monsters have gone now. They are scared of me."

The thought suddenly hits me. I spent more nights than I care to remember hiding under that single bed, safe in my cocoon of soft toys, eyes closed firmly so that I couldn't see anything. I would even hum a familiar tune in order to block out their noise as they moved around the room. It was a simple defense, but one that worked for me. I stand as an adult now, looking around this imaginary world from my past. There is no sign of monsters of any sort in the room.

"No, they are still here. It is not safe."

I am beginning to think, this was one of the days that I defiantly refused to come out from my hiding spot. I must have missed what would have been the most incredible night of my life with my father. I shake my head as I consider just how foolish I was as a child. Without considering the stupidity of my actions I begin to move towards the single bed.

"They won't hurt you Cupcake, not while I'm here. I'm big enough and ugly enough to handle those mischievous ratbags that invade your room. They are nothing but pussycats, all bark and no bite," my father says in his usual comforting though confused manner.

As I seat myself on the floor next to the bed, I hear my younger self laugh a little between sobs. We both say in unison like we are twins, "Dad, cats don't bark!"

I lie on the floor and peer beneath the bedspread draped over the bed. I see a pair of glowing eyes blink shrouded in the dim light amongst the toys. To my surprise she flinches backwards a little then spits defiantly, "Stay away from me! Are you one of them? Leave me alone!"

I am dumbfounded that she can see me. I struggle to contemplate how this is even possible. I struggle as I search for the right words, "I am……I am…..I……"

"Who are you? What do you want? Leave me alone……..please…….leave me alone."

"Darlin', please little darlin'. I mean you no harm," I stammer. "I am just a friend, come to help you feel safe."

A kitten spits in my direction, hidden in amongst the soft toys next to my younger self.

Oh my God! Socksy, dear Socksy. I had forgotten all about you. We were inseparable in our day. How could I ever forget you?

"No!" she whispers as her eyes burn with terror. "You are one of them. You have come to trick me. You are going to hurt me. My heart hurts. I am scared. Please leave me alone."

I remain focused on the task of reassuring my younger self, though I am concerned by this revelation that she may be in pain, "Are you hurt darlin'? Why don't you come out and I can help to fix you up? I am your friend. I will make the monsters go away."

"No," she whispers as her body shakes involuntarily. She struggles to gasp for breath as she begins to have an asthma attack. She breathes awkwardly for air as she tries to state her case, "they will......come and get me....they.... will grab me......they will hurt me.......they will not leave me.....they hurt me.....they hurt me all the time.......they will.........."

"Hey darlin'," I implore. "Slow your breathing. C'mon Baby. Breathe slowly and carefully. Focus on breathing in and out. You are safe here. I won't let anyone or anything hurt you."

I watch as she tries to control her breathing. She coughs and splutters as she struggles to remain in control. She looks so fragile and scared witless. Was this really how I was back then? Was I so terrified of monsters? Was I looking for attention from my father? Did I feel that deprived of his company? This is surely something more than that. How could something imaginary provoke such terror in someone so innocent? I wonder if there was something else going on. Was there something real that was scaring me senseless back then? Maybe the only way I could explain it was to call them monsters? Were the monsters just adults in my life?

I shudder as I feel sick to my stomach. Was someone hurting me? Was I being abused in some way by someone trusted by my parents? Was it a family member of a friend close to us? What did they do to me? Think, what did they do to me? Was I......?"

A hand reaches out and grasps me by the shoulder.

"What the hell?" I scream as I clamber to my feet, arms flailing out like a thrashing machine.

"Hey, hey, it's just me," Peter yells as he stumbles backwards. "It's just me. What's going on, anyway? Why are you lying on the floor?"

"I.......I......" My heart pounds vigorously as I look around the room seeking clarity. Everything is normal. My childhood bedroom has gone, so has the bed. Little Julie has vanished. I sigh as I realize my father has gone too, taking with him the wonderful comets I missed seeing as a child. "I......I....."

Peter laughs as he tilts his head on the side, a bemused expression spreading across his face, "Is that all you've got? You're not making any sense. Do you know that?"

I feel the anger well up inside me from a dark place that I didn't know existed: a place hidden deep within my being. I push Peter roughly with both hands as tears well in my eyes, "You've ruined everything. That is what you've done. You've ruined everything."

"What have I done?" Peter asks as I storm from the room. "Hey Sweetheart, what have I done?"

I choose not to answer as Peter's question sticks in my head, echoing over and over again. I search desperately for a place to run and hide; a place where I can find solitude, a place where I can get my head together, a place where I can find an answer to Peter's question.

I run from the house, my bare feet skimming over the rough stones leaving a trickle of blood in their wake.

I find no credible answer.

I feel so foolish.

I wish my Dad was here.

'Warning'

Cherish their laughter,

Share their abundant joy.

Marvel at their wonderment.

Look at the world as it sparkles in their eyes.

Enjoy this time so short.

Guard their innocence well.

For ever present in the shadows,

Darkness lurks ominously, while deceit dwells.

Chapter 1

Monday, February 13th, 2006.
Early Evening.
Toorak, Victoria, Australia.

A summer breeze passes silently, though with an unmistakable, underlining strength and urgency to its movements. It causes the first batch of Autumn Oak leaves to dance like subservient puppets; subtle movements controlled by an omniscient being through invisible strings. They rustle, scamper and race across the manicured pathways and lawn. Some even become airborne; pirouetting elegantly before they fall limp to the ground. All becomes still as a strange breathless calm descends over the garden.

Cassandra skips lightly across the dew covered grass. Dutifully Toto, her faithful Scotch Terrier, marches close behind her. He is unperturbed by the cardboard ears now dangling awkwardly from his collar; remnants of an adventure they have shared less than an hour ago. He has endured far worse indignities over the last few months, not that he is worried. He simply loves any opportunity he gets to play with Cassandra in their spacious wonderland she refers to as 'the front yard'.

"Mary has a little lamb, its fleece is white as snow," Cassandra sings cheerfully as she moves towards the roses her mother has tended lovingly for so many years. The garden bed holds over a hundred different colored bush roses interspersed with a straight line of standard 'Iceberg' roses at the front. She is well aware of the rules; she can look but not pick any of the flowers here. However, the little daisies flourishing intermittently in the lawn are fair game. Neither of her parents seem greatly concerned by her regular daisy harvests which she uses to create exquisite 'fairy bouquets'. She never gets in trouble for her floristry. To her parents, they are simply weeds, little more than fodder for the lawn mower.

"Darling, it's time to come inside. It's getting cold," her mother gently calls from the second floor balcony. There are several hours of daylight left; however, the cloud cover is increasing and the cool night air will soon be closing in. She doesn't want Cassandra to get a chill. Not again. She has spent the last four weeks recovering from the flu. Maybe, in Cassandra's eyes, her mother is a little over protective. However, that is her role and her right. After all, she is a mother and knows first-hand just how cruel this world can be.

"Yes mom," Cassandra calls back politely. She knows it is rude not to answer when spoken to. She has learned the hard way what the consequences of ignoring her parent's instructions are; a most painful experience for her backside. One she is not keen to revisit.

Cassandra plans to obey her mother precisely; as good girls always do. With a mischievous grin engulfing all the features of her lily white face, her crafty mind slowly formulates a plan as to how she is going to achieve this goal. She hasn't come all the way across the front lawn to miss out on smelling some of the wonderful perfumes emanating from her mother's precious garden. Surely she can risk incurring the wrath of her mother and yet still have time to reach the flower bed without being caught. All she has to do is hurry. She quickens her pace, her blond ponytail bouncing behind her as she continues to walk away from the house.

A sudden gust of wind encircles the little girl, pulling at her light cotton dress and ruffling her hair. It is fleeting in its disturbance, though vigorous enough to grab and hold Cassandra's attention. In amongst the low murmuring whoosh, Cassandra hears a familiar voice whisper, "Beware!" The mysterious voice is soft and enticing, a friendly tone which remains untarnished, even as it delivers its fearful warning of danger.

Cassandra brings a finger to her lips as her eyes dart this way and that, searching for the owner of the voice. She appears unperturbed that there is no one in the garden which surrounds her. Earnestly she whispers, "Shhhhhh! Mom doesn't like you and anyway I am too busy right now to deal with your nonsense!"

Cassandra continues on her way, walking towards the garden, at a slow yet steady pace. She knows she will be in trouble if caught disobeying her mother's simple instructions. She also knows her punishment will be far worse if her mother catches her talking to her imaginary friend once again. Her mother simply doesn't understand; there is no way she can. From Cassandra's limited experience she has gained enough knowledge to know that all adults seem to lack the ability to believe in what cannot possibly exist. This ability appears to be a child's talent. It requires the untainted pureness which comes from possessing a truly open mind. A gift for the young; it allows them to recognize the strange and unusual, while embracing all its joyous wonderment.

She stops, crouching to smell the red roses planted at the front of the bed, just behind the 'Icebergs'. They are her favorites. The blood red roses have a dark black center. They have a strangely hypnotic effect which draws the curious to move ever closer. Their strong fruity perfume makes Cassandra's nose tingle as she inhales their bountiful fragrance. Closing her eyes, she exhales prior to drawing a second deep breath through her nose. She smiles as the familiar fragrance wafts in, triggering a pleasant, satisfying sensation once more.

Perfect!

Cassandra tries to ignore the racket Toto is making. In her mind he is being very bad today. For some unknown reason Toto is barking aggressively behind her, trying unsuccessfully to capture her attention. The only thing the agitated little terrier manages to achieve is to break the tranquility Cassandra is trying so desperately to savor. It is uncharacteristic of Toto to bark so much. He is normally so quiet and docile. Finally, Cassandra's frustration overwhelms her.

"Shhhhhh, Toto. I'm trying to concentrate!" she yells, scrunching her freckled face. Cassandra stays firm while admonishing her usually loyal pet. She refuses to grant him the satisfaction of distracting her, even for an instant. She refuses to acknowledge his unrelenting insolence. Standing up, she smooth's the wrinkles out of her bright floral dress and prepares to move to the next line of roses.

The little dog takes no notice. His rampant barking continues unabated. Slowly he begins to growl intermittently between his nippy barks. Though greatly annoyed, Cassandra decides to continue to ignore him; she knows she doesn't have much time left. She moves towards the next rose, bending down and breathing in its more subtle fragrance. This particular pink rose generates a gentler, musky scent which swirls up from deep within the heart of the flower. Cassandra, however, is unimpressed. Her face contorts as if she is in great pain as she shakes her head vigorously.

Not as good!

Cassandra jumps to her feet and turns, in a single fluid movement. The frown on her face disappears in an instant, replaced by fear and confusion. Wide eyed, she watches in horror as Toto begins to run down the driveway, towards the front gate. She is just in time to see his tiny white paws flying across the blue stone paving as he skates rapidly away from her. Toto slides around the corner of the drive, barking ferociously, before regaining his footing and scurrying down towards the main entrance leading to the road. He disappears, hidden by the elegantly manicured line of box hedges. His barking, however, still resonates throughout the spacious garden.

"Toto!" she screams as she gives chase at a much slower pace. Her open toed, leather sandals make it awkward for Cassandra to run. Toto has never behaved like this before and she is eager to discover the source of his distraction. She is desperate to catch him before he reaches the road, fearful that he may escape from the grounds and run straight into the traffic outside. There is no time to go back to the house and change into her old, scruffy runners. She has no choice but to run as fast as her footwear will allow for she fears in her heart that Toto is in great peril.

Cassandra comes to an abrupt halt. She concentrates, listening intently to the first of three distinct sounds. The first mysterious sound is made up of two short pops; a little like party balloons bursting, some distance away. She suspects, however, it is not balloons. It is a sound she can't quite place; something completely foreign to her innocent mind. It is a sound which seems strange and out of place in this quiet leafy suburb. A sound she has not heard before. She frowns as she wonders what it might be.

The second sound she knows all too well. There is no mistaking it, nor the trepidation it stirs in her heart. It is the sound of Toto, some distance away, emitting a short, blood curdling squeal of pain. She has heard this sound once before when her father accidentally walked backwards, stepping on Toto's paw as he cursed, "That damn stupid dog!"

Cassandra is confronted by a far more disturbing sound, a sound which sends a chill coursing down Cassandra's spine. It is a sound which radiates outwards, touching everything in the garden, changing the atmosphere in a most detrimental manner. It is the sound of all-encompassing silence.

She pauses where she stands for what feels like a lifetime. Listening, waiting, yet there is no sound, just silence.

"Toto!"

Her heart beats vigorously; tears begin to cloud her eyes as Cassandra runs to the front gates. Peering through the solid iron bars she tries desperately to look up and down the road, searching for her dog, to no avail. The gates are recessed back between two giant, red brick pillars. Her vantage point only allows a limited view in either direction up the street. She can see a portion of the road, the footpath, the nature strip and some parked cars. Toto, however, is not in plain sight.

Fearing he has disappeared down the street and maybe even been hit by a car she pauses, considering her options. Her mother will soon be looking for her; she knows there is not much time. She has been warned so many times, by both her parents, to never open the gates, not even in an emergency. However, she knows if she obeys this rule, she may never find out what has become of Toto. After all, he may be lying on the road, injured. Worse still he may be dying.

Her mind races as she tries to grapple with the predicament of her situation and come up with a acceptable solution. Finally she reconciles her conflicting thoughts. She is going to get into trouble for disobeying her mother anyway. Surely it won't be any worse if she opens the gates too. If she is quick, her mother may never know the mischief she has been up to today.

I need to find Toto.

"Beware little one!" hisses the breeze as it passes Cassandra's ears before lovingly caressing the nape of her neck.

"No!" yells Cassandra defiantly. "I need to find my dog."

Cassandra scampers to the back of the brick pillar which holds one of the huge, wrought iron gates. Standing on her toes, she can just reach the electronic keypad. She flicks open its outer casing to reveal the numbered buttons on the touch pad. She has seen her father punch in the eight digit code many times. It is a little game she plays; watching him type the code as she memorizing its sequence. Last week she surprised her father by proudly reciting the code to him before he typed it into the keypad.

On that particular occasion, Cassandra's father had turned to face her with a shocked and thinly disguised disapproving scowl which spread quickly across his face. Slowly, regaining his usual unflappable composure, he bent down on one knee and addressed her face to face. Though quiet and calm in demeanor, his face exuded his infamous 'this is serious' look. Cassandra knew she was in trouble, though chose to remain still and silent, waiting to be chastised for whatever misdemeanor she was guilty of. Her father's weather hardened features gave no indication that he might be amused, not even in the slightest. Anyway, Cassandra doesn't believe he has a sense of humor. She has never seen this side of him displayed, not even in private. He is a hard man who deals with hard people, in his line of business. If he has a softer side, he certainly hides it well.

"That is very clever, Angel. I hope you will keep that as our little secret," he drawled in a softer tone which Cassandra was unaccustomed to. "However, Sweetheart, I need a special favor from you."

"What is it Daddy?" Cassandra asked, barely containing her excitement.

"You must promise me you will never open these gates yourself or tell anyone else what the code is, no matter what they say to you. No matter what they do. It could be dangerous. Very dangerous!"

Cassandra was pleasantly surprised by her father's milder tone. She has been in fear of him at times. He makes quite an imposing figure when you consider he stands at 188cm tall and combines his imposing stature with a severely terse manner. Though, on that day, she was not overcome by any feelings of apprehension.

She said sweetly, "I promise."

She was so proud that her father had noticed her and had taken the time to talk to her face to face; such a rare event. He is a very busy man, usually completely preoccupied with his work. Some weeks she doesn't see him at all. She just hears the sound of his arrival, coming home late, during the dark hours of the early morning. His black Lexus glides slowly to a halt over the loose cobble stones outside the front door. She peers through the curtains from her second storey bedroom window, trying to catch a glimpse of him as he arrives home. It is hard to make out his features in the dull moonlight, as he moves swiftly to the front door and out of sight.

Cassandra's mind drifts back to the task at hand. Placing a finger on her mouth she thinks carefully. Tongue sticking out between her teeth, she concentrates. She types quickly onto the keypad.

Eight, Seven, Three, Six, Nine, Two, Two, One.

The mechanism buzzes into life, clanking and screeching as the cogs spring into motion and the gates begin to separate. Cassandra claps her hands excitedly as she watches with delight. She runs, squeezing through the central gap as a minimal opening appears. Anxiously she continues to run down the driveway, towards the footpath. Once there she looks to the right, scanning the horizon. Nothing, absolutely nothing!

Spinning on her heal, looking to the left, she gulps, trying to remove the knot which has suddenly surfaced in her throat. Her brain races as her tender mind tries desperately to work it all out. She has a clear, unobstructed view of the scene laid out in front of her. However, she comprehends nothing of what she sees. It just doesn't make any sense; who are these people? What do they want? Eyes wide open, heart skipping a beat, she tries to rationalize the scene before her.

A shiny black limousine is parked at the curb, two men standing alongside the vehicle. One is dressed immaculately in a black chauffeur's uniform, complete with peaked cap and highly polished black shoes. At first glance he looks like a taller version of 'Parker' from the 'Thunderbirds' with his wispy grey hair protruding from under his cap. He is standing near the car, holding Toto in his black leather gloves. Toto is limp in his arms. Cassandra watches the smartly dressed stranger as he walks around to the passenger's side of the car and gently places Toto on the front seat. As he leans towards the car, the sleeves on his suit jacket rise up to reveal multi-colored tattoos extending from his wrists. Though the top of the tattoos remain hidden, enough of the picture is exposed that Cassandra can clearly ascertain the image they portray. To Cassandra the tattoos seem to be babies climbing the stem of a tree. However, they are actually cherubs with golden wings, clinging desperately to a bloody dagger with a skull handle. Even though she fails to comprehend the inspiration behind the drawing, she still finds the image is a little scary.

The man stands up and turns to look squarely at Cassandra. He studies her from head to toe, assessing all her features. A disturbing smile slithers across his wrinkled face. He winks at her as he runs his tongue across his lips from one side of his mouth to the other, like he is preparing to partake in a bowl of delicious ice cream smothered in chocolate syrup. Cassandra feels uncomfortable. She feels the man's smile is deceitful. She senses that this guy is creepy; someone not to be trusted. Cassandra always trusts her instincts.

The second man is shorter, much shorter, even though he still towers over Cassandra. He has dark, short cropped hair and is slender and fit. He is impeccably well groomed, dressed smartly in a dark blue, Armani business suit complete with a white carnation positioned in his lapel. In Cassandra's eyes, he looks a little fake. He is a bit scary too, particularly with the deep scar that runs from the corner of his mouth, across his cheek, all the way up to his ear. Her eyes remain transfixed on this scar as she wonders what type of accident could produce such a hideous injury.

Scar man walks slowly towards Cassandra as she stands, feet glued to the footpath. Sensing the movement towards her, Cassandra instinctively wills herself to take a few hurried steps backwards, as she prepares to run. She halts abruptly, somewhat curious, as the man says with a syrupy, disarming tone to his voice, "Wait, I just want to help."

Cassandra stands still, her eyes watery and fluttering somewhat, as she hesitantly lifts her arm and points towards the man who placed Toto into the car. The chauffer moves slowly and deliberately, closing the door, thus sealing Toto inside the car, out of Cassandra's reach. Shaking a little, her voice wavering and uncertain, she pleads earnestly, holding out both her hands to emphasize her request, "Please.....Give me my dog!"

Scar man crouches down in a deliberate manner. He is aware the little girl is scared. He attempts to reassure her by coming down to her level. He smiles broadly, exposing a mouth filled with gold capped teeth. One tooth in the front sparkles in the sunshine exposing the diamond that is embedded into its surface. Softly, Scar man calls out, "Don't fret little one. We were just about to take him to the vet for you. As you can see, he's not well."

Cassandra remains wary of the stranger, her parents cautioning words ringing in her ears. She doesn't understand what Scar man means. Toto was healthy a minute or two ago, why isn't he healthy now? Have the strangers done something terrible to him? Or has he been in an accident?

The man's accent sounds similar to some of the strange men who work, from time to time, for her father doing what he calls 'errands'. They are scary too. If possible she tries to avoid them whenever they come to the family home. When she does encounter her father's part time employees, she chooses to ignore their attempts to engage her in polite conversation. Instead she runs like the wind, back to the security and safety of the house.

Bewildered, she asks clearly, hands planted firmly on hips, "What's wrong with him?"

Scar man pulls a packet of cigarettes out of his inside pocket, pausing as he considers the reaction of the girl in front of him. Deciding to err on the side of caution he replaces them back into his jacket pocket. Looking at the pavement, trying to hide the evil lurking behind his eyes, he considers his words carefully. His goal is to use words that will be easy for the little girl to understand. He keeps his sentences short and to the point, only providing essential information that he wants her to know. He speaks softly, with a convincing air of sincerity, "He ran out in front of us. Chasing a cat, I suspect. We had no time to react. Our car hit him. He's not well. He needs to go to the vet. Don't worry, little darlin', the vet can fix him up."

Toto hasn't moved since Cassandra first caught a glimpse of him in the arms of the chauffer. Now he is in the car and she can't see him at all through the tinted glass windows. She is increasingly concerned about the state of his health. Her five year old brain is desperately trying to work out what she should do next. Her parents cautioning words, about strangers continue to ring loudly in her ears. She asks nervously, "Will he be okay?"

Scar man smiles more broadly, sensing he is making progress with the girl. He begins to feel confident that the task bestowed on his shoulders won't be so difficult after all. He speaks to Cassandra slowly, not wanting to rush or startle her, "Of course he will, Darlin'. But we need to get him to the vet straight away. There's not much time. We haven't even got time to boil an egg."

"I'll go and get Mom," Cassandra says acknowledging the gravity of the situation. She turns and begins to run back towards the gates and the driveway leading up to her house. She runs for the briefest moment; no more than a few steps taken.

"No!" Scar man yells, halting Cassandra in her tracks. She slowly turns back around to face him, fear visible on every feature of her face. She does not like the stranger's abrupt and aggressive tone. Scar man inhales deeply as he calms himself, knowing full well that the innocent eyes of children can see deceit and danger more readily than the tainted eyes of an adult. He continues more softly, realizing he has made a crucial error. Speaking softly, he tries to salvage the situation, "No need for that. You don't want to upset your mom when there ain't no good reason. I'm sure she gets angry with you when you do something wrong."

Cassandra nods, thinking back to the terrible tongue lashing she received once when she picked a large bunch of roses for her mother. Her current situation is far worse and she remains worried that she will be in trouble for a number of misdemeanors. She knows she will experience an appropriate punishment once they are discovered by her mother.

"Yes, she gets mad at me, sometimes."

Scar man smiles, sensing he is back on the right track. He wants to push forward his advantage; hoping victory is close at hand. "I'm sure she will be happy, when you do something good. We can take Buster here...."

"Toto!" Cassandra declares defiantly. With courage beyond her tender years, she maintains a safe distance from the Scar man.

"What's that?" Scar man asks, confused and taken aback for a second by Cassandra's sudden change in demeanor.

"His name is Toto!" Cassandra declares more earnestly, placing her hands on her hips to emphasis the point. "Not Buster!"

This was the name she chose for the dog when she first laid eyes on him as a tiny pup, carried in by her father in an open shoe box filled with tissue paper. In her mind, he looked like a living ball of cotton wool back then; so terribly cute. There was no way in the world she would ever contemplate a complete stranger calling him by the wrong name, for any reason. This was simply intolerable.

Scar man smiles, realizing quickly that this isn't another impossible problem rearing its ugly head. Just a small misunderstanding which he can easily rectify, "Yes, of course. We can take Toto to the vet and get him fixed up good and proper. I'm sure your mother will be so happy."

Cassandra studies the smiling face of Scar man, trying to determine if he is indeed a good man, a man she can trust. She feels certain, in her heart, that Toto needs some help from the vet. However, a sticking point remains. A problem she cannot reconcile in her mind. She labors over whether or not she can trust these men while her problem weighs so heavy on her mind. After a few moments of reflection, she shakes her head and says simply, "I can't."

Scar man is fearful he is losing her attention. He finds children such a frustration to deal with; that is why he has actively chosen to have none of his own. Kids are simply an unnecessary nuisance; of no conceivable use at all. He decides to try and keep her talking. If he can keep her talking for long enough, she is bound to reveal what her concerns are. Once her concerns are exposed to daylight, he knows he can use his glib tongue to twist her words around to his advantage. Even if he can't allay her fears, maybe his stalling techniques will give him a chance to move closer to her. Maybe he can move close enough to be within striking distance; time will tell.

"Don't you want to help Toto get well?" he asks as he slowly stands up, stretching his body back to its normal height.

Cassandra reacts swiftly as she nods vigorously in response, "Oh yes, mister. It's just that I'm not allowed to go with you."

Scar man stands pensive, with one hand on his chin. In an instant, a thought flitters into his brain. It produces a mixture of adrenaline and hope to begin coursing through his veins. He starts to smile in a manner that barely hides his sinister intent. He now realizes what the problem is. He has no doubt this little girl has been well trained by her rightly cautious parents. They know the inherent risks associated with their particular line of business. They have surely instilled some measure of safeguards into the brain of their only child. They would have taken these precautionary steps in the hope of protecting her if she ever found herself alone in a situation, just like this one.

He asks simply, "Have your parents told you not to take rides from strangers?" Cassandra nods vigorously, sadness clearly evident on her face. Scar man holds out his gloved right hand and says in a friendly manner, "Well that's easily fixed. I'm Steve and I'm glad to make your acquaintance, my Darling."

Cassandra smiles as relief spreads through her entire body. Steve is not a stranger anymore. According to her parent's strict rules she is now free to go with him and get help for Toto. Her parents will be so pleased with how 'adult' she has behaved today, once they find out. She curtsies rather than taking his hand; she feels it is the right thing to do.

"Hi. I'm Cassandra and I'm 5 years old."

"Well Miss Cassandra, how about we take Toto to the vet. We can have an ice cream while he is being fixed, if you like," Steve says, his eyes glistening with evil delight. He knows success is close at hand.

"Can I have strawberry? That's my absolute favorite!"

"Strawberry happens to be my favorite too," Steve chimes, barely able to contain his excitement. However, if the truth be known, strawberry ice cream makes his skin come out in hives. He avoids anything he suspects may contain strawberries. It is not a life threatening problem; he simply loathes anything with strawberries in it. This has been his way since he was a very young child. Anyway, he knows it won't be a problem. No one will be eating ice cream of any flavor on this day.

Cassandra skips merrily beside Steve as he walks towards the open back door of the luxury car. She pauses as she looks into the car. From where she is standing she cannot see who is sitting in the back seat. However, she can clearly see someone is there, lurking in the shadows. All that is visible is a pair of female legs with a green and red tattoo, a distinctive image of an Iris flower bearing sharp teeth. This tattoo is clearly visible to Cassandra on the lady's right thigh. The woman is wearing black, leather, knee high, lace up boots with stiletto heels. Her upper body and face are obscured by the darkness of the vehicle's interior.

"Don't be afraid, Honey. I won't bite," she says in a husky, sultry voice. The mystery lady's words beckon Cassandra towards the seat, even though she still has grave reservations. She likes the lady's mothering, soft tone of voice. She sounds just like one of her Aunties. They are always kind towards her and shower her with the most amazing gifts on her birthday and at Christmas.

Looking up from the car, Cassandra spies a dark haired lady in a floral cotton dress, standing on the opposite side of the road. This mysterious lady has a dark shimmering shadow, just a yard or so behind her. Oddly enough, this shadow seems to be able to stand of its own accord. To Cassandra the shadow appears to be hovering in midair, lacking a structure, such as wall, for support. It is like the shadow is not a shadow but rather something or someone standing behind the lady.

That's odd. Shadows don't usually do that!

Cassandra's attention becomes focused on the mysterious dark haired lady for some unknown reason. She is standing about twenty feet behind the car. Her shoulder length, glossy black hair billows in the non-existent breeze. At her feet, a large black cat with a droopy right ear sits calmly, looking directly at Cassandra, blinking occasionally. The lady is a stranger to Cassandra but somehow she feels drawn to her. Cassandra feels a connection, a familiarity, even though she doesn't know the lady's name nor can recall having ever met her. Cassandra feels a warmth filling her body as she watches her. She feels in her heart she must be a friend.

Awkwardly Cassandra waves to the mysterious lady.

The lady standing on the path remains stationary. She looks on passively as proceedings unfold. Cassandra watches her closely.

"Cassandra, remember this...... hope is a waking dream!"

Cassandra is startled. She can hear the softly spoken words of the woman clearly even though she is some distance away. However, Cassandra remains confused. The lady's mouth doesn't open as she speaks; it doesn't move or twitch a muscle. Cassandra is almost sure of it. She looks at Steve for guidance. He simply nods and points at the open door. He acts like he hasn't heard the words of the cat lady, nor even caught a glimpse of her.

Looking back across the road, Cassandra notices the lady and the cat have vanished. Both have silently disappeared without trace. Drifting out from within the car she can smell the tattooed lady's perfume. As it wafts around her, Cassandra's fears are steadily washed away. It is a fragrance she knows. It is a fragrance she loves. It is a fragrance that makes her feel content and safe.

Red Roses!

Cassandra shrugs her shoulders and jumps in, bouncing on the car's comfortable seats. As Steve begins to climb into the car next to Cassandra he looks over the door and winks at the chauffeur, "Too easy."

The chauffeur smiles as he shuts the passenger door. Moving swiftly, he takes his seat behind the wheel. Slowly the limousine pulls out from the curb, moves over the hill and glides quietly out of sight. No witnesses are wandering Meadowview Street this day. Nobody sees their departure. It is not until much later that someone notices a single white Carnation lying on the driveway of Cassandra's palatial house. Even when it is found, the police have no idea of its significance. They pay no heed to its importance. It is not even collected and bagged or photographed as a piece of evidence.

In the mansion, Cassandra's mother begins to search for her daughter. "Cassandra?" she calls anxiously, with no reply.

On the front lawn a small white dove sits calmly, blinking its grey eyes, as it stares across the lawn. Just an average dove, maybe someone's pet. Most of the doves around this region are grey, after all. Cassandra's mother ignores the dove as her eyes scan a different part of the garden from the second floor balcony.

"Cassandra!" she calls more loudly now as she tries unsuccessfully to calm herself.

The dove sits silently, staring towards the front gates. With a swish of air, a large black Raven sweeps in, dive bombing the lonely dove. The dove squawks once as the giant bird grasps it by the neck in a flurry of feathers. As the Raven lifts the dove up off the ground, a loud cracking sound can be heard. The dove's neck is broken, crushed between powerful talons. The Raven flies over some bushes, releasing the dove's lifeless body as it goes. It glides effortlessly in a circle, returning to where the dove had been. It lands smoothly with several hopping jumps before it comes to a halt. Instead of watching the front gates, it faces the opposite direction. Its glowing red eyes watch Cassandra's mother intently.

"Cassandra!" the lady calls desperately, as her eyes frantically search the whole garden.

Silence is her only reply.

The Raven spreads its wings and flies off into the distance as dark clouds gather rapidly on the horizon, carried effortlessly by the strong, upper level winds. It flies towards the East, following the limousine, maintaining a respectable distance.

"Cassssandrrraaaaa!"

'Blind Eyes'

Red roses abound,
Chocolates a tempting sight,
The fragrance of love fills the air,
On this magic night.

A distraction too great,
To closed eyes it appears right,
Yet beware what is lurking,
On this magic night.

Chapter 2

Summer.
Tuesday, February 14th, 2006.
Valentine's Day, Afternoon.
Kinglake, Victoria, Australia.

Ahhhhh!

This is my 'Dreamtime'. It is my time to shine like the brightest firework on a dark, still, balmy night. My time to stop, to breathe slowly, peacefully inhaling all the subtle fragrances of life, deep into my soul; enjoying each aroma for its diversity and uniqueness while cherishing the pleasurable sensations they provoke. My time to savor everything the world has to offer.

Ahhhhh!

This is my time to live, my time to love and, most importantly, my time to be loved.

My time to be!

My journey to this blissful state of nirvana has been a long one. A life long journey, one might accurately say. My mystical awakening occurred, I guess, for two reasons. The first was waking with a start one fateful morning, feeling overcome by a nauseous feeling of emptiness. I was bothered by a nagging thought that I was living a life of abundant potential, though most of it had thus far remained disappointingly unfulfilled. This thought was quickly followed by a powerful urge to assess everything. By the way, when I say everything, I mean EVERYTHING! Every last detail of my life, however great or humble, past, present or future was fair game in my stocktake of my misspent life. Nothing was shielded from intense scrutiny.

This self-evaluation was, of course, undertaken in an appropriate climate of relaxation and tranquility. Locking myself in the lounge room, I built my sacred den of contemplation. Rod Stewart crooning softly in the background and Frangipani candles scattered throughout set the mood. My luxurious, though frayed, old leather arm chair positioned just so in the center of the room. Provisions for my inner journey included a half-eaten packet of Tim Tam's, some Salt n' Vinegar chips in a woven basket and a bottle of Coke Zero, to be healthy of course. Curtains drawn, paper and pen in hand, my silent oasis from the maddening world was complete.

It was the perfect spot. A place where I could consider what had been and what was still to come. The perfect environment for me to contemplate what, in my heart of hearts, I want from this foggy haze which is my future. No, that's not quite right. What I NEED the future to be would be a far more accurate description. This is the moment when I, age 32, decided to give up my haphazard life for something more structured, more determined, more decisive.

I guess you could call it 'the dawn of my life's plan'. As a writer, I should have a more exciting title however, in the end, it is what it is. Many elements were already present in my life back then. I just needed to identify the most important, hold onto them with both hands and never let my vice like grip falter. I decided, that day, that my time had come. Then and there I made a solemn pledge to myself to ensure that I would make the most of my life. I wanted to squeeze every last drop of vitality and excitement from every day. Live life to the fullest, achieve my goals and enjoy every second of the journey.

My second reason for my new life beginning at this time is a little corny, as life often is. I fell in love with Peter. Though fearlessly independent, I found myself increasingly yearning for his companionship, his company and strange outlook on the world. He makes my life complete, stable and oh so right! He doesn't negate my being; not in the least. I remain who I am, Julie Mahoney; proud and strong. On the contrary, he makes me stand a little taller and walk with a little more purpose. At night I find myself dreaming wonderful, technicolor dreams of my hopes and wishes, carried in the arms of golden angels. They are illuminated in flight by the subtle, summer moonlight and serenaded by a chorus of harps playing the same classical tune in perfect harmony.

Told you it sounds a little corny.

As you might have gathered, my life with Peter couldn't be better. We are fast closing in on our third anniversary of officially becoming 'a couple'; the day we decided to move in together. Our relationship has never been stronger. Our feelings for each other remain fresh and vibrant.

I catch myself smiling, thinking about Peter and our plans for the coming weekend. Curiously nervous, just like a school girl patiently waiting to experience the joys and terrors of a first date. The anticipation of seeing a mischievous glint in his baby blues as he stares lovingly into my eyes. Waiting for his fingers to slowly seek the company of mine, entwining in a strong and loving embrace. This is what I live for.

Every kiss feels like our first; the slow motion of our lips, the meeting, the sensuous touch, lingering for a moment, or three, while we lose ourselves in the beauty of our love. Refusing to be parted, even for an instant, we spend our day waiting for the next time we will see and be with each other. We live our lives in heaven, just the way it should be.

Maybe our behavior could appear a little sickly for the unwary who, through no fault of their own, unwittingly view our unbridled displays of affection as silly. We don't care. We love each other and choose to reaffirm that fact whenever and wherever the urge overtakes us. Of course, Peter surprising me with tickets to the sold out John Farnham, Valentine's Day concert at the Melbourne Arts Centre certainly helps to incite the flames of our passion to greater heights. I don't think our feelings for each other have ever been as strong as they are today. Whenever I look into Peter's eyes I see a man brimming with confidence and hope for the future. There is no doubt or uncertainty, no hint his feelings might flag with time. Hopefully they never will.

The human heart has been indelibly linked to love since the first poet dipped his quill in ink to scrawl some idle thoughts on a crudely formed sheet of papyrus. I live my life believing that these early scholars got it right. I believe this is why a heartbeat slows, races or even skips when you are lucky enough to be with someone special. It allows you to live longer lives together, cherishing each other's company, drowning in the precious sweetness of two unique individuals, living their lives as one.

I remember fondly, my heart skipping a beat or two on that landmark day when Peter first broached the subject of buying a place together. He knew my hopes and dreams for the future revolved around buying one of the few houses to come onto the market at Kinglake in recent years. I had talked about it so often, recounting all its intangible aesthetic qualities. Qualities which, to anyone else, would appear almost indiscernible under the thick veneer of sanding, repainting and other essential maintenance required. I, at least, could see the potential.

Kinglake is such a perfect area. Close enough to Melbourne, for work commitments, as well as the Yarra Valley if we require some well-earned

R & R. It is a quiet hamlet where I can concentrate on my writing, so peaceful and liberating.

Not wanting to harp on the point, however, the thing I liked most back then, as I do now, is that the place I had my eye on was a real gem. Brick veneer, eighteen squares, two bathrooms, 3 bedrooms and quite a sizeable backyard. The kind of place I would have loved as a child, yet sadly could only dream of during my childhood. It was the type of place where I could see myself spending the rest of my life, building a family, growing old serving Creamy Soda in tall glasses to over exuberant grandchildren. When I first saw it, I knew; this was MY home, my forever home!

Little did I know that for weeks Peter had been thinking that our relationship was going fine, better than fine. In fact, he was feeling so good about our life together, that he was giving serious thought to the possibility of raising the subject of moving in together. I know that sounds funny, yet this is Peter. He has never done anything without a lot of planning and, when it is something as momentous as this, becoming very self-conscious and nervous.

The idea had been playing on his mind for weeks, frustrating him as he valiantly searched for the right words. He wanted to talk about how he felt, without messing up a good relationship by seeming too pushy. Like most men, talking about his feelings doesn't come easily. Finally, with much trepidation, as sweat poured down his brow, he summoned all the adrenalin and courage he could muster and began to speak, blocking fearful thoughts from his mind.

Clearly and precisely, in fluent 'Peter-speak', he stated, "Well Julie, Angel, I've been thinking. You know, how about it?"

After a moment or two reflecting, trying to comprehend the meaning of his meagre words, my brain started to register the enormous implications of his questions. With a couple of quick fire questions, to ensure I was fully understanding his proposal, I jumped into his lap, kissing him like there was no tomorrow. Peter was so relieved, beginning to breathe for the first time in several minutes.

It certainly doesn't feel like three years since we made the offer, signed the papers, took out the loan and then promptly panicked about the re-payments. Wow, three amazing years since we bought the house of our dreams. I guess that's a good sign, we're not bored with each other's company just yet. We are still in the passionate beginning of our relationship, still hoping for kids someday, still living the dream.

Returning from the pleasant haze of my daydream, I casually glance at the time in the box on the lower right side of my computer; three thirty.

Damn!

I sigh, resigned to the fact that my leading lady, the notorious Jemima Jones, will have to remain in her dire predicament for another day or so. I am not making any progress today, anyhow. I have too many wonderful thoughts distracting my mind.

You see, currently I have my much 'critically' acclaimed heroine, of eight best-selling crime novels, hiding in the basement of a gangster's hideaway. The hideaway is set in a, as yet, undisclosed secluded location, somewhere in the Dandenong Ranges. She has been searching the house for clues as to the location of the stolen 'Edinburgh Pheasant', a solid gold statue of some historical importance which also just happens to be valued at around a million dollars, U.S. Until recently the statue has been held in the possession of one Cynthia Huntington-Smythe, a well-known shipping heiress. Now it has been stolen from her palatial Toorak mansion in somewhat mysterious circumstances. Jemima has been hired by the socialite due to her reputation as a no-nonsense, go getter who always gets the job done, no matter what, no matter how many laws have to be broken in the process.

I raise my arms and stretch, loosening the tensed muscles in my upper back and neck knowing full well that Jemima will have to wait till tomorrow for me to help her escape from the gangsters. She is a good lead character, very patient with me and my fluctuating inspiration and occasional writer's block. I simply have no further time for writing today. I have to meet Peter somewhere around Clifton Hill by 7pm.

Glancing over my shoulder, I check the grandfather clock to my right; twenty to four. That gives me a little under three and a half hours. With one hour's travelling, I now have only two and a half hours to get ready! Just enough time, I hope. After all, Valentine's Day is something special and I must look my absolute best for my sweet man.

Standing, I walk briskly as my 'to do' list steadily materializes in my head. Some inspirational music on my stereo; Gwen Stefani would be suitable. Hot bath with essential oils while taking care not to relax too much and fall asleep, like I usually do. Shave my legs and rub coconut body cream over my entire body. Apply just the right amount of perfume and makeup; I don't want to look like a tart. Straighten my hair to accentuate the shimmering gloss of my natural jet black color.

That will be a start, all the tedious though less important preparations taken care of. The important decisions are yet to come. Selection of outfit will be tricky and probably involve spreading most of my wardrobe across the bed. I will try to mix and match until I come up with the perfect combination that screams style and elegance.

My outfit will have to be practical, yet sexy. It will need to be cool enough for the early evening, yet warm enough as the night air cools. It must be captivating to Peter while not too revealing to any other lecherous guys we encounter. After all the toing and froing, the rejecting and further rejecting, I will still have to find jewelry, earrings, clutch purse and shoes to match whichever outfit is judged to be a winner. What a task! Sneaking a peek at the clock I see the minutes continue to tick by; ten to four. I sigh, hoping I have enough time.

*   *   *

Five thirty P.M. and I am ready for a romantic night on the town! It is bound to be a night to remember. I stand, rotating slightly, checking my look in the full length mirror. I smile as I check every line. A thought, powered by adrenalin, yells out in my mind.

You look hot!

My glistening hair is shimmering to dazzling effect in the late afternoon sunlight. I am draped in a full length, red ball gown complete with thin shoulder straps. The bodice is plunging, though somewhat ruffled. Its design creates the expectation that flesh will be exposed, particularly as the fabric shimmers when I move. However, the loose, overlapping fabric maintains modesty at all times. Thus the dress should create an allure that no man, not even my Peter, can escape.

I opt for dangling gold earrings which, from their lowest point, a tiny diamond tear drop swings inside a loop. These are my favorites as they also have special sentimental significance to me. Peter presented these to me as a surprise gift last Valentine's Day. Sentiment is important to me.

Adorning my wrists are several simple, yet elegant, bracelets; again in gold. My clutch purse is a cream colored Armani knock off with imitation gold buckles and locks. The final part of the puzzle is my shoes. I look at the seventy three pairs stacked neatly, taunting me as they rest patiently on the specially built shelving in the walk-in wardrobe. After a while, my eyes fix on the perfect pair. Gold, strapless, high heeled, French shoes I bought during a writer's block shopping spree, six months ago. They are overdue for their first outing into the real world. I pick them up with two fingers, admiring their beauty.

Ooh la la. How sexy is that!

Taking my purse and a red silk shawl, for later, I check my watch as I rapidly prepare to leave the house. I'm doing fine for time. Anyway, Peter never expects me to be on time. I do a quick lap of the house, switching off appliances and checking all the windows are closed and securely locked. You can't take any chances. Even in an idyllic town such as this, several burglaries have occurred in recent months. The last one was at Mrs. Johnson's house, little more than half a mile down the road. Pulling the front door closed behind me, hearing a reassuring 'click' as it fastens tight, I make my way towards the car.

Walking on air, I fumble through my purse, searching for my car keys. Tonight I am travelling light. Usually, as Peter tells me incessantly, my handbag is overloaded with all manner of junk. Makeup, three different lipsticks, mirror, Ventolin puffer, diary, mobile phone, Panadol, brush, crumpled receipts dating back six months, lots of plastic cards including local library, Target, Subway, Muffin Break, an iPod, ear phones, tissues, Band-Aids, pens, mini torch, face wipes and, somewhere hidden amongst it all is the only essential item; my keys. Even with my more modest clutch, to my astonishment, I fail to find my keys.

Finally, success! Like a magician pulling a rabbit from a hat, I produce the set of keys from the palm of my hand, gleefully looking at them as they dangle between my fingers in the sunlight. Suddenly, I have an overwhelming feeling that I am not alone. I turn and face the street. The bewildered look I am receiving from the two women power walkers, paused on my front pavement, is priceless. I smile politely, nodding an acknowledgement as I quickly open the car door and slip inside. Sitting in the seat, allowing the leather to contour around my waist and legs, I smile, shaking my head as I imagine how foolish I must look in their eyes; the ultimate airhead. I start the car and reverse out of the driveway as the women continue on their way.

It is a pleasant day to drive, quite mild really, probably around twenty five degrees Celsius, at a guess. Within twenty minutes I have traversed the winding road, which leads down the mountain, to the more sparsely treed township of Whittlesea. All the while, I keep to the speed limit as I sing along badly to the songs on Nova. Plenty Road is dry, glistening like a mirage into the distance. The road works at Mernda will be finished for the day by the time I make it down there. At least that's what I hope. Though necessary, they have become somewhat of a nuisance over the last few months.

As I leave the outskirts of Whittlesea, I open the glove box, flicking through my collection of loose CDs. One hand on the wheel, I occasionally glance back at the road ahead to ensure I am keeping some sort of reasonable line. My speed is fairly constant at fifty miles per hour. I eventually find the one I am looking for; John Farnham's 'You're The Voice'.

Adjusting my line, to move back to the correct side of the shimmering white line, I insert the CD. As the first track begins, I reduce the volume slightly so the speakers in the back aren't vibrating so vigorously. My little Festiva was only built with a more primitive sound system in mind. Just as I get the volume level to my comfort zone, my mobile phone begins to ring. Pressing pause on the CD player, I put the phone on hands free.

"Hi honey," I say without checking the display. I know full well who this will be, calling me at this time, on this particular day.

"I hope you were expecting me," Peter says sarcastically.

"Actually I was hoping it was my lover, but I guess you'll have to do," I laugh as I turn a slight bend. The bright sun reflects on the windscreen, glinting in my eyes. I reach for my sunglasses on the seat beside me. Awkwardly, one handed, I position them successfully on my face.

"I don't mind you taking lovers as long as it's the anorexic, pimple faced, trolley boy rather than a Ferrari driving muscle builder with plenty of credit cards. That way I don't have to be jealous. I'm sure your mother would find the trolley boy a better catch for her Princess, too."

"That's a little harsh. Don't pout, Hun. I think I can still squeeze you into my busy schedule for dinner and a show. Where do you want to meet?" I enquire with more than a subtle amount of excitement noticeable in my voice. I can't believe the concert is so close now.

"Well, I'm just passing through Fairfield via Albert Street at the moment. Can you hear me?" Peter's voice crackles down the line as I frown, concentrating on his words.

"Yes, you're a bit patchy but yes, I can hear you."

"So where are you anyway? How far away are you Angel?" Peter asks.

Taking note of my surroundings I continue, "I'm still on the other side of Mernda, probably about half an hour behind you considering how the traffic will be from South Morang towards the city at this time of the day."

"Well, why don't we meet at the corner of Bourke and Swanston and I can surprise you," Peter suggests. The tone of his voice makes me imagine that a devilish grin is spreading across his face as we speak.

I frown, "Surprise me? What are you up to Babe?"

Peter laughs, "Yeah, I guess there's no harm in letting you in on a small secret. I've booked a table at this great little cafe that serves hot and spicy Mexican food. They have live music. Well there's a bloke singing with a guitar. Anyway, the place has a lot of ambience."

I laugh at Peter's turn of phrase, "You must have been around me for too long if you are starting to use terms like 'ambience'."

"Hey, Angel! I'm an educated guy. I know about things such as ambience and.... and... and Shabby Chic."

"Shabby Chic!" I say incredulous. "Now I am amazed. Where on earth did you hear about that?"

Peter laughs, "Well, don't tell the blokes but I think it was on 'Better Homes and Gardens' or one of those renovation shows which I stumbled upon while channel surfing, looking for the football."

"That would be right!" I knew it would be something like that. Peter has showed no interest in my home decorating at any time in the past.

"Anyway, back to the cafe. It looks nice. I think you'll like it too. Is that good enough for you?"

Funny, I don't think they forecast rain.

A little distracted, I look at the storm clouds gathering outside the car as the light levels begin to drop rapidly. I remove my sunglasses, throwing them on the seat beside me. The clouds billow as if they are being moved by a gusty Northerly wind yet the trees next to my car are barely swaying. I flick my headlights on, just to be safe. While peering through the windscreen at the rapidly developing storm, I am struck by a sudden sharp stabbing pain in my chest. I reel back in agony, grabbing my chest with one hand while trying desperately to control the car with the other. Eyes bulging, car swerving, I use every ounce of determination to regain a steady line and to remain conscious. I stop myself from screaming out loud. All the while, I panic.

Oh God! Is this a heart attack? I can't die. Not today! Not today!

The sound of thunder reverberates through the car, followed shortly by the sound of heavy rainfall. My curiosity is aroused by the pelting rain. I wonder why I can hear the rain lashing the roof of my car when there is not a single drop hitting the windscreen. The aroma of post rain air is prevalent, though mixed with the smell of smoke like there is some sort of massive fire somewhere close at hand. A fire at some type of factory, maybe. For the air smells acrid and stings the receptors in my nose.

"That's strange," I say out loud, trying to work out exactly what I see unfolding in front of me. The pain in my chest is terrible, though appears to be non-life threatening. At least I hope so.

If this is a heart attack I should be dead by now. I certainly shouldn't be able to drive a car. Maybe I have just strained a muscle or something.

I try to relax, drawing in deep breaths of precious oxygen, holding them for a second before slowly releasing the carbon dioxide from my lungs. My heart pounding, little by little, I regain composure.

"What is it?" Peter asks from down the line. I guess from the urgency in his voice, he has become aware something is amiss.

I answer slowly and deliberately, trying to explain what is occurring without scaring Peter, "I'm travelling through some sort of storm. I can hear rain but I can't see it. I can also smell smoke coming from somewhere, I don't think it's something fusing in the car; it smells more like wood and chemicals burning somewhere. Shit! This pain is unbelievable."

"What pain? What's going on Angel? Are you hurt?"

Suddenly the sky in front of me opens up, allowing bright sunlight to come streaming through. As the cabin illuminates, something strange begins to occur. Everything around me seems to slow. It is like I am in a cinema, viewing a film. However, a malfunction with the projector has caused the film to play at just one tenth of its normal speed.

Whoa! What is happening here?

I draw precious breath and survey the scene ahead. I can see a smartly dressed lady standing on the edge of the road, a hundred feet in front of me. She's in her late fifties. Her grey hair cropped short and styled in such a manner as to imply class, sophistication and status.

Her clothes reflect and enhance this image further. She is immaculately dressed in a stylish pink jacket, buttoned neatly over a white shirt with a yellow rose in her lapel. This is offset by a snug, not tight, fitting skirt of a completely respectable length. The hem line falls slightly above the ankles. Her ensemble is complete with a pair of expensive silver, Italian, handmade, low heeled shoes. Her image exudes a mixture of elegance refined with maturity.

The lady has a mobile phone held tightly to her ear. She is smiling, waving her free hand as she speaks. She steps forward, onto the road, without a sideways glance. I watch her walk, step after step, as she remains fully engrossed in her phone conversation. I am mesmerized. I know what is about to happen though, somehow, I am unable to react. I am unable to avert the impending catastrophe. Somehow the crucial message is not being passed from my brain to my feet in order to generate some sort of emergency stopping procedure. I continue to drive towards her without slowing.

I hear her scream; a horrible, prolonged, gut wrenching scream. She turns and faces me, still on the phone. I am close enough to see the fear in her eyes. I am drawn to her eyes. I can see deep into her soul. I can see her hopes, her dreams, and her life about to be swept away. She is scared, she knows she is in trouble; she is not ready to die. Her eyes are pleading for mercy, for salvation. Divine intervention seems to be scarce. My stomach knots, my mouth is dry.

I begin to brake only as my car collides with her. I hear the horrible sound of flesh hitting metal, the gruesome sound of many bones breaking all at once. The lady's body, limp and misshapen, tumbles over the bonnet. Her head smashes into the windscreen which shatters into a spider's web pattern yet refuses to break. For a brief second I catch her eyes once more as she lies on the bonnet. They are fully open, staring at me, accusing me; so blue, so glazed, so lacking of any essence of life. I feel the bile surging up into my throat as I am overcome with nausea. Everything is moving so slowly.

The car lurches. With some effort I pull the car to a screeching halt. My head bounces onto the steering wheel with a heavy thud as I hear the lifeless body sliver, then tumble, off my bonnet, crashing to the pavement with a gut wrenching thud. She falls some feet in front of my car. I see her prone lifeless body lying on the concrete in front of me. I feel additional pain beginning to register in my brain. As I reach up and tentatively touch my forehead, I find its source. I am aware of my heart pounding at an extraordinary rate. I look down in disbelief at the large amount of blood on my hand.

Oh Shit!

"No, no. This can't be," I say incoherently, shaking my head as tears roll down my cheeks.

I hear a young girl's voice filtering through the car. Her voice is somehow familiar, though her words confuse me. In a shrill voice she beckons, "Julie, please Julie. You just have to believe. There's always hope."

"Wait..... help......," I call. I hear her footsteps fade away to my left as she giggles. I search my mirrors and windows. I see a ball bounce, behind the car, off into the grass. I search more urgently. No matter how much I seek her, I can't find the little girl. I know she is there somewhere, for I can hear her singing some sort of child's lullaby. Her voice echoes, appearing to come first from the left then the right.

Where is she? How does she know my name?

I begin to hear other sounds. A baby cries out. Not clear, but unmistakable none-the-less. It sounds muffled like it is inside a house or car nearby. I hear footsteps of an animal, possibly a possum, as it's claws scurry across the roof of my car. Finally I hear a man laughing.

Shit! Who is that?

I frantically search my surroundings for the source of the manic laughing. It resounds for a split second and is gone. I am not mad, I know what I heard. I just can't see the person responsible.

A cold sweat forms on my brow as I notice a couple walking in the paddock in front of me, hand in hand. Their faces are shrouded in darkness. From this distance away it is hard to establish any detail at all.

To me they look like they have stepped out of a nightclub, straight into the grassy paddock.

I watch as the woman tries to pull away from the man. He refuses to release her hand, pulling her back into his arms. He grasps her blue party dress by the shoulder with his free hand, preventing her escape. The material tears as she returns to his clutches.

Shit!

A small object bounces off the roof of the car with a thud before falling to the ground. I have no idea what this is. It simply passed by too quickly for my eyes to even pick up some sort of general shape. Turning my attention back to the couple I find, to my surprise, they have gone.

My mind vaguely registers the faint sound of Peter calling out my name, over and over again, more desperate each time. I don't respond. I am too far gone. Too gripped with fear about what I have done. Too confused about what is happening around me. I am overwhelmed by the stabbing pain in my chest.

Peter? Where are you? Are you here? Peter? I need you Peter!

The excruciating pain in my chest and head remains, yet I suddenly feel just a little more comfortable as I look through the side window. My heartbeat slows as I see a doctor standing in the garden of a house, complete with white jacket and stethoscope.

Surely he is here to help. He must be helping the lady. That's why he's covered in blood. She must be alive. If he's helping her, she must be alive.

My eyes flutter. I drift slowly into unconsciousness, trying desperately to force my eyes open with all the inner strength I can muster. I stop breathing. My brain becoming hazy as carbon dioxide fills my body. For some reason I am unconcerned by any of this. My brain's only function at this point is to try to unravel the images and sounds around me and organize them into some sort of logical picture that makes perfect sense. My brain continues to fail in its quest.

The doctor disappears, without trace. I look forward and see that the lady's body has disappeared from the pavement where she lay a minute or two ago. The smell of smoke has gone. The sky is clear and blue, just like when I started my journey. Most of all the pain in my chest has completely dissipated almost as if by magic.

Peter continues to scream my name over the phone.

I don't respond.

I don't breathe.

Where have they all gone?

I don't breathe.

Confused, I drift further towards unconsciousness.

What is going on?

I don't breathe.

Everything becomes black.

What?.....

I don't breathe.

Everything is quiet.

"Julie!" Peter calls through my mobile, provoking no response.

Everything is peaceful.

I still don't breathe.

My eyelids flutter as I stare at the passenger's seat. I can't believe what I see. It simply doesn't make sense.

Where did you come from?

"Meeeoww!"

My eyelids flutter, then close.

No more time for questions.

Everything disappears...............

"Jullllieeeee!"

'Future Looms'

Strange and curious powers,
So misunderstood,
Must be kept hidden,
For the better good.

Lives on the line,
There can be no doubt,
Swimming in murky waters,
Searching for a way out.

Chapter 3

March 1683.
Delaware, New Jersey.

Spring Festival is the annual celebration for the town of Delaware; a time when strangers and longtime friends come together. In fact, it is a time when the whole town gathers as a community in order to eat, drink and dance; usually to excess. The hardships of the past year are forgotten, at least for a day, while the townsfolk become absorbed in the frivolities on offer. Hope for a plentiful crop and a prosperous future is abundant. It is an exciting time when all the townsfolk are joyous and relaxed. A wonderful day which later transforms into a magical night when anything can, and does, happen. Sometimes, just sometimes, it is an opportunity for new partnerships to form; a favorable climate for romance to begin to bloom. It is a night when people meet and dance with their neighbors in a celebration of life and rejoice in all its bountiful pleasures.

It is during this festival that Mary first lays eyes on Thomas, a gangling, shy, be-freckled, yet well-heeled newcomer to town. Mary is sixteen; a mere slip of a girl who has been blessed with piercing emerald green eyes. Her jet black hair is brushed for hours daily till it is straight, hanging just below her shoulders. She is a stunning beauty who is starting to acquire many admirers amongst the young lads scattered throughout the town. Alas, as the eldest daughter of a poor farming family, she has no time for romance. She has a more pressing task, bestowed on her by her parents. Her sole responsibility is to ensure that her two younger sisters are safe and stay out of trouble. This is a full time task at the best of times. However, her parents remain blissfully unaware that Mary, rather than assisting with this chore, is the mischievous influence in her sister's lives. If the truth be known, she is an excellent teacher, training her two young apprentices thoroughly in all the dark arts of skullduggery.

The girls' latest plan is simple yet elegant in every detail. It has worked before. It will surely work again. The day is fast declining. Seven o'clock and the light from the sun has fully disappeared behind the hills to the west. Most of the adults and older children are scurrying along the dirt road, heading haphazardly in all directions though steadily edging their way into the heart of town. The men are handing out lanterns and taking them to the central light keeper to be lit. The mayor, resplendent in his new cotton shirt, is trying to gather everyone together in preparation for the parade. The women are adjusting bonnets, dusting off their clothes and those of their children, spitting on kerchiefs and wiping down faces.

Everyone is busy. Everyone, that is, except Mary and her two sisters. They are hiding under a table in the soup tent. Dresses filthy from lying in the dust, they patiently watch the shuffling feet from beneath the overhanging tablecloth, as the towns folk fuss around in preparation. Only the three girls are aware of the cunning plan that is about to be hatched.

"Let's go," orders Mary as she grasps Sarah by the shoulder of her dress and drags her out from beneath the table. They take just a few steps before they peer back for Amy who, they discover, hasn't moved. Whistling to distract her from playing with her rag doll they begin waving their arms earnestly, trying desperately to encourage her to come forward. Slowly Amy crawls out from under the table and joins her older sisters. They speak in whispers for a second then, hunched over, they walk briskly, though nonchalantly, towards Mr. Fitzpatrick's stall. As they reach the front bench they each take an apple, stand upright and, hearts pounding, run like the devil himself is chasing them.

Mr. Fitzpatrick, spotting the heist, grabs his walking cane with his left hand and a machete, used for cutting watermelons, in his right. He hobbles to the front of his stall yelling unintelligible abuse with a thick Irish accent as he waves the machete for full dramatic effect. He stops in the middle of the street just as he sees the last of the girls, little Amy, disappearing in amongst the massing crowd. He smiles to himself while continuing his tirade of insults for the benefit of his customers. He's not greatly perturbed by the loss; food is always a profitable enterprise. He can spare a couple of apples here and there. He just doesn't want his customers to know about his generous side. That would be bad for business.

The girls run hard, giggling all the time, yet fearful they are still being chased. They don't have the courage to stop for a moment to sample their ill-gotten gain. Not just yet. Dodging and weaving they keep moving. They continue to sprint until they run into their older brother Michael. With a thud they literally run into him like dominoes into a wall. Mary and Sarah, still smiling, take a step backwards. Instinctively they hide the apples out of sight, behind their backs. Amy just stands there, looking up at her brother, holding the apple in her hand as she smiles, innocently blinking her eyes.

"Hello Mary, Sarah, Bub, having fun?" he asks sarcastically as he scowls, placing his hands on his hips. He watches their faces for some sign of guilt. Spotting their filthy dresses he knows instantly they have been up to some sort of mischief, he just can't quite work out what. Slowly his mind reluctantly sets aside its suspicions. He remembers his manners and promptly introduces the stranger accompanying him, to his sisters, "This be Thomas. He be new to town. I art his guide this day in Delaware."

Mary looks up at the stranger in front of her. He is wearing an oversized canvas hat and new looking tan cotton shirt with cotton trousers.

Thou doth appear to be a farmer, yet thou be too well dressed.

She guesses Thomas would be about eighteen, the same age as her brother. Mary is smitten at first sight. Thomas smiles and presents his hand to Mary, "Glad to make your acquaintance.''

Mary glances sideways at her sister Sarah as she rolls her eyes. Turning back to face Thomas she accepts his hand, laughs and curtsies like she is greeting the most noble of royalty.

"What has prompted thou mirth? Have I said something to amuse thee?" Thomas asks, perplexed.

"Sir," Mary says with a wry grin, thinking about the pomposity of the language Thomas has chosen to use. It is a style of language which is not common in these parts. She wonders if it means he is well educated. "Every word thou Majesty doeth speaketh be funny."

As Mary speaks, Amy takes a large bite of her apple. The resounding 'crack' draws the attention of all those gathered around her.

Michael's demeanor changes in a heartbeat on hearing Amy's teeth crunch into her apple. He becomes furious, his cheeks turning a flaring shade of red. His eyes bulge as he begins to rant, "Stealing apples again! Pa will tan thy hides for this."

He leans forward, trying to grasp Mary but she is too quick. With a shimmy and a side step she moves a few steps away from Michael, just out of reach. Cheekily, Mary takes a bite of her apple, smiles and exposes the apple between her teeth for Michael to see as she chews.

"Why you!" Michael screams as he reaches for her again. Once again Mary dodges his outstretched hand. She pokes out her tongue as she turns and begins to run, diving in and out of the crowd, her sisters following close behind. Michael decides the chase isn't worth it. After all, the girls have to come home sometime and their father will be well aware of what they have been up to by then.

It has been a great day. A day of innocent mischief filled with laughter and smiles. It is a day that will be cherished, fondly remembered during the harsh days to come. Though she doesn't realize it just now, Mary will someday let her mind drift back to this day in order to find some miniscule amount of comfort and a safe place to hide. She will treasure these memories when times of trouble appear to be looming close on the horizon.

This wonderful day is the day when a line will be drawn in the sand. It is the day before she realizes her life has changed forever. Her life will no longer be carefree. For tonight is the night when everything changes irrevocable. Tonight is the night that the dreams begin. Tonight is the night on which she becomes both blessed and cursed with an ability that no one else could ever hope to fully understand.

The dreams become so real, like the worst nightmares imaginable. Night after night she sees the same thing. All the local children, dressed in their Sunday best, playing on a tenuous swing, constructed from a crudely woven rope with knots tied at regular intervals. The rope is draped over a branch of a Weeping Willow tree which extends over the river. Thus it allows the children to swing from the river bank, out over the water. They either swing back to shore or, the more daring, curl into a ball as they let go, diving into the murky waters as they unleash a wild scream of excitement.

The dreams are so realistic in their depictions that Mary sometimes forgets they are not real. Mary has witnessed their message over many nights for several weeks; reliving the sequence of events over and over again. The images change slightly each time. One thing that remains constant is that it is always the same scenario. However, she witnesses the drama as it plays out from slightly different angles. This provides her with a fairly clear understanding of proceedings. Children are playing on the river bank one second. Suddenly, after a brief discussion, two children begin playing on the swing as they are encouraged by the cheers and laughter of their friends. The dream always starts cheerfully enough though it changes rapidly as the branch holding the rope swing creaks loudly before snapping, sending the branch and the two children hurtling awkwardly into the water. This is followed by chaotic scenes as the children appear to be dragging two lifeless bodies from the river. Mary always wakes in a cold sweat at this point, like she is cursed by the 'fever'. The first thing she spies as she tries to regain her breath is her new black kitten, curled up at the foot of the bed, purring contentedly. Jezebel is there watching over her.

Mary's parents don't understand her relationship with Jezebel and how important she is to keep her from going mad. They have tried to keep the cat out of the house for fear that it might be responsible for her nightmares. Her parents are regular God fearing people who are wary of black cats and their familiarity with witches. They fear the cat must be a servant of the devil himself, particularly considering the fact that the kitten appeared from nowhere on their doorstep one day. It is about this time that Mary's mother gifted her with a wooden crucifix pendant on a leather cord. Mary is in rapture over the present. It is the most beautiful gift she has ever received. She decides then and there to wear it each and every day. Her parents are glad of this fact. They are a little more at ease, hoping it provides her some protection from the evil forces they imagine are beginning to circle her.

Jezebel arrived the night before the nightmares began, a situation noted by Mary's parents. The cat, however, is a strange one. It adopted Mary only, refusing to be handled by anyone else. If someone was foolish enough to venture near the cat, drawn in by its apparent friendly disposition, they would soon discover the error of their ways. Once they are within striking range, Jezebel attacks, scratching and hissing for all it is worth. It is because the cat can't be trusted, with this split personality, that it has been bestowed the name Jezebel. Mary adores the cat and chooses to call it by a more affectionate name; Jezzie.

Mary is tired and drawn due to lack of sleep over a period of weeks, fast drawing on a month. She sees the level of concern her parents have for her health. They are simple people who work hard, long hours producing and preparing the food for their young family. They know they are good people living an honest, righteous life. Mary's nightmares visibly scare them; she can see it in their faces. Just the way their facial muscles tense when they discuss issues using thinly veiled, deceitful whispers tells her she is an outcast, bringing shame down upon her family. How they force a smile as their paths cross. The way they avoid talking to her in general, maybe they just don't know what to say. Maybe they are beginning to hear some of the talk spreading in the town. Maybe they think she is possessed. Maybe.... they think she is a witch!

Mary's mind is made up. She decides to try to hide what is happening. The problem is that she sleeps in the same room as her parents and siblings, for the house only possesses one room. However, she always makes sure the curtain is drawn between her and her parents. She stuffs her nightshirt into her mouth and tries to breathe through her nose. This technique makes it harder for her to fall asleep initially, though it works in that it allows her to successfully muffle any screams prior to waking. To her surprise this plan has worked so effectively that she hasn't even woken her sister Amy, a notoriously light sleeper, who beds down on the bunk below her.

Although she can limit the effects, she can find no way to prevent the dreams. In fact, as time goes on, the dreams change, becoming progressively worse. She does not understand them. Oddly, the dreams are becoming visible to her while she is awake. For the first time in her life, Mary realizes she is alone. She is one of six people living in the same room, under the same roof but, in her fear riddled heart, she is undeniably alone. There is no-one she can confide in. She knows too that there is no-one in the village who she can trust; that path only leads to fear, misunderstanding and danger. She has seen first-hand, the reaction of the local minister when her parents sought advice on exorcising her nightmares. The gaze he delivered to her was filled with dread and loathing; no compassion or promise of hope was on offer. She knows trusting any member of the local clergy can be life threatening, particularly if she is denounced as someone bedeviled. She has heard stories of witch burnings in faraway towns. Though she doesn't care to believe them, she is not foolish enough to discount these stories as false either.

Over the coming weeks she hides it well. So much so, her parents and siblings are completely convinced she has recovered from the 'fever' and no longer has a 'familiarity with the devil'. It surprises Mary when she hears her mother speak openly about her ailment, now cured, using these grievous terms. She seems so pleased the unpleasantness has righted itself, on the back of all their prayers. It re-enforces their strong belief in God and their standing in an overly superstitious community.

On this particularly sunny, spring day, Mary and Sarah are coming back from the surrounding bush, laden with eggs, talking vigorously. The new blue sky is cloudless. The birds are chirping and all seems right with the world. Suddenly Mary stops, just for a second, as if startled by something terrifying, before regaining her stride. It is enough time for Sarah to take an extra step forward. Sarah spins around to confront Mary who has quickened her pace and moves swiftly past Sarah.

"I be well," Mary says, answering the unasked question from her sister as tears begin to form in her eyes.

Sarah knows what she has seen. She also knows exactly how to interpret Mary's skittish behavior. There is not much that Mary can hide from her. She knows her sister has seen or felt something, something that Sarah lacks the power or unnatural ability to distinguish. She is obviously having one of her 'dreams' while fully awake. Sarah decides in an instant that she will not let the matter pass. It is far too grave a circumstance for her to remain silent. Dropping her basket to the ground, her face is tense as both confusion and knowledge mix together at the same time. She runs, forcibly wrenching Mary around so she can confront her face to face.

"What be it? Tell me! Tell me or I'll tell Ma what I hath seen."

Head still bowed, visibly distressed, Mary's body shakes with overwhelming fear as she considers her words carefully. She is determined to prevent a 'witch hunt' from beginning, though she isn't quite sure how she is going to achieve this ambitious goal. She sighs, filling her lungs with much needed oxygen and hopefully a smattering of confidence. Unfortunately, when she speaks, her words are nervous, hesitant and most of all, hollow, "I be well. I doth not see anything, nothin' at all. Not a thing."

Sarah watches Mary closely. She is completely shocked, having no faith that there is some truthfulness in her sister's feeble words. She is only two years younger than Mary. However, Sarah has always acted much older. Sarah feels that they are closer to being twins with similar tastes, likes and dislikes. This is precisely why Sarah knows when her sister is lying. Sarah releases her grip and takes a step back, hand over her mouth, "Thou doth see things in the daylight, whilst thou be awake? This be madness. This be madness or ....."

For the first time Mary stops staring at the ground in front of her lace up boots. She looks her sister squarely in the face, tears pouring down her cheeks. Earnestly she pleads with her sister as she drops to her knees, "Nay, I be not bedeviled. Nay, thou can't mistrust me, thou be mine flesh and blood. They shall thinketh I be afflicted with the 'fever' once more. They shall thinketh I be familiar with the devil. I am not, yet they shall still think it be so. Pray don't tell of my affliction."

Sarah is distraught, conflicted as to what she should do. She loves her sister with all her heart and soul. Yet she is a young, impressionable girl who fears God's wrath. She feels overcome with an impossible decision to make. Seemingly destined to be damned either way, no matter what choice she makes. Pulling her sister to her feet, embracing her and beginning to cry too she says, "I'll shall stow thy secret, keep it silent within my beating heart. It be my solemn vow to thee as my blood. I shall not tell of thy visible appearances. Words of thy bedevilment shan't pass my lips."

Mary smiles as she begins to cry harder. Her sobbing is more characteristic of an outburst of relief rather than fear. She now has a confidante; a trusted one at that. She hopes she has an ally in fighting this most unholy of curses.

From that fateful day Mary continues to see, hear and feel things that aren't there. Blood stained rocks, the shadow of a swing, the sounds of children playing, the sounds of children screaming and crying. She is able to keep all of this hidden with the assistance of Sarah. If Mary accidentally pauses, Sarah reacts. She distracts those present by pretending there is a mouse or a spider which has startled them. With time and practice, she is becoming quite convincing in her role playing. They work brilliantly as a team. Mary knows she owes Sarah a debt of gratitude she hopes, some day, she can repay.

This concealment of Mary's visions continues, with great success, for several months until one day when Mary is near the barn, collecting eggs. Something new occurs, something which unnerves her just as she is becoming more comfortable with experiencing the visions. Two white doves land with precision on Mary's right shoulder.

Nay, thou be not there. Thy evil talons claw not at my soul. Thy bedeviled coo fails to reach my pure ears. Nay, I see thou not. Nay, thou be not there!

She stands frozen to the spot. Terrified, her only conscious movement is to close her eyes while her whole body shakes involuntarily.

Amy walks from behind the barn. She sees her sister with the doves and promptly drops the pail carrying the goat's milk, spilling the entire precious contents in the mud. Her eyes bulge open in wonderment, at the amazing sight before her.

Mary opens her eyes and stares squarely at Amy, blinking several times rapidly. The tension eases instantly as confusion spreads over her face. She asks, somewhat elated, "Thou doth see this unholy vision too?"

Amy offers her outstretched hand and pleads with eyes filled with innocent wonderment and hope. She doesn't perceive these creatures as evil. To her they are simply messengers from God. She nods towards Mary, "Pray may I hold one?"

Mary doesn't answer, she is lost in thought, her mind unable to determine what it all means. Her dreams have felt so real though she knows from her discussions with Sarah that they are not. They are simply the manifestation of false images which swirl around in her subconscious mind. Now she is confused.

Amy can see these birds; is she having visions too? Maybe the birds are real. Maybe they are a message, a sign of some sort. That has to be it; a sign. What on earth can the sign mean? What on earth?

Finally, her eyes widen and her skin becomes ashen as the blood flows away from her face, "It be a sign. Something bad comes to pass. Something bad comes to pass this day!"

With this realization reverberating in her head she begins to run. The doves take flight, shedding several feathers which flutter reluctantly down until they sink in amongst the goat's milk sludge. Amy twists around to see her sister running up the hill towards the Johnson's farm which stands high above the river. A light gust of wind brings with it the muffled sounds of children's excited voices to Amy's ears, for the briefest of moments.

"Mary?" she says with uncertainty, unable to fathom what is going on.

Mary doesn't stop. She sprints as hard as she possibly can while encumbered with her long flowing dress. At one point she stumbles, falling awkwardly in the mud and rocks, badly grazing her knee. She doesn't flinch nor cry out in pain. She simply regains her composure, stands up, lifts her dress slightly and begins running earnestly once more. Her muscles strain with every step she takes up the steep and awkward slope. She knows that no matter how her muscles are aching, she has to keep going. She has to get to the river as quickly as she can. She has experienced her visible dreams for too long. Though still sketchy she knows basically what is going to occur and she is determined to stop it. She just has to, for if she doesn't, friends will die today. She has foreseen it. She has to make it on time. In her heart she has no choice.

She reaches the top of the hill and pauses for a moment. Hands placed on hips, she finds herself gasping for fresh air to fill her depleted lungs. The hill top is cleared. From her vantage point she can see all the way down towards the willows growing by the river's edge. She can see her sister Sarah and about six to eight of their friends gathered around the creek watching activity which is hidden behind a tree. She sees a young lad climb down from the tree with a big grin on his face. He beckons in an exuberant fashion for the others to move a little to the side as he takes a few steps backwards. Mary gasps and places a hand over her mouth in horror as she realizes it is Thomas. He sprints, taking a flying leap towards the creek. Instead of a plunging headlong into the stream, she watches as he swings back into view on a rope the children must have tied up earlier this morning.

Mary runs down the hill, waving her arms and screaming every forced breath from her lungs in a noisy and incoherent manner. The children, startled, turn around just in time to see Mary lose her footing and roll several times down the hill, scraping her knees further and tearing her dress before coming to a halt in amongst some rocks. Thomas, hearing the commotion swings back onto the bank of the river. He releases the rope to land expertly on dry ground, under the willow. He is the first person to sprint up the hill to see if Mary is alright.

"Well what doth we have here; an angel that hath fallen from heaven?" Thomas laughs.

"I be well, that is not the issue. It be thou who art in danger. Thou all be in danger!" Mary says earnestly.

The gathering crowd of children is bewildered by Mary's outburst. There is a general lack of concern from the friends who are simply out to have some fun. They place no credence in the words of the disheveled wretch in front of them. She is obviously a bit shaken by her fall. Eventually one of the boys says, "She's fine. It be my turn next!"

As he turns in preparation to run back towards the river, closely followed by everyone except Thomas, Mary screams, "No!"

The children take no notice of her protest as they run. Paul is the first one to get to the riverbank. He launches himself effortlessly into the air, landing with precision onto the makeshift swing. Mary lowers her head into her hands and begins to sob, "Why doth thou not listen. I see what will be. Death is close at hand. It reaches out to touch all that hath chosen to be here on this day. Mark my words with heed. No good shall come of this day."

Thomas reaches down and lifts Mary to her feet. Patting the dust from her dress he smiles as he says calmly, "Nay, there be nothing to fear here. We art but friends enjoying a beautiful day by the river. That be all."

Mary tries to get the words out, "Nay, thou art mistaken. A terrible accident shall befall us. Much heed needs to be granted. I fear thou may be hurt, nay even die this day. There be a problem with thy swing. It be unsteady."

Thomas, unconcerned, steadies Mary and escorts her towards where the children are playing with the swing. Mary begins to shake involuntarily, her terrified eyes remain fixed unswervingly on the swing. Fear fills her heart. She knows her words sound like madness yet she knows she speaks the truth. A truth which she needs to make heard.

"Let me show thou, the swing be safe. We have a good, strong rope. There shall be no problem. I will show thee."

Thomas relinquishes his hold on Mary's arm. He leaves her standing on her own, looking at the unfolding scene from a distance. Thomas briefly speaks to Johnny who smiles and nods. To Mary's dismay, Thomas takes a giant running leap onto the rope, followed by Johnny on the return swing. The two of them look back towards Mary smiling. Thomas waves as he holds on one handed. His skylarking fails to have the desired effect of placing Mary at ease.

They swing backwards and forwards, using their legs to propel themselves to greater heights. Mary watches this scene attentively, wary though growing a little calmer as the seconds go by and nothing happens. As she relaxes little by little, she looks deep inside her own mind, searching for an answer to her waking dreams. Self-doubt grows rapidly as the seconds grow steadily into minutes without incident. She raises her arms outwards, forming a human cross. She looks skywards for answers as thoughts scamper through her troubled mind.

Maybe all is well. Maybe thy swing be true and sturdy. Maybe there be no cause for my alarm. Maybe this be naught but madness. Am I afflicted by a madness? Oh God, please send me a sign. Am I but a fool to believe such fanciful visions? Or are they a sign, a sign of that which is yet to come to pass? Please God, send me a sign. What be true, what be false? Is this the devil's work? Please God, send me a sign. What be thy plan for me? What doth thou expect me to do?

Inexplicably, at this particular moment, both boys look up. Mary gasps as everyone hears a large creak from where the swing is tied to the branch. Both boys grip the rope more tightly as it swings forward again over the creek. Their knuckles are white, their eyes filled with fear as they both pray that they will be able to swing back to the safety of the river bank. It is not to be.

As the swing reaches its widest arc, deep over the river, the branch breaks with a fearful sound, sending both boys into the river. The large limb follows, landing squarely on top of them, dowsing the onlookers in water. Thomas and Johnny are completely submerged in the bubbling, rippling, murky waters of the river. Only the large branch protrudes as loose leaves and twigs ride the waves off into the murky distance downstream.

The children stand together on the bank immobile as the enormity of the accident washes over them. There is no way the two boys could have survived being thrashed onto the rocks which lie on the river bed or pounded by this huge branch which now pins them helplessly underwater. The witnesses all stand like statues, looking at the spot in the river where the boys have disappeared. Nobody takes the initiative to launch a rescue. Mary is the first to spring into action. While clutching her crucifix pendant tightly, rubbing it with her thumb, she screams, "Help them for pity's sake!"

Several of the boys step up, diving into the river. They swim into the middle of the stream, trying to establish exactly where they should be searching. They clamber over the huge branch, bending small limbs as their quest becomes more urgent. Mary and the other girls stand on the bank screaming, "Save them!"

"I cannot see them," Paul yells as he sits on the branch, soaking wet. "The waters be too murky.'

Mary takes a deep breath, picks up a stick and points, "Over to thy right, Thomas be under that branch. Hasten! Paul, Johnny be over there, just under thou main branch."

Paul looks at the spot Mary is pointing, unable to see anything among the leaves and muddy water, "I see naught."

"They be there!" Mary implores shaking her finger at the spot under the branch. "I know it to be."

The boys jump into the water and dive below the surface. The four of them are under for a few seconds searching the spot Mary has indicated. One by one they resurface, shaking their heads. They each take another deep breath and dive again into the swirling waters. This time two of them resurface, dragging Thomas awkwardly to fresh air. Like his rescuers, Thomas is badly scratched and bleeding, coughing and spluttering, gasping for breath. Mary doesn't care about that at all, at least he is breathing. They bring him ashore as the others surface screaming for help.

"We've found him! Johnny be trapped under the log. Quick, we need more help."

Thomas's two rescuers dive back into the river. Thomas sits in the mud, coughing and spitting murky water out of his lungs. He watches, through half opened, bloodshot eyes the scene as it unfolds in front of him. The children go down two at a time, feverously working to free their friend. Two come up for air just as another two dive back in. After what feels like an eternity, a miracle occurs, three children surface. Finally, it is done; they have Johnny!

The children clamber to the shore to the cheers of the girls on the bank. Only Mary stands there silent, looking down at her feet where a pure white dove has fallen from the sky. She reaches forward and lifts the beautiful, lifeless, bird up into her hand. She studies the bird closely; it weighs heavy in her palm as if it too has just come from the river. Its head is bloodied. A trickle of murky water drips from its open beak. She says quietly, knowingly, with dread and certainty in her voice, "It be a sign!"

The boys lay Johnny on the bank and stand around him, looking in disbelief. Johnny's head is split with a deep gash across his forehead. Blood trickles down his face and onto the boulder that supports his limp body. Everyone has the same thought; there is too much blood. His skin is pale, a little bluish in color. His eyes are wide open, sightless and scary. They stare directionless at the sky above. He has a strangely peaceful expression on his face. An unsettling air of serenity has befallen him.

"Be he dead?" Sarah asks, not particularly wanting to hear the answer.

Paul lowers his head respectfully and nods. Sarah begins to scream, pushing away her friends as they try to comfort her. Turning away from the grisly scene, she runs up the hill as she tries desperately to create some distance between herself and the site of the accident. Most of the other girls run too, leaving to seek help. The boys shake their heads in disbelief. They stand or sit around Johnny's lifeless body as they try to understand how this could have happened.

Mary tosses the bird disdainfully aside. There is nothing she can do. There is nothing she can change. She sits next to Thomas on the riverbank. He is covered in mud, sore, cut and bruised yet breathing more regularly now. She looks out across the river at nothing in particular. Without looking, she reaches for his hand. Their fingers entwine and grip tightly.

Thomas looks at Mary as he asks, "Thou knew, didn't thou?"

Mary gazes, devoid of emotion, out across the river. On the other bank a group of gray sparrows forage amongst the grass for seeds, oblivious to the human drama unfolding opposite. Mary realizes the universe doesn't care; life goes on, no matter what. She nods her acknowledgement to both Thomas and God.

Thomas sits beside her, lost in thought for a few moments. Eventually he leans over and whispers in her ear, "I shan't ever question nor doubt thou again. Not as long as we both shall live."

They sit silently for what seems like hours, gazing at nothing in particular, nothing more to say. They are still there, sitting hand in hand, like this when the adults from the village start to clamber down the hill. Mary is exhausted, her heart filled with disappointment as she contemplates a life unnecessarily lost.

On the hill above the creek, Jezebel sits silently. Calmly she watches the foolish human melodrama being playing out by the river bed, mindful at all times of Mary's precise location. She remains content, happy in the knowledge that Mary is in no immediate danger. Not at this point in time, anyway.

She stands guard, hidden from curious human eyes, just to make sure. She is ready to intercede should this situation change rapidly. She is well aware humans are notoriously fickle, unpredictable creatures with irrational, violent tendencies. Mary is the only one she trusts. Mary is the only one worthy of her benevolence. After all, Mary and Jezebel have a familiarity that other humans could not possibly comprehend nor understand; certainly not with their feeble closed and superstitious minds.

Jezebel watches………

'Scared'

Lost,
Dark,
Confused,
Scared.

Awake,
Bright,
Confused,
Scared.

Chapter 4

Wednesday, February 15th, 2006.
I guess???????
Location unknown.

Where am I? Oh God, where am I?

I feel a cold sweat dripping down my brow. Liquid fear somehow begins to replace the blood racing through my veins. Something is not right here; that is obvious. My surroundings are just so different. My body is not working as it should. Everything is dark, far too dark. I try to concentrate, to move my eye muscles. However nothing happens. My eyes remain firmly shut and obsolete. I find myself trapped, trapped in my prison of darkness; surrounded by a foreign world with unknown dangers. I am an eyelid width away from visual freedom yet that feels like a world away. My brain begins to spin. I am terrified. 'Terrified' is too weak a word to describe how I feel at this point in time. However, I am at a loss as to what word would be apt in this situation.

What the hell is going on? Am I safe here? Why can't I see? Why can't I move? Is this it? Is this all I have left? Will I be trapped in this darkness forever?

My breathing increases sharply as I lie wide awake, though reluctantly immobile. Frantically I try to move every muscle, one by one, in a very systematic manner. My efforts fail to provoke a response. My body appears to be, in layman's terms, paralyzed, though I know these medical problems are never that simplistic. Maybe it is a result of the trauma I have suffered during the accident. I guess that's at least plausible at this stage with the limited information I have at hand.

To my left a sound emanates. At first I pay it no heed, though now it intrigues me greatly. Maybe it holds a clue as to where I am. It is a quiet, artificial sound, a regular pattern of beeping, soft though insistent. It appears to remain at the same pitch, at a fairly steady, repetitive rate. I know that I can use my curious mind to work this out.

What is that machine? Am I hooked up to it? What on earth is it for?

I can sense little points of pressure on my skin. They feel like circular stickers. Maybe they fasten, strategically, some type of sensor to my body in all the relevant spots. I can discern the machine's rhythm changing tempo as my breathing and heart rate increases along with my level of anxiety. Maybe these stickers connect me to some sort of heart rate monitor. It's possible, though I can't be certain in this damn infuriating darkness.

I prick up my ears, concentrating hard, searching for any other sounds that might provide some clues in this void. After all, my ears and mind appear to be the only survival mechanisms at my disposal at present. In the distance I can hear a mixture of incoherent sounds, mixed chaotically together. I concentrate, struggling to decipher what they are. At a basic level, the faint sounds appear to be fragments of numerous conversations, occurring all at once. I quickly find that trying to comprehend their tangled messages is a fruitless task, a foolish exercise which provides me with no new useful information. I am left with a frustrating sensation that these incomprehensible conversations could be important.

Damn I need my eyes!

Listening closely I can determine that the sounds are moving, indicating that the people are talking while walking. Their words come closer before trailing off just as quickly. The more I try, the more impossible I find it. There is simply no way to determine what the voices are saying other than for a few futile words. I am just so damn frustrated. It is infuriating not knowing where I am, what precisely has happened and why I'm being kept here; wherever here is. I feel I need to try harder, look deeper for clues and unravel this mystery which has now engulfed and imprisoned my life.

I must work this out!

I take note of the strong smell of antiseptic mixed with lemon as it wafts through the air. I begin to wonder if some sort of detergent is being used to try to hide the overpowering smell of sickness. I have had an overwhelming sensation, since the first moment I woke, that I was in an extremely clean environment. This smell is an aroma I am all too familiar with, having been employed in a doctor's surgery while I was working my way through University. My analytical mind knows exactly what these clues mean. Cleaning on a more concentrated level, combined with a heart rate monitor can only mean one thing; I am definitely in a hospital of some sort. It just shouldn't be so dark with all this activity going on around me.

Stop! Concentrate and work this out. Why can't I open my eyes?

I take a deep breath and consider my plan of attack. All I can do is use what I already know to find questions I need to answer.

A hospital; where?

No clue at all about where I am.

Why?

Oh my God! That's right. I was in a car accident. A lady was hit with my car. Oh Hell! I hit a lady with my car. I can still see her terrified eyes pleading as she bounces over the bonnet. It makes me sick just thinking about her. I never imagined in my wildest nightmares that I would ever be responsible for hurting someone in this way.

How did I get here?

I must have been transported by an ambulance. I don't remember seeing one. There were no colored flashing lights or loud sirens. Why were there no sirens, even in the distance? All I remember is the doctor who tried to help by the roadside. That's it; the emergency crews must have arrived on the scene after I blacked out. I guess the doctor must have placed the call; that is the only logical solution. Yes, I remember hitting my head then everything fading as I slowly drifted into a state of unconsciousness.

I still can't open my eyes though I am wide awake and seemingly coherent enough. Why? Why is such a simple reflex action so impossible to execute? Why has my brain disconnected from my nervous system? Why?

Must be due to the trauma I suffered as a result of hitting my head on the steering wheel. That's got to be it. I remember the blood. There was so much blood. So much blood! To hit my head that hard must have done some internal damage, some bruising of the brain perhaps. Though, now that I think about it, I don't recall any pain. Maybe that was just how my brain responded to protect me in a dire situation such as this. Every receptor was instantaneously switched off.

Am I really that badly injured?

I guess so. That would have to be bleeding obvious. Otherwise I wouldn't be lying here completely incapacitated. There seems to be only two possible reasons why I am in this predicament. Either my body has shut down as a result of the trauma of the accident or I have been placed, by the doctors, into an induced coma of some sorts in order to assist and speed up my recovery. I have heard they resort to drastic action such as that these days. It can produce miraculous outcomes in cases of severe trauma to the brain. Or maybe I'm simply paralyzed as a result of horrific injuries. Maybe my spine was broken. Jesus! No, that can't be. If I were paralyzed I could still open my eyes. No, this is unlikely, I hope. I hope I am right.

I feel so tired. I don't know what day it is or how long I have slept. It feels like I have had no sleep at all. The only thing I know for certain is I must stay awake. Sleep leaves me confused and vulnerable. I need to think, to listen, to hear, to smell and decipher the clues my available senses are receiving. I must not sleep, though my will to achieve this goal is feeble.

Instantly I realize something frightful. I am not alone. From some distance away I can hear footsteps on a hard, uncompromising floor; more likely to be concrete than wood. My pulse quickens as I sense the unidentified person is approaching. They are edging closer, not running, though moving with conviction and purpose. Their footsteps halt as the person reaches the edge of my bed. I tense as I consider the intentions of this unknown person. I wonder why they are taking such an interest in me. I feel the stale air move slightly as the person roams stealthily around my frozen body. Their intentions remain undisclosed. I hear a metallic rattle. I wonder. I just wonder if that might be a pen on a string swinging into a metal clip board. I would imagine there is usually a clip board at the end of a patient's bed. That is what I have seen on all those American T.V. hospital shows. Maybe it is something else, something my fanciful imagination cannot grasp at this time.

One thing is certain. The mystery person hovering around me is a woman. I can be positive about that much, at least. She is wearing some sort of pleasant, flowery perfume. However, the name of the fragrance eludes me. I am usually an expert at identifying fragrances too, as they are one of the things I research and include in my novels. It smells like jasmine. Maybe it is something new on the market.

I feel contact, though remain unable to react, as the woman reaches out and gently lifts my hand. My heartbeat increases with her touch, sending the heart rate monitor into a mild frenzy.

Why can't I see you? Why can't I pull my hand away?

"C'mon honey," she says in a caring, soothing voice. Her English is relatively good. I would deduce from this that she is educated, to some extent. However, there is an underlying accent which suggests to me that she may have been born overseas. Or maybe she has grown up in a household where English was a secondary language. Anyhow, she sounds like an adult, probably in her twenties or early thirties. Her fingers feel small, yet are warm on my skin. Her hands are smooth and gentle like they have been spared from heavy manual labor. She has a light and caring touch. "Calm down, Sweetheart. No need to panic. We'll look after you. Just take it easy and rest. That is all you have to do. Trust in the Lord and let your body rest and heal. We'll take good care of you."

I try to calm myself somewhat though it is difficult being trapped in complete darkness. However, my spirits rise as I listen to the unfamiliar stranger with the soothing, friendly voice. Maybe I am safe here, wherever here might be. At least that's my hope. I'm not in any position to defend myself if I am wrong, anyway. All I have to save me is hope. Of course, if they were going to do me harm, they would have already had plenty of opportunity.

Surely I am safe. Surely she is just trying to help. Surely.

As my breathing begins to slow and my heart beat begins to fall back to its normal resting rate, I hear the beeping machine slow its tempo. It is definitely a heart rate monitor, there can be no doubt. This has to be some sort of hospital. I am beginning to lean towards the idea that they have induced a coma to help me heal. I wonder what drugs they would use to do that. I have been told some stories of people making incredible recoveries, from hideous accidents, using this technique. I hope they are more credible than fairytales. That would at least make sense with what I am experiencing with my body. I wish I could ask some questions.

I need to remain cautious in case I am wrong. I don't want to draw any unnecessary attention to myself while I work out what my predicament actually is.

"That's better," the stranger whispers as she continues to go about her work. "They tell me I be stupid for talking to people in comas. I have no time to listen to them. I believe what I want to believe and no fool is goin' to change my mind. I know you can hear me. Just take it easy, Sweetheart. Everything is going to be fine."

Coma! Finally some confirmation. I guess that was really the only thing that would make sense. It would explain completely what I'm experiencing. I wish I could just ask some questions, get some answers as to why I am conscious and alert yet unable to open my eyes or move a muscle. I want to know what the doctor's think my prognosis is. Am I going to recover from this? No, I should be more positive. When am I going to recover?

I decide to try a simple experiment. Unfortunately it fails miserably. The muscles around my eyes just won't flinch in the slightest as I strain to invoke some movement. I remain frustrated. I can't think of a way to signal that I am conscious, to signal I can hear. It's like the connections from my brain, through my nerves, to every part of my body are disconnected. Everything should work. I'm here, I'm alert. Yet nothing, save my mind, is working. Why would my body shut down like this? Why?

I become aware that a second person has entered my room as I hear someone gasp audibly from a distance away. The mystery lady, who I now believe to be a nurse, twists slightly making her rubber soled shoes squeak as they brush against the floor.

"Can I help you?" she asks with enough authority to suggest that visitors are frowned upon. I wait in anticipation to receive some small clue as to the identity of the person she is confronting. I hope with all my heart it is someone I know.

There is swift movement. Footsteps shuffling closer, though still some distance away. Someone sniffs as if they are suffering from the flu or, more likely, have been crying. The steps are somehow familiar. This is definitely someone I know, it must be. Who is it? Who dammit? My excitement builds. I feel I am smiling though I suspect no one close to me can see any evidence of that. My muscles refuse to display my emotions.

Is it...... ?

"I am Julie's boyfriend, can I come in or is this the wrong time?" Peter asks hesitantly.

Peter! I'm here. Come quick. I need your help!

Overcome with emotion I scream out for Peter as I feel my body shiver and become filled with fear that I will break down and cry. I suspect by their reactions, that Peter and the nurse are completely unaware of my excitement. They both continue with their conversation without giving me a second thought. I keep forgetting my actions purely exist in the prison that is my mind.

The nurse leaves my side as she walks towards Peter. Her tone is noticeably softer as she whispers earnestly, "Of course, come in Darling. It's not visiting hours but I think it be a good thing to bend the rules a little. In my experience, I have found it can help sometimes. I have never been one to play by the man's silly rules anyhow. Life is too short."

I sigh as I hear the footsteps of both Peter and the nurse moving towards my bed. All I want to do is sit up, reach out, hug and kiss my man endlessly. No matter how much I try, I remain immobile, trapped in my dark purgatory.

How long must I endure this?

"I.... I just wanted to be close to her, to let her know she is not alone," Peter offers, his voice quivering with emotion. I know how much he loves me; we both feel so strongly for each other that, at times, it's overwhelming. However, I have never heard his voice so scratchy, so worried, so uncertain. I hate hearing him so upset. Maybe he knows more than I have been able to establish; he must. Maybe he knows just how dire my current predicament really is. After all, he can see my body, no doubt battered, bruised, broken and scarred after the accident. He knows exactly how bad my condition is and his tentative words reflect his assessment of my health.

Oh God, I wish I could see again! What the hell is wrong with me?

"It's okay. You're right. Just hearing the voice of a loved one or feeling their touch can have a drastic effect. I've seen it before. I don't know if you have been told; it's probably not my place to tell you. Anyhow, I don't care for rules. So let me tell you. The doctors don't expect Julie to be in a coma for all that long. In fact, they are not quite sure why her body has drifted into a coma in the first place. There isn't a great deal of trauma associated with her accident. Normally, something like a sharp blow to the head is required to cause this sort of reaction. Anyhow, I talk too much. I've been told such on numerous appraisals. I don't care much for what they have to say anyway. I am who I am, and I won't be a changing for anyone. Certainly no fool man who thinks he be superior to me."

I am startled, for an instant, by the unexpected sound of something wooden being dragged across the floor towards my bed. I suspect this object is some piece of furniture, maybe a chair, being moved closer to where I am lying. I suspect Peter is intending to sit next to me.

"I'll leave you two alone for a while. I'll try and make sure you're not spotted by one of the other nosey nurses who have no business here. They be always trying to stick their noses into my business, trying to get me in trouble with the boss. I don't care about his rules, I be no slave to no surly white man. He's not superior to me with his jive talk of love and commitment when he be cheatin' on his wife. No sir; I don't care for his damn rules or consequences. I just try to help folk who need help. God knows I be a good soul who harm no one. That just be me and I won't be a changin' for anyone. No sir," the nurse says as I hear her leaving my side and walking away.

The nurse moves quickly as she glides lightly across the floor. I hear her pause briefly at the edge of the room before she leaves. Her footsteps merge momentarily with all the other sounds that linger beyond my room. With a click all the background noise is suddenly diminished as the door shuts behind her, sheltering Peter and I from the curious gaze of others.

I lie in the bed motionless and frustrated, yet with little choice. My body remains prone and obsolete. I can't even mouth a few words. It just doesn't make sense. Alas, this is my plight. I am injured and this is part of the natural healing process I guess.

For a moment I forget that Peter is still in the room, he is so quiet. It is only when I feel the roughness of his hand reaching out and picking up mine, that I realize he is there. I try desperately to speak, to let him know I am fine, to ease his concerns in some way. However, no words are spoken. The heart rate monitor picks up a little pace for a second before I calm myself down. I resign myself to rest and tolerate my current predicament. I will tolerate it for the moment, until I can work out how to fix this, if I can.

Peter holds my hand gently in one of his, rubbing the back of my hand like he is patting a fragile new born kitten. For a long time he doesn't speak. I know he is upset. I suspect he is coping badly by the way his hands shake as he tries to comfort me. I wish I could communicate to him, let him know that I am aware of his touch, can smell that awful cologne that he likes so much, can hear every sigh he breathes. I want to be able to comfort him as he comforts me.

Peter sighs deeply. With some effort he says, "There are just so many things I want to say to you. There are thousands, no millions of thoughts and words I have going through my head, conversations yet to be had, thoughts yet to be shared. I just hope I still have the opportunity to .... to ...."

What does he know that I NEED to know?

I hear his words taper off, unable to continue to express his emotions and fears clearly. I sense he is struggling to hold back his tears. I have never experienced this depth of emotion with Peter in the four years I have known him. If the current situation fills Peter with fear, then it grips me with terror.

My frustration increases as I hear Peter begin to cry. His sobs are at first muffled, like he is trying to hold back the inevitable flood. Eventually he succumbs to his feelings and begins to sob uncontrollably, squeezing my hand tighter as he does.

I begin to feel like crying too. Like my speech and movements, nothing works, nothing happens. Tears refuse to form, no matter how upset I become. Time in this predicament is impossible to measure. At the very least this scene has played out for some minutes now, maybe longer. The sadness I feel weighs heavy, draining my already depleted energy reserves further. Eventually, overcome by my emotions and frustrations, I fall towards sleep. Peter continues to hold my hand tight, unaware of the change in my state. It happens so quickly, I fail to realize that I am beginning to drift. Maybe it is for the best. I need sleep to get better. Maybe my situation will improve when I wake.

Maybe...........

'Daylight Perhaps'

Daylight approaching,
Too bright for these eyes.
A strange era dawning,
Filled with senses that lie.

Uncertainty runs rampant,
The air reeks of doubt.
Too much for my feeble brain,
To consider and work out.

Chapter 5

Saturday, February 18th, 2006.
Location unknown.

I glance nervously over my shoulder without missing a step. I am flying, my sneakered feet slipping, struggling for traction amongst the loose gravel on this barren slope. My body aches as if I have run a marathon. Though my muscles scream for respite, I don't dare rest. That would be foolish.

I can't see them, though I have no doubt they are there. They are never far away, always lurking, creeping, hidden in the shadows. They are ruthless, relentless in their desire to do me harm. I must escape. I just must. They must not catch me. If they do, I know, all hope will be gone. They will be merciless.

I pause, laboring to catch precious breath. Heart pounding in my chest, I spy a refuge. Maybe it will prove to be a safe place to hide, a haven for the innocent. Who knows, maybe they are not so brave. They might be scared of the dark or wary that I have a surprise prepared, waiting for their arrival.

My opportunity is a narrow cave, hidden slightly by some loose rocks. On closer inspection, I find that beyond the mouth, the cavern widens to a much larger space. From my vantage point I fail to establish precisely how spacious the cave is. It is, at the very least, long enough for me to climb inside. I wonder if it has an alternate entrance. No matter. It is my only chance of putting up a credible fight. A chance I must take. The cave is pitch black inside. At least that offers me some sort of miniscule advantage.

Rrrrrrowwww!

I spin as I catch my breath. Looking down the slope I see nothing, just remnant scrub here and there, grasping a tenuous foothold on this God forsaken moonscape. That wild noise is unmistakable, however. The beasts are close, too close for my liking. Skilled hunters, I am sure they have picked up my scent. Their mouths will be salivating, hungry for blood, my blood. My mind is made up. I am out of options. I scamper into the darkness of the cave. This will be the site of my last stand against the evil that circles me with murderous intent.

Once inside, I look around the fortress that is mine. To my surprise the cave is indeed quite spacious. There are numerous small fissures in the walls, none of which seem large enough for me to crawl inside and hide. Loose rocks, of various sizes, lie on the floor indicating recent instability. However, as I stand there, hands on hips, gazing around, it seems stable enough for my needs. I nod as I deem it to be an adequate hiding place, a place where I have a chance to survive. I hope to live to see the day when I sing its praises. At least, that is my frail hope.

Rrrrrooowwww!

Instinctively, I squat in a ball, arms crossed over my chest. I begin to shudder, each cell in my body agitated, nervously anticipating my fate, whatever that may be. The beasts seem so close now, too damn close for my liking. They have definitely caught my scent. There can be no doubt. They have probably been watching my movements for a while now. Eyes wide open; I search the horizon, though I fear they are closer. I begin to wonder what they have in store for me. Are they smart? Are they toying with me? Hell, I just don't know. In fact I don't even know what they are or how they operate. I do not know their motivation. I am very much in the dark, in every respect.

Mmmmrrrrr.

Shit! Shit! Are they outside, just to the side of the cavern? They are so bloody close. I thought I had more time to prepare my defenses. What the hell do I do now? What have I got to defend myself with; just a few loose rocks, my bare hands, my mind and precious else? Shit! What do they want? Why are they chasing me? How can I reason with something as primitive as pure evil? I just can't. SHIT!

I search the dimly lit cave for who knows what. I crawl around the floor looking for something, some form of inspiration. Anything I can use as a crude yet effective weapon. Just something that will give me a fighting chance. Realistically, I am unlikely to find a loaded gun or Excalibur discarded in the dampness, waiting for my arrival. I remain hopeful that there is something here, something I can use or forge quickly into a weapon. My mind is distracted. I am intently aware my time is running out. However, I'll be damned if I'm going down without a fight.

My right hand grasps a rock from the floor which has captured my interest. It sits snugly in the palm of my hand. I test its weight; solid, yet light enough to obtain a good velocity, hopefully a deadly velocity. My fingers trace over its jagged, misshapen surface. I feel its razor sharp edges cut my skin with precision, just like a surgeon's scalpel. I lift my finger in front of my eyes. Catching some filtered light from the cave entrance, I see a thin trickle of blood sliding down my index finger. I smile to myself. This will do nicely.

Mmmmmm.

I freeze as a large shadow falls across the entrance of the cave. They are here. My heart races as uncertainty grips my mind. What the hell would make a shadow like that? Is it some sort of devilish beast, something not of this world? What sort of unholy creature can it be? Is it alone? How many are there? Why are they stalking me? Am I nothing more than a quick snack?

The shadow traverses its path slowly across the cave entrance until it reaches the other side, disappearing out of sight. I wait for the beast to attack. Surprisingly, as seconds go by, I realize it has chosen to remain outside the cave. Bewildered, I frown as I wonder if it knows that I'm here lurking in the darkness with my rock. Like all wild creatures, it can smell my scent. At the very least it knows I have passed this way. Maybe it is searching for my trail. Or maybe it is playing with me, stalking me. A third possibility is that it is fearful, apprehensive of what surprises await it in the darkness? I hope it is scared. That means I have a chance to hurt it, maybe even incapacitate it. I wish I knew what the beast was thinking.

Suddenly, I feel a shudder, gentle at first, though growing in intensity. The floor begins to vibrate as I see a fissure in the wall to my left open up before my eyes. Small rocks begin to fall from the ceiling, pelting me in the head and shoulders. I drop my weapon and cover my head in a desperate act of self-preservation. For the moment, all thoughts of the beasts at my doorstep are forgotten as my life is in more immediate danger from my former safe haven.

Within seconds the quake abates. Coughing and spluttering, I steadily regain my senses. Slowly, through the dust haze, I stand, assessing the structural changes to my surroundings as they become visible, searching for imperfections which could further endanger my safety. I quickly establish that something strange has taken place. The interior of my little cave has more light for some reason. The air is musty, filled with fine dust. Things are not right; not as they were moments ago.

Shit. Shit!

I stare at the entrance in utter disbelief. It is now completely blocked by massive boulders, dislodged from the surface during the earthquake. Turning my attention to the walls of the cave I see the source of all this light. Plastered on the walls throughout the entire cavern are millions of fireflies, glowing luminously in the pitch darkness as they clamber over each other striving for the best position.

I begin to sob. Then fall to my knees as I realize my predicament. I am trapped. I am trapped.

"Noooooo!" I scream as I hear my words reverberate throughout my prison.

Boom, boom, BOOM!

*   *   *

I wake with a start, body immobile, blood racing through my veins. Everything is bright, far too bright. It is like I am looking directly into the sun on a cloudless summer day. Everything is blurry. As I squint, taking quick glimpses of my surrounding world, I can see colors and vague shapes. It is so difficult to adjust my eyes to recognize and comprehend exactly what I am looking at.

I frown, closing my eyes completely. I hold them shut for a few seconds, protecting my fragile irises from the scorching light. Eventually, with some effort, I force them open again. Just for a few seconds. Just long enough to allow them to adjust to my surroundings. The light is still too bright. It inflicts a sharp stabbing pain which extends from my eyes, deep into my brain. I close my eyes quickly once more, seeking temporary shelter, though knowing I need to persevere with this process till I can see, unhindered by the glare or pain. I begin to repeat this process over and over again, sure that I will eventually be able to keep my eyes open. I'm just not sure when.

Each time I try, my eyes, little by little, become more adjusted. The length of time I can keep them open is steadily increasing. However, visibility and perception are still lacking. The pain from using dormant eyes is steadily abating as they become more accustomed to normal wavelengths of light. Eventually, the glare eases and I find I can keep my eyes open. I find myself squinting, blinking more often than normal. Some clarity begins to appear, though this is distorted by the increased moisture welling in my eyes. I finally get my first look at the place I have been reluctantly kidnapped to, the place which, for better or worse, has been my darkened home for the past few days.

How many days have I been here?

At first I can only make out the larger shapes. My blurred vision restricts the level of detail yet, from what I can see, there appears to be another bed in my room. The occupant of the bed is snoring loudly. I guess, by the verbose nature of the snoring, that my roommate must be a man, though I can't be a hundred percent certain. I assume he must have arrived in our room sometime while I was sleeping for I haven't heard any sounds before this time. I am a notoriously heavy sleeper at the best of times so I can understand how he was brought into the room without my notice.

Everything is very white; this is unmistakable. For my poor sore eyes it is all a bit too bright. Somehow it matches my dreams and thoughts of what it will be like when I die and walk hand in hand with a guiding angel towards heaven. One thing I know for sure, I am still on earth. I am certain of that. I have not died. This is a hospital of some sort, not a pathway leading to the pearly gates.

The whiteness does not assist the clarity of my sight in the slightest. I wish there was a little more color here and there providing a contrast my eyes can latch onto. I continue to struggle to identify the individual objects in my current surroundings.

I raise my head slightly and look beside my bed. A dark brown wooden chair is pulled close, though, alas, it is vacant. Peter must have finally gone home. I wonder if it was his decision or the doctor's. He has been here every time I have been awake over the last few days.

Being comatose appears to heighten one's senses. I could hear his soothing words and most certainly recognize his distinctive Bulgarian cologne. That cologne's aroma is something unique, which only Peter loves. It has a strange twang to its odor, which I tolerate more than adore. He bought gallons of it from a dubious character at the local pub, one drunken evening. He claims he got the bargain of the century. Though personally, I can't wait till the day when he runs out of the stuff.

I chuckle slightly as I think about Peter being here while I was unconscious and gone now that I am awake; what are the chances? My smile wanes as I consider how he must be coping. His emotions have been frayed during my stay. He has not been the tower of strength that he usually is. Normally, he is the rock our relationship is built upon.

He must be so worried.

Peering around the room further I notice a splash of color sitting atop of what is probably a small fold out table. I squint, trying to get a better look at the object. Eventually I work it out. The object looks like it could be a bouquet of beautiful flowers, held in a tall, grey metal vase. I can't make out their variety. They just appear to me as a fuzzy mixture of reds, yellows and white. I shake my head in disbelief.

That would have to be the perfect gift for someone like me who is comatose and unable to open their eyes!

I glance towards my left, where the sound of music is softly emanating. I can vaguely see the dark shape of a compact disk player resting on top of the set of drawers, by the bed. It is quietly playing one of my John Farnham CD's. I assume this is so it will not disturb the other patient in my room. Other John Farnham CDs lie nearby, in a neat little stack. I first noticed the music while I was comatose, though had given it little thought. I considered it was just my mind playing tricks on me, making the most of idle time. My mind often drifts, remembering favorite songs, songs which I sometimes sing along with as I am driving. This habit greatly annoys my family and friends. I have heard how people who are in comas can be brought around by comforting words or familiar and loved sounds. Maybe that is what the CD player is all about. Maybe it helped, who knows. It certainly didn't hurt.

At least someone thought a little about what music I liked.

Over in the distance, a little to my right, there is an open doorway. I can discern the fuzzy colors of people as they pass by every now and then. There are sounds of metal trolleys and the like going to and fro. Eventually, a person dressed entirely in blue walks in. They block the doorway completely as they lean against the wall. As the person stares in my direction, I tilt my head slowly, trying to gain a better look. Alas, my sight has not returned enough to discern facial features clearly. I cannot work out whether the person is male or female.

Are you a nurse or an orderly perhaps?

"Well then, what have we here? Sleeping beauty has finally decided to grace us with her presence," she says as she displays her gleaming white teeth in a broad smile and walks steadily towards me. I can roughly make out her features as she moves closer; her dark skin, freckled face, dark wavy hair and her sparkling teeth so prominent.

"What...?"

"What's up Honey? Take your time. You've probably got a couple of questions you want some answers for. Anyways, I know your name is Julie but I don't think ya know mine. I be Nurse Pamela, here at your service," the nurse says using the sweet reassuring voice I have heard so often while in my coma. The familiar smell of her perfume wafts into my nostrils as she takes my arm, checking my pulse.

"What......what day is it?" I gargle hoarsely. My painfully sore throat feels as if it has never been used to make speech before. I gulp, trying to lubricate it somewhat, as the nurse pours and offers me a plastic cup of water. "Thank you."

"That's okay, Sweetheart, you've been no trouble as a patient, no trouble at all. Not like that damn fool of a cheating, married, sorta boyfriend of mine. If you only knew the trouble an' strife he is a causin'," Pamela laughs as she speaks.

"What day is it?" I ask again, more clearly this time.

Pamela stops her fussing as she holds my hand and says "Sorry Sweetie, I been meaning to get to that. It be Saturday, February the 18th. Honey, you've been out cold for four days straight. Gave us a right scare, didn't ya?."

I frown, feeling groggy and disorientated. I knew I had lost track of time, however I had convinced myself that it was not that long, "Four days?"

The nurse releases my hand and lays it gently back down, tucking it under the blanket as she gives it a friendly pat, "Count yourself lucky Darling, comas are funny things. Sometimes people never come out of them. In your case we still don't know why you went into one. There be no obvious signs of trauma. The way the mind works is a tricky thing. I make no claim to knowin' how the man's brain functions, if it works at all."

I rack my disorientated brain for answers. Pieces of information are jumbled together in an irrational fashion. A child's lullaby, a sense of fear, a man covered in blood, a couple passing by, insane laughter, a babies muffled cry, the smell of smoke and a woman hitting my windscreen with an incredible, gut wrenching force.

Shit! That is it; the accident.

"I must have banged my head during the accident," I offer, convinced I make perfect sense.

Pamela stares at me with a quizzical expression on her face as if she has some problem with what I am saying. She remains frozen in thought for a few seconds. Abruptly, she bursts out laughing. It is a hearty, genuine laugh which doesn't seem to match my honest appraisal of how I ended up in a coma. "That's a beauty, Honey. You have a great sense of humor."

"What are you talking about? It's quite simple. I banged my head during......."

"Julie!" comes Peter's shrill voice. He cannot restrain his relief as he looks into my room and spies that I am awake. I smile, hand outstretched as I desperately seek his embrace. Running the few steps across the floor, he takes my hand in his as his free hand pulls the chair out from under the bed. Holding my hand tightly, as if he never wants to let me go again, he bends forward and kisses me on the lips. We part slowly as I run my fingers through his hair. Tears of joy begin to form in my eyes. It has been frustrating being so close to Peter, though with an insurmountable impasse between us. Peter whispers softly as he pulls away, "I love you."

I smile as I whisper back, "Love you too."

Peter sits as he regains his breath, looking smug like a cat after catching a mouse. He falls silent, as he steadily composes himself, gathering and savoring the happy thoughts which flood his mind. His face beams with excitement. He places his free hand on top of mine, securing it completely between his two tradesman's hands.

The nurse saunters around the bed, placing a hand on Peter's shoulder causing him to turn slightly and smile at her. She says, "She's a right card, this one. Thinks she's been in a serious accident. The funny ones always are the best catches. Someone who makes you smile. Mmm, mmm. How I wish my Frederick had just a smidgen of a sense of humor. I wouldn't let this one get away. Hold her tight, Gorgeous. Don't let her go."

"I don't intend to," Peter chimes with enthusiasm, turning his smile and focus back to me. "I don't intend to lose you again. Ever!"

Nurse Pamela turns, looks towards the heavens and mumbles to herself, "Mmm, mmm. All the good ones are taken." She looks Peter up and down, "Particularly the ones with good butts. Hallelujah, Lord, ain't that the truth. Just the married and unfaithful for little old Pamela, hey? What did I do to deserve this life? I go to church every Sunday and this be my reward? Ahhhhh! I guess when it's all boiled down you're nothing but a God in man's image anyway. From where I stand, that's not much better than a donkey's arse. That's just what I believe and I ain't changin' my mind for no man or his God. So you'll just have to lump it."

I laugh as the nurse walks briskly out of the room leaving the two of us alone for the first time.

What a hoot she is, a veritable firecracker, difficult for any man to try to tame.

My sight still has room for improvement, though even I can see the features displayed on Peter's pale, gaunt face. Dark bags sag under his eyes making him appear years older than I remember him. His hair is unkempt and a little tangled. It is dark and unwashed. His face is covered in stubble that is more than a day old. It is clear he has not coped well with my hospital stay. I guess I would be disappointed if he seemed unfazed by my predicament.

Looking into his eyes, I express my concern as he smiles foolishly back at me, "You need to look after yourself, Babe."

Peter laughs, a hearty laugh, throwing his head back in an exuberant, involuntary response. With tears in his eyes he retorts, "You should be the one to talk! Fancy giving us a scare like that. Four days in a coma!"

I close my eyes and frown. Tired, overwhelmed and most importantly, still very much confused. I need equal amounts of rest and information desperately to ease the ache in my brain. For someone who has slept so much, I feel like I have been deprived of a good night's sleep for days.

I realize I cannot sleep and seek answers at the same time. I decide to try for the latter first. I ask bluntly, "Peter, what exactly happened to me?"

Peter looks a little bewildered, uncertainty evident in his expression. I watch him closely. Maybe he is struggling to find the right words to explain my predicament; words which will not alarm me. I am confused by the odd expression on his face as he speaks, "The doctor was hoping you could fill in those gaps for him. He doesn't seem to have a clue."

"What do you mean? Surely it has something to do with the accident, doesn't it?"

Peter is confused. He shakes his head in a negative manner as he opens his mouth to speak. He is stopped from expressing his thoughts as the doctor strolls cheerfully into the room. Grinning broadly, he moves towards me, Nurse Pamela following close behind. He moves forward like a sprinter. With not so much as an introduction, he flicks on his little torch, promptly shining it deep into my eyes. My poor eyes scream out in pain as they react defensively, squinting in a desperate attempt to get away from the sudden brightness.

"Hey!" I call out, shocked at his aggressive bed side manner. The doctor seems completely unperturbed. He continues his examination at a break neck speed. Finally he switches off his torch and replaces it in his breast pocket.

Smiling first at me, then at Peter he says, "There we are, never in doubt! I thought you would come out of this in your own good time. Good responsiveness. Everything seems to be in order"

Peter stands, pushing the chair backwards with his legs causing it to squeak on the hard floor. He shakes the doctor's hand vigorously as he seeks some clarification. He squints at the doctor's name badge as he explains, "Doctor Khan, Julie was wondering what happened to her. I wasn't quite sure how to explain it to her."

As Peter returns to his chair and I regain his hand in mine, the doctor turns back to face me. I can see he is young, maybe early thirties at most. He has an olive complexion and dark hair. It appears he might be of Indian extraction. He certainly speaks excellent English, without a hint of an accent. This suggests to me that he might be Australian born and raised, maybe second or third generation considering the confidence with which he speaks.

He leans on the back of Peter's chair as he consults me, "That is the million dollar question. It's the reason I come to work each day. I just love the bizarre and unexplained situations that crop up in medicine. Yours is a most unusual case."

Struggling to focus on more than one person talking in the room I ask the most detailed question my frazzled brain can formulate, "What.....?"

Dr. Khan, seeing the odd expression on my face takes a more professional stance and says earnestly, "Well, to be honest with you, we are not exactly sure what happened. Your case is something of a conundrum. We've run a full gamete of tests. We have studied everything from your blood work all the way through to the electrical activity of your neural synapses. However, in the end, we have found very little other than a slight fluctuation in your brain's electrical impulses, when you were first admitted."

"What does that indicate doctor? Some sort of tumor perhaps?" Peter asks, completely confused. Medical matters always seem to be beyond his scope to grasp. He has a tendency to latch onto the worst possible scenario, particularly when a simpler explanation readily presents itself. A prime example of this was when he suggested I may have contracted Bird Flu last spring when I merely showed symptoms relating to a mild touch of hay fever.

I punch him gently in the side as I glare at him for even suggesting I might have a tumor of some sort.

"Sorry," he offers meekly as his smile reveals he has realized the error of his thoughtless tongue.

"Not necessarily. Actually, I don't think so. The ECG settled down fairly soon after Julie arrived here. In fact within the first three or four hours her brain waves began to appear normal. We did a CAT scan and found nothing out of the ordinary as well. It's a complete mystery as to the reason for the spike in electrical activity. It seems that your body decided to shut down for a while. It is as simple and complex as that. Why it took this drastic action, we don't know. It is quite extraordinary, really."

I watch the doctor while he is trying to explain what has happened to me. His turn of phrase is making it slower for my bedraggled brain to comprehend what he is saying. Then again, maybe it is just me. As I watch him I become a little distracted. There is something about him that is familiar, something I can't quite figure out in my current frame of mind. His face is still a little blurry, even at this close distance.

Where have I seen you before?

"Don't worry," the doctor continues. "We'll do more tests and get to the bottom of this. The main thing is you're on your way to recovery. The best thing you can do is try to relax and get as much rest as you can. Sometimes the body knows what to do and heals itself, in its own good time. I'll be back a bit later to see how you're progressing."

I nod to him. The doctor swivels on his heal as Nurse Pamela moves sideways, out of his path. He briskly strides away and out of the room. The nurse follows, as best she can. Peter smiles and says simply, "I'll be back in a second, Sweetheart."

Peter alights from his chair and runs from the room. He stops the doctor in the hallway and begins an earnest discussion with him. I wonder what he has on his mind. The sounds in the hallway are too jumbled to decipher any individual conversation. I watch them carefully, as Peter waves his hands about, wondering what they are discussing.

With a concentrated effort I focus my attention on the doctor. My vision clears substantially. So much so that, even though I am some distance from the hallway, I have an excellent view of the doctor and can clearly distinguish his features. His dyed dark hair; visibly grey on the sideburns, the lean, athletic structure of his face, his bony fingers protruding from his long white overcoat.

I watch him intently, perplexed as to why he is so familiar to me. Eventually, he turns and smiles in my direction before shaking Peter's hand and walking away down the hall. It is in that instance that I make the connection; I know where I our paths have crossed.

You were at the accident. But, but why were you there? I don't understand; you would have been at the hospital, not the accident scene. I don't understand. It makes no sense at all.

Confused and tired, I close my eyes tightly as I try to sort out my fragmented thoughts. Everything is just so confused. I don't know what is real and what is little more than jumbled fragments of my dreams. Suddenly, I feel a pain in my chest, a sharp pain which cuts deep inside. Just like the pain on the fateful night of the accident. This pain is accompanied by the sound of a ball being bounced next to my bed. Opening my eyes I see a shadow move towards the open doorway, straight past the young boy holding a tennis ball in his hands. He is a chubby boy, no more than about ten years of age, I guess. He is casually dressed in a horizontally striped red and white T shirt and blue cotton shorts.

"Hey Julie, want to come out and play?" he enquires as the smell of putrid smoke reaches my nostrils.

Who are you?

The pain suddenly disappears. Averting my gaze from the boy for a second, I search for the source of the smoke. The acrid odor has now vanished. There is no evidence of anything burning. Turning my gaze back, I search for the young boy. He too has disappeared.

Was he really here, was something burning or are my senses just playing tricks? He seemed so real. But I am still so tired and groggy. He spoke to me didn't he? What did he say? What the hell is going on with me?

I don't have the chance to ponder my bizarre visitor for too long. I am startled by movement and the arrival of a solid weight jumping onto my legs which are held tight beneath the bed sheets. Changing my focus, I look down towards the end of the bed to find out precisely what this lump is. To my surprise I see a large, jet black cat staring back at me as he slowly massages the blanket, preparing a place to settle. He is a fairly young cat, little more than a year old. His individuality is distinguished by a white stripe extending down the full length of his chest and a droopy right ear. Intriguingly it has beautiful, iridescent emerald green eyes. The cat exudes contentment and seems well fed, not at all what you would expect of a stray. It finally settles, watching me intently as it begins to purr vigorously. I am surprised as the cat seems to wink at me.

Do cats wink? Is this real or just another trick of my eyes?

"Where did you come from?" I ask the cat, not really expecting a reply. The cat just continues to stare at me, purring, not in any sort of hurry to move on its way.

"I see you've found a friend." Peter says, re-entering the room. "Do you want me to take him away?"

You can see him too!

I shake my head and smile, comforted that I am not losing my mind. Not completely at least, "No, not really. He's not any problem. In fact, I quite like him. He seems to have a ......"

"Seems to have what?" Peter asks bewildered, as he tickles the cat under the chin. The appreciative cat purrs more vigorously.

I laugh, "He seems to have a pleasant disposition."

"Fair enough, I can't argue with logic like that. However, I don't think the nurses will be impressed when they find him here," Peter says, moving back to the seat and taking my hand in his once more.

I don't care. He seems to have a strange calming effect on me. I need that more than anything in my life at the moment. It is nearly like we have some sort of connection, soul mates perhaps. Anyway, I want him to stay. I hope he stays a while. I won't let them take him. If no one comes to claim him I will keep him, I have decided and that's final. If I can, I will keep Serenity with me as long as I remain in this place. Maybe he will help to get me through this.

'A Door Ajar'

A door ajar,

Light streaming through,

A brave new world beckons,

The scent of hope lingers too.

A dish waiting to be savored,

Filled with tranquility,

Garnished with a little hope and peace,

Free of ignorance and stupidity.

Chapter 6

Winter 1691.
Christmas Eve.
Salem, Massachusetts.

Thomas stops the wagon as it reaches the top of yet another mountain rise. The horses are grateful for the respite. Each day they have travelled such a long distance and the grass is green and lush in this clearing. It has been an arduous trek over the past four weeks. They have encountered many obstacles during their journey through the hills and valleys, travelling along many crudely made roads. These roads, in most cases, are simply little more than wheel tracks. They are the worthless souvenirs, discarded by earlier explorers, etched deeply into the rock and mud of this predominantly inhospitable terrain. It is but for the grace of God that their journey has not been afflicted by illness as it has for so many other travelers they have passed. The makeshift, rock covered graves, adorned with primitive crucifixes made of kindling and twine, are a constant reminder of just how difficult the crossing can be for the unwary. They have somehow remained healthy, though all are exhausted and praying that their final destination is close at hand.

Thomas surveys the valley below. The pots and pans strung up along the side of the wagon continue to clatter, though less vigorously now, as they begin to slowly settle. Silence is a rare treat, usually only savored at night fall. Thomas releases his vice like grip on the reins, allowing them to slide effortlessly through his fingers. Placing the reins on the edge of his seat, he stands in order to gain a better view of the glorious panorama laid out in front of his disbelieving eyes. Thomas grants himself the opportunity to smile. Not for the welcome respite his ears are receiving.

His smile is a manifestation of the feelings stirring in his heart as his eyes remain transfixed by the beautiful valley ahead.

Mary's black cat is hanging onto the canvas, claws fully extended. Jezebel is a wild creature which shares neither affection nor good will with Thomas, even though Thomas is the main provider of scraps during meal times. Their contempt for each other is comparable in size to Jezzie's love for Mary. The cat has been her constant companion, for as long as Thomas has known Mary. It must be eight years old if it is a day.

Mary loves Jezzie even though she isn't what you would call a 'work of art'. Half an ear missing, deep scar across its nose and a pearl colored, blind eye just add to its fearsome mystique. Jezzie's loyalty is unquestionable, though. In fact it is by far her most appealing attribute. The cat is more loyal than a dog. Jezzie has an aloofness you expect from cats. However, she is different in that she never strays too far away from Mary's side. She always seems to have a happy knack of being around to alert Mary when danger is close at hand, ready to attack if required. As with the rattle snake they encountered at their previous home. The poor snake didn't stand a chance as Jezzie pounced from behind, placing two paws on its neck before ripping its head off in one swift and vicious movement. She is indeed an unusual cat.

The sound of owls nesting peacefully echoes out of the nearby trees and across the hill top. Jezabel arches her back, looking around at the grasslands ahead as if searching for danger. Her whiskers twitching as she breathes in the unfamiliar fragrances of her new surrounds. Satisfied of her safety, she leaps from the top of the canvas and scurries off into the lush grass. In an instant she is gone, hidden somewhere amongst the thick undergrowth, close to the track which leads to the forest. The forest falls silent, as word is passed and the indigenous wildlife become aware of the new danger lurking within their midst.

Mary, sitting in the back of the wagon, looks at her girls waiting contentedly opposite her. Life would be so different if God had not chosen three of her children to join him as angels in heaven, prior to their birth. Still, with all that has happened she is grateful to God for allowing her the opportunity of seeing her two girls grow and develop into young women. Sarah and Edward have not been granted such a gift. It appears as if they never will, without the intervention of a divine miracle. For alas, it appears Sarah has been cursed by being born barren.

Both Mary's girls have their long, jet black hair pulled into ponytails. Their freckled faces glowing. They pray silently, hoping they are going to stop for the night. Bright green eyes, wide open and alert. They struggle to hold back their excitement, just waiting for the word that they can alight from the wagon. They are curious by nature and love exploring each and every new site they encounter. They love seeking out hidden treasures or exotic flowers at every stop.

Mary looks outwards from the gap in the canvas cover. The sun is high in the sky. There is still plenty of daylight left before they need to forge a camp for the night. She is puzzled by their unplanned, early stoppage. Slowly she emerges from her shelter in order to ascertain the nature of the problem. Surely it isn't another stint of inaccessible terrain which ultimately requires more back tracking. She peers out from under the canvas flap fluttering in the cold southerly breeze. She pulls her shawl tight around her as she descends via the three metal steps to solid ground. As she strolls around the wagon, her hair held tight in a bun, all she can see is Thomas standing tall next to the wagon, reins at ease on the vacant seat. She is surprised by the broad grin on his face. He appears revitalized and at peace. It is such a long time since she has last seen him this happy.

Confused, Mary asks, "What be it, my Darling? Hath our path been blocked?"

Thomas smiles at his wife, his face visibly excited and full of joy. He reaches over, grabs Mary under the arms and drags her forcibly forward and up onto the coachman's seat. She squeals her protests and punches him repeatedly in the arms to little effect. She is no match for Thomas who doesn't loosen his grip in the slightest. His strength is sufficient to lift Mary's tiny frame effortlessly onto the seat. He jumps up next to her and kisses her firmly when she is close enough, ignoring her groaning protestations.

Finally Mary wriggles out of his grasp, slaps him squarely across the cheek before straightening her rumpled clothing. "Mr. Murphy! What devil doeth possess thee? Why doeth thou feel thy hath the right to take such liberties?"

"Well, Mrs. Murphy," Thomas says. He is enjoying the day and all it has to offer. He has waited patiently for this day to come to fruition and, though tired, is ready to celebrate. He waves his hand highlighting the view across the hill top, down into the valley ahead of them. "I thought you would like to celebrate our arrival. For this will be our home."

Mary's anger begins to ease as she joins her husband looking, wide eyed, at the expanse in front of them. The valley below is heavily wooded with the odd clearing as you look farther up the next hill. The vegetation at the top of the hill seems sparser than the lower slopes. In the distance a couple of small plumes of smoke are visible from cottages nestled in amongst the trees, hinting that the next town is close at hand.

Mary wonders how many people are in the village. Maybe there aren't too many. Maybe it will be okay. Maybe?

"We be here?" Mary says clambering towards the front for a better look down the mountain, into the valley. "Thou be sure? Be it as the dream I hath at night?"

They both like the look of the vegetation here. There appears to be a good number of trees suitable for obtaining timber to build a farm house and later fences and a shed for the grain. There is a large stand of Western Red Cedars to the east. To the west there seems to be a mixture of Maples, Oregon Ash and Pine. Thomas has brought many of the tools he will require with him and with the help of his brother-in law Edward, he knows he can build a home here. Thomas is sure he can make friends with the settlers who belong to the plumes of smoke in the valley below for anything else they may need. He knows he will have to be selective, acquainting his family with only the less curious of neighbors. He is a good judge of character which, as it has in the past, will help him in his quest to determine who he can trust. Hopefully that will be enough to protect his family.

In the eyes of Thomas, the sight before him is perfect. Close enough to town for supplies and trading, though still a little isolated. It is ideal for their needs.

"I doeth think so. Sarah and Edward have long told us of Salem and this does bear a likeness to their words. We shall camp here for nightfall and I shall ride into town on the morn. We doeth need to be careful."

Sarah moved from Delaware to Salem nearly five years ago now, shortly after she married Edward. Her husband's family has always farmed in this area and as such he was keen to bring up his own children in the community he knows and loves. They were not to know that she would remain childless. Her longing for 'blood kin' is small part of the reason why Mary and Thomas have decided to uproot their family and make the great trek to Salem.

They have spoken kindly of this place in all of their letters, of how the towns folk are somehow special here. They spoke also of how everyone helps their neighbor without so much as a second thought. Mary and Thomas welcome the notion that the inhabitants of this town may be friendlier than those in Delaware, particularly after the events surrounding the fire.

With Sarah's heart yearning for her family to be close and Mary and Thomas looking for a new beginning, the time was right to make the move to the safety of Salem; to make the move towards a new, brighter future.

"Where shall we live?" Mary asks as the excitement, building in her heart, overflows into her words.

"If this place be Salem, I shall build us a house here. It is close to town yet beyond the gaze of prying neighbors. I think water is at hand for I hear the sound of water passing through the valley. We shall dream a little longer here, I suspect."

"Yes, it be but a dream, our dream. I think our trouble in Delaware be distant now, a lifetime ago. Yet it be prudent to be distant of the town and it's folk. People doeth not understand."

Mary thinks back to their last few weeks in Delaware and the terrible nightmares she endured. During the day as well as the night, she had visions of the stables next to the local Inn catching fire. She saw the drunken skirmish which led to a man left bruised and battered amongst the straw. She couldn't, however, make out the face of the perpetrator. She saw the vile man take the lantern and deliberately set fire to the stables in a vicious, murderous act. She heard the screams for help, not only from the bashed man but also from the fifteen people trapped in the Inn. Though Mary gave much warning of the impending danger, she was considered mad and her words went unheeded.

Twenty four days after her dreams began; sixteen people died a most despicable death. Before the coals had time to cool, fingers were already being pointed in Mary's direction. Her words were finally considered, after the event. There seemed to be two schools of thought circulating through the town. One said she was a witch who had brought this misery on the town out of sheer contempt. The other opinion was that she had started the fire in order that she could be seen as having a 'gift'. Either way, the town was under no illusions as to who was responsible for this tragedy.

Mary and Thomas packed up all their belongings that night and left town under the cover of darkness. A wise move, for the lynching was already being planned for later that week.

Thomas looks squarely at his wife and says, "Mary, this shall be a new dawn. They know us not here, we have no history. Sarah and Edward's words foretell that their hearts be pure. They are neither fearful nor filled with superstition. Evil does not dwell in their hearts here. We will be safe at last."

Mary nods in agreement as she thinks about the future of her girls, "Aye. Yet we be duty bound to nay revisit our trouble in Delaware. I fear our fate hath we not fled that night. I dream for naught save my blood be safe."

Thomas nods as well, "That be my dream too. Thou doth know I will always protect thee yet....."

Mary knows exactly what he is going to say even though Thomas is clearly struggling for the right words. She turns to face her husband with a stern scowl on her face. With heartfelt urgency she implores, "Thou knows I doeth not summon these apparitions. They be an affliction, an affliction I may be burdened with until my demise, I know not. All I can do is be silent as thou must be too. We must let others know naught of what has been. I be not a witch nor devil's helper. Thou doeth know me. Thou know who I be."

Thomas takes her hand as he sees the tears forming in her eyes. He squeezes firmly, yet in a loving manner, as he seeks her understanding, "I know thou be not evil. Thou art my wife and mother of our girls. I love thee. I think we can keep our distance from this town. We have a chance to build our lives, free from inquisition or careless thought. Life shall, God willing, be good."

"I agree with thee; we must keep a distance always."

"We must," Thomas says as he jumps from the wagon. He walks around to Mary's side and pulls her from the seat, into his arms. Carrying her he says, "Let us have a closer look at our new home. We must find this water that I hear."

Mary calls out as she laughs, "Girls, come and look. It be our new home."

One by one, two little heads materialize from under the canvas. Their ponytails sway to and fro as they move. Violet and her younger sister Rose clamber onto the front seat with the agility of monkeys before scrambling their way to the ground. A task they have achieved many times before. This time their excitement quickens their movements. As the girls reach the grassy fields, Jezebel suddenly reappears from the undergrowth, keeping its distance, though stealthily stalking the two girls in a half serious, half playful manner.

The girls run to join their parents. Violet catches up first before running a short distance past them. She stops momentarily to pick some of the red berries that are on a small tree growing on the hillside in front of her. She is cautious as the fruit is unfamiliar to her.

"Ma, can I eat these?"

Thomas places Mary back on the ground and she strolls over to her young daughter and picks a berry from the tree, popping it in her mouth.

"Of course, Darling. These be Bearberries. They be of some use with our cooking. Maybe we can maketh some jam. Their leaves be good as a tea of sorts. It be wise that thou asks first. This be a new place with unfamiliar plants and animals. Tis sure to be many unforeseen dangers here."

Violet nods as she throws a berry into her mouth, chews on it for a few seconds before her face begins to change drastically. Initially her face begins to frown, then it contorts before she spits the berry out onto the grass, "I doeth not like that. I doeth not like that at all. It be poison!"

Violet runs down the hill, dodging the patchy snow, to join her sister Rose in exploring her new surroundings. Thomas smiles and walks up to Mary, placing an arm around her shoulder. As they watch their daughters playing and discovering new and exciting things Mary says, "I thinketh she shall hath plenty of time to get acquainted with their taste. This will be our home for many happy, safe years."

Their journey from Delaware has been lengthy and eventful. They have had many challenges to overcome. Mountains, rivers, dense forests, a broken wheel, snow over the last month and the ever present hunger and possibility of illness or danger. All these trials as well as the tension and frustration they have provoked are now long dissipated from all of Mary's family. After all, this is a new beginning, a fresh start.

Mary skips away from Thomas. She twirls, doing a little dance with her arms raised in the air. She looks completely at ease, embracing all her surrounds.

"Merry Christmas Mrs. Murphy," he says quietly under his breath as his mind begins to savor this happy place.

Maybe life will be less complicated here. Maybe it will be different. Maybe it will be perfect. Maybe it will be safe. At least on this fine day it is and everyone plans to make the most of it. Tomorrow will have to wait till tomorrow. They can only hope and pray it will be just as good as today.

Time will tell.

'The Unreal'

The world gone mad,

Images twisted and distorted.

Believe what you see,

Believe reality has been thwarted.

Nothing is real,

Nothing is false.

Unravel the mystery,

Of the lady with no pulse.

Chapter 7

Sunday, February 19th, 2006.
South Morang Regional Hospital, Victoria, Australia.

I continue the charade. Eyes shut, motionless, as if I am sleeping peacefully. I am well rested having devoured a full night's sleep with glee. The weight of my concerns has been lifted from my shoulders, now that my sight has miraculously been restored. Panic no longer dominates my emotions to the exclusion of all other feelings. I am ready to gather the scattered pieces of my life from five days ago, and put them back together in some form of coherent work of art. I yearn to be released, to be allowed the freedom to continue on my life's journey. I shall be undaunted, moving enthusiastically forward with renewed velocity and energy. I will not look back, nor let anyone block my path. I regard these last few days as just a blip, an unscheduled pit stop in my wonderful life, nothing more.

Eyes voluntarily closed tight. I am well aware of the fact that my mother is in the room. Her rose bouquet perfume is unmistakable. It is inexpensive. No. Let's get that right. It is cheap, overpowering and quite easily identifiable. I assume my sister isn't far away. She has become my mother's volunteer chauffeur of late. My mother only drives short distances these days and considers it an indignity to use public transport to travel anywhere further afield. It isn't that she is a snob. Public transport just brings back too many memories of the jobs she once needed to take in order to feed, clothe and house her two young daughters when father left our lives so suddenly all those years ago.

I feel a breeze rustle across my face as my mother moves away from the bed, heading towards the doorway. I wonder if she is leaving temporarily, for a coffee or some tea perhaps. Maybe she is leaving for the night, considering I appear sound asleep. I wonder if it is time to open my eyes and sneak a peek at what they are up to.

Anyway, *Is it day or night, I've lost track?*

"Hi sis. I know you're awake. You never could keep a secret from me," whispers Gina in my ear.

I open my eyes and smile. My sister Gina is standing over me, a broad grin dominating her face. I watch as she flicks her dark black, shoulder length hair off her lightly freckled face. Her gold earrings dangle and reflect the fluorescent lights above. Her complexion is enhanced by just the right, subtle application of makeup. I have never seen her in makeup before. She has always been my little sister, given that she is two years younger than me. Though, as I take the time to look at her now, I can see that gap is becoming negligible. I hadn't noticed till now how fast she is growing up. While I have been busy with my own life, she has undergone a complete metamorphosis. She has changed from a cute little sister to a beautiful woman in the space of just six months. Married life seems to suit her. The butterfly within has been released; yet another heart breaker fluttering through this world.

My vision wanders further, angling towards where my mother has strayed. I am a little anxious to see what she is doing. The sound of her raised voice travels effortlessly to my bedside. As I look towards the corridor, I can see she has stopped by the doorway. She is dressed in a blue floral dress with a dark green, woolen cardigan, to stave off the cold. Even at this time of the year she feels the cold on her arthritic bones. Her outfit is complemented further by a green beret, tilted on an angle, hiding most of her grey, short cropped hair.

To my disappointment, her face is tense. Her face confirms what I already know. My mother is extremely unhappy about something. I can see, from my vantage point, that she is involved in a fierce discussion with Peter. In fact, this is the only form of conversation they seem to be able to conduct, particularly in recent times. My mother has never thawed to Peter. I guess she has always held tightly onto her dream that I would someday fall deeply in love with a doctor or some sort of rich professional. Not to be. I have no regrets that I fell for a 'tradie'.

With a defiant hand, placed squarely on his chest, she is successfully preventing Peter from entering into the room. Her tirade of words is ferocious as she lays down 'Heather's Law' as she sees it, "There is no way you are coming into this room!"

"But...." Peter tries to interject to no avail. He glances towards me offering a hesitant smile in a feeble attempt to reassure me everything is alright. Peter is a very patient man who tries his best to avoid confrontation with my mother at all times. He knows it upsets me when they fight. I know it is not always avoidable, particularly when my mother acts like a junk yard dog with a bone.

"No buts. Julie is in a fragile state and needs ONLY her family and rest at this point in time. I will thank you to remember your place, young fellow."

Peter's face darkens as his self-control waivers in the face of belligerent contempt. I hold my breath as I wait for his response with trepidation, "I'm a large part of Julie's family...."

I know exactly what she is thinking as my mother takes a deep breath. Her face reddens several shades. There is no way in the world Heather is going to tolerate such a provocative statement as that, just uttered so recklessly by Peter, "You are NOT part of this family yet and have no right to be so presumptuous about such matters. You are just lucky I'm only telling you to leave this room and nothing else. I should be telling you what I really think."

As my head begins to ache, the early symptoms of a migraine forming, I turn to face Gina. She is smiling, shaking her head, enjoying the sideshow. I frown as I softly implore her, "Can you please go and separate them. I can do without all this stuff today. Really, why can't they behave as adults for once."

"Sure, sure," Gina says as she begins to take the argument more seriously. I can tell she is worried about how the fighting is affecting me, as I lie here recuperating. She moves towards Peter and my mother before I have even finished talking. Her footsteps are reticent, giving her a chance to carefully consider her words of persuasion. In her mind she is seeking the most diplomatic approach she can take with Heather so that her words will not exacerbate the situation, increasing hostilities. Gina has adopted the role of peacemaker many times before and has become quite adept at the task.

"Mom," she tries meekly.

"What?" Heather responds tersely.

Gina gestures towards me, trying to distract our mother from ripping Peter to pieces, "Julie's awake and wants to see you."

Heather's face softens as she spies me lying on the bed, forcing a smile. "Darling.," she says as she outstretches her arms and runs across the concrete floor, desperate to embrace me.

While enduring Heather's bear hug, I can hear Gina clearly as she quietly encourages Peter, "Just go. You can see her after mom leaves. You know what she is like, it's not personal. She's just over protective."

I watch as Peter relaxes his shoulders. He speaks with resignation in his voice, "I know; no guy will ever be good enough for either of her daughters."

Gina smiles, winks mischievously and pats Peter on his chest, "Don't I know it, Honey. Don't I know it? My Sebastian would back you up on that score."

Peter looks at Heather holding my hand. Sadness fills his puppy dog eyes. Shaking his head he says, "Well, she had better get used to it because I love Julie and have no intention of leaving her either now or in the future."

Gina takes Peter's hand. She glances at me before saying softly, "Julie knows that. I just think this is a battle for another day. Julie needs to relax and rest. Can't you please leave, just for the moment? There will be plenty of time for you to catch up."

Peter nods as he pulls away from Gina and moves reluctantly towards the door. He looks longingly towards me as he speaks to Gina, "Can you tell Julie I love her and will see her later."

Gina holds the edge of the door, ready to close it. Peter stands in the corridor, vainly hoping for a reprieve from his exile. "You know, I will," she promises as she gives Peter a kiss on the cheek. She begins to close the door before she is stopped by Peter.

"Wait."

Watching Peter, standing outside the door, smiling with sad eyes, I wonder if he is planning to cause some trouble. I am reassured to see Peter pause as he looks sorrowfully towards me. I watch closely as he points to his eyes before placing his hand deliberately over his heart. Finally he points in my direction. As Gina closes the door, excluding Peter from my limited world, I smile, knowing full well what his simple sign language implies.

I love you too.

For the first time I turn and begin to focus on what my mother is saying. To this point in time her barrage of words has been lost on me. I was too engrossed in making sure Peter was alright, "Darling, Darling. Are you feeling a little better? Are you okay? You're not saying very much. Are you tired? You're a little pale. Are you okay?"

I blink, searching for the right words to stave off the verbal avalanche, "Yes, yes. I feel fairly good, all things considered."

Heather smiles, "You gave us such a scare. Have you been eating enough?"

I tilt my head and frown, staggered by how stupid my mother's question sounds, "I've been comatose for four days. I guess they fed me through a drip while I was unconscious. I don't know. I don't feel hungry, if that's what you're asking."

"That's not what I mean," Heather explains. I can tell by her tone she is not at all happy with the attitude exuding from my response. "I meant prior to blacking out in the car. Were you eating enough then or were you on some sort of foolish celebrity diet? You know what I mean, something which encourages you to eat carrots and drink water and nothing else?"

A little perturbed, I state, "Mom, I can't believe you're on my case. You know I'm not on one of those sorts of diets. I always try to eat regularly and sensibly. I'm not an airhead!"

Heather tries to calm me with a cynical, soothing tone. It is a tone I have heard many times before during instances when I have done something wrong and been unwilling to admit it. It is a tone I can first remember hearing when I was about five years old. Back then she used the tone when she discovered the clean laundry covered from ceiling to floor in washing powder, "I don't mean to imply anything. It's just the doctors have done numerous tests and they can't seem to work out exactly what caused your little episode. They can't work out why you blacked out. Drifting into a coma is even more confusing to them, as it is to us. There appears to be no reason at all for your condition. I was just thinking you might be working too hard and not eating right."

"Has the world gone mad?" I enquire rhetorically, not expecting an answer. "I would think what happened to me was fairly obvious."

"Julie!" Gina says as she takes up a position, standing next to her seated mother by the bed.

Heather interjects, waving Gina to stop talking, "What do you mean, luv? What is obvious?"

A little weary I look at the two confused faces before me and ask, "Do I have to spell it out?"

Gina shrugs her shoulders, "Julie, we don't know what you're talking about."

Taking a deep breath, I decide to humor them, "Okay, I'll play along. I saw the lady walk out onto the road. It took a few seconds for my brain to register that someone was on the road in front of me. By the time I braked it was too late and I hit her. She bounced onto the bonnet and rolled off, landing on the pavement with a sickening thud. At some stage my head hit the steering wheel with a fair bit of force. I cut my head.

There was lots of blood. I don't remember much more so I guess that's when I blacked out."

I look at Heather and Gina as they stare at me, listening intently to my explanation. Their faces remain confused. In fact, rather than my words being logical and to the point, it appears they have had the opposite effect. Both Heather and Gina seem scared. To ease their fears, I continue to calmly explain my position, "I guess I drifted into the coma, as a result of the trauma to my head, sometime after that."

Both Heather and Gina remain silent for a considerable length of time, curious expressions on their faces. Heather eventually releases her grasp on my hand. She stands and walks silently towards the doorway and out of the room. I can see her as she stands in the busy corridor, lifting her hand to cover her mouth. I am startled and confused as I watch her begin to cry.

Gina takes up the seat as she whispers to me, "Julie, there was no trauma."

Startled, I look at my sister's face. She gives every indication that she is serious. I am furious she is treating my accident so lightly. After all, a lady died at my hand, "You've got to be kidding me. This was a horrible thing to live through, very painful and traumatic."

Averting her gaze Gina says simply, "There was no accident. That is why....."

I interrupt, horrified, as a chill runs up my spine, "What are you telling me? Did that lady walk out onto the road, in front of me, on purpose? Was she trying to kill herself?"

Gina lowers her head and shakes it vigorously, signaling a negative response. She offers no words of confirmation as she cringes away from me.

What are you so scared of?

"I don't understand. What is the problem? Has the lady died or not?" I state, confused as to what is going on. To me it seems quite simple, just another fatal car and pedestrian accident.

Gina looks up, tears clearly visible in her eyes. "There was no accident," she repeats.

"What are you talking about? Of course there was an accident."

Gina shakes her head, "There was no accident. You didn't hit any lady. You didn't bang your head. You just stopped the car in the middle of the road, blacked out and then drifted into a coma."

In disbelief I look at my sister as if she has told me the world is flat, "Are you mad?"

Gina lowers her head once more; she seems unable to work out exactly what to say.

"I was in an accident. I cut my head!" I implore as I reach up and touch my forehead. To my astonishment, my fingers feel nothing. There is no bandage. I run my hand across my forehead and scalp in a desperate self-examination. To my dismay, I find no evidence of any large cut or stitching.

"Julie....."

"Hand me a mirror!," I demand sharply.

"But Julie......"

"No, Gina, I need to see for myself," I say, softening my tone, somewhat.

Slowly Gina reaches into her handbag and pulls out a compact mirror, opening its case before passing it to me. With trembling hands I stare wide eyed at my shakey reflection in the mirror, searching for any sign of a scar or a wound. There is none. I hand the mirror back to Gina.

"I told you, you weren't in an accident. You weren't injured at all." Gina says as she replaces the mirror in her bag.

"But I was. My doctor was there too, I think he was trying to help. Go ask him. He will tell you I was hurt."

Gina shakes her head and begins to cry, "He wasn't there. It's all just a dream in your mind. It's not real. You were found by the driver behind you who called the ambulance. Doctor Khan only helped treat you once you reached the hospital."

"That's not right! Gina!" I scream as my sister leaps from her chair and runs from the room. "Gina!"

Exasperated, I run my fingers through my hair. Lying back down, I stare blankly at the ceiling, gathering my frazzled thoughts. My mind races with numerous conflicting images merging all at once. I am unable to grasp what is occurring. It simply makes no sense at all.

This is madness. I was in an accident. Why else would I be in hospital? What is going on? I know what happened. They know what happened. I'm sure I know what happened. Surely I do.

The more I think, the more certainty disappears, only to be replaced by fear and confusion. Even so, I have no choice other than to continue to process my thoughts as well as sift through my memories of the accident until it all make sense.

I must work this out!

I become aware of numerous footsteps running towards my bed. I turn on my side quick enough to see three nurses dashing into my room. They gather around my bed; one on either side and one at my feet.

"Calm yourself, Honey," one of the nurses soothes as they reach out and pin my arms and torso to the bed. The nurse at my feet lifts a large needle up to her eyes and squirts a little liquid out of its tip in order to clear any air bubbles. Distraught, I struggle valiantly for my freedom, though the two nurses remain resolute, pinning my arms ruthlessly to the bed. "This will help calm you."

I feel the needle pierce my skin and the liquid begin coursing through my veins. I struggle to free myself for a few more seconds before being overcome with drowsiness. I look sideways and see Serenity, crouched under the bed next to me. He must have been there the whole time, hiding from all my visitors. His luminous green eyes stare at me as he flicks his tail in obvious agitation. I watch him wondering a ridiculous thought.

Are you upset with what they are doing to me?

I fight to stay awake as the nurses release their grip and step back. It is no use. My muscles relax and I quietly drift off to sleep.

'The Real'

Insanity proclaimed,
Without a second thought.
Assistance is lacking,
Alone I am caught.

Family surrounds,
Their concern I feel.
If only I could make them believe,
That what I see is real.

Chapter 8

Sunday, February 19th, 2006.
Afternoon.
South Morang Regional Hospital, Victoria, Australia.

My lonely teardrop falls silently in the dust.

No one bears witness.

I am nothing, if not trapped and solitary.

Boom, boom, click.

Startled by the sudden noise behind me, I swivel on the spot. My denim jeans tear on the loose, sharp rocks which litter the floor beneath me. I stare at the tiny fire flies and their flickering light as they crawl en masse over the walls of my cavern. Some take flight, frolicking around my head in blissful curiosity. They appear intelligent, trying to investigate and understand the strange creature that has invaded their home in such an unwarranted and provocative manner. I do not fear them or their inquisitive ways. They appear harmless enough. In a strange fashion, they offer some form of reassuring company while I am trapped in this purgatory.

Boom, boom, click.

I stand and stroll towards the loose rocks from which the sound emanates. The mysterious noise sounds somewhat industrious, man-made perhaps, though, in this strange world, maybe not. I will have to be careful. Silence engulfs the cavern as I walk slowly towards the pile of rocks. As I near the limit of my realm, I notice two bizarre things. The first is a trickle of water, seeping from the top of the wall, gently cascading down some of the rocks, forming a small pool on the floor. This stream is unusual simply because of its color; bright fluorescent yellow. I reach out and cup some of the water in the palm of my hand. Under closer examination it feels and smells like water. Bravely I decide I have nothing to lose. I taste the water. Though a little sugary, it tastes like normal water.

My attention is drawn to the second curiosity. Amongst the many rocks piled up at the edge of the cavern, one stands out. It is partially hidden, though clearly has some form of writing scrawled on it. Reaching out and taking this rock in my hand, I pull it free from the masses, causing a small, yet safe, landslide. With a moist finger I gently wipe away the dust to reveal its message. It becomes apparent quickly that the message is a simple sentence, written surprisingly in English. It reads:

'Hope is a waking dream'

How curious, I think to myself.

A luminous light filters through into my cavern from a football sized gap I have opened up while acquiring the message rock. Intrigued, I move closer. Bending down, I strain my neck searching for the source of the light. Standing in the dimly lit cavern, it is hard for my eyes to adjust to the brighter light streaming through the hole. Though detail is hard to establish, one thing is certain. Beyond the rock wall appears to be a larger space. Excitement builds in my heart. A larger space with bright light might be the path to my freedom.

Furiously, I pull at the pile of loose, sharp rocks. I discard them behind me, with little care, as I steadily increase the size of the hole. As the gap widens, my excitement grows. Already I can tell a strange world awaits me. I wonder if the light will prove to be a road map, highlighting escape routes which lead to the surface. I catch my breath, hands torn and bloody. Finally, the portal is large enough for me to crawl through.

As I step into the multi-colored fluorescent light, I catch my floral cotton shirt on one of the rocks, causing a long tear to form from my shoulder down to my elbow.

Damn!

Disgusted, I examine the damage to my shirt for just a second before I am distracted by a curious occurrence. What can only be described as a gentle snow storm forms around me. The snowflakes fall dry on my skin and clothes, disappearing without trace, as if they were never there. As the snowfall gets heavier, I am aware of a magical transformation taking place. My damaged shirt, jeans and shoes have all evaporated into thin air, only to be replaced by a light, lacy, see through, tight fitting dress and comfortable, open toed Roman-like sandals. The snowfall eases then stops.

The material of my dress is unusual in the extreme. It is very fine, soft to the touch. Though airy and light, its fabric has a tensile strength unseen in any man made fabric I have thus encountered. Strangely, it is colored in the same shade of emerald green as the large tree fern which grows next to me on this crudely made track. To my right there is a huge purple lily, about six foot by six foot in size. It is a unique botanical specimen which draws me closer. As I near the plant I am stunned to see my outfit change color, adopting the dark purple shading of this incredible flower before me, just like the skin of a chameleon.

Boom, boom, click.

The sound is coming from somewhere deep in the shrubbery which lies before me. I have little doubt now that the sound appears to be industrious, maybe something to do with construction. Maybe someone is building with timber in amongst this amazing forest. The path I am following leads, in a winding manner, towards the sound's source. I hope the sound is an indication that there is a town of some description some short distance ahead. If I am lucky, these strangers may be able to help aid my return to the surface.

As I begin my descent along the path, I take a closer look at my surroundings. The cavern is huge, soaring some hundred or so feet above me. Its walls grow out of sight into the distant horizon. There is all manner of exotic flora growing in the brown loamy soil that is mixed with the rocks. Small streams of the fluorescent yellow water are visible passing in and out of the undergrowth.

It is a strange paradox indeed. However, all the plant life is familiar while being completely foreign to me. There are giant lilies in a myriad of translucent colors, orange conifers sporting red Bromeliad like flowers and reed like grass which sways to create an unobstructed path for me to move through. A carpet of blue daisies covers the floor here and there. They produce a strange whistling sound as they launch tiny spores up into the air. These spores have an innate ability to land on adjoining flowers each and every time, with pin point accuracy. Once a flower receives its spores, it closes and shrivels back down, hiding in amongst the golden foliage.

I suddenly realize I am not alone. I become aware of creatures flying around me as I feel a soft breeze pass my face. My eyes follow the source of the air flow, off into the distance. I see an array of strange butterflies of every possible color combination. Some are bright, some are dull. Some are one distinct color; others are a combination of eight or more colors. The only uniformity they have is their form. They have huge bulging eyes and thin spindly legs which seem three sizes too big for their bodies. As I watch them playfully move throughout the flowers in the forest, I hear a blood curdling scream resound from the bush, further down the track.

Turning sharply, I discover what looks like some sort of flying elf. He stands about a six feet tall, if that. His thin athletic body is covered in a scaly green skin which sparkles in the unnatural light. He has a narrow face with large puppy dog brown eyes that look fearful. His wings, crafted by nature in clear crystallized lace, are folded behind his back. They appear longer than the rest of his body. As I move towards him, he blinks nervously a few times before expanding his wings, displaying their impressive ornate structure.

"Wait," I call out to no avail as, with a single swift movement, his wings spring into action, fluttering at such a rapid rate that they become invisible. With a flourish and a swirl he flies off down the track, into the bush, towards the source of the screams.

For a moment, my curiosity outweighs my better judgment and I begin to run down the track, deeper into the bush. I fight my way through the overhanging branches, for what seems like several minutes, finally forcing my way into a clearing. I pause as I look in awe at the magnificent view in front of me.

The land before me continues to descend, with numerous streams cascading over the edge of a large cliff, about a hundred feet away. Throughout the cavern in front of me are hundreds of giant red mushrooms. Each mushroom has about twenty large brown spots on its upper surface. As I watch, these strange spots open one at a time, for little more than a second. They reveal an amazing flower of shimmering metallic color before retracting once more. There appears to be no sequence as to which flower opens next. The random nature of their opening seems to be frustrating the dozen or so flying elves which are *trying to steal nectar from the center of the flowers. If they succeed, they land, pausing to savor their ill-gotten gain. If they are too slow, they scream out in pain, as they wriggle, trying to extricate their arm from the closed spot on the mushroom.*

The flying elves are unconcerned by my presence. Either they are too pre-occupied with their attempts to source sustenance or they have the ability to sense that I represent no threat to their wellbeing.

Suddenly the earth begins to shake, though it is not like the previous earthquake. It is more like a herd of elephants running in step. I barely have time to turn as a large brown streak rushes past me. I fight the urge to scream as I see one of my monsters, for the first time, in all its glory. Between two of its large, hairy fingers it holds one of the elves by the throat. I slowly move backwards, crouching down under a mushroom. I can see the distress the elf is in as it makes its futile attempt to escape the clutches of its predator. Overcome with sadness and horror, I witness the fear hidden within its beautiful eyes. They are a mirror, reflecting an image of my own, as I cower in the shadows.

The monster stands some fifteen feet tall and appears to be some type of mutant ape. Its skin is hairy, though patchy as if it is suffering some horrible ailment like the mange. On its bare skin, open sores weep foul smelling, purple puss. The beast turns to face me, revealing its rotten, misshapen teeth in an alarming devilish grin. I immediately discover the monster's breath is far worse than the smells coming from its skin. Bubbling drool flows readily from the creatures' mouth, some falling heavily on the poor trapped elf. Its evil glowing red eyes mesmerize me as I hunch, frozen with fear. Unexpectedly, the creature turns, takes a few steps and bounds into the deep crevasse and is lost from sight.

Within a few minutes the elves cautiously flutter back to the mushroom patch. They congregate near the edge of the cliff, staring down into the distance, before separating to continue their foraging. I surmise that, to them, this is the natural order of things. They know their place on the food chain and they know it is not worth worrying about. They can do naught to change their lot in life. This is their fate, sooner or later. They might as well make the most of life while they can.

A little nervously, I edge my way towards the cliff for a better look. At the precipice, my view is unobstructed. A short distance down in the gully, the monsters appear to have set up camp. Four of the monsters are sitting on fallen logs around a huge, glowing camp fire. Scattered around the camp are several wooden boxes. Nectar from the mushrooms is positioned loosely on their upper surface. I wonder to myself what purpose these boxes perform. As I watch, an elf moves boldly towards one of the boxes, hungrily searching for an easy meal.

Boom.

As the elf lands on the lid of the box, a trap door opens, sending the elf and his food tumbling into the trap. He squeals in pain as his wings bend awkwardly under the weight of his body as he crashes to the floor.

Boom.

The trap door springs shut preventing the elf's escape.

Click.

A copper colored lock swings into place ensuring there is no possible escape for the unfortunate elf. His futile screams resonate throughout the valley, ignored by all, including the monsters. He is simply a meal, stowed in their makeshift pantry for later.

As I cast my attention back to the gathered monsters, I see the monster from the mushroom forest stroll casually back into camp, elf in hand. He is greeted by the rapturous growls of approval from his compatriots. They appear excited that his hunting expedition has been so fruitful.

I watch in horror as he nears the campfire. Reaching down he grasps a crudely fashioned spear. He thrusts the spear deep into the stomach of the elf whose shrill scream of pain burns in my ears. I watch transfixed as the monster takes the skewered elf, somehow still alive, and places him over the fire like a marshmallow. I forget where I am for an instant.

"Nooooo!" I scream, my voice echoing throughout the valley.

The hairs on the back of my neck stand up instantly as I realize the gravity of my mistake. For a moment the five monsters pause, searching for the direction of my voice. Then, as the echoing abates, they all stand and stare in my direction. Dropping the smoldering, lifeless elf to the ground, the five monsters begin to move swiftly towards me. I turn searching for a hiding place. All I see is the frightened expressions on the faces of the elves. They scatter, hiding in the forest once more. I sigh deeply. As I begin to run, I can hear and feel the monsters' footsteps drawing ever closer.

* * *

I wake with a start, sweat beading on my forehead. Nervously, I look around, searching for the monsters; they are gone. Clarity eventually dawns as I realize I have just escaped from another meaningless nightmare. All I have experienced is pure fantasy. The hospital ward has returned in all its whiteness and clinical cleanliness, to save me from the demons which prowl my dreams. A little disappointed at the lack of adventure, I resign myself to my fated real life.

It is hard to know exactly how long I have slept; there is no reference point. My watch is gone, removed from my wrist by someone at some stage, probably when I was first admitted. There is no clock in my room either. The absence of windows and my irregular sleeping pattern have combined to cause me to lose track of the number of days I have been here. I guess it could be five days, possibly a week. I doubt it is longer than that. I refuse to admit to myself that it might be longer, though really, I just don't know.

While I was asleep, I was blissfully unaware that my room had become somewhat of a speakers corner. Maybe their incessant chatter is what has caused me to wake. All I know is that my mother, as always, is front and center, firing questions at Dr. Khan in quick succession. Gina is more passive in the discussion, listening and chiming in only when she feels there is a need. As I try to eavesdrop on their conversation, a sense of unease washes over me. They are so engrossed in their discussion that they fail to notice I am wide awake. I feel it is important to understand what is going on rather than alert the doctor and my family to the fact that I am awake and aware. To this end I decide to fain sleep, listen intently and establish the nature of the conversation taking place, so vigorously, between my family and the doctor.

"Are you sure there is nothing physically wrong with her?" Heather says in a surprisingly calm and controlled manner. It is strange to hear my mother so calm while standing, front and center, in the middle of a family crisis.

Dr. Khan is forthright in his assessment, "Quite sure. Sometimes the brain acts in an odd manner when a tumor is growing, placing increased pressure on certain crucial areas of the cerebrum. A tumor can even grow from the brain cells themselves, causing natural functions to be distorted or lost as a result. Fortunately or unfortunately, depending on your perspective, our tests have given Julie a clean bill of health. Her brain and the surrounding tissue appear completely normal. However, considering the clarity and vividness of her delusions, I would have expected to see a large abnormal mass, possibly the size of a twenty cent piece, growing somewhere in the front cerebral cortex. Contrary to this, our tests show there is nothing out of the ordinary. There appears to be absolutely no damage or foreign object placing untoward pressure on her brain."

Delusions! I don't suffer delusions. I'm not mad. I know what happened to me. I know what I saw. I know what I felt!

Apparently perplexed, Heather asks, "So Doctor, what do you think the problem is?"

"Well, as part of our examination, we did a full blood test and found no hallucinogenic drugs in her system."

Gina can barely contain herself, offended by the not too subtle allegation from Dr. Khan. She says bluntly, "Julie has never had anything to do with drugs. I should know. She is my sister after all!"

Imagine even contemplating such a thought!

Dr. Khan makes a hasty retreat, trying to retract his careless words, clarify his statement and appease Gina, "I didn't mean to question your sister's integrity in the slightest, however drugs were certainly a consideration we had to evaluate in order to rule them out completely. The mere nature of your sister's delusions is such that they manifest themselves as a blur between that which is real and that which is imaginary. This imaginary aspect of these visions has no reasonable link to the reality of life. The images she thinks she sees are simply disjointed shards of remnant information thrown haphazardly together by her dysfunctional brain. Unfortunately your sister appears to have lost the cognitive ability to distinguish between what is real and what is not. That is essentially the crux of the matter."

Silence engulfs the space around me as both Gina and my mother struggle to make sense of the doctor's explanation. Finally Heather asks the question on everybody's lips, "What do you mean doctor?"

Dr. Khan sighs, "It is quite simple, really. Consider the aspect that Julie thinks she has been involved in a hit and run car accident of some sort. As we all know, this situation is ludicrous. The fact of the matter is that this didn't occur at all. Julie simply blacked out for some unknown reason after she stopped her car in the middle of the road. It is then reasonable to assume that this alleged accident is a complete fabrication, concocted by her addled mind."

I did have an accident. I ran over a lady for heaven's sake! And what is this crap about an 'addled mind'?

"You mean she made it all up?" Gina enquires.

Confidently Dr. Khan replies, "No, that's not exactly right. I don't think she is actively inventing a fictitious story. Though with her background as a successful author, I would presume Julie would be extremely capable at tackling such a task. No; Julie genuinely believes that she saw and felt everything which played out solely in her mind. However, none of the sensations her senses experienced were real."

"And you thought this....., this......, this delusion my sister is suffering from is the result of taking some form of drug?" Gina says calmly, seemingly acknowledging the possibility of the doctor's hypothesis.

Gina, for goodness sake! You know who I am and what I believe in. You know I don't take drugs. I don't even drink alcohol. I treat my body like a temple. Having a clear mind is how I make my living. Tell him. Tell him how it is.

The doctor continues, "It was certainly a consideration. We have seen many cases in the past of drug induced hallucinations which provoke crippling side effects. Distorted reality is a common symptom in drug affected patients. Many widely available recreational drugs such as Ecstasy, GBH, LSD and the like will do this. You only have to attend our emergency ward on a Friday night to see first-hand what I mean. It can be a daunting task for an author to come up with a fresh storyline to meet the needs of their publisher. I just thought there was a chance that Julie had tried to self-prescribe some creative stimulation or was researching a character and the experiment had gone somewhat pear shaped."

Gina says determinedly, "Well, you could have asked me. I'm her sister. We are VERY close. I would have known if Julie was taking drugs. She isn't taking anything like that. In fact, if she could hear us discussing this stupid notion right now, she would be mortified!"

Thanks Gina.

"That's the interesting aspect of this," Dr. Khan continues, undaunted by Gina's vigorous protestations. "In these cases it is usually the family that is last to know. Something changes in the lives of their daughter, their sister and they start to experiment with some form of drug they receive from a friend or at a party. They find it helps them to relax, to escape the everyday, to a world more wondrous. Unfortunately, with time, they find it necessary to increase the dose they take in order to get the same rush or to try to ease the pain of whatever is going on."

Rubbish!

"But you said you found no drugs in her system?" Heather asks, breaking her silence. She sounds surprisingly calm, almost pensive. I wonder what she is thinking. She has had plenty of time to gather her thoughts.

"That is correct, absolutely nothing. Not even a trace of Panadol or the like. The tests are quite conclusive. The system we use is quite complex, it is able to detect trace elements of drugs consumed several weeks prior to the blood sample being drawn. The tests show clearly there is absolutely nothing in her system."

Hesitantly, Heather asks, "So, what does all that mean? What does that leave as an answer to her illness? What do you think is wrong with her?"

With a deep sigh the doctor continues, "Well, that's the concern. The visions Julie is experiencing appear to have no rational explanation whatsoever. They appear to be purely psychological in nature. For this reason it is imperative that Julie be evaluated to ascertain whether or not she is suffering from some form of degenerative psychiatric illness or has undergone a complete mental breakdown."

"My sister's not mad!"

Good girl Gina! Tell this imbecile exactly what you think of him.

"Please, calm yourself. I do not mean to offend."

Could have fooled me!

"So what exactly are you saying doctor?" Heather asks while maintaining her new found composure. I don't think there has ever been a time when I have heard my mother so calm in a crisis. This is completely uncharacteristic and more than a touch scary.

"To be perfectly frank, I think Julie is suffering some form of psychiatric problem which should be left to the specialists to diagnose accurately. Our specialist team is best placed to develop the appropriate treatment program to manage her condition satisfactorily. Her illness may be a nervous breakdown or an undiagnosed mental illness, something which has been triggered to manifest itself in an aggressive manner for some, as yet unknown, reason."

The room falls silent as my family considers the gravity of what has been said and its possible implications. I wait to hear them defend me, to vouch for my sanity. I wait for Gina to tell the doctor he is wrong. I wait for Heather to ask for more tests.

I continue to wait.

I open my eyes. Gina and Heather do not notice.

I can see the fear clearly in their eyes as they look to each for some inkling as to what they should do next. Their faces are blank, devoid of inspiration.

Hey! Tell him he's wrong. Tell him I'm fine. Tell him……… tell him something at least!

"So what do you suggest from here doctor, how should we proceed?" my mother asks softly, drained of all emotion.

"I would suggest that you admit Julie to our psychiatric ward for assessment. Once assessment has been carried out by our team of highly credentialed specialists, a program of treatment options can be considered including medication and shock therapy. This state of the art treatment may ultimately allow her to return home in a supervised manner. She may even be able to regain some sort of semblance of her previous life, with time that is."

Has the world gone completely mad!

"April, May?" my mother asks as I lay watching, aghast that this insane conversation is even occurring.

Dr. Khan sighs again, "Nothing is certain when it comes to the human brain. There is much still to be learned. Julie may have to spend the rest of her life hospitalized. That is a realistic possibility. However, we should only be considering that when the time arises. It may not be that bad. There may be a simple explanation as to what is causing her to behave like this. The main thing, at this stage, is to focus on getting her assessed. That way we can help her to overcome her illness with the appropriate treatment."

Fear and rage well up inside me as the doctor speaks. I struggle to control myself. I want to defend myself, to convince the doctor that I am not delusional. I hesitate, wondering what is going through my mother's mind. I cannot read the expression on her face. I have never seen her like this before. She is almost zombie like, as if her mind is on auto pilot.

After a further silence, I shudder with fear as I hear my mother speak unthinkable words, "Are there any forms I need to sign?"

"Yes I have them right......"

"No, I'm not mad," I scream as I lose my restraint. I begin to pull the electronic senses from my skin, releasing me from the web of wires which attach me to an array of diagnostic monitors. In a swift motion I pull back the sheets and leap out of bed.

"Security!" Dr. Khan yells at the top of his voice as I grapple with the open flap at the back of my gown. I desperately try to regain modesty before attempting to walk towards my family.

"Julie!" Heather yells as she moves backwards, startled by my sudden advance. I stare at my mother in disbelief, as rage fills my heart. Slowly I move towards her, shaking my head, hoping desperately to convince her of my sanity. The look in her eyes tells me that task will be hard to achieve. Maybe it will prove impossible. Still, I need to try.

"I'm not mad. You know that mom," I call out, my lips quivering with sadness. I reach out with both arms seeking a warm embrace, though none is forthcoming. My mother continues to back away.

Heather shakes her head. Her eyes are bloodshot and tearful. She has a maniacal grin on her face as she tries desperately to reassure me with a smile, "Darling you're ill. That's all I know."

I stare at my mother in disbelief. How could she, of all people, believe this garbage? I don't have all the answers myself; however, I am sure of one thing.

I am not mad!

I stand beside the bed, frozen in thought, searching for the right words to explain what I have seen and lived through. I know that I have been in an accident. I just don't understand why no one is willing to acknowledge this fact.

Two large men in blue skivvies rush into the room. It is instantly clear to me that they are determined, completely single minded in their purpose. Without a word, they move with obvious aggression towards me, barging past Dr. Khan who drops his clipboard in the ensuing fracas. I have no opportunity to defend myself. Running at me, they aim for my midriff with their broad shoulders. Winded from the well-executed tackle, I find myself thrown violently, back onto the bed.

"Nooooooo!" I scream feebly from deep inside my battered diaphragm. I fall silent as my brain registers a sharp, sudden pain in my side.

My ribs!

As I continue my futile struggle for freedom, they use their full weight to pin me to the bed. In a deliberate manner, Dr. Khan nervously moves around the bed. Systematically he takes hold of the restraints attached to the bed. One by one he places them over my body, pulling them tight and locking them in their belt clip. Within a few tense seconds he effectively constricts my arms, legs and my body as a whole. Once the three ties are securely in place, all I can do is squirm, yell and move my head from side to side. I wince with the pain pulsing from my damaged side.

The task completed, both security guards relinquish their grip and walk away from the bed. One of the guards takes the time to bend down and retrieve the clipboard. Dr. Khan straightens his ruffled coat and accepts the clipboard with a nod of thanks as the guards walks past him and out of the room. The doctor says, "Please wait outside. We might need your help with the boyfriend."

Both guards nod and silently march from the room.

Dr. Khan turns to face Heather. He sighs before saying earnestly, "This is why it's important to have her diagnosed. This type of violent outburst can become more common and increase in severity as time progresses. We will need to maintain this level of restraint until such time as we are convinced that Julie has no self-harm issues or suicidal thoughts, just to be safe, of course. We can't have any harm coming to her or my fellow co-workers."

I look at my mother for much needed support. Softly I plead, "I'm not mad! I'm not suicidal!"

Heather smiles oddly my way before calmly walking the three steps it takes to reach the doctor. Stealing the clipboard from his hands, she averts her gaze from my pleading eyes. Instead, she is fully focused on the words printed on the slip of paper before her. Dr. Khan reaches into his shirt pocket and removes a pen which he clicks as he presents it to her. Heather scrawls her signature on the bottom of the form and hands the clipboard and pen back.

"Why don't you believe me?" I ask as tears begin to roll down my face.

Heather strolls over to my bed and takes my hand in hers. My arms are numb, pinned to the bed. She caresses my hand as she speaks from the heart, "They will help you dear. They will get to the bottom of this and help you. I am sure of that. I believe this to be true. As God is my witness, you will be okay."

I shake my head, "I don't need any help!"

Heather releases her grip. Her fingers slowly slide between mine until all contact is lost. Turning, she walks solemnly over to Gina, taking her hand and whispering something unintelligible to her. Gina nods in agreement.

An orderly, hiding near the doorway, moves towards the bed. He works swiftly, lifting the side guards and releasing the brakes from the oversized caster wheels. Getting behind the bed he starts to push my trolley towards the door.

"Gina, you have to stop them, please!" I rasp as I pass my sister. Her head bowed, gaze cast downwards, she refrains from saying a word. My mother's arm extends around Gina's shoulder, comforting her as her body starts to shake. Gina begins to cry vocally. Heather watches me impassively, as I am wheeled from the room. This is my last vision of my mother and sister as I am wheeled away to goodness knows where. It is a vision of betrayal that haunts me in my moment of greatest need.

Why can't you understand how much this hurts me?

We reach the corridor and a commotion begins. "Hey, where are you taking her?" Peter yells as he rushes to meet me.

One of the security guards grabs his arm, preventing him from getting any closer. I watch as the guard says something to Peter, something which is too soft for me to make out. The guard's words of explanation appear to be received as unwelcome. Peter at first seems confused, then upset as he tries desperately to reach me. Both guards struggle to maintain their restraint.

The orderly pushes my bed down the corridor, away from Peter. Dr. Khan walks beside the trolley. He turns his head every now and then as he keeps a watchful gaze on Peter. He says hesitantly, without any measure of certainty in his token words, "Don't worry Julie. We'll take good care of you."

Stretching my neck, I can see Peter. The two guards are now successfully holding him at bay, preventing him from running to my aid. He looks completely lost.

A door slides open behind my head. With a solid push, I find myself in the elevator, facing the corridor. The orderly pushes the button for level three and stands back whistling, waiting for the journey to commence. Down the corridor I can still see Peter, restrained by the guards. I see his arm outstretched, trying to reach for me. I try to move my arm to return the gesture. It remains pinned tight to the bed. Unfortunately, I am the best part of fifty feet away; a distance that tears at both our souls.

Peter's torment reverberates around the walls of the elevator, "Julie!"

The doors slides silently closed, blocking my only chance of salvation from view. I am separated from Peter's love and assistance in a most emphatic manner. For the moment, at least, I have no choice but to remain calm, keep breathing and go along with this journey to the psychiatric ward. I must be strong. I must hold on to what I know to be true. At least I know one thing for certain.

I am not insane!

'To The West'

Dark clouds gather,
With foreboding,
To the West.

Danger comes lurking,
Look for the signs,
To the West.

Chapter 9

Winter, 1692.
Late February.
Salem, Massachusetts.

Under an ochre shaded sky, framed by the deep green woods, the homestead is clearly taking shape on the grassy fields in amongst the patchy snow. Thomas stands on the slope above, his bronzed arms glistening with sweat. He stands quietly while having a well-earned break. Taking a swig from his canvas water bottle, he admires the view.

With the assistance of his brother-in-law Edward and their new neighbors, the cottage is complete. Two weeks have now passed since the clay was added to waterproof the thatched roof. It has been tested three times by rain and snow since then and has been proved successful each time.

Their attention and skills are now focused on the walls of the large barn, just to the east of the house. They have been lucky over the winter. Though it has been bitterly cold it has been what the locals of Salem call 'a dry un''. There have been fewer days of snowfall and a lighter covering settling on the ground than would normally be expected. Such conditions, though harsh, have proved a blessing while they try to build in winter. The day length, however, has been short. To compensate, the men have worked at a feverish pace. All their efforts are beginning to show. It is starting to look like the farm that Thomas and Mary have envisaged in their dreams since they first began courting all those years ago.

It has been hard work, even for something as simple as a one bedroom cottage and barn. George Williams, a neighbor from down in the valley, offered his labor and tools in trade for Thomas repaying him in kind by helping to sow his crops for the spring. His dray and harness have proved invaluable. They can only cut and drag one large log to the barn at best during a day, sometimes it takes several days. Without the horses it would have proved impossible to move the wood as the terrain is riddled with pot holes, stumps and rocks.

Once the logs are dragged to the site, they need to be cut into smaller lengths and slotted into the next rung of the wall. As the wall for the barn progresses, each level has its gaps sealed with mud that is carried in pails, by hand, from the creek. This seemingly simple task has presented even more challenges to overcome. The creek is located down a steep slope, two hundred yards into the bush. In order to gain access to the water they needed to create a better pathway by cutting some of the lush undergrowth with machetes. The construction of a few steps to make the journey safe was also a priority. The path has had much use since its construction as they also require a regular supply of water, gathered from the river daily, just for their domestic use.

While the men are building the barn, Mary and her girls are contributing in their own way to developing the farm. They are concentrating their efforts on getting the land ready for sowing their first crop early in spring. This is particularly important now that they are starting to see the first signs of the late winter rains. They remove rocks, creating a stack near the unusable bush. Small branches are dragged clear of the paddock and piled near the house so that they can be used later as firewood. As well as these arduous tasks, all their regular chores, like washing clothes, cooking, cleaning and collecting the eggs from the scrub, have to be completed too.

Mary rises before dawn to cook breakfast while also making a start on the preparations for the evening meal. Breakfast consists of fried eggs and salted pork. Thomas helps by carving the pork from the bone, next to Mary's fire and pan.

She bakes daily. First she starts by heating the crudely built clay oven. Two hours later it is ready for use. While she is waiting for it to heat, she prepares her short term supply of breads and pies. Both her girls help, in their own way, once their chores are done. Violet, just turned seven, is becoming quite useful for Mary with the preparation of ingredients. Every now and then she spends time with her Aunt Sarah, learning different techniques which she shows off, with much pride, to her mother.

Rose, only four years old, loves baking with a passion. Though at her tender age the results take the form more of 'mess creation' rather than 'bread making'. She is keen as mustard with little if any technique. This doesn't matter; Mary knows she has all the time in the world to teach her how to bake. She will one day be as good as her mother in this respect.

Once the baking is underway they concentrate on washing the clothes down by the river. They remove the excess water by beating the clothes on the large rocks before bringing them back to the homestead and hanging them to dry on some of the small saplings growing in the sun.

Mary then prepares berries and a small amount of vegetables ready for the evening meal. If she has time, she churns some of the goat's milk into butter; a task which can take several hours.

On this particular day Mary decides to take a break from her regular routine. She is resting on a stump close to the front of the house. Over the last couple of weeks she has been unwell. She has begun to experience visions again, mainly at night, in her sleep. At first they are infrequent. However, they are now beginning to occur on a daily basis, sometimes in the daylight hours. At night she sees the same vision from various angles. Over the course of a few weeks she has established that the situation involves a large, hostile mob and two people dressed in black. These two individuals have their identities concealed effectively with black hoods shrouding their faces. She wakes at this point, heart palpitating wildly, drenched in a cold sweat. Mary is also overcome by an unnerving sensation of being cold and alone. Unfortunately for Mary, this is the extent of the detail she has at her disposal. To her consternation, the subsequent visions have failed to provide any clues as to the identities of the two hooded people and their fate. As such, she is unable to help with their predicament. This is a situation which frustrates her no end.

Mary is looking drained; exhausted due to the lack of sleep she has endured in recent weeks. She has initially hidden her visions from Thomas, a task which has proved surprisingly easy. After a long, hard day in the fields he goes to bed early, falling asleep with ease. He is a notoriously heavy sleeper. Once he is asleep nothing will raise him from his slumber till the cock calls.

Thomas only realizes, to his dismay that the visions have returned when, one day, he spies Mary standing frozen in the sunshine. She is staring into the distance intently, like she is watching an invisible play unfolding before her eyes. Thomas knows it is a play that only Mary is privy to, a play staged by either God or the devil. They discuss her visions that night for hours, falling asleep in each other's arms, tears rolling down their faces. Thomas remains ill at ease yet comforted by his love and undying faith in his wife's judgment.

Both Thomas and Mary are worried by the recurrence of her visions. They make a pact to try to mask their fears from both Violet and Rose as best they can. They are too young to understand what is going on. Any discussion would only serve to place fear in their innocent hearts.

George has encouraged them to see the doctor in the village. He is worried about Mary's pale skin and weariness. They decline his offer of transport and try to lie that it is just something Mary has endured for years. They don't dare tell George the truth about Mary's visions or their joint fear that these will, with the passage of time, be events which come to pass. George would never understand her curse, no one ever does. To try to explain their plight would simply result in the loss of a new and valued friend. There is also the danger his mind could be swayed by the prevalent stories of witches and their evil deeds against the teachings of God. He could, in these circumstances, prove to be the instigator of their demise.

Mary's visions and apparitions have, up to this point in time, followed the same sort of routine. They become more regular and detailed as the time of some great catastrophic event draws nigh. This continues until a certain number of white doves appear. The number varies each time yet seems to correspond with the number of innocent people whose lives are under threat. She is heartened by the fact that no doves have appeared in Salem thus far. This means she still has time to work it all out, time to make a difference. Maybe........

Mary sits, looking dejectedly at the clothes still to be collected off the trees, all energy drained from her body. Jezebel strolls casually in front of her, tail in the air, looking up at the sky, as Mary rests. The cat rubs her back affectionately against Mary's leg. At precisely that moment Mary's tranquility is broken by a fluttering sound somewhere close behind her. Instantly the hairs on the back of her neck stand up. A pain stabs deep into her chest. Her vain hope that her family will incur no drama as a result of her visions in Salem, due to the small population and their relative isolation from the town, is now fully shattered. She is well aware the visions will never stop; they will follow her wherever she goes. She is well aware that the time of her next vision coming to pass draws near.

Slowly she stands and turns around in order to identify what type of bird has chosen to land behind her. Fear engulfs her heart. Her eyes are fixated by the white dove feeding peacefully on some seeds in the dust, a short distance away. Just beyond the dove her eyes are drawn towards two wooden coffins lying on the grassy slope. They look so out of place on her beautiful homestead. Goose bumps spread through her body as the lid of one of the coffins begins to swing open without any human assistance. Mary holds her breath as she waits to see who is inside. Her face contorts into a frown as the lid falls awkwardly, half off the coffin, just as a cold gust of wind rustles through her hair. To her horror and dismay, the coffin is empty.

What doth that mean? Oh, Lord, what doth that mean?

Mary turns back around. She sees young Sam Williams, off in the distance, with his mop of unruly, red hair. He is sprinting across the hill to where his father George and Thomas are trying to drag a particularly obstinate log towards the half constructed barn.

Mary watches, wavering a little as George drops the reins of the dray he is leading. She sees him run to meet his son, grabbing him by the shoulders as he tries to discover what news he brings. Thomas is edging closer to the pair, wiping sweat from his brow. Mary watches as Thomas squats down as he listens to the boy and his story. Sam is quite agitated, waving his arms around as he tells his news to the two men. Thomas is quite animated in the discussion too. Not at all like his usual friendly, unflappable nature.

Suddenly all three turn and look straight in Mary's direction. She feels the full enormity of their deathly gaze as it drains all the remaining energy from her body. Horrified by the unsaid implications of their unified glance, she begins to feel faint. Succumbing to the nausea, she falls backwards onto her tree stump stool. She sits meekly, watching helplessly as George and Thomas begin to run towards her.

Mary feels the continuing pain in her chest. A pain like none she has ever known. It feels like someone is driving a knife deep into her heart. She dreads the news that is approaching. She knows it is not good. Her befuddled mind races trying to unravel the meagre clues her visions have provided. As she searches her mind for the answer as to what the calamity could be, she hears the footsteps getting louder as Thomas and the others run towards her. Thomas is the first to reach Mary. He raises his hand, pleading for a second's grace. Hunched over, he tries to catch his breath, breathing in several large gulps of air to fill his depleted lungs. His face is bright red as his lungs search for precious oxygen. His body is shaking uncontrollably.

Mary can't wait, "What in God's name be thy news?"

Thomas, still breathing heavily, weakly voices a single word, "Sarah."

Mary is horrified. Reaching up she takes her crucifix pendant in the palm of her hand. The pain in her chest intensifies as she leaps to her feet and embraces her husband. Somehow she vaguely hears the desperate sounds of a baby crying, followed closely by raised unintelligible voices.

She ignores these ghostly sounds as she pleads with Thomas, "Please, what be it? What ails her?"

Thomas looks up, tears in his eyes, fear clearly visible on his face. He chooses his words carefully as he says simply, "She has been denounced as a witch in Salem. They be trying her. She will be hung if found guilty. If she pleads guilty they shall be swift and humane with their deliverance of punishment."

"And if she pleads innocent?" Mary asks knowing the answer is something she doesn't want to hear.

Thomas shrugs his shoulders as he speaks truthfully, "Her life shall be forfeit just the same."

Mary falls to the ground, "It can't be. She hath never experienced visible appearances. It be a horrible mistake. She is truly innocent of such crimes."

"That may be so, but the town feels there be much justice required. There be a strange affliction that the children hath been enduring. Their hearts are filled with fear, their minds poisoned with superstitions. The towns folk feel there be witches and want them found."

"We must help her," Mary says defiantly as she tries to move away from Thomas.

Thomas grabs her arm, "No, we can't"

Mary tries to free herself from his grasp. Thomas is defiant. Mary says, "We must!"

Thomas says just as vigorously, "No we can't! We must stay here. They are arresting the kin of accused if they be known to be familiar with witches. They be trying them too. It be far too dangerous for us to visit Salem whilst all this be happening."

"So what are we to do?"

Thomas has no answer for Mary's question. They stand frozen with fear, looking at each other with an overwhelming silence for several seconds, unable to find the suitable words for either a solution or for comfort. Mary is beginning to realize how impossible Sarah's predicament is. She is beginning to realize there is naught they can do.

Mary looks over her husband's shoulder as the pain in her chest subsides. The tormenting sounds disappear from her ears, replaced by the birds in the woods. The two wooden coffins have disappeared from view as well. Everything has returned to normal. This latest vision has gone. Only the dove remains, staring towards Salem. Mary shakes her head and sobs as she pounds the back of Thomas with her fist. He refuses to relinquish his grasp on her.

George stands silent, scratching his grizzled chin in deep thought behind Thomas. He speaks in a booming voice, offering the only logical idea for how any of them can help, "We can but pray and pray we shall."

Mary remains silent as faith slowly weeps from her heart.

'Darkest of Nights'

Evil scurries about,

With devilish delight.

Guarantee of no sleep,

On this, the darkest of nights.

Weak but conscious,

So ready to fight.

All my hopes seem futile,

On this, the darkest of nights.

Chapter 10

Sunday, February 19th, 2006.
Afternoon.
Psychiatric Ward.
South Morang Regional Hospital, Victoria, Australia.

The most important thing in life is to know when you're beaten. It's good to 'put up a fight' or 'try your best'. That way, at least, you can claim that you had a go. Occasionally, however, you simply know in your heart that you have no chance. It's just easier to sigh, sit back and relax. Sometimes there is nothing you can do to change your situation for the better. Trying will only make things worse. In this situation a tactical retreat is always a wise move. A chance to regroup, recharge the batteries and plan a little strategy before going on the attack.

My current predicament is surely one of those situations. It doesn't take a genius to work that out. I am strapped securely to my bed, protestations ignored, being wheeled into my new domain, a domain in which I am certainly not Queen. Beyond that, I don't feel like I am Julie Mahoney anymore.

This ward is built like Fort Knox. It exudes a completely different vibe to my open room where anyone and everyone appeared to have access at will. A buzzer sounds prior to the opening of the double doors. We pass through two doorways like this prior to entering the ward itself. Armed security guards stand, hand on holster, in the recess between 'the normal wards' and 'the psychiatric ward'. They watch me closely as I pass. One has a dressing on his cheek, covering a recent cut or scar. They are big, strong men who look like they can handle any situation that arises. However, their eyes tell a different story. They show the fear that they harbor, deep down inside their souls. I guess they are wisely fearful of every new arrival. After all, anyone admitted here is crazy. All must be considered unstable and dangerous. Though in my current restraints I can't imagine how I could possibly be a threat to anyone.

As I am escorted through the second set of keypad encoded, sliding, security doors, I feel a tightening in my stomach. There is no escaping the stark reality of my situation. Escape from this place will be difficult if not nigh on impossible. The wire mesh embedded in the plate glass windows is testament to the fact that my new home is the South Morang Regional Hospital's equivalent of Alcatraz. I pass the nurses station to my right. Behind this desk I can see a locked cabinet laden with syringes, bottles of pills and, of course, numerous vials of sedatives. I guess that is how they keep control in a place as chaotic as this.

I don't want to be sedated again. I want to be awake in here. I must be awake in here if I am to survive.

My senses absorb every aspect of my new environment as they push my bed through the main common room. I search for weakness, something I can use to my advantage in order to escape. However, at this stage, nothing startling is evident. This room is quite spacious. Its decor is quite bland save for the odd solid wooden table combined with chairs curiously bolted to the floor. This area appears to be inhabited by numerous patients of dubious mental health. They seem to be allowed to wander at their own discretion. Some stand quietly, staring into the distance. Others shuffle to and fro. Some are restrained in strait-jackets. I wonder to myself if this is for their own protection or for the protection of others. Maybe it is a little of both.

This ward is not as clean as my previous lodgings. The stench of urine and feces aggravates the nerves in my nostrils to the point that I have to fight to prevent the bile from my stomach jumping up into my throat. The smell makes me think that this place is a Hell-hole, where the damaged refuse of society are dumped, hidden away behind firmly locked doors. Nobody really cares what happens to the mentally ill, anyhow, these days. They represent too difficult a challenge.

I must be calm. They might untie me. I can't escape like this.

One of the 'statues' standing in the middle of the room starts to scream like an air-raid siren for no particular reason. Others become agitated, some swearing voraciously as the room erupts in riotous sound. Two nurses try to quell the maelstrom. They are largely ineffective. I try to distract myself from the turmoil that abounds by focusing on the layout of my surroundings. To the side are the sleeping rooms. One of which, I assume, will be my final destination. As I pass several of these rooms I can see there are other patients strapped to beds.

At least I have company in this predicament.

As the commotion subsides, I notice most of the patients roaming the room are unhindered by any visible restraints. They all have the same peaceful expression on their face, combined with glazed, sightless eyes. Even as the orderly pushes me through the riot of noise, I do not feel threatened, not for an instant. Curious is the term I would use to describe how I feel. Particularly as I observe all the patients seem to exude the same persona of unnatural calmness. They behave like they have been placed under a magical spell which maintains them in a trance-like state.

Drugged, I bet.

One patient catches my attention as my bed traverses its way through the maze of lost souls. This man is quite tall, a giant amongst the other patients. He is muscular and fit, though not in a sexy way. He is too old for that. I guess he is aged in his sixties with thin, wispy, receding grey hair which appears beyond the help of even the most accomplished hairdresser. He is different to the other patients in that he is bound tightly in a secure looking strait-jacket. I have a strange sense that he is familiar to me, though I can't quite place his face. As I look at him, he sneaks several sly sideways glances my way. His lazy eye disturbs me a little as it makes him appear even more creepy. I guess that description fits everyone in here, one way or another. However, as I watch him I can't help but wonder if he recognizes me. I can't be sure, though I think I even observe a hint of a smile flickering at the edge of his mouth as I draw nearer.

Does he know me?

My vision remains fixed on this strange man, as my bed is pushed closer to him. I rack my brain searching for some clue as to where, in my past, I have encountered him. Alas, I find no clue. I am conscious of the fact he is walking on a slant in my general direction, shortening the time it will take for me to reach him. As I get within six feet of him, he lunges violently at me, screaming at the top of his lungs. I feel his salvia splatter across my face as he is pushed away roughly by the orderly. The man in the strait-jacket staggers backwards briefly before falling awkwardly to the floor. From my vantage point I can see him getting frustrated, flailing around on the floor, arms trapped in the jacket, desperately trying to regain his footing. Startled, my heart begins to pound at an excessive rate. The orderly, seemingly with some prior knowledge that this was going to happen, laughs as he pushes my bed onwards.

"Yeah, thanks Chris. You've had your bit of fun for the day. Scared another 'fresh vegetable'; pop another notch on the wall."

'Fresh vegetable' is such a strange term. I have never encountered it before. I assume that's how the staff refers to a new admission to the psychiatric ward, an 'in joke' perhaps. Not a particularly endearing term. One I would like to take them to task over, once, that is, they have seen the error of their ways and choose to release me from these ties. I will have to wait for that time to come. I am not in a great position to be debating the professionalism of the nursing staff. Not at this moment, at least.

My mind latches onto something else that the orderly has said. I feel the simple statement is both a revelation and a worry. I am filled with a strange mix of excitement and dread. As the seconds tick by my emotions edge more towards dread. If my suspicions are true, it would explain why I vaguely recognize the man restrained in the strait-jacket. I am compelled to discover if my suspicions are correct. With much hesitation in my voice, I ask, "Chris..... Chris Hagatie?"

The orderly smiles at me, a little surprised that I know something about this vile piece of filth. He confirms what I already know to be true, "Yes, that's the infamous Chris Hagatie, a recent acquisition to our collection. Though he has only been here a few days, he is already causing his fair share of trouble. Did you know he raped fourteen girls under the age of sixteen before they caught the bastard? His lawyers thought he would be more comfortable residing in here rather than a prison cell. He'll be staying in these luxurious digs till he receives a fair trial and they lock the bastard away in some dark hole for the rest of his abhorrent life. You need not worry about him though."

"No?" I ask, completely at a loss as to why I shouldn't be concerned about being locked in a psychiatric ward, strapped to a bed, with the most callous rapist of this century calmly wandering around.

Images begin to flash through my mind of his victims. Their glowing faces and bright innocent eyes haunt me from photographs taken in happier times. I remember their faces from the heartfelt news bulletins which frequented my television screen during his reign of terror.

He lured his young victims away from their parents as they played in seemingly safe, crowded, suburban parks, in broad daylight. He did this successfully by luring his victims with the promise of their choice of ice cream. This is how Chris Hagatie became dubbed with the unfortunate label 'The Mr. Whippy Rapist'.

The orderly whispers softly to me, "No Miss Julie, he's completely safe. They keep him drugged to the gills, enough to knock out an elephant. Anyway, he only has an inclination for very young women; you're far too old for him. What are you twenty three, twenty four maybe? Far too old to attract his interest, I suspect. His preferred age is about eight."

I feel sick to my stomach as I contemplate the depravity of this truly evil man. It just isn't right. How can an adult treat defenseless children with such contempt? Children are to be treasured, nurtured and protected. They are the vessels of joy to this world and demand our absolute respect. The barbaric things this man has done during his lifetime are beyond rational explanation. All punishment for his actions seems grossly inadequate.

Somehow, I don't feel reassured by the orderly's assumption that my safety is certain. The notion just doesn't hold water. Chris appeared to know exactly what he was up to when he lunged at me. In fact, by the sly glances and hint of a grin, I would suspect his actions were premeditated. If he was heavily drugged he wouldn't be able to plan, let alone instigate, an attack such as this. I cling to the slim hope the orderly is right about the drugs. I guess in my current situation, my only hope is that Chris Hagatie IS harmless. I am certainly in no position to defend myself if the orderly is wrong.

I need to be free to be safe.

"Room 5," the charge nurse calls out from across the other side of the common room. The orderly doesn't slow his steps, just nods and continues walking at a steady pace. Though he seems outwardly calm and collected, I suspect he doesn't want to spend more time than he has to in this ward. I don't blame him.

He should try being strapped prone, to a bed in here!

Finally the orderly turns the trolley towards an open doorway to the left. We enter a vacant room with bland, lifeless white walls. Nothing is attached to these walls. Not even a soothing poster or a picture of a calming waterfall; just plain white walls. Though this room is bland, I am glad to be here away from Chris and the others out in the main room.

The only fitting in the room is a window, made of thick plate glass infused with wire mesh. I suspect by its sturdy construction that it would survive, unscathed, if someone got the idea in their head to take a run at it and test its strength with their shoulder. The hospital isn't taking that chance, anyway. Outside the window, visible through the opaque surface, a thick wire grill is positioned as a secondary deterrent to escape. They seem to have thought of everything.

The orderly spins my bed around so I am left facing the open doorway. I relax a little. At the very least, I will be able to see who is coming into my room.

"There you go little miss. Hope you enjoy your stay. Caviar and Champagne will be served in the dining room at 5 pm precisely. Dress code is formal, though hospital gowns will do in a pinch," he says as he kicks the wheel locks into place. He chuckles to himself as he leaves the room hurriedly.

What a comedian!

Now alone, in my room with no door, I have no choice but to lie back and contemplate my options. Escape seems impossible. Convincing the doctors I am sane might be equally so. I have no choice, though. I must use my time effectively and choose the right words that will prove my innocence, prove I am of sound mind. After all, I am a writer. I should be able to offer a reasonable argument in defense of my sanity. My musings shouldn't lean towards the pessimistic, particularly considering the fact I am not mad. I am not even slightly unhinged. I have all my faculties. I know the details of what has occurred. The horrible images run rampant through my waking thoughts. I was in a terrible accident where a lady lost her life. That is certain. I know what I lived through. I just fail to appreciate the reason why no one believes me or acknowledges this fact. Time, hopefully, will help me resolve this mystery to a satisfactory end. Time is what I have in abundance. At this moment, time is my only weapon, feeble though it may be.

I don't know the rules in this place. Can I receive visitors here? Oh, I hope so. Peter must be beside himself by now. I long for nothing more than for him to be beside me. Feeling his body embrace mine would at least ease my troubles a little. I would certainly feel much safer, having him around. We have never found ourselves in a situation where we have been forcibly separated. It simply feels unnatural. I wish I could find some way to reach him, to get a message to him. This is so frustrating.

I watch the doorway, hoping the next person to appear will be Peter. Every now and then I catch a glimpse of a patient shuffling by or a stressed nurse rushing to her next problem. No matter how long I wait,

Peter fails to appear. I steal my resolve so as not to give up hope. Peter is resourceful; I know he will find a way to reach me. I just know.

I must stay quiet. I must be released from these bonds.

My heart begins to beat faster as adrenalin courses through my veins. The hairs on the back of my neck stand up in unison. My eyes bulge, filled with equal measures of disbelief mixed with fear. I realize, starkly, the gravity of my predicament. Pure evil has taken an interest and come to visit my room. The intentions of this manifestation of Satan are unclear. The feeling in my gut, however, cannot be ignored. This feeling screams at me that no good will come from this visitation. Evil does not bring fresh flowers when it turns up on a blind date.

Leaning in the doorway with a smug expression on his face is Chris Hagatie. He seems quite relaxed, with all the time in the world to stalk and torment me. Grinning broadly he stares at me like the psychopath he is. His jet black eyes cannot hide the devilish thoughts that rule his deformed mind. Every now and then he glances over his shoulder, then back at me again. He seems conscious that the nurses are close by. However, he is well aware that they are lax with their assigned task of tracking his movements. The nurses appear more interested in the movie I can hear, playing on the tiny television positioned at the front desk.

A vein in his neck twitches involuntarily every few seconds. It is unnerving having such an evil creature keep watch over me while I am incapacitated. I don't have to suffer for long. Chris makes his move. Swiftly he glides over the floor to the edge of my bed. I can smell his foul breath as he stands uncomfortably close to my chest. To my disgust he begins to rub his head against my neck like an affectionate dog. Salvia dribbles down my neck and into my cleavage.

"Don't fret, my little Buttercup. I be trapped in this damn jacket. I can do thee no harm," he says, showing no inclination to move back from my personal space. "They give me tablets to remove my urrrrrges. I be completely safe."

Chris finishes his words as he stands upright. For some reason he wants me to see his face clearly. Using his tongue, he picks up the tablet he has hidden in the back of his mouth. With as much force as he can muster, he spits the little yellow tablet in my face. I flinch, closing my eyes. The tablet lands on my cheek, slowly sliding down my face in its river of yellowish-green saliva. I shake my head from side to side, trying unsuccessfully to dislodge the tablet from my skin.

"I'll scream blue murder if you don't leave me alone," I whisper with venom, hoping his only intention is to scare me. My fear, however, is that he has entered my room with more sinister intent in mind. I hope my hollow words are enough of a threat to make him reconsider his advance and move away from me.

"Don't worry. I will not hurt you," he laughs, showing no fear of me whatsoever. He moves closer once more, his eyes wide open and menacing, "How could I in this. All I want is to smell your perfume. Yes, to smell your lovely perfume. It reminds me so much of my childhood and the children I have played with in the past. Such marvelous days indeed, days I long to return to for a break from the reality of life. Maybe, just maybe I can taste it too. That would be wonderful, just dandy my sweet Buttercup."

I am aghast that such an evil creature could have a similar thought in his head as mine; a yearning to return to the joys of childhood in order to escape the realities of life. Do we have that much in common? Does everyone possess a familiarity, even a miniscule one, with the devil himself? I shake the ludicrous notion out of my head. Our visions of childhood are so drastically different. My vision is filled with innocence and wonder; his is filled with little more than darkness and pain. The void between black and white is stark. There is no grey. I could never envisage a situation where I could be drawn upon to harm another person. I never will harm another. I have nothing in common with this unholy creature.

Chris moves closer, flicking his long tongue in and out of his mouth like a thirsty Goanna. I can feel his hot breath on my neck moments before he begins to lick my skin. I feel the roughness of his tongue as he slowly licks his way up my neck towards my face. His crotch touches my hip. To my disgust, I can feel a large bulge pressing against my skin. Paralyzed with fear, I begin to feel a pain growing in my chest. I try to hold onto my scream. However, the agony is too much. The pain increases rapidly, becoming unbearable within seconds.

"Mmmmeowwww!" comes the fearsome warning from the foot of my bed. I look down and see Serenity standing on his hind quarters, eyes dilated, front paws raised with claws fully extended. He is ready for a fight.

"Ahhhhhh!" I scream out into the room. Chris is startled by both the cat and my fearsome cry of anguish. He stands up smartly and shuffles quickly away from me. In an instant he glides out of my room and is little more than a half forgotten nightmare.

The charge nurse comes running to my rescue as Serenity slides off the side of the bed. The nurse mistakenly sees a psychotic patient having some sort of violent fit as I writhe about in agony. I try desperately to free myself from the restraints. My efforts are futile in the extreme. All my thrashing about and incoherent screams just send a stronger message to her that I am dangerous and need to be drugged.

"It's okay. Calm yourself," the nurse says coldly as she fills a needle with the same clear liquid I have experienced before. I continue to thrash around as she administers the liquid into my upper arm. Within seconds I begin to calm, though the agony in my chest remains.

I lie back in pain as the energy steadily fades from my body. The drug begins to circulate, causing the onset of drowsiness. In the doorway I can see Dr. Khan standing behind a young couple, a strange look on his face. Could they be the couple who witnessed my accident? Maybe they have come to set the story straight. Maybe they will tell him the accident was real. Maybe he will listen.

There is a calendar on the wall near the doorway. It is positioned next to a clock in the shape of a wooden birdhouse. Just below a panoramic photograph of the South Morang Regional Hospital, the twentieth of February is circled in thick red marker. A window in the clock opens abruptly and a plastic bird pops out twelve times, announcing the hour. Even in my drowsy state I know something is wrong with this picture. Something is not quite right.

The clock and calendar weren't there when I came in were they?

My attention falls back to Dr. Khan. The couple has disappeared, leaving an unobstructed view of the doctor. He seems to have some blood on his neck and on the front of his lab coat. He smiles at me as the charge nurse leaves my room. She walks directly towards him. To my astonishment, without slowing her step, she passes straight through Dr. Khan like he is a ghost.

Oh my God!

I gasp as I struggle to breathe. The asthma which has stayed dormant since I was a child suddenly recurs. The nurse takes no notice of my distress. She has her back to me, some distance away, heading back to her station. I have a clear view of Dr. Khan now. His stomach is covered in blood, though it is clearly not from a patient. From my vantage point I can see the blood continuing to pulse out of an open wound. A second wound pulses from his neck sending blood gushing down his left side and onto the floor around him. His face is pale, very pale. I am not medically trained yet I know he is going to die if someone doesn't do something fast. He is losing far too much blood.

Breath coming in gulps. I struggle to remain calm and fill my lungs. My vision begins to blur, due to the lack of oxygen and the effects of the drug. I sense I can smell smoke; putrid, acrid smoke. I look around the room. I see no evidence of a fire. No alarms or sprinklers are activated.

Surely that wasn't a child singing a nursery rhyme, not here. No children would be safe in this ward.

To my surprise I see a little girl standing at the end of my bed; her light cotton dress fluttering in the gentle breeze. Her eyes look sad. She must be lost.

"Please, help me," she says before turning and walking from the room.

"Wait!" I scream. "It's not safe out there. Come back, come back. Please come back!"

What was that, a fluttering sound outside the window? Is that a bird or maybe a bat? Who are you? What are you doing here?

I drifted into unconsciousness, deeply troubled by what I have just seen. A dark shadow, in the general shape and size of a man passes along the wall and out the doorway. However, I do not see the person who generates this shadow. They are not here. It was certainly not the nurse; she is back at her station, out of view. Dr. Khan has disappeared too, as has the blood he spilled on the floor.

The pain in my chest stops abruptly. As my eyes flutter, steadily losing their fight against sleep, I see a small shape walking towards the bed. I smile as I recognize the black cat with the strange droopy right ear as he jumps onto my lap. My breathing becomes more regular as I gain control over the asthma. As I pat Serenity under his chin, I drift further away.

You're real! Not some trick of the mind. I don't know how you got here but I have a feeling you will watch over me. Make sure I'm safe. You will, won't you?

A final thought drifts into my head before sleep takes hold.

If Serenity can find an entrance into such a secure facility as this, then maybe Peter can too. Even better, maybe I can find a way out.

Unconsciousness descends upon me like the dew in the night; I can feel it taking possession of my being, numbing my insecurities.

Serenity curls up by my side and begins to purr. It is such a pleasant, peaceful sound. A sound that makes me feel completely at ease. I feel so sleepy. I drift into quiet darkness, away from the maddening world.

Blissful...... unconsciousness.....

'Riddles'

A kind heart beating,
A lie that is told,
A merry dance taken,
As a story is sold.

A risk that is taken,
A deception conceived,
A play being written,
Filled with hope and intrigue.

Chapter 11

Monday, February 20th, 2006.
Morning.
Psychiatric Ward.
South Morang Regional Hospital, Victoria, Australia.

Grrrrooowwwwww!!!

I stumble and fall in the dust as a strap breaks on one of my sandals. Searching the path behind me, I see no sign of the monsters. I quickly discard the other sandal and clamber to my feet. I can tell by their fearsome cries, that they are gaining on me. I know I cannot out run them. Though, at this point in time, I have no choice but to try.

Barefoot, I make my dash across the sharp rocks hidden in amongst the dust on the track. I feel every cut as the jagged edges tear at my feet with uncompromising brutality. I do not stop to consider the damage. I know if I do, I will die. This is a fate I still hope to avoid, somehow, today.

Grrrrrooowwwww!!!!!

They are closer now. I turn and look over my shoulder just as two of the monsters crawl out of the ravine. They drool with hunger, their powerful muscles glistening with sweat. I focus on taking clean steps, searching the horizon for some form of refuge which may provide protection from the rampaging beasts. I find none.

Time seems to slow as the seconds steadily pass one by one. I feel the ground shake as their footsteps bear down on me. I brace myself for their attack. I pray my death will be swift. I dare not turn around for I know they are right upon me. All hope is lost.

Grrrooowwwww!!!!

As the lead beast lunges for me I fall down a steep hole, hidden by the shrubbery. Instinctively I crouch into a ball in order to try to protect myself, somewhat, during my rapid descent. I bounce viciously off the walls until I find myself winded, lying at the bottom of the hole.

I wince as my nerve endings begin to register the great pain I am in. I am alive, barely. My quick self-assessment is not good. I have multiple cuts that are bleeding badly and, I suspect numerous broken bones. I fear my spine may have been damaged too as I no longer have any sensation in the lower half of my body. As the dust settles I begin to cry. I have escaped the clutches of the monsters only to be condemned to a slow painful death, alone, at the bottom of a deep hole.

Whispers echo through the dust filled air as my eyes dart, seeking their source. My stomach tightens as I realize I am not alone. Numerous eyes stare back at me from the darkness over by the far wall. As the dust settles, the fireflies reappear, adding some semblance of light to the darkened cavern. Finally, I can see the dirty, scared faces of thirty or so frightened people, huddled against the wall, seeking comfort in numbers. I smile, dumbfounded to see human faces staring back at me in this strange, savage world.

Far above my head, I am aware of much movement and agitation as the monsters examine the hole through which I fell. They walk around the top making grunting noises, searching desperately for a way in. They seem reluctant to admit defeat, yet admit it they must; for the hole above me is too small for them to use as a conduit. The hole is also too deep for them to reach in and pluck me out. Save for an alternative entrance there is no way their hairy claws can reach me. I may be seriously injured but, at least for the moment, I am safe.

"Hi," I whisper as I nervously try to break the ice. By the look of their stunned faces, I suspect they don't speak English. As the air clears further I can see there are about twenty adults and maybe a dozen children. They all appear petrified. I guess that comes as a consequence of living your lives in the realm of the monsters. I hope I can communicate with them somehow. However, I doubt they can offer the medical assistance I so desperately need, considering how primitive they look.

Suddenly I am aware of movement around me. Something soft and wet is slivering underneath me. As I watch in horror, a purple leaf vine begins to wrap itself around my body from all directions. I am unable to fight off its advances as it slowly binds tight around me. I shriek in pain as it manipulates my broken bones back into place. Tiny spines puncture my skin, injecting some sort of fluid into my veins. I am overcome by the tingling sensation of this foreign substance coursing through my system. The liquid is cold, sending a chill through my skin.

Cocooned, I have no choice but to relax. The people cowering opposite me seem strangely at ease with the creeper that is attacking me. Maybe they know something I don't. After a few minutes I notice something curious. The vine begins to shed some leaves. Then the stems start to whither and fade away. Within a minute the vine has shriveled up and died leaving me free once more. I smile as a most extraordinary thing occurs. Sensation spreads through my body as my blood begins to circulate to all my extremities. I stand up, feeling no pain, as I examine my scar free arms. I am miraculously healed.

Looking into the distance I see a small hole at the end of the cavern. Beckoning the group to follow, I lead them to the other end of the tunnel. Within seconds I have removed sufficient rocks so that I can squeeze through, back into the world of the monsters. I implore the others to follow me. Reluctantly, one by one, they crawl through. As I assist the last child to escape the hole, I turn around to see where we are. I sigh and shake my head in disbelief. Will this nightmare ever end?

We are standing at the edge of the monster's camp, down by the riverside.

*   *   *

I wake slowly from my deep slumber, unable to determine precisely how many hours have elapsed since the second injection. To my astonishment, I feel fairly good. My vision is clear. I'm not drowsy at all. In fact I feel rested and alive. The terrible pain in my chest has abated too. My breathing is calm and normal. Only the dull ache in my head reminds me of the commotion earlier.

The room has changed since I last saw it, though one thing remains the same. I continue to be imprisoned in my bed by three secure straps which bite into my skin, cutting off the blood flow a little. The walls of my room are again white and bland; lacking any form of decoration or adornment. The calendar and clock, previously hanging near the door, have disappeared completely. I find this curious. Is someone playing games with me, trying to mess with my mind?

Were they ever really there?

I wince as I feel some soreness from a dead weight pushing on my bruised ribs. I look down the length of my body. Sitting, curled up on my stomach, Serenity blinks his iridescent emerald eyes as he watches me rouse from my slumber. He purrs contently, exuding confidence into the room. The cat's calm demeanor is infectious, a virus my body and soul welcomes readily. My life has been so tumultuous in the past week that I crave a little security and peace. I smile, unconcerned by the pain produced from his gentle rhythmical massage. I know he means well.

"So you decided to stay around this time. How did you get in here, anyhow? They invest thousands of dollars into all those security measures and they can't even keep a stray like you out. There is something special about you isn't there? I just can't quite put my finger on it. I'll work it out eventually. Anyway, I'm glad you've stayed to keep me company."

Serenity sits watching me, quietly purring, not offering any answers. Suddenly he begins to stir. He puffs up his tail to twice its normal size as if he fears attack from some undetectable foe. He releases a deep guttural growl for additional effect as he slowly stands up and faces towards the open doorway. The cat arches his back and prowls towards the end of my bed before sitting, ready to pounce.

"What's wrong mate? What's the problem?" I ask, unable to move my arms and comfort my new found friend with a pat. I am a little concerned that the problem may be with me rather than someone or something else. After all, the Serenity was looking at me when he first began to growl.

I catch my breath as I spy Chris peering around the edge of the doorway. Only a small portion of the right side of his face is exposed from my vantage point. I feel relieved that my new found friend hasn't turned on me. At the same time I am greatly unnerved by Chris lurking around my room again while I remain strapped to this bed. I search my mind for something that will deter his advances for a second time.

Oh God, make him go away.

Without warning, Serenity emits a sharp, horrible spitting hiss. Startled by this act of aggression, I jump. To my surprise, so does Chris. Head down, he walks sullenly away, past my doorway. I guess he simply decides there are easier patients he can bother on this ward; patients without cats. As he walks past, I notice the left side of his face as it becomes visible for the first time.

I look straight at Serenity as he turns and walks up the length of the bed towards my chest once again. As he begins to settle I ask, "I don't believe it. Did you do that?"

As I speak, the cat pauses, standing directly in front of me. I see the cat's eyes change from dark black to their normal vibrant green color. He begins to purr once again, more vigorously this time. Just like in our earlier meeting, in the recovery ward, he winks at me as if to acknowledge that everything is fine now. There is no more danger. Serenity then proceeds to turn in a circle three times in a smooth fluid movement. He finishes his dance curled up completely on my lap. A patch of sunlight streams through the window, pin pointing the exact spot where Serenity has made himself at home.

This cat seems to know more about what is going on than I do.

Chris's face has become badly scarred while I was sleeping. On the left side there are deep, narrow, open cuts. They extended the full length of his cheek, from level with his eye all the way down to the area just past his mouth. The scratches are swollen slightly, like they are infected along the edges. They look for all the world to me like cat scratches, three or four on top of one another. If they are indeed from Serenity, then he has put up one heck of a brave fight in my defense.

Maybe you've been watching over me after all.

Outside my room I hear heavy footsteps coming towards me. Two people are engaged in a vigorous discussion about something. It is hard to discern exactly what the discussion is about. I decide to fain sleep again in case they come into my room. I want to avoid another injection, if that is at all possible. Closing my eyes, relaxing my body, I begin to lie there, waiting. I hear them walk through the doorway before they move to the end of my bed.

"Don't worry about her; I gave her an injection about five hours ago. She should be out cold for a little while yet," the charge nurse makes no effort to lower her voice as she is unaware I have woken from my chemically induced slumber.

"What about that? Should that cat be on the bed?"

The charge nurse laughs, "No he shouldn't. You know the regulations about animals as well as I do. Lord knows how he found his way in here. Anyway, you're most welcome to try to get rid of him, if you want. Though let me give you the tip. I've got some pretty nasty scratch marks down my arms from when I tried about an hour ago."

Don't laugh. Hold it together.

"I don't think he worries me," the second nurse says deciding wisely to let Serenity be.

"What the Hell....?" exclaims the charge nurse as a noisy fracas resonates from beyond the main room. I open my eyes to see both nurses rushing from my room, bewildered as to what is occurring.

Raised male voices can be heard, in heated discussion, just outside the security doors. Though their tone is loud, the clarity of their words is muffled by the thick, heavy security doors. The booming sound of pounding on the security doors echoes through the ward and into my room. I can see the two nurses standing just outside my doorway, stunned, watching the security doors intently.

Suddenly the verbal brawl gains much needed clarity. I hear the security doors swish open and several angry people clamber through. The argument has now entered the psychiatric ward. It appears someone has talked, or rather yelled, their way through the two sets of security doors. I can now hear the conversation clearly as all the participants seem very loud in expressing their forthright opinions and thoughts.

"I'll take it from here Phil," the charge nurse says with authority, dismissing the guard who has followed the intruder into the ward. I can tell by her stance that this is her domain and she is determined to defend its security procedures at all cost. "So what is going on here? Who the Hell are you?"

"Sorry for the interruption but this fellow wasn't going to take no for an answer," the security guard offers feebly.

"What is the point of having security if you grant access to this ward to anyone who is a bit more voracious in their verbal application for entry?"

"Sorry," is all Phil can offer, though it seems grossly inadequate considering the circumstances of what has transpired. I hear the doors swish open once more as the security guard makes a quiet, though hasty exit from the ward.

"I have not begun to be voracious yet, Madam," I hear the intruder say. Though his words are out of character, I think I recognize the owner of this voice. I smile, hoping my theory is right.

That couldn't be Peter, could it? Surely it is. But what on earth is he up to?

"I want to make you very clear on three points, Sonny, so that you can be left in absolutely no doubt. One, I will not tolerate you stating your business here to me in that tone of voice. Two, I most certainly will not be tolerating your presence here for much longer if you don't start adding the term 'Sister' to every sentence you utter."

"Got it, what is your third point?" I hear Peter pause for a second. I assume he is re-thinking his approach as he adds quickly, "Sister."

"And thirdly," the charge nurse adds with much emphasis. "I run this ward. While I'm on duty, you will have to deal with me and let me tell you, my word is law."

"That may be so," Peter says, showing absolutely no sign in his voice that he is backing down in the slightest. "However, I feel you and your hospital have committed a grave injustice against my client. I must warn you that, as a party to this restriction of basic human liberties, you may be liable as a co-defendant in any compensation hearing my client may seek in the future, Sister."

That is Peter isn't it? What is he going on about?

"I will have you know I am not in the habit of letting myself be badgered by the likes of you," the charge nurse retorts pointing a finger at Peter. She is a formidable foe and I fear Peter is standing on thin ice trying to win an argument with her. Particularly considering the approach he is adopting.

"My only concern is the harm that may be occurring to my client, Sister." Peter's words are so different to how he normally talks. They sound so professional; just like a lawyer. I wonder who has helped him put together this bizarre idea. I guess I shouldn't criticize him, he has made it to just outside my doorway. That's not such a bad effort, all things considered.

"Your client, whoever they may be, is completely safe here. No harm can come to them. In my ward, my nurses strive for the highest possible standards of health care. To this end we have developed and incorporated the strictest safety procedures of any psychiatric health ward, in any hospital, in any state or territory in Australia!"

Peter is undeterred, "That may be the case but that doesn't explain why my client is being held against her will. The mental scarring that could result from an inappropriate incarceration in a psychiatric hospital such as this, has the potential to be enormous. A payout to my client in relation to your incompetence could be astronomical. I can assure you that she will, on the direction of my advice, sue all those responsible for this travesty of civil liberties, Sister."

"She?" the charge nurse muses, curious as to which patient has provoked such a vitriolic tirade. "Who is this client of yours anyway?"

"Julie, sorry Miss Julie Mahoney. It is my understanding that she was admitted to your ward without her consent. That represents a severe breech ...."

The voice of the charge nurse rises, just a fraction louder. Her body language suggests to me that Peter's questioning of the hospital's competency is starting to irritate her greatly. Her words make it crystal clear that she will not stand for her authority, or that of the hospital, to be undermined by a belligerent interloper as she continues, "Now just hang on a second. I was just starting my shift when Julie Mahoney was brought in to us. All her paperwork seems to be completely in order."

"What are you saying? Did she sign herself in? That would be an amazing effort considering her arms were tightly strapped to her bed at the time she was admitted."

Now angry, the charge nurse places her hands on her hips as she continues to argue her point, "Of course not! Her mother admitted her on the advice of the Doctor who oversaw her initial admission."

Peter turns up the heat, twisting the nurse's words to his own advantage, "Are you telling me that my client, who still has all her faculties, was admitted to your ward on the basis of a signature from a vindictive mother and a quick superficial examination by a Doctor! The courts will have a field day with this."

"Now hang on just a minute!" the nurse states as she points aggressively at Peter with a quivering, yet forceful finger. "The proper admittance procedures were followed in this instance. In fact, they were followed to the letter. There is a great deal of anecdotal information to suggest that Julie is afflicted by some sort of psychiatric disorder. Her belief in her delusional episodes suggests she has temporarily or otherwise, lost her grasp on reality. With this in mind, she represents a danger not only to others but also to herself. In fact, she was so agitated when she was first brought in that we had to administer a standard sedative in order to calm her."

Peter ignores the insinuation that I have lost my mind and continues to berate the head nurse, "This just gets better and better. Administering a sedative to a patient who never should have been admitted in the first place is unforgivable. It could also be very costly for you and your hospital. In fact, this case could even turn out to be the biggest lawsuit in Victoria's history."

The charge nurse sighs. With an air of smugness in her voice, she says, "As I told you Julie was admitted correctly, in my opinion, and you may have to take your complaint to the courts."

Peter steps forward into my field of view. He reaches into his jacket pocket and produces an A4 piece of folded paper with some typing on it. From this distance it is impossible for me to see any of the words printed, let alone decipher the document's sentences. He looks confident as he continues "Well, as it so happens, I already have a court order. As you can see this is from the Melbourne Magistrates Court."

"Can I see that?" the nurse asks softly as Peter flashes the paper briefly before her eyes. To me, the paper looks like an official document of some sort, complete with a logo or design like a coat of arms at the top.

Surely he hasn't engaged a lawyer and gone to court. There wouldn't have been sufficient time for that. So, what on earth has he got in his hands? What scam is he trying to pull, I wonder?

"You're most welcome to, Sister. However, I would prefer to read it to you, so that there can be no misunderstanding as to the seriousness of this situation."

A hint of resignation, mixed with frustration surfaces in her voice, "Do as you please; just make it snappy. I have a lot to attend to."

Peter continues, pausing momentarily to clear his throat, "The Melbourne Magistrates Court on this day, Monday the twentieth of February, 2006, grants a temporary injunction against the South Morang Regional Hospital and all its employees in the case of Miss Julie Mahoney. She is to be released with the utmost haste and cannot be re-admitted until such time as a hearing of her case can be held with all concerned parties. Currently this hearing is scheduled to take place at 10 am on Friday the fifth of May, 2006. Signed Judge, John Farquat."

The charge nurse says something to Peter though it is impossible to make out her words. She has lowered her voice considerably so as the other staff cannot hear what she has to say. Her body language shows fear and uncertainty, particularly as she glances my way several times during the hushed conversation. It is only when I hear Peter's voice once more that I realize things might be taking a turn for the positive.

Peter glances my way and winks with his right eye before addressing the nurse once more, "That is not necessary. If you provide me with the appropriate wheelchair I will give an undertaking to ensure that my client leaves this facility without any further harm. I personally want to ensure that her exit is swift and safe. It is better for all concerned if she doesn't stay in this ward a moment longer than she needs to."

Somehow he's done it. I can't believe it! They are going to let me go.

I hear several pairs of comfortable shoes scurrying towards the nurse as she beckons. After a quick conversation, they run into my room and begin to untie the restraints which have held me fast for so long now. I feel the blood flow back into my lower arms as the first strap is released. Serenity remains curled up on my chest. Both Serenity and the nurses watch each other suspiciously though neither party seems eager to start a war. Somehow the cat must sense that the nurses are here to help.

"Thanks," I say as they continue their feverish work.

One of the nurses smiles and says, "No worries love. He can't see you like this, anyways. You know what them lawyer folk are like. All our jobs will be toast."

They hand me my red dress which they have extricated from a cupboard hidden well beyond the range of my gaze. I drape the garment over my torso while my legs remain strapped down. The nurses form a physical barricade, protecting my privacy. I try to straighten my dress, though I know, even without the aid of a mirror, that I have only partially succeeded. I must look quite a sight. Silver high heeled shoes on lap, disheveled and overdressed in a psychiatric ward setting. I'm glad no one has a camera.

I hear more footsteps moving towards my room. The nurses hear them too. They quicken the pace of their work, unhitching the last of the straps before standing back so as not to obstruct the visitors. Peter walks into view, framed by the doorway. I smile broadly as I see he is dressed to the nines. Dark blue pin striped suit with a matching tie over a brand new business shirt, dark, shiny black Windsor Smith shoes with laces. These shoes are a rarity for Peter who usually wears work boots exclusively, even when he is lounging around the house. All these clothes are unfamiliar to me. I was unaware Peter possessed clothes of this quality. The two junior nurses have slunk out of the room. They are not in a position to see him smiling. They also fail to see him put a finger to his lips, encouraging me to stay silent and to resist the urge to laugh.

Freed finally, I rub each of my arms in turn, trying to increase the blood flow to my extremities. After having some success with this I lean forward and start working on the circulation in my legs. In doing so, I disturb Serenity who leaps off my bed and runs across and out of the room. He dodges and weaves past numerous legs with unabashed efficiency, causing somewhat of a commotion out in the common room as some of the patients are delighted by the sight of a cat.

"Excuse me, sir," the nurse says as she brings the wheelchair into my room. Peter steps aside to let her pass. The nurse brings the wheelchair to the edge of the bed, facing it towards me, placing the brake firmly on. The nurse and Peter then move either side of me, lifting and steadying me as I climb into its seat. My legs feel wasted, somewhat, from the lack of use over the last few hours. As I stumble awkwardly into the chair, I'm certainly grateful for its availability.

Once seated, the nurse moves to push me away from the bed. Peter steps forward and reassures her with a smile, "I'll take it from here."

Reluctantly the nurse looks at Peter, unsure as to what the hospital regulations are in a situation like this. She knows enough to realize this isn't normal procedure, not even close. However, she remains silent, fully aware that she is only a junior nurse and that she is dealing with a lawyer with a court order. All the nurses on duty in the psychiatric ward have no intention of standing in the way of such a person and risking involvement in any costly or job threatening litigation which may occur at a later date. The nurse stands aside, offering the handles to Peter.

Peter turns the wheelchair around and pushes it towards the door with vigor. As he wheels me through the main area, I realize the psych patients I encountered on my arrival aren't dangerous at all. In fact, they all seem completely docile. This might be just a change in perspective on my behalf. After all, I came in completely helpless. Everything was new and a threat. Now that I'm leaving the ward for good, everything feels so much safer. Or it may be because with all the yelling between Peter and the charge nurse, the landscape has changed. Many of the patients now appear frightened, seeking shelter in their rooms or cowering near the walls. Even Chris doesn't make an appearance as we make our way to leave.

The charge nurse sends a long, cold, glaring stare my way as we pass by her desk. She knows she is beaten. I know she is uncomfortable with the taste that leaves in her mouth. A taste she has not savored very often in her working life. She signals for the security doors to be opened with little more than a quick flourish of her arm before returning her concentration to the pile of insignificant papers in front of her. I feel I represent a great deal of unpleasantness to her and that she can't wait to see the back of me. The feeling is mutual.

As we wait for the guard to activate the doors, my eyes are drawn to something by the far wall. I concentrate, trying to work out precisely what the mass might be. It looks initially like a pile of discarded laundry. With further examination, that doesn't seem quite right. Eventually it comes to me. It is a discarded strait-jacket.

That's odd for the nurses to leave that on the floor.

The security doors buzz into life and we begin to move forward. We pass through effortlessly, without interrogation or suspicion. The guards bear witness, reluctantly passive, on either side of the narrow room which separates the psychiatric ward from the open access of the normal hospital. The sound of the electronic doors receding is an exhilarating revelation to me. Hearing each of the two sets of doors close and lock behind us is even better. I sigh with relief.

Peter continues to walk briskly towards the elevators. It is only when we reach the elevators that I realize something is wrong. Peter is normally a very patient person. However, as we stand before the closed elevator doors waiting, he seems rather anxious, pressing the button repeatedly for service. I can see sweat starting to build on his forehead. He seems to have lost the ice cool veneer he displayed so well in the presence of the charge nurse. Maybe he has simply held it together for as long as he can. I don't know.

"C'mon!" he yells through gritted teeth as he pushes the button vigorously a few more times.

"What's wrong, Hun? What is it?" I enquire, baffled by his behavior.

"Shhh, not yet" he pushes the button four more times. He looks apprehensively over his shoulder, as if he suspects we are being followed. I continue to watch him, wondering what on earth is making him so jumpy. It is only when the elevator arrives that he seems to relax a little. We enter and he pushes the button for the ground floor. The metal doors begin to close. Before they slide fully shut, Serenity runs through the narrowing gap, leaping deftly onto my lap. As he settles, he starts purring as usual.

"So your friend is still following you around, I see," Peter says as the doors close finally. The stiffness appears to ease from his shoulders as he leans casually against the wall.

"Don't change the subject," I say patting the cat. "What's wrong?"

"Nothing, now I've got you out of there," Peter says, his eyes sparkling like he is reminiscing about a dirty joke that is too rude to share.

"There must be something, though. I've never seen you so agitated."

Peter smiles, silently fishing the piece of paper out of his coat pocket, "Well if the truth be known, it appears I upset the charge nurse so much that she let me read out the court order rather than look at it in detail herself."

"I don't understand. What's wrong with the court order?" I ask blissfully ignorant of what Peter is trying to convey to me.

Peter laughs as he passes the order to my trembling hand, "Have a look yourself. Tell me if you can see a problem with what the court has ordered."

I stare at the document in disbelief. I shake my head as I read through each sentence. I stare at Peter who is grinning from ear to ear. I can't believe what he has done. It is just so incredibly dangerous, he might have been arrested for ...., for something, I guess. It is just so stupid. My frown evaporates into a grin. So stupid, it actually worked.

"You used this to get me out?"

A smug look on his face, Peter gloats, "Sure did."

"They could have locked you in there with me."

"Yep, I guess they could have."

"They could have called the police and charged you with various things. Fraud, deception, maybe trespass, maybe....."

"Yep, I guess so. But they didn't. They didn't have a clue did they, Angel?"

"I just can't believe you got me out of a secured mental health ward of a major hospital with nothing more than a speeding infringement notice."

"Strange things happen sometimes. Look at this damn cat following you around over three floors via elevators, through security doors. By the way we're not taking him home with us. You know that don't you?"

"Hsssss!"

Peter moves to pat Serenity as the cat warns him off. Peter moves back to the wall. Serenity feigns sleep, keeping a watchful eye on Peter while he evaluates whether he is friend or foe.

"We can't leave Serenity here, not after all he's been through. Anyhow, I don't think we have a say in the matter."

I can see by the look on Peter's face that he knows not to argue the point any further. Once I have named a pet there is no point discussing the issue. Peter knows me well enough. I also know Peter. I know that he has wanted to get a cat for some time now. This one will have to be the one. I'm sure they will get used to each other, eventually.

'Wildfires'

Harsh family judgments,
From ignorance conceived,
Rise to the surface,
So quickly they breed.

Sharpest of tongues.
Satan's vile words freed,
Confrontation unavoidable.
So quickly intolerance breeds.

Chapter 12

Monday February 20th, 2006.
Afternoon.
South Morang Regional Hospital, Victoria, Australia.

Our exit from the hospital is amazing in its simplicity. Peter pushes me casually out through the front doors. We pass numerous staff members; nurses, orderlies, security guards. No one gives us a second glance. No one tries to question our speedy departure or strike up a conversation. I am just another patient who has completed her treatment and is being discharged. A common enough occurrence, something that happens hundreds of times a day. I guess I expected someone to discover the 'scam' Peter has perpetrated. In reality, now that they have decided to allow my discharge, no one appears to be concerned about the circumstances surrounding my release. They are all too busy with their own lives.

The loading bay is a hive of activity, as usual. I glance to my side and my heart stops as I sense I have been caught. A woman in a bright floral maxi dress stares at me for a moment. Our eyes lock as she seems shocked to see me sitting in a wheelchair, at the edge of the pavement. Her wavy hair billows in the gentle breeze.

"Shit, is that the nurse from your original ward. Does you think she recognizes you?" Peter asks with much trepidation in his voice. We've come so close to freedom, it would be heartbreaking to be caught now.

I wave to Pamela and smile, "Yes that's her and I'm sure she recognizes me."

"Do you think she's going to cause trouble?" Peter asks.

"No," I reply calmly as Pamela smiles and waves back. I know exactly how her mind works. "No, it's okay. She be no slave to no surly white man and his rules. She makes up her own rules as to what is right and what is wrong. She won't call security on us."

"What?" Peter asks, completely confused.

I laugh a little at the in-joke, "Don't worry. We're fine."

We are both relieved to see Pamela turn and walk towards her car. As she disappears across the car park she rejects the temptation to look back. She doesn't want to know anything more about our escape to freedom.

The hospital car park is permanently full. There is no meaningful option for patients other than for their drivers to park directly outside the entrance. Several cars are double parked at the moment. Peter leaves me sitting in the wheelchair, on the edge of the pavement, while he goes to collect our car from the South Morang Shopping Centre car park, some distance away. Serenity is awake, curled up on my lap.

Peter was one of the lucky ones who managed to pry a space free, earlier in the day. It is a patience game, looking for someone with keys in their hands as they head towards their car. I watch Peter now as he half walks, half jogs, dodging slow moving traffic, on his way to collect the car.

"I'll give you a hand, missy."

I turn to see a complete stranger standing next to me. His hair is a little scruffy. A thin layer of bristle graces his chin giving the appearance that he hasn't shaved for twelve hours or more. He looks fit though a touch weary, dressed neatly in his red and white ambulance officer's uniform. He looks for all the world like he has just completed a marathon shift. His smile radiates a warmth which indicates a caring nature; though obviously exhausted. He winks at me, "I'll give you an' your fella a hand when he gets back. Wheelchairs can be a tricky thing for the inexperienced."

"Thanks," I say reaching out and grasping the stranger's hand. I squeeze gently before releasing it once more. I am feeling a bit washed out and lethargic, a bit uncertain about the prospect of standing on my own two feet. It will be good to get some extra assistance. After all, Peter is enthusiastic though just a tad awkward at times. He gets flustered easily too. Sweat forms on his brow as his shoulders visibly tense whenever he is placed in potentially embarrassing situations. I'm sure he won't mind a bit of extra help in this instance.

I turn my focus back to the car park, searching for Peter. He is nowhere to be seen; lost somewhere in amongst the masses of cars waiting in parallel bays. On the pavement opposite I spy a woman in a drab, brown overcoat which covers a simple white cotton dress. Her long, mousy brown hair appears unkempt as it flutters in the wind. She looks drenched, as if she has been caught in a late summer storm. However, that cannot be, as today is a bright sunny day and the soil in the garden beds is cracked, giving the impression there has been little, if any, rain in the past week.

Her gaze is unsettling as she stares right at me. Her eyes are unflinching and cold. I feel her thoughts directed silently at me, harsh and spiteful. She gives the impression that she wants to do me some harm, waiting patiently for her opportunity to move in and stab me with a knife perhaps. I shake my head. This is a stupid thought. I try to push this idle thought from my mind. Even though she is a stranger, she somehow seems familiar to me. I rack my mind yet I can't place her specifically. I smile and send a wave her way, hoping she has no quarrel with me.

Serenity stirs on my lap. Glancing up at me, blinking it eyes as it produces a low guttural roar.

"What's wrong mate?" I ask as it becomes patently obvious what is wrong. He has noticed the woman too and is not at all comfortable.

The lady responds to my wave with a startled look. To my surprise she begins to march, at a brisk pace, straight across the roadway towards me. A car narrowly misses her as it passes by. She spares no sideways glance to check for further traffic. Her actions show a complete disregard for her own safety. She is determined to reach me. I tense and shut my eyes, expecting the inevitable impact of our bodies. The pace she is walking is both steady and fast. The distance between us shrinks rapidly.

"You Bitch!" she hisses as I open my eyes to see her face only an eighth of an inch from mine. She is so close that I can feel little droplets of saliva hitting my face as she spits her venom. "Why don't you do something? You're just so useless! For God sake do something!"

I brace myself for an impact as she stands upright, towering over me. Strangely, she walks straight through me. I feel a tingling sensation on my skin as she passes through my body and out the other side. Gasping for breath, I turn desperately trying to find her yet, she is gone, disappearing into thin air just like she was never there in the first place.

This is madness! Why is my mind playing tricks on me?

"Hey, are you okay?" I hear a voice to the side of me call as I return from my drowsy ether, back into the real world.

I turn and stare at the ambulance officer beside me. His expression has changed from jovial to somewhat fearful. I realize I must appear a tad insane through his eyes. My behavior, while encountering a 'ghost', must have seemed curious at the very least. Considering, of course, that I suspect he didn't see this mysterious apparition for himself. I slow my breath and force a smile to my lips, trying to restore confidence to my outer persona as I lie, "I'm fine, really, just itching to get out of here."

He nods, seemingly accepting my explanation. However, I am well aware my words are feeble and lacking any semblance of credibility. I can see by his face that he too is not convinced that I am alright. His body language suggests that he is unlikely to make an issue of it. I hope I am right. I have had enough people question my sanity for one week.

It takes Peter just a few minutes to traverse the intervening distance and retrieve our humble chariot. The minutes seem to last forever as an uncomfortable silence falls between the ambulance officer and myself. As Peter brings the car around to the entrance, the ambulance officer grabs the handles of the wheelchair and pushes me closer to the door. Peter runs around to the passenger side and opens the front door.

Serenity takes advantage of the open door, jumping off my lap, into the car and over to the back seat. He quickly makes himself at home, curling up in the middle of the back dashboard, beneath the rear window. He seems quite content in amongst the warm, plush covering and my hug of teddy bears.

The ambulance officer graciously assists me into the car, taking one arm and steadying me while all the time holding onto the chair. Peter and I thank him briefly before he smiles and turns away, taking the wheelchair back into the hospital for us.

"You two take care," he says as he forces an insecure smile while he looks my way with questioning eyes. For a moment he is lost for words. He seems to be searching his mind for the right thing to say. Eventually he whispers, so that only I can hear, "I hope you feel better soon. Take it easy."

"What's up with him?" Peter asks as he takes his seat behind the wheel and fights with the retractable seat belt.

"Nothing," I lie as I watch the ambulance officer walk away. He glances over his shoulder at me with a frown on his face as the hospital doors automatically slide open. "I guess he's just tired after a long shift."

"I guess that's probably it," Peter says as his attention span wanes rapidly.

My thoughts return briefly to what I have just experienced. I know I have not changed. I am confident that I have not had a breakdown nor lost my sanity. However, with that in mind, I remain perplexed as to what is happening to me. The lady in the coat seemed so real yet, in the end, she disappeared just like some sort of ghostly apparition. I am beginning to reluctantly acknowledge to myself that some of what I have seen in recent days is not real. I am finding it difficult to sort the real from the imaginary at the moment. The visions I see are just like dreams which have come to life during the day, 'Waking dreams', for want of a better term. I know that sounds insane, though I am certain I am not. Maybe I am just attuned to the spirit world in some way. Something is going on, that much I know for certain.

I do not let my dilemma dwell too heavily on my mind. I feel completely relaxed as we begin our journey out of the car park. Peter is absorbed in the task at hand; getting me as far away from the hospital as quickly as he can. His shoulders are rigid and tense. I assume it will take a while for him to believe we are truly home free. Delicately I reach over, placing a hand on his knee. He turns and smiles. The deep furrows in his forehead disappear as he is distracted from his thoughts momentarily. The tension rapidly ebbs from his body. We kiss briefly, forgetting that the world is around us. He caresses the nape of my neck soothingly before sighing, checking his mirrors and setting off.

Watching the suburbs outside my window disappear and change into green, sparsely treed paddocks is a dream come true for me, particularly considering I was bracing myself for an extended stretch, trapped inside a psychiatric ward, less than an hour ago. I feel completely at ease. No concrete, few cars, no people. My problems of recent days are beginning to drift rapidly away. I am free. I cannot ask for more than that at the moment.

"You're very quiet," Peter says as he glances my way prior to turning right at the South Morang roundabout onto Plenty Rd. We are making good progress.

I smile as I stare out the window at the passing scenery, "Just catching my breath, Hun."

I savor every tree, every cow, and every bale of hay sitting peacefully in the paddocks as we roll by. These are everyday items, things which I have become very nonchalant about up till now. Insignificant constants in my life, always part of the back ground scenery. I pass them over and over again each day without appreciating their significance. In the scheme of things they are of no importance whatsoever. However, after my experience incarcerated in the psychiatric ward, I am taking nothing for granted. Not anymore. I plan to enjoy the freedom of being a 'tourist' in my own back yard.

Looking over my shoulder I check on Serenity. He is curled up, asleep on the back ledge, completely unfazed by the motion and noise of the car. His name certainly seems apt as I look at him now. Our previous cat was not such a fan of car travel. The last time we transported Felix to the vet, we finished up having a devil of a time trying to get him down to

Whittlesea. For the duration of the journey he hid under the front seat, moaning loudly. Once at our destination, it took a full ten minutes to extricate him from this position. His remittance for our services was a horrible, steaming mess in the most inaccessible of spots under the car seat. We spent several days trying to remove the smell, though never really succeeded. Looking at Serenity now I realize how much I miss Felix, my second black cat. He passed away only a month ago after a long and eventful life. He always seemed to be around when anything exciting was occurring. An appealing trait I can see in Serenity's makeup as well.

Serenity's just so unbelievably relaxed.

Coming up 'the hill' just outside Whittlesea, I feel I am home. Still thirty minutes from our house yet my senses are telling me 'we are home'. The kangaroos grazing peacefully in the paddocks to the left, the sensation of elevation, the smell of Eucalyptus wafting through the open window and my ears popping all add to a welcome feeling stirring in my heart. I am definitely home.

Nothing but bush from here on. In the past, living in Kinglake has felt, at times, so isolated from the rest of the world. After the problems I have experienced with numerous people over the last few days, I am looking forward to enjoying as much isolation as I can find. A gentle breeze, the sound of a Wattle Bird looking for its mate in the nearby gully and the absence of people with opinions are the only conditions I seek. That would be heaven for me.

We glide into the driveway, my mind completely at ease. It will take time, yet I know the events of the last few days will eventually drift into the mists of time. I will reclaim my life; I will be unscarred by my treatment and the accusations which accompanied it. Today is a new day, the day I start the rest of my life.

Finally we arrive at our home. I notice Peter's ute in the driveway. For the first time it dawns on me, a curious, unexplained question as to how Peter collected my car after I blacked out, leaving it parked in the middle of the road? I guess he asked Gina or a friend to help. I wonder if it was still at the side of the road or if it was towed? Doesn't matter, I guess. He fixed the situation somehow.

Peter opens my door and assists me from the car. Serenity scoots past, running straight for the safety of the shrubbery.

"Hey, Serenity!" I call out to no reaction. The cat is lost deep in amongst the dense foliage.

"Don't fret, Sweetheart," Peter offers. "I'm sure he will be fine. He's a very independent creature, though he seems to have a happy knack of staying close to you. I'm sure he won't go far. Just exploring his new home, I guess."

"I guess you're right," I say without much confidence. I reluctantly turn my attention away from the garden. Instead, I look towards the grey stone path leading to the front of our house.

Peter is so attentive. He is treating me like I am fragile piece of porcelain, ready to fall and break at any moment. I guess he may be a little guilty that he has let me down by allowing me to be incarcerated in the psychiatric ward. I don't think that way. He shouldn't feel guilty at all. After all, he was the one who saved me. What transpired was not his fault. I am determined to ensure that I make this clear to him over the days and weeks to come. I love him so much. I will make sure he knows that too.

With Peter's arm securely around my waist, I stumble up the cobbled pathway towards the front door. My feet slip, their steps uncertain, as I walk on the loose, uneven stones. I know my home hasn't mysteriously changed at all in the last few days. However, from this angle it has never looked as good as it does today.

"Just as well I don't drink," I joke, as I find each step I take surprisingly difficult. I pride myself on my fitness though, so far, this hasn't aided me in my quest to regain my 'land legs'. I am sure, given a few days, my jelly legs will strengthen and normality will resume.

I lean against the wall to steady myself while Peter unlocks and opens the front door. We wobble down the narrow hallway, turning left into the living room. I flop onto the couch, exhausted by the short walk. I laugh as I conclude that the cleaning and dusting will have to wait another day.

Peter, standing upright, asks, "Would you like a cup of tea or coffee or something cool?"

How cute. He's still fussing.

"Something cold would be lovely."

"Do you want some ice, maybe?" he yells as he disappears into the kitchen and opens the fridge.

I laugh, wondering how long he will wait on me. Somehow, I rather like being treated like a queen, "That would be nice, if it's not too much trouble."

Out in the kitchen, the phone begins to ring. It is a wall phone which was broken by the previous owners of the house. It now has only one setting for the volume of its ring tone. It is loud, very loud. Not only can you hear the phone ring from every room in the house, you can also hear it from the furthest corner of the backyard with all the doors and windows shut. We have found it very useful, except, of course, when it rings while you are standing right next to it.

"I've got it. Hello," Peter answers "No, we're fine."

Peter hangs up the phone.

"That was quick," I yell back to the kitchen, seeking some clue as to who just called.

Peter comes into the lounge carrying two glasses of Diet Coke on the rocks. His grin tells me everything I need to know before he opens his mouth to speak, "That was your mother."

"Oh," I say recognizing the tone in Peter's voice, a tone which I do not approve of at all.

"Oh indeed. She knows you're out of hospital and is not, how should I put it?" Peter considers his words carefully before continuing, "She's not overly rapt about it."

"Oh," I say simply, knowing I can well do without the fallout that is sure to follow. My mother doesn't change her opinions very readily. In fact, once she has a strong opinion on a topic, she expresses it vigorously until she has convinced all doubters that she is correct. She usually gets her way.

The phone rings again. Peter looks at me as he raises his eyebrows in a disapproving glare. I stroke his arm affectionately as he hands me my glass. He places his glass on the wooden coffee table before sprinting back to the kitchen. He answers the phone calmly, "Hello."

He hangs up without saying another word.

"I hope that wasn't my mother," I scold Peter as he strolls back into the lounge.

"Actually it was," Peter answers honestly, unashamed by his rude manner.

"Oh Peter," I half smile, half frown. I certainly don't approve of his childish behavior even though I fully understand where he is coming from. In the whole time we have been together he has never been fully accepted into the family fold. Worse than that, my mother sees Peter as a major obstacle in her unfulfilled dreams that I find a 'real husband'.

"It wasn't my fault," Peter pleads with a mischievous tone to his voice. His eyes are sparkling with life as he savors what he has done. "You see, when she started to yell, the hand piece simply slipped out of my hand, falling back into the cradle on the wall. As you can envisage, hanging up on dear old mom was a complete and unmitigated accident."

Scolding him I say, "You can't hang up on my mother, Peter. You know that won't stop her."

The phone rings again. Peter jumps up and runs to the kitchen once more. He picks up the phone, waiting a few seconds, before placing it gently back in the cradle without uttering a word.

As Peter comes back into the lounge I playful throw one of the small couch cushions at him. Startled, he catches it and laughs, "You'll have to do better than that."

"C'mon Peter. She's just concerned. You shouldn't treat her like this."

"Actually," Peter says, re-entering the lounge and sitting cross legged next to me on the couch, a smug expression on his face. "She won't be phoning back, I disconnected the phone."

I look at Peter in stunned disbelief, "You know that only gives us five minutes before she's around here in person!"

Heather lives in Glenburn Rd, just behind the Kinglake Hotel. It will take her ten seconds to get her car keys; they are always in the basket near the front door. The brisk walk to the car will take a further ten seconds. Starting the car will take a minute, at most, if she hasn't driven it today. Thirty seconds, if it has been warmed up. The two mile trip from her house to our home will only take a few minutes, particularly at the speed she drives when angry. My estimate of five minutes might be generous.

"Enjoy it while it lasts, Angel," Peter says, completely unrepentant. Watching him I can see he is trying desperately not to laugh. I shake my head, not wanting to give him the satisfaction of laughing at the horrible treatment he has delivered to my mother.

Ah, well. What's done is done. I guess mom is coming to visit.

Peter and I sit on the couch enjoying our drinks, talking like we haven't seen each other for weeks, rather than just a day. I am surprised how good I am feeling. I seem to be suffering no ill effects from the accident, other than a little tiredness.

There was an accident wasn't there? It couldn't have just been a dream.

Watching through the window, we cannot fail to see my mother's blue Camira pull into the driveway at high speed, scattering loose stones onto and across the lawn. Heather moves rapidly to exit the vehicle. She slams her door not only to release some of her pent up frustration but also to send a clear message to Peter. Message received, he springs into action.

"I'll just put these out in the kitchen," Peter says nervously taking the empty glass out of my hand. His arrogant confidence has deserted him in little more than a heartbeat, now that Heather is close at hand. She is not so easy to fob off in person.

"You're not scared are you?" I grin.

Peter just laughs as he scurries away, seeking refuge in the kitchen.

Without knocking or waiting for an invitation, Heather storms into the house. Instantly she calls out for me. Her desperation is clearly evident in her loud, quivering voice, "Julie!"

She flits from room to room as she carries out her search. It only takes a few seconds for her to find me. My house is not an unassailable labyrinth. She peers around the corner of the doorway. The lines of frustration on her face slowly give way to relief as she sees me reclining and smiling on the couch.

"Are you okay, luv? Do you need anything? Where is Peter? Shouldn't he be looking after you?" Heather fusses as she enters the room. She rushes to the couch and takes my hand in hers, holding it firmly as you would if this was the last time you were going to see a loved one before they passed away.

"I'm fine mom," I state, feeling just a tad suffocated by this display of close personal attention.

"Hi mom," Peter says with some sarcasm as he returns from the kitchen. His words are suitably provocative considering she doesn't like nor allow Peter to call her 'mom'. She never allows any exemption to this rule. Never. Combine these simple words with the stupid, childish grin on Peter's face and you have a truly volatile situation which is ready to explode without warning.

Heather jumps to her feet as her rage bubbles to the surface, uncontrolled. She moves towards Peter with unbridled menace as she begins to unleash her venomous spray, "You irresponsible idiot! Julie is not well, can't you see that?"

Peter remains cool under pressure as he stands his ground and points vaguely in my direction, "Have a look for yourself. She seems okay to me. Does she look like she's ill to you?"

Heather turns and looks at me with bewilderment. She continues a little more hesitantly, though still strenuously trying to make her views clear to Peter, "She looks fine at the moment. However, neither you nor I are doctors and as such we are not qualified to make an educated judgment on her state of mind. The, ...the things she is seeing and telling us about are not right. They are not right at all. She needs to be professionally assessed."

"Not in that Hell hole, she doesn't!" says Peter loudly as, red faced, he jumps to my defense. It is hard for me to listen to my mother's words. After all, I am her daughter. I should be the one person she believes in no matter what.

Why do you doubt me so?

"Since when do you have the right to make that decision? I am her mother and you are not family. You.............."

A haze begins to envelop my mind as I begin to drift away from the vigorous debate raging. I am not yet strong enough to successfully moderate this fight to an uncomfortable truce, like I have, so many times before. I feel unwell. I wish they would stop bickering so much. Why can't they see what it does to me?

A sharp stabbing pain begins to build in my chest. My pulse races as I fear for my health. I begin to panic as I try to voice my alarm that something is wrong. Nothing comes out. My eyes dart from one to the other. They have forgotten I am in the room with them. Peter and Heather are too engrossed in their argument to be aware that I am in trouble.

Please God, let them stop. I don't want to have a heart attack.

I clutch my chest as the pain increases a notch or two in intensity. My concentration is captured by something unusual, something lying motionless on the floor on the other side of the room. I am intrigued by the object, curious as to what it may be. I can't quite work out what it is. For a moment it distracts me from the awful unrelenting pain. I start to walk slowly, awkwardly towards it in order to gain a better look.

The mystery object is about 8cm long, skin colored and doesn't appear to match anything I can think of that should be in the room. It is something indiscernible, as it is partly hidden by the low hanging lounge room curtain. Even so, I can tell as I near it that it is something foreign, something that shouldn't be present in this room at this time.

What on earth is that?

The argument is lost to me now, just babble in the background. Peter and Heather are so entrenched in their discussion that they fail to see my movement towards the curtain. My footsteps are slow and unsteady. The pain in my chest is increasing unabated, though I don't allow it to impede my progress. The sound of a child, a girl singing a lullaby, suddenly resounds in my head. I look around but there is no one there.

Continuing to move forward, it takes me just a few seconds to reach the curtain. Looking down at my feet, I still find it impossible to determine what the object is. With much trepidation I begin to lift the curtain in order to reveal more detail. Vaguely, I register Peter calling out my name softly, though I don't react. I can feel both Heather and Peter eyes piercing the back of my head. I don't know if this is a foolish notion. I do not turn around to see if they are staring at me. I am fully focused on revealing the object. Like a magnet, it draws me in. I must know what it is.

Finally, it is done. I can see exactly what the object is. My eyes bulge as I raise a hand in an attempt to stop myself from vomiting as the bile rises up into my throat. I can't believe my eyes.

I begin to yell while holding firmly onto the curtain, "Get it out. Get that blasted thing out of here before I'm sick."

Peter runs to my side and looks at my feet in astonishment, "I can't see it. What is it? What are you looking at?"

I turn and look Peter in the eye, astonished that he can't see what is in plain sight. Pulling the curtain higher so that he can gain a better view, I say, "That, the severed finger! Quick, it's dripping blood all over the carpet!"

Heather says smugly, looking on from a distance, "See. I warned you. Now what have you got to say for yourself, Peter?"

Peter hisses, his face turning a deepening shade of red, "Shut up!" His voice softens as he speaks earnestly to me, "Julie, there is nothing there."

I look at Peter in agony from the cutting pain in my chest. In utter disbelief, I say as tears begin to form, "Don't be stupid, it's right there in front of you. Can't you see it?"

Peter shakes his head. In a quivering voice he says softly, "Angel, there's nothing there."

Confused, I stagger away from Peter as I struggle to accept his words, "Why are you doing this? Are you trying to make me feel that I'm going insane?"

Peter walks towards me, reaching out to take my hand and rescue me from my bitter torment. I pull away. Peter says, "Angel, there is nothing on the floor."

Tears roll down my face as I shake my head and continue to walk backwards. I don't know what to say, so I stay silent. I pause looking around the room as I hear a familiar sound echoing down the hall.

Where is that coming from? It sounds like a child.

The lullaby draws my attention to the window next to Peter. My bloodshot eyes widen as I begin to shake my head in disbelief once more. Peter is watching me with a curious expression. I know that he realizes I have seen something else. He turns and looks through the window, into the yard outside. He searches the garden, seeking something unusual or out of place. As he turns back around, I can tell he has seen nothing out of the ordinary. He asks quietly, "What is it?"

I shake my head, confused and terrified. Peter is my beloved confidante, yet I fear he will forsake me if he realizes the extent of my visions. I want to tell him everything, though I am cautious of his reaction to the truth as I see it. I hate withholding information from him. Distraught, my words fall weakly from my lips, "It can't be."

"What do you see?" Peter pleads with urgency. His thirsty mind is desperate to be quenched by the delectable liqueur of knowledge.

How do I explain this to Peter so that he knows I'm not insane?

I struggle to believe what I see. The vision in front of me makes no sense at all. It is simply impossible. The woman I killed in the accident is standing outside the window. She is unhurt. Her clothes are immaculate. She is perfect in every way. I flinch as I hear a loud bang, like a car backfiring or a gun shot. The child's voice, singing the lullaby, fluctuates like a fading echo throughout the room before it disappears, leaving nothing save silence.

She's dead. She must be. I hit her so hard with my car.

I gasp for air as the mysterious woman takes a step forward, straight through the glass window. She doesn't appear to see the glass nor be hindered by its presence. She moves forward like she is in a different universe, a universe where my window doesn't exist. The lady is distracted as she continues her conversation on her mobile phone. She seems unaware of me or anyone else in the room.

I struggle to regain my breath. Wide eyed and desperate, I take short, sharp gasps in the vain hope I can replenish my depleted lungs. I know unless I calm myself and concentrate, filling my lungs will remain an impossibility. Producing words, to explain what I am seeing, is also an impossibility; at least until my asthma subsides.

I need my puffer!

"She's having an asthma attack!" Heather says with an air of hysteria creeping into her voice.

Suddenly the lady moves violently sideways, as if some unseen force has reached out and pulled her away. She disappears through the solid plaster wall without uttering a cry for help. The wall is undamaged by the episode. Not even the slightest blemish to its paintwork.

On this wall there is a mirror. I have a nagging suspicion something is wrong with it though, at first, I can't imagine what. Then it comes to me. As is normally the case, the mirror shows all the items in the room reversed. All the images, that is, except for the clock and the calendar. I wonder why they appear as normal in the reflection. The calendar is open to February 25th, five days from now. The clock is just as curious. It is reads 11.35 pm when the current time is about quarter past twelve in the afternoon.

I look at the wall opposite. Everything that is present in the mirror's reflection is there, everything except the calendar and clock. I look back at the mirror and they are gone from the reflection too. I sense the smell of smoke, putrid black smoke. It is the type of smoke that you would expect from an oil or tyre fire. The smell burns my nostrils. It begins to fade away at about the same time as the pain in my chest eases. Within seconds I become pain free once more. Able to focus now, I bring my breathing back under control.

Blinking, I look at Peter and Heather's stunned faces for some support. I know they have been watching me. I wonder what they think of my little floor show, stomping around the room in my trance like state, looking at things which aren't actually there. They know only a little of what I have seen. Unfortunately, I can tell, they suspect I have seen much more than just the severed finger. Peter looks concerned and confused, though not ready to run just yet. Maybe he wants answers. Heather looks completely terrified.

"Mom," I say reaching out for my mother. She spurns my gesture.

Heather flinches backward, shaking her head. There is a distance in her eyes, a distance too great for me to reach out and touch her soul. She stares at me like I am a stranger to her. Heather directs her words to Peter while she watches me intently, "Julie is ill. She needs medical help."

"She just needs our support," Peter chimes in, with little confidence evident in his voice.

Heather looks away from me and gives Peter a steely gaze which leaves him with no misunderstanding of the gravity of my situation, "No! She needs medical help. I can't handle this. It's too much. It's not right. I need to go. I'll have nothing to do with this madness again. It's not right. I need to go."

"Mom?"

Heather doesn't reply, she just turns and runs from the house leaving the door swinging open behind her. Peter walks over to me. I let myself drown in his tight embrace. I lower my head onto his chest and cry as a mixture of fear and relief flood my heart. I'm comforted that at least one person in the world doesn't feel I'm mad. Peter provides me with much needed strength. I will need this if I am to successfully diagnose and cure this curse that ails me. I need him more than ever. Though I do not consider myself especially religious, I find an idle thought repeating itself over and over again in my brain.

Please God, don't let him run.

'Trouble'

Peace gives way,
As visions return,
Trouble draws nigh.
As sanity wavers,
And reason burns.

Evil lurks ominously,
Spreading its feathered wings,
Ready to fly,
Destruction of hope,
Is all it shall bring.

Chapter 13

March 14th, 1692.
Salem, Massachusetts.

Thomas sits quietly at the table, pulling apart his bread and dipping it into the soft warm yolk of his eggs. Every once in a while he glances up at Mary. Mary moves like a whirlwind, busying herself with all manner of chores to be done. She glides from one job to the next. Cleaning the frying pan and bench top then sweeping the floor. She occasionally sighs as she pauses for an instant then moves straight into the next job. Thomas is well aware she is busying herself in order to try and ease the thoughts about her sister's predicament. He can see by her expression, it isn't working.

Mary knows it would be dangerous for her to visit Sarah, particularly with her visions returning. The townspeople just wouldn't understand in this climate of fear and hate if they discovered her secret. Though she knows she can do naught but wait and pray, the drama unfolding still weighs heavily on her shoulders. She feels that she should make an attempt to visit her sister. 'How?' is the question she has no answer for. Thomas knows a little piece of her hates him for not allowing her to visit. Their relationship is steady though under enormous pressure. It is the toughest of times for both of them.

Mary has barely uttered a word over the last few weeks. It worries him that she is stowing her emotions away from his curious gaze. He feels she will eventually speak, when it suits her. At least he hopes that will be her way. He has never seen her like this before. At this point in time Thomas is more concerned about her meals. Mary has eaten sparingly over the last two weeks. She is looking pale and gaunt and tires easily. Looking at her now he knows he has to intervene. This situation can't be allowed to continue.

Mary clears the breakfast plates away, throwing them roughly in the trough. She hunches over the sink looking tired and deflated. Thomas watches her silently, not knowing the words he should use to comfort her. Rose is on the floor playing. Violet is sitting at the table looking at the front door, a puzzled expression on her face, "Ma?"

"What be it, Darling?" Mary asks absent mindedly without looking up from the trough. A pail of water hangs from a nail in the wall just next to the trough. Using a ladle she draws water from the pail, tipping it over the plates before she begins to scrub them furiously.

"Something be wrong with Jezzie. She be staring at the door."

Mary drops the ladle breaking one of the clay plates. She freezes, reluctant to turn around yet somehow, feeling compelled. Eventually she wipes her hands upon her apron and turns to look at Jezebel. Jezebel is crouched down on the dirt floor, nose touching the sliver of light intruding under the front door. Her head bobs to and fro as if she is watching something moving about on the landing. In the silence the faint sound of doves 'cooing' can be heard by all. Mary glances at Thomas. The anger on his face is undisguised.

Thomas chooses his words carefully as he looks at Violet. He does not want either of his girls asking questions he is not willing to answer. He doesn't want his girls to be placed in the position where they might accidentally pass on some gossip to someone in the village. That could result in danger for all of his family. He says in a soft, firm voice, "Take your sister and go and collect the eggs."

"But I...."

"Now!" Thomas says with a force that shocks everyone, including Thomas himself.

Mary watches the tears beginning to form in Violet's pure eyes, the fear on her face and the trembling of her body. Thomas has never raised his voice to her before. She is clearly shaken. Mary says calmly, "Go. Your Pa and I needeth to talk."

Violet nods and slides off the kitchen chair. Taking her little sister's hand, she drags her up from the floor. As she opens the door, Jezebel charges out, chasing the doves who promptly take flight. As Violet is about to leave the house she looks back at her father; his head bowed, banging the table repeatedly with his fist. She wonders what she has done to upset him so.

As soon as the girls are outside, Mary tries to calm the situation. She walks towards Thomas still wiping her hands on the dish cloth. With conviction in her voice she says softly, "Doth thou believe I possess a choice in this matter. If I could desist I would. It be not up to me."

"I shan't put up with this foolishness," Thomas drawls. "Thy vile wickedry needeth not happen."

Mary takes a chair and sits opposite Thomas, reaching out and holding his hand, "There be naught here but per chance fate comes a calling. I be obliged to nay turn away." Mary shakes her head, "Nay, I hath no choice. It be God's will."

Looking back at Mary he says through gritted teeth, "No, thou hath to ignore these things, now more than ever with the madness that abounds. It be too dangerous. Thou cannot help thy sister by being denounced as a witch."

Mary becomes uncertain, wondering how her words will be taken. She knows she has to tell Thomas, he has a right to know. Taking a deep breath she tries. Almost silent she says, "There be more to my visions than just Sarah."

Thomas looks blankly at Mary trying to fathom some logic from her words, "There be more? Why did thou not tell me? I love thee with all my heart and soul. I can help thee, if thou let me into thy world."

Mary shakes her head. More relaxed now her secret is out in the open, she speaks more calmly in a clear soft voice, "No one can help me with these visions. They be my blessing and my curse."

"Blessing! In God's name how can they be a blessing?" Thomas rages.

"Maybe they allow me a chance to change what will be," Mary explains simply.

Thomas pauses for a second. He has never considered this idea before. He wonders if this might be the reason for Mary's affliction, "Maybe thou art right. Yet to do so, may be at thou own peril."

"I thinketh I shall try," Mary says. "I doth need to."

Thomas stands up from the table and begins to pace up and down the room, scratching his chin as he often does when he is lost in thought. He turns to Mary and asks succinctly, "What art thou new dreams? What doth thou see?"

Mary lowers her head, her shoulders stiffening visibly beneath her light cotton dress. She says simply, "I dare not utter them out loud for I fear what I doth see."

Thomas moves swiftly back to the table. He seats himself down taking Mary's hand in both of his. He kisses her hand before he says, "I shall help."

Mary pulls away, takes to her feet and moves a short distance away from the table with her back turned towards Thomas, "I dare not utter them. They be hideous."

Thomas implores her, "Please Mary. I doth needeth to know."

Mary pulls out a kerchief from her sleeve to wipe away her tears. As she stows it away she spins around and walks back over to the table. She leans over and looks her husband directly in the eyes with a manic stare, "I hath warned thee yet, thee still persist in thy need to know."

Thomas nods, a little wary of Mary. She has a crazed look to her that is unfamiliar to him. It is the first time his considers the option that these visions might be no more than the onset of madness. He brushes this thought aside for the moment as he continues to seek the truth about her visions.

"Yes, I want to know what thou doth see."

Mary laughs a strange sort of crazy laugh, throwing her head backwards as she does so. It is the laugh of a woman on the edge of her sanity. Leaning closer to Thomas she whispers into his ear, "I see many things. I see people marching. I see a great leader, not from this time."

"A leader of people?" Thomas asks, confused.

Mary pulls away and sits back down at the table. She reaches out and clutches Thomas's hands firmly, "I know not what it means yet I see more things too, things that be horrid. Unspeakable horrors which invade my dreams."

"Pray tell," Thomas says not knowing if he really wants an insight into Mary's visions anymore. He knows he must be strong. He needs to believe in his wife. He needs to know everything about what ails her in order to help. He wonders, though, if there is any way he can protect her from going mad.

Mary takes a deep breath then continues, "I see people dressed in black. I see two coffins, one be a baby's. I feel hatred so strong. I see my blood being driven away in two wagons to parts unknown. I smell smoke."

"They are but visions......," Thomas offers feebly knowing, as he utters his words, that they provide no real comfort at all.

Mary stops Thomas mid-sentence, "Nay, they be the truth that will come to pass......"

Mary pauses staring at Thomas blankly searching for her words but none are readily forthcoming.

Thomas watches her intently wondering what she is struggling to say. He asks compassionately, "Is there more? What, pray tell, troubles thou so?"

"I see more," Mary's whole body begins to shudder, slowly at first, then gaining more intensity. "I see a knife. I see a room full of blood."

Mary pauses for a second to regain her composure. Finally she sighs and continues, "I see my hands covered in blood. I hear her screams. I feel my body go cold."

Thomas squeezes her hand more tightly, unwilling to let her go, "You are not cold, but warm."

As a tear rolls down her cheek, Mary shakes her head, "Nay, I only feel cold. I only be cold."

Thomas offers some hope, "Nay, that doth not hath to be the way. Thou can change what is yet to be."

Mary shakes her head as her shoulders sag, "I fear I cannot change that. It is beyond my hands. I am not a God. I be merely an obedient servant."

"Mark my words," Thomas stresses. "God shall not forsake thee."

"I hope thou art right," Mary says acknowledging her plight. "For only God can save me."

"God shall not forsake thee," Thomas repeats.

Mary shrugs her shoulders, "Death comes to take me. That is all I know."

'Enlightenment'

Only those few,

With their eyes wide open,

Their minds unencumbered,

By preconceived notion.

Can be considered to be,

Truly Enlightened.

Chapter 14

Tuesday, February 21st, 2006.
Morning.
Kinglake, Victoria, Australia.

I stretch out and feel the bed next to me. To my disappointment the sheets are empty, Peter is gone. I look towards the foot of the bed and see Serenity curled up peacefully in a ball on top of the bed spread. He stretches out one paw, clawing at the fabric, as he yawns, opening his mouth wide to display his immaculate set of razor sharp teeth.

"Hey, sleepy head, how'd you get in here anyway?" I ask as I watch the cat fall back to sleep. "You're very secretive, you know that? You don't give much away."

I flop back onto the pillows, shutting my eyes, hoping to enjoy just a few more minutes of sleep. If Serenity is allowed to do it, so am I. I realize quickly this is a forlorn hope. I am now wide awake. Sleep has deserted me, preferring to go into hiding. I know it won't reconsider visiting me until at least dusk is upon us. Drowsy or not, I must resign myself to the fact that day has come in all its shimmering glory. The day will simply not be denied.

Lifting myself onto one elbow for a better look, I see the time displayed on the digital clock. 9.03 A.M. It is most unusual for Peter to rouse first, especially without setting the alarm. He is a notoriously heavy sleeper. Nothing can wake him from his peaceful slumber. Most weekends he will sleep in till eleven A.M., sometimes noon. I am the light sleeper in the household. I sleep well until first light appears. By then, I am usually wide awake, no matter how tired I feel. I get so frustrated watching Peter sleep soundly next to me when I so desperately crave a sleep in. I throw pillows, make a racket, kick him solidly under the sheets, yet he still doesn't wake. When it comes to sleep, Peter is a machine.

Peter has been behaving differently, not that I am complaining. He has always been caring. That, I feel, is one of his most endearing qualities and one of the reasons why I love him so much. Somehow though, at the moment, he is even more so. He is more attentive to my needs, more cautious in his approach to me, more diligent; doing every little thing he can to make me happy. I guess this is just his spin on how he should approach my problem, a problem which he can't hope to ever really understand. He's trying his best to help, to ease the tension that I am burdened with. I couldn't possibly ask for more than that.

Last night was a prime example of this. We talked and cuddled after my mother's dramatic exit from our house. This affection transformed into something wonderful as we retired to the bedroom. Our love making was incredible. We took our time, savoring the moment. Peter seemed to appreciate my need to be held, to be close to someone who cares. I had an overwhelming need to be intimate with someone who loves so passionately, so unconditionally. Peter was everything that I desired.

Usually Peter's idea of foreplay is asking if I am ready for bed. However, last night was very different. We continued to talk while he held me tight, sharing our most untamed feelings and emotions. For once it was me who was the instigator of our lovemaking. We made love slowly, tenderly, gently. It was a side of Peter I have not seen before. He seemed to know exactly what I needed and delivered to my complete satisfaction. He was determined to do everything he could to calm my confused mind and slow my beating heart, at least for a time. Afterwards we fell asleep in each other's arms, completely at peace. It was truly special.

I don't know what is going on with him. No matter, I will work it out sooner or later. I know I will.

Getting out of bed I realize that my battered muscles are not so bad this morning. I lift my nightie for a closer inspection in the full length mirror at the end of my bed. I smile as I see very little bruising. I feel a weight has been lifted now that I know for certain my ribs aren't broken. I take my robe from over the back of the chair. I drape it over me, covering my lavender lace nightie. Tying the belt firmly around my waist, I walk from the bedroom out into the kitchen. I yawn, releasing the remnants of sleep as I open the fridge and reach for the milk. Once I pop the top and smell its contents I realize instantly that it has gone off.

Resigning myself to a less than healthy breakfast, I light the gas jet and take the fry pan off the hook on the wall. Searching through our scant provisions I find what my stomach yearns for. I crack open two eggs and drop a rasher of bacon into the pan. At least the bacon seems to be fresh. Well, fresh enough, anyway. I like my bacon cooked until it is crispy, so it shouldn't be a problem. My personal cooking technique, honed through years of unsupervised practice, should ensure any possible bugs are burned off to an edible level.

I am frantically sizzling away at the stove as Peter, to my surprise, suddenly walks in through the backdoor, his arms laden with shopping bags full of supplies. "I thought you'd gone off to work already."

He raises his eyebrows, "Not yet. The boss is letting me have a late start."

Peter drops the bags onto the table and walks over to me, carrying a bunch of multi colored daisies. I know they aren't the most expensive flowers at the supermarket. I don't care about that. They are a welcome surprise which brings a smile to my face.

"What's this?" I ask pleasantly bemused.

"Just thought I'd do something nice," he says placing the flowers on the bench next to me. Peter is a man's man and carrying a bunch of flowers is simply unnatural for him. His hands now free, he embraces me around my waist from behind. As I continue to cook my breakfast he hugs me tight. Slowly he twists his head and kisses me on the neck, steadily working his way up to my ear.

"You're up to something aren't you?" I say, trying not to show how much of a distraction he is.

"Maybe," he says backing away and leaning against the bench smiling.

As I keep the eggs and bacon moving with the spatula, I give him a sideways glance. It is hard to figure out what he is up to. Peter is leaning against the cupboard dressed in an old scrappy T shirt and work jeans. He is watching me as I cook with a strange grin dominating his face.

What are you up to?

Turning my full attention back to the pan I enquire, "Well are you going to tell me what's going on or not?"

"Maybe, maybe not," he teases.

Placing the fried delights onto my plate, I turn and walk towards the table, "Well in that case you can make your own breakfast."

Peter grabs a carrot out of the crisper and takes a seat at the table opposite me. He leans back in his chair, watching me eat. "I'm fine," he says, his gaze unwavering.

I laugh, "Yeah, nothing going on here. Since when have you started to eat raw carrots?"

Peter just continues to smile, "Just wanted to change the monotony of life."

I shake my head, trying not to become frustrated by his arrogant behavior. I know he is up to something yet I simply have no clue as to what. At the present he is just being annoying. To prove to him that I am not interested in his games, I take the remote control from the edge of the table and flick the television on. I turn the volume down slightly as the latest news blares through the speakers.

"And in breaking news, a psychiatric health patient has escaped from the high security ward of The South Morang Regional Hospital......."

"Oh my God, Peter. I'm on the news!"

"Always knew one day you would be world famous, Angel," Peter says as he sits upright in order to listen more closely to the reporter.

"Shhhh, this is serious," I say as I wave my arms about seeking his silence. For my escape to make the news, it must be regarded as a serious breach. What we did must have been illegal in many ways. I turn the volume up a little as I try to absorb what the reporter is saying and the possible implications for us. I wonder if we might need the services of a good lawyer.

"At approximately noon yesterday, convicted child sex offender, Chris Hagatie, also known as 'The Mr Whippy Rapist', escaped from this maximum security psychiatric ward. He had been placed in this unit in order for a full psychiatric assessment to be carried out prior to his upcoming trial over a series of recent sex offences against ten children under the age of fourteen. Somehow, either with or without the assistance of another patient, he was able to extradite himself from his protective straight jacket........."

Peter and I look at each other dumbfounded, "I thought this was about me."

Peter laughs, "Sweetheart, you're so unimportant, you don't even rate a mention."

I belt Peter in the arm as he flinches.

"Allegedly, Chris was able to arm himself by stealing a steak knife from the duty counter where the charge nurse was eating her meal. Hospital officials are refusing to confirm or deny this as it would represent a grave breach of protocols, particularly considering how he used this knife to escape........"

My skin turns cold and clammy as I listen to the reporter's words. The image of the bedraggled woman in the brown overcoat suddenly springs into my head. I see her face, her critical stare. Most of all I can hear the words she spoke to me outside the hospital as they begin to echo in my head.

"You Bitch! Why don't you do something? You're just so useless! For God sake do something!"

"Dr Khan," I whisper as I sit, eyes glued to the unfolding news report.

"What was that, Angel?" Peter asks as he looks back and forth from the television to me. "Were you saying something about your doctor?"

I stare blankly at the reporter, not answering Peter's question. I don't know what to say. I just hope I am wrong. Serenity leaps onto the table in front of me, blocking my view of the television. I swipe him away with frustration as I focus on the detail of the news being shared.

".......unconfirmed sources say the mad man took a hostage, one Dr. Wasim Khan, a highly credentialed practitioner of seventeen years' experience, in a headlock, threatening him with the knife. He then demanded the two security doors be opened and all security to be absent from his escape path. Once the doors were opened by security, he exited with Dr. Khan in tow before disabling the doors by smashing their electrical system......"

"A clean cut to the jugular and four stabs to the back," I say calmly, aware that Peter is watching me. "He had no chance with his lung and kidney damaged in the attack."

"Hey, Angel. You don't know......"

"...... once security and nurses were securely locked away, Chris then proceeded to carry out the blood thirsty, execution style, murder of Dr. Khan, the now obsolete hostage. His attack was most violent. Again unconfirmed sources say Dr. Khan was stabbed from behind several times. Chris Hagatie then slit his throat, severing the jugular artery. Even without this neck injury, doctors say the internal injuries to Dr. Khan's right lung and kidney were enough to cause life threatening internal bleeding. Security, coming to the aid of those trapped in the ward, found the unfortunate doctor slumped dead by the closed security doors in a massive pool of blood. Chris Hagatie, however, was somehow able to make his escape, stealing an unattended taxi from the car park. Police say due to his unstable and violent behavior, he represents a great danger to the community and should not be approached under any circumstances. Mike Jones reporting, for Seven Morning News."

We both remain breathless at the news of the day. I think back to my experiences with Chris Hagatie and shiver. I knew he was unhinged, yet to murder a doctor when he has already escaped, that is simply barbaric.

"......And in other unrelated news, Police fear the Melbourne gangland war could be set to erupt again after the execution style murder of Giovanni Camerleri on Sunday night. Police found Mr. Camerleri slumped behind the wheel of his black Lexus about 11pm........"

"You saw that didn't you, Angel?" Peter asks cautiously. "That was part of your dreams?"

I nod, struggling to find the right words to explain how I knew about Dr. Khan's murder, "Yes, I saw that he was hurt. I didn't see it was Chris. It was all so confusing. I didn't know the details of when he would be injured. I didn't know he was going to die."

"........He was parked on St. Kilda Rd. Police are non-committal about whether or not this is yet another in the series of recent gangland related murders. However, sources close to police suggest that Mr. Camerleri was shot with a small caliber bullet at close range through the side of his forehead. This would bring the current number of deaths in this new gangland war to sixteen.......'

I can do without further bad news today.

I switch off the television wondering if I could have helped. The dream didn't make any sense to me at the time; it was far too confused with other images, images which don't equate to what has occurred.

Are there several events that are somehow blurred together?

I try to block my random thoughts from my head. I need to rest. I need to forget about all this nonsense and get on with my life. I simply had a dream which bears some resemblance to reality, nothing more. I am not seeing fragments of the future. That is too insane to even give a moment's thought.

I cut and eat another portion of my breakfast. Peter seems to be lost in a state of deep contemplation. He is chomping away loudly on his carrot, eyes staring vacantly into the distance. I try to distract my troubled mind by flicking through the pile of mail he has collected. Most of what I find is just the usual bills. They can all wait for a little longer. I know, in his own annoying way, he hopes his silence will help me gather my thoughts rather than get frustrated by the strange predicament I seem to find myself in at present. He must sense I don't want to talk about my problems. He knows me well.

Looking at the first letter I eye the bin over in the distance. I look towards Peter. "American Express wanting to give me a Master Card with fifty thousand dollars credit. Filed," I say flicking the letter towards the bin. It flies straight for a second then does a loop, hitting a cupboard and falling to the floor.

"Readers Digest, filed. Telstra, keep for later. Wombat printer cartridges, filed. What's this?"

Peter takes the plain envelope out of my hand. Turning it over for further inspection he looks at the back, "No return address. It could be from anyone. Want me to file it?"

I snatch the letter back, looking at Peter ruefully, "No, not yet. Let me have a closer look. It might be something important."

The letter appears to be a normal, plain tan envelope. It lacks a window like the ones we occasionally receive trying to sneak junk mail through our well-developed filtering system. The letter is addressed using old fashioned writing which reminds me of how my grandmother would write before the rheumatoid arthritis took hold, causing her hands to be disfigured so horribly. The envelope feels heavier than a normal letter. By feeling through the paper I can tell there seems to be two small objects roaming loose inside. The letter has me stumped. My curiosity is aroused.

Tearing it open, I pull the letter free. It consists solely of a single page of lined paper, folded unevenly in half. Its edge is rough, as if it has been crudely torn from an exercise book or the like. Hand written words are visible, written in blue ink, as the light causes the poor quality paper to become translucent. I place the paper on the table in front of me without reading it. My attention is drawn to the other objects in the envelope. I hold my hand, palm up, in front of my eyes and tip the remaining contents out into clear view. Two small, silver, old fashioned keys fall into my hand. They are about 8cm long. Each has an oval shaped handle decorated with a rampant ivy vine. They look identical, just like twins, with rounded shafts leading to a fan shaped head. Placing them together, I observe a subtle difference in the shape of their head. Otherwise they are identical.

"This is interesting. Two old keys, I wonder what they are for?" I say dumbfounded. I can't imagine why someone would be sending me two old keys.

Peter states the obvious, "The letter's bound to make it clear what they're about."

A thought suddenly leaps into my brain. I begin to smile, wondering if I am on the right track. I push the keys across the table towards Peter, "This is what you've been up to, isn't it? What are you up to?"

Peter pushes the keys back towards me as he shakes his head, "This is nothing to do with me, Angel."

I watch his face, looking for a glimmer, a hint that I am near the truth. To my surprise Peter keeps a remarkably straight face. Not his usual forte. Usually he breaks quickly once I have discovered a surprise he is hatching. However, though I see no corroborating evidence in his expression, I suspect I am right. I think these keys are part of Peter's elaborate scheme, whatever that is.

Frowning, with nervous anticipation, I open the letter. I don't believe Peter at all. He has been acting strangely of late. He must be up to something.

My smile disappears, replaced by a frown as I realize Peter is telling the truth. He knows absolutely nothing about the keys. My elation is replaced by confusion as I read the letter, silently to myself, twice.

The letter is brief, lacking the clarity I so desperately crave. It is written in the same scrawled, old fashioned hand writing as the address on the envelope. It reads simply:

Dear Julie,

'Sorry for not sending these earlier, what was I thinking? Anyway I hope you enjoy the treasure, it should help to answer some of your questions.

P.S. If you want to meet me, just follow the signs.

At the Bendigo Safeway you will find an interesting advertisement for a Pet Rock on the notice board. I would highly recommend that you purchase this item as it will lead you down the path to enlightenment.

Bye, Joe.

I stare at the note failing to comprehend its meaning. Completely bewildered, I read through the note a third and fourth time just in case I have missed something crucial. My impression after a few seconds is the same as my first; I have precisely no idea what the keys and note relate to. For the life of me I don't think I know anyone named 'Joe'.

"This is odd," I say turning to Peter as I shake the letter in front of him.

"What are the keys for?" Peter asks with enthusiasm. He always likes a good mystery. Whenever I am working on a new Jemima Jones novel, he always tries to sneak a look at my early drafts. Once he begins to read the story he becomes obsessed. He is a real pest, hounding me for details about how she is going to get out of her current predicament and solve the case. He is like a dog with a bone once his curiosity is sparked.

"Well that's just it. I have exactly no idea what the keys are for, the note doesn't say. In fact, they were sent to me by someone called 'Joe'. Do we know anyone called Joe?"

Peter has a quizzical look on his face as he considers the possibility, "I don't think so; not that I can remember, anyway. Maybe it is one of your literary friends, sending something to amaze and inspire you."

I consider this for a few moments before I discount the notion. I have not met anyone named Joe at any literary function. I don't think anyone I know would use a playful pseudonym to disguise their true identity.

"No, no I don't think so. I suspect this is someone new, someone I haven't met. I just wonder how they know about me."

I sit pensive, not sure what to do with the letter. Maybe it is addressed to the wrong person; maybe it isn't meant for me at all. I know it is addressed to me but maybe Joe is looking for someone else. Maybe he got my address from a phone book. Maybe these keys are meant for a different Julie Mahoney, one who knows precisely what they are meant to open. There are just too many 'maybes' for this situation to get satisfactorily resolved at the moment.

I fold the letter once more, placing it and the keys carefully back into the envelope. Rising from the table, I stow it in the empty fruit bowl on the bench for safe keeping.

It'll be safe there. Just in case it turns out to be important to someone.

Suddenly, a noise resonates through the house. Clearly it is someone knocking on the front door. I deduce from the type of knock that the person is cautious, maybe polite in their approach to greeting us. I turn and look at Peter wondering who it might be. Instinctively I adjust my dressing gown to increase modesty, tying its cord tighter around my waist to prevent any possible fashion mishaps.

"Who do you think that is at this hour of the day?" I ask Peter as he shrugs his shoulders and begins to walk towards the front door. I follow, hiding behind Peter's solid frame a little.

As Peter opens the front door I see a couple, strangers aged in their early twenties, standing on our veranda. They are dressed casually, both wearing jeans. The man is wearing a pale blue T-Shirt with several holes and a pair of scruffy white runners. The girl is dressed in a floral blouse loosely draped over a white T-shirt. She has one arm around his waist, the other in front holding his hand. She is leaning in, head tilted onto his chest. They look like they are very much in love, a little too much in love for this hour of the day.

I study the couple as my mind muses over the strange first impression I am feeling. My impression is simply that they are false. Their stance seems a little too 'staged for effect'. It is a little too wooden to feel authentic. Wondering who they are and why they are standing outside my front door, I quickly become uneasy. Involuntarily I pull the dressing gown tighter around my neck.

"Hi, we saw your light on and felt we just had to come over and say 'hello' straight away. I hope you will forgive the intrusion." The man says continuing to grin like I should fully understand what he is talking about. It has been a most confusing morning. I can see they are both of Asian appearance though the man's pronunciation is excellent, suggesting that he, at the very least, might have been born in Australia.

I fold my arms and lean against the door jam. With a look of bewilderment on my face I raise one eyebrow and say blandly, "Hi."

The girl digs her long, blood red finger nails into the man's side, gaining his attention as she whispers something into his ear. She hides her head shyly from our curious gaze. Her secret words cause him to laugh and shake his head. "Oh sorry, I don't think I'm making myself clear."

I smile awkwardly as I nod. Peter looks over his shoulder and winks at me. He turns back to the couple and says, "No you're not, mate. How can we help you?"

"Sorry, we need to introduce ourselves. I am Malcolm and this is my wife Emma. We have just moved in, to the place next door. In fact we moved in last night to be precise. I guess we are just so excited, you know adrenalin pumping and all that. We didn't sleep a wink though we are utterly exhausted. I guess we simply wanted to say 'hello', get acquainted with the neighbors. I'm sorry if we interrupted anything, we didn't check the time. I hope we haven't disturbed you?"

Peter reacts instantly. He leans forward, extending his hand in friendship for Malcolm to shake. Malcolm responds, reaching forward and grasping his hand. I know Peter. I know he is up to something.

Peter's grip is firm and unrelenting, dragging Malcolm forward into the house as he speaks, "Glad to meet you mate, I'm Peter. The statue behind me is called Julie. Don't be worried about the time; it's never too early for a beer. You do drink, don't you?"

I raise both my eyebrows, glaring at Peter as Emma scurries shyly past me, following Malcolm into the house. I see Peter's eyes momentarily lower, running down the length of Emma's tiny frame, checking her out from behind. My mouth gapping open, I slap Peter playfully on the arm. He merely smiles, shrugs his shoulders then runs behind his guests as they stroll aimlessly into the house. I follow, head lowered, smiling in disbelief as to how this morning is playing out. In a haphazard fashion we all make our way towards the kitchen.

Inviting strangers in for a beer at nine in the morning when I am barely dressed! I guess he will jump at any excuse for a Crowny.

Malcolm and Emma are seated at the kitchen table by the time I arrive in the room. Peter is scouring through the open fridge searching for refreshments. He fishes out two bottles of Crown Lager, tossing one to a startled, though thankful, Malcolm. Malcolm hesitates prior to opening the bottle. I wonder if he is a drinker or not. Peter didn't give him the opportunity to decline his offer. Malcolm's thoughtful consideration of the liquid offering in his hands suggests much indecision. Maybe he is a reformed drinker, I don't know. Finally, he cracks the top off the bottle and takes a sip from his beer.

Emma's eyes watch Malcolm ruefully with much sadness as he savors the beer like it is liquid gold. His tongue caresses his lips, allowing his taste buds to sample each and every drop. As I walk past Emma, I lean towards her, saying quietly, "How about we show these Neanderthals how it's done at this hour. Would you like a coffee?"

"That would be great. Some milk and two sugars would be fantastic. Though I probably shouldn't; I've had four cups in the last few hours. I do love coffee. It has such an aroma. I just love the taste of the roasted beans. It really perks me up," Emma says with much exuberance.

I guessed that.

"So you did a moonlight flit?" Peter jokes casually as he opens his bottle. I have my back to our guests as I prepare the coffee. An audible, awkward silence lingers throughout the room. Finally Peter tries to rescue the mood as I turn around to see what has happened. "Did I say something wrong?"

Emma is staring at the table in front of her. Malcolm looks uncomfortable, eyes darting between Peter and me. He speaks slowly, nervously choosing his words carefully so as to remain vague, "No, it is nothing like that. We just felt it was time to move to a new area, time to start afresh, clean the slate, so to speak. Isn't that right Em?"

Emma raises her head. Timidly she tries to avoid eye contact with Peter and me as she offers an unconvincing smile. "Yes, that's right. A new start," she says without any conviction as she lowers her head once more. Her body language is poor, her shoulders suddenly tense. For a girl who walked in so bright and bubbly just moments ago, this represents a drastic change in persona.

There's something going on here. Why is she so tense and evasive? Is it just nerves, being in a strange house answering personal questions to complete strangers? I guess it's none of our business. We shouldn't be so nosey. I'm always prying into other people's business. It's a bad habit I've fallen into lately which I defend with the excuse that I am a writer.

Trying to hide the fact that I have observed Emma and Malcolm's unease, I turn, focusing my attention on making the coffees. I try to lighten the heavy atmosphere which has rapidly descended upon the room, "Well I think you'll find Kinglake different to what you've experienced before. It's certainly less intrusive than the suburbs. You can have as much space as you need out here."

Peter chuckles, "Actually, if you look around you will find it's just like the suburbs. No foot paths, two street lights for the whole town, no traffic lights, no shops open after five. No, I can't see any difference to the suburbs at all."

I turn around slowly, carrying the two steaming hot coffee mugs as Malcolm continues, "Well Emma and I don't worry about such things. We are mainly just looking for somewhere quiet and private. Everyone needs a little space at times. There can be too many prying eyes in Melbourne. Kinglake should be good for, ... what's the word I'm looking for? Reinvigorating, that's it. Yes, reinvigorating our souls. Don't you think Emma?"

Malcolm reaches out, placing his hand on Emma's as he speaks. She flinches noticeably, pulling her hand away from his touch. She takes the coffee mug from the table in front of her, holding it with both hands. I can't but wonder if this is an attempt to cover up her sharp reaction or to stop Malcolm from trying to hold her hand once more. She is a little flighty. She certainly appears a little claustrophobic in this kitchen with the three of us. Her face shows the strain as she forces an awkward smile, "I hope it will be better."

Taking a seat opposite Peter I can see the conversation is turning steadily towards silence. Peter glances at me, looking for some inspiration, wondering what topic we should raise in order to spark the conversation back into life. He looks like a man who knows he has made a mistake, inviting complete strangers into our home. I know this look; he is searching for a way to send them home without offending them. He always has this look when guests have overstayed their welcome at a party. However, I have never known him to become bored with visitors so quickly. As I search for a topic, I suddenly realize something silly; I haven't added sugar to Emma's coffee.

"Oh, I'm sorry. I didn't add any sugar….."

"That's alright….." Emma says reaching for the sugar bowl as I push it across the table towards her. Her fingers touch mine lightly as she takes the condiment out of my grasp, causing a sharp, unexpected pain in my chest. Grabbing my left breast in agony, I watch her hand in disbelief. I struggle, as I try and fail to fully comprehend what is occurring before my very eyes. Looking up, I see a strange expression on Peter's face as he silently mouths a question towards me, "What's wrong, Angel?"

I shake my head as I look directly at Malcolm. Startled, I jumped back from the table violently, knocking the drinks crashing to the floor as my arms flail around. I step backwards till my back is pressed hard against the plaster wall. Peter, Malcolm and Emma have all flinched with my sudden movement. They stand before me now, watching from a safe distance, dumbfounded and nervous. They fail to see what I see. As my heart beats rapidly, I know there is no way I can explain what is going on. Any words I choose will simply be regarded as insanity. Even Peter, with his open mind, will not understand this.

"Julie?" Peter calls out to no response.

Peter's heart felt plea rings in my ears. Though, at this point in time, I am too intent on watching the play unfolding before me. I fail to acknowledge his call. As my hand touched Emma's, while passing the sugar, an impossible chain reaction of events is set in motion. A ghost like apparition disembodies itself from Emma. It begins with the hand, then the arm, shoulder and torso. This process continues until there is a complete transparent image of Emma standing beside the genuine Emma.

However, the ghost version of Emma has some noticeable differences. She is dressed in a long flowing blue dress, torn slightly at the shoulder. Her face is severely bruised. A steady trickle of blood pours from her cut lip, down onto the light fabric of her evening dress. Her mouth looks a mess, suggesting that she has several teeth missing.

Oh my God, I know you! You were there when I had the accident. You were the couple wandering casually by. Was that just a dream? How can that be? You seemed so real though completely out of place wandering in the paddock in your formal wear.

The terrified apparition has its hands clasped together, loudly pleading her case for forgiveness as she spits tiny droplets of blood from her mouth, "Please, no more. I'll change. I promise I will change."

It is only then that I see the second ghostly figure, an alternate Malcolm, walk through the kitchen wall and into the room. He is wearing a white shirt, sleeves rolled up to the elbows, and black trousers. Malcolm looks like he has returned home from a night on the town. He moves towards Emma at breakneck speed, his face beaded in sweat, vein prominent, pulsing from his neck. He reaches out, grasping her violently by the shoulder, "I'll teach you how to behave, you cow. What were you thinking? Get on your knees now and show me how sorry you are."

Vaguely, my brain registers the sound of Peter trying to explain my behavior to the real Malcolm and Emma. To me, this premonition is far more important than what is going on around me in real life. I focus on the detail, trying desperately to work out what the ghostly Malcolm is holding in his hand. Emma sprawls on the floor in front of him pleading softly, "Don't hurt me. Please, don't hurt me."

"Julie's been ill of late, not her usual self. Please excuse…"

"I think we had better go. C'mon Em," Malcolm cuts Peter off as both our guests make a hasty retreat from the kitchen table. Hand in hand, eyes wide open and frightened, they walk straight through the ghostly apparitions without any sign of hesitation.

"Please don't be alarmed….," Peter tries, to no avail. Our two guests run down the corridor and out of the house, slamming the door behind them. The ghostly apparitions, however, do not follow them. They have other, unfinished business to attend to. I watch their movements as the stinging pain in my chest shows no respite.

Finally, to my horror, I discover the truth about the object Malcolm is brandishing at Emma's head. It is a small handgun, held at a distance that would ensure deadly accuracy if discharged.

"When will you learn? I'm the man of this house and you will obey and respect me at all times, without the slightest question. What do you have to say for yourself?"

Head lowered, she cowers, subservient on the floor. Flinching with the expectation of great pain, ghost Emma says meekly, "Yes."

Unrelenting rage explodes, without provocation, as Malcolm belts Emma across the side of her head with his clenched fist, holding the loaded pistol. She falls to the floor in a quivering, anguished mess. I move forward, unable to restrain my anger at this brutal assault. I position myself between Malcolm and Emma, protecting Emma from any further onslaught.

"Get away from her!" I yell, propelling both my arms forward in order to try to push Malcolm backwards. My attempt fails miserably as ghost Malcolm is unaware of my presence. Both my arms pass effortlessly through his chest as he proceeds to walk straight through me.

I gasp in horror, realizing I am interacting with a figment of my own imagination.

Jesus. They seem so real!

"Julie! What is it? What do you see?" Peter yells.

I turn one hundred and eighty degrees then stand frozen, watching the one sided argument between the two quarrelling apparitions. My mind races, unsure as to what my next course of action should be. A voice in my head whispers softly to me, telling me there is nothing I need to do. After all, none of this is real. I decide to watch, to note and to remember. If this is indeed a premonition of what is to come, then I owe it to Emma to be forearmed with the only weapon I have to defend her in her hour of need; knowledge.

The ghostly image of Malcolm remains highly agitated; his face ruddy, beaded in sweat. He flourishes his hand around as it grips the gun tightly. Accidentally, the gun passes straight through my stomach as I look down in disbelief. I feel no pain from this, just the continuing agony pulsing in my chest. Malcolm continues to press his point in a most aggressive manner, "What did you say?"

Emma spits some more blood onto the floor. She says faintly, her voice semi coherent due to her injuries, "Yes, sir."

"I can't hear you? What did you say?" Malcolm screams as he looks straight at Emma. From my vantage point I can see the madness that lies behind his eyes. He is the epitome of evil itself. I fear he is willing and capable of anything.

In a louder, quivering voice Emma repeats herself with defiance, "Yes, sir."

Enjoying his dominance over Emma, Malcolm asks again, as he waves the weapon around for effect, "I still can't…."

I feel sick as I see the cockiness evaporate from Malcolm's face. The gun discharges with a deafening roar. He stands immobile, silent, trying to comprehend the enormity of his actions. Eventually he starts to mumble as he falls to his knees, "Oh my God! What have I done?"

I take three steps sideways, shut my eyes as a silent prayer passes over my lips pleading for this horrific vision to go away. I hear Peter's footsteps and feel his arms surround me in his loving embrace. As I begin to cry I am comforted that he is here with me. His soft words act to calm my troubled mind somewhat, "Hey, hey. It's alright. There's nothing there. It's alright, I tell you."

I open my eyes. To my surprise I find the will within me to stop crying. I look at the fear etched deeply into all the lines on Peter's face. I know full well, an explanation is needed. However, I find myself lacking the appropriate words which Peter will accept as the truth. My ears continue to ring with Malcolm's protestations behind me. I turn, determined to see for myself what I already know to be Emma's fate.

Sighing deeply I watch on as Malcolm holds Emma's lifeless hand in his, rocking to and fro. It is clearly evident he is overwhelmed by grief and remorse, though I have no sympathy for him. His compassion has come too late. Emma's body lies on the floor at an awkward angle. Her head is obscured by Malcolm. By the rate at which the pool of blood is increasing around both of them, it is obvious that Emma is dead.

As I watch, the two apparitions begin to fade. Startled, feeling the pain in my chest dissipate, I look back at Peter. Over his right shoulder I see the reflection in the microwave. It is a clearly defined image which is instantly familiar to me. However, I am left feeling curious as to its meaning within the context of my vision. It is a clue of unknown significance which, as I watch, evaporates, leaving no permanent trace.

What was that? XII. Twelve? What does that mean?

"Peter! We have to stop this," I say with certainty as my eyes dart around the room. I search for some clue as to when and where this murder is going to occur. I think back to my vision of Dr. Khan and the clues I ignored that were right before my eyes. I can't make the same mistake again. Emma's life is on the line.

There must be a calendar, a clock, something that gives me a clue as to when this is going to take place. I must stop this. What have I missed? What have I missed?

My search proves fruitless as everything in the room appears completely normal. The pain has now gone, leaving no lasting after effects. I am left frustrated and alarmed. I flinch as Peter places a reassuring hand on my shoulder.

"Shhh. Hold on a second. Whatever you saw is just from your imagination. You've been under a lot......"

I cut Peter off bluntly, "You have to believe me. If you don't, how will anyone else believe me?"

Peter looks unsure as he stammers, "It......It's just I don't see what you see."

I come back to reality with a thud. My visions are so realistic that I now consider them to be true. However, Peter does not see them as I do. As such he does not fear their clear message as I do. He doubts their authenticity. It is unreasonable for me to expect more than this from him at this point.

I calm myself as I strive to explain the situation in a clear and concise manner. Choosing my words carefully, I speak succinctly, "Listen. I saw Malcolm hold a gun to Emma's head and shoot her at close range."

Peter pulls away from me, shocked at the gravity of my allegation, "Now hang on just a minute. That's complete madness. You saw them. You don't know them. They seem like a normal, everyday, happily married couple."

"We don't know that," I interject. I wonder how, if I can't convince Peter I am sane, I can sway the opinions of anyone else.

"We don't know they aren't either," Peter says looking directly into my eyes with a steely glare. "You don't know they are having problems. You don't know Malcolm has a gun. It might just be your mind playing tricks on you. You've been through a lot of drama of late. It's got to take its toll, somehow."

I sigh as I avert my gaze, "Listen, my vision about Dr. Khan came to pass."

"Maybe that was a coincidence," Peter offers with caution. I can tell from his voice he is struggling to understand how I knew about Dr. Khan's demise before the reporter outlined the horrible story.

Angrily I scream, "How can you say that was a coincidence? I had the same pain in my chest. I saw the stabbing to his stomach. I saw it all. It is just the same. I know Emma will die too. I know it will come to pass."

Raising his hands in an effort to placate me, he says, "Listen to yourself, please. These visions are not normal; no one understands them, not even you. If you try to do something to stop a murder, which has yet to occur, for a reason we cannot fathom, they'll lock you up again. It's just not rational. Can't you see that? There is no evidence. This is all just in your head."

I fall silent for a few moments, knowing full well Peter speaks the truth. No one understands what I am going through, no one, including me. However, I feel the weight of knowledge weighing heavy on my shoulders. I feel I need to try to do something to change what will be. I stress the importance of my vision to Peter, "We can't choose to do nothing. An innocent life may be at stake!"

Peter takes my hand in his, "That's exactly what I'm saying. You know we have to do nothing. We can't get involved in a situation that might or might not happen. Everyone will think you're mad. They'll lock you up. I won't be able to visit. There'll be absolutely no way I'll be able to get you out a second time. I couldn't live with myself if I let that happen to you."

"I see what I see, I can't help it. It must be for a reason. Some good must come from my torment, it can't just be meaningless," I say in a quieter tone trying to appeal to Peter's sense of logic with a statement I know is completely illogical.

He sighs, "You don't know why you are seeing these images. All you know at this point is that other people will not understand. To put it simply, they will think you are mad. You must keep silent about what you see. Promise me, Julie, you will keep silent, won't you? Please, Sweetheart?"

Looking deep into Peter's baby blue eyes I feel uncomfortable, for the first time, in the surety of our relationship. My stomach knots as the enormity of Peter's words hits home. I am not scared by the opinions and thoughts of others; I don't care what anyone thinks. It is the underlying statement seeping between Peter's spoken words that frighten me. It is an unspoken statement that I hear clearly and understand its chilling ramifications.

He doesn't believe me!

Considering this possibility for a few seconds I bite my tongue and lie, "I guess you're right. I'll keep silent and try not to do anything foolish until I can work out what is going on."

Peter embraces me tightly once more, swallowing my false statement. The knot in my stomach grows tighter. Talking over my shoulder he says softly, "Good girl. You know it's for the best."

Staring at the wall behind Peter transfixed, I feel horrible about my deceit. I feel as if I have cheated on him. I know this feeling will not fade. It is something I will not grow comfortable with as time moves on. However, I know also, I have important business to take care of. A life is in danger and I cannot stay idle. A plan is forming in my mind as to how I will prevent this murder.

I feel Serenity rubbing against my leg. I am strangely comforted by her affection.

I must be able to change things. Why else would I be having these visions? It must be my destiny; Emma's fate rest squarely in my hands. This is the only thing that makes sense. It must be why I'm seeing what I see. Surely it is, surely.

Serenity begins to purr loudly.

'A Woman's Touch'

A burden too heavy,

For a kind soul to hold.

A task too complicated,

For a clever mind to solve.

An impossibility too certain,

For a man to succeed.

Only a woman's pure heart,

Can clear the smoke and set the truth free.

Chapter 15

Thursday, February 23rd, 2006.
Morning.
Kinglake, Victoria, Australia.

The journey from my bedroom towards the kitchen is usually an unexceptional experience. Today, however, is very different. From the moment I leave the bedroom I can tell something extraordinary has happened while I was sleeping.

A dusting of multi-colored rose petals leads down the hall towards the kitchen doorway. Momentarily I pause, wondering what on earth is going on. The tension in my body begins to ease as I let myself go, imagining the romantic surprise which must be at the end of this floral pathway. I pull my dressing gown cord tight as I follow the trail, smiling broadly as I tip toe along the hall, through the deliberately discarded blossoms.

Maybe I'll finally find out what you've been up to!

As I stand in the doorway, I can't believe my eyes. My mouth agape, I stare in disbelief at the arrangement Peter has laid out as my surprise. It is simply breathtaking. The kitchen table is engulfed entirely in red rose petals. In the center of the table a bottle of Champagne awaits, chilling on an angle in an ice bucket, filled to the brim. The note attached to the bottle is visible from this distance. It reads simply, in large letters, "For later, Sweetheart. XXX"

Next to the Champagne is an unsealed envelope. Spotting it, I move swift across the short intervening space, grasping it in my excited hands. Like a fool, I do a little victory dance, on the spot, before I calm myself somewhat. I open the envelope, pulling free the hand written note. With gusto, I read it out loud:

'Happy anniversary Sweetheart,

You've got two days to pack,

So don't panic.

I've booked a room at the Crown Towers.

(We leave Saturday morning)

As you can see, I have everything well planned.

So….

Get plenty of rest and I'll see you tonight.

Love you always,

Peter.   XXXXX

I grasp the note tightly to my chest as I smile to myself. I can't believe it. I am always the one who remembers our anniversaries and plans something special. Our first date, our first kiss, our first day living together as an official couple, they are all important to me. How could I, of all people, forget that fateful night when Peter stumbled through our dinner date acting like a foolish school boy. There was obviously something pressing on his mind. I just wished he would 'spit it out'.

He was so nervous that night, though there was no reason to be so. The look of relief on his face when he finally gathered enough gumption to ask me to move in with him was so sweet.

I must have been 'away with the fairies' in the last week or so. How could I forget such an important anniversary? Poor Peter. He must feel so neglected.

Suddenly, I hear the front door of our neighbor's house slam shut. I move across the lino floor swiftly in order to gain a better look from the kitchen window. I stand, leaning on the sink, peering out through the closed lace curtains. Serenity jumps onto the bench beside me, curious as to what has caught my attention. He sits upright on the bench, silently twitching his nose in the air as he looks out onto our neighbor's front yard from an angle. He is well aware that Peter has left for work, so he is safe to break the house rules, just a little. Peter can't stand Serenity's habit of jumping onto bench tops and other furniture. It doesn't bother me that he acts like he owns this house and we are no more than visitors whose presence is tolerated. We are mere servants who top up his feed bowl. I know my place on the household ladder and I am comfortable with that. Though he wouldn't like it, Peter is a distant third.

We both watch intently as Malcolm walks the short intervening distance to his car and leaves quietly. The only sound which heralds his exit is the crackling of stones under his tires as he slowly drives towards the tarred road. For the moment, I forget our pending celebrations. There are far more pressing matters at hand. For it has been two days since my vivid premonition of the deadly altercation between Malcolm and Emma. It has been two days since I have seen Emma. In that time she has not once strayed from the sanctity of their home. It has been two days since I was last at ease.

I consider my options carefully, with much reservation. It is hard to do what is right when all the options available involve some elements of wrong. I know I have promised Peter not to talk to Emma, and I always try to keep my promises. I would feel terrible if that turned out to be a lie. However, I feel I cannot possibly leave for Melbourne, on a holiday with Peter, without doing something first. How could I live with myself if I didn't try to help? The thought of something happening to Emma while I am in Melbourne would certainly play on my mind. I just wouldn't enjoy the vacation at all. It would ruin all Peter's plans too. It might even put a wedge between us. Peter would surely understand that circumstances have changed now and that I need to talk to Emma, while I have a chance. Surely he will understand? Of course he will.

Having convinced myself that I am doing the right thing, I turn to Serenity for confirmation, "Well, what do you think? Should I go and have a chat with Emma, check everything is okay?"

Serenity looks at me with his wise emerald eyes sparkling in the early morning sunlight. He winks once then begins to purr. In fact it nearly appears like he is smiling.

Can cats smile? No, don't be so silly.

"Right," I say as I charge back to the bedroom. I dress quickly, discarding the dressing gown and nightie for a plain oversized T-shirt, faded jeans and some well-loved runners; nothing too fancy, simply practical and convenient. Walking through the house I consider the words I need to say. I must find the right way to explain what I have seen without losing all credibility or appearing insane. After all, the last time, the only time I met Emma, I was behaving like a complete mad woman. Lord knows what sort of impression that left with her.

I pause at the front door, wondering if this is such a good idea after all. I'm filled with a sense of trepidation and unease. I don't allow this emotion to take hold, this is too important. Defiantly, I pull the door closed as I exit.

I walk the short distance to my neighbor's front door and rap vigorously on the woodwork. From inside the house I hear the sound of slow footsteps, trudging in a tired manner across the carpet. The shuffling continues until the person inside slows to a halt, just on the other side of the door. The deadlock unbolts and the door opens slightly.

Emma is hidden in the darkness of the hall. She glances into the daylight to see who has arrived unexpectedly on her door step. Her features are indiscernible in the darkness that abounds. From my angle, there appears to be no lights switched on within the house. Only the dim flicker of light, emanating from a candle somewhere in a side room, provides any light at all. Almost immediately the door begins to close again as Emma realizes I am the visitor who has come calling. I jam my size six runner into the narrow gap in an effort to keep the door ajar. I feel the door bite into the side of my foot as Emma continues her attempts to shut the door.

Glad I didn't wear my Joanne Mercers!

"I don't want to talk to you," comes Emma's sad, tired voice through the narrow gap. She is holding me at bay rather than trying to close the door completely. My foot is grateful for the respite.

Taking a deep breath, holding the edge of the door so that Emma can't suddenly break my foot, I plead my case, "Please, I need to talk with you about what is going on."

Quietly, Emma replies, without any emotion evident in her voice, "I can't talk to you, it's not your problem. You must understand, please."

I persevere, determined to try to help. It is all I can do considering now I have confirmation there is a problem of some sorts. I also remain burdened by the potential gravity of my horrible vision, "It is my problem too. I know what is going on and will not rest until I help you with your problem. I must ensure you are safe. Are you safe?"

There is an uncomfortable silence building, creating a sinister void on the other side of the door. I am uncertain as to what I should do next. I know I am not welcome here yet, somehow, I feel it is my duty to continue my attempt to help. As I wait for Emma's response, I wonder whether I should I continue to talk or should just be patient, for I have said more than enough. I decide to wait a few seconds longer. As I wait, I think to myself that this could go either way. All my efforts could be for naught.

Suddenly, to my surprise, the force holding the front door closed on my foot evaporates. The door swings open. Emma is revealed, walking slowly away from me, her right hand clenched over her mouth. She is wearing a loose fitting T shirt, baggy grey tracksuit pants and no footwear. After a few steps she halts, face hidden in the shadows, silent. She seems lost in thought, wondering what to say next.

"I don't believe you know what is going on," Emma says finally through clenched teeth as she keeps her back to me. I get the impression she is hoping I know something about her situation. That would be so much easier for her. She would not have to risk a verbal explanation and potentially be exposed to Malcolm's retribution for disloyalty. I sense she is scared of Malcolm. I sense she is scared witless.

"There is no easy way to explain this to you," I say as I try to choose my words carefully. A careless combination of words will only serve to confuse and scare Emma further. I want Emma to see me as a friend, not as an extra danger in her life. Considering the nature of what I have to say, my task is an onerous one.

"Try," Emma says curtly. She appears to have no time for long, drawn out conversations.

I pause for a second, take a deep breath and try to explain myself satisfactorily, "I was in the South Morang Regional Hospital after a car accident about a week ago. My injuries were minor and are of no consequence to you. Anyway, while I was in there, a doctor was stabbed to death by a patient who ran amuck."

Emma moves both her hands onto her hips in a defiant stance. Her muscles tense as she shakes her head in short, sharp jolts as she speaks, "Well, that has absolutely nothing to do with me or Malcolm!"

Raising my hands apologetically I try to correct myself, "No, of course that has nothing to do with the two of you. Well, actually, it has a lot to do with Malcolm and you."

A hard edge surfaces in her voice as Emma says, "How does it have anything to do with us? We have never been to that hospital."

I hesitate, knowing how my words will sound. I choose to shroud my explanation in a little bit of fog in order to hide anything that could be unsettling. Closing my eyes, hoping Emma will understand what I have to say, I continue, "Well, prior to the doctor being stabbed, I saw the attack occur."

"You mean you witnessed the attack?" Emma asks a little confused.

I take a deep breath, knowing I need to be more honest with her though fearing the consequences. Opening my eyes, I look straight at Emma's back, "No, not exactly."

"Just say it, for God's sake. What are you are trying to tell me?" Emma screams as her patience wears thin. She waves an arm around, emphasizing each word, as she remains with her back to me. The time for diplomacy has long expired. I know I must be more direct.

"Before the attack occurred, I had a premonition that the stabbing would take place."

Emma falls silent as she ponders this statement for quite a few seconds. Finally she turns a little, revealing the left side of her face.

Calmly she asks, "What? Was it a dream or something? I have nightmares sometimes."

I nod, hoping I am making some progress towards much needed credibility. I need Emma to believe I am genuine and my assistance of help is heartfelt, "It's hard to explain, though that's fairly close. At the time I didn't realize what it was or what it meant. Unfortunately, I did nothing. I don't want to make that same mistake twice."

Emma stands at angle, blinking. Finally she asks slowly as she makes each word a sentence in its own right, "Did. You. Have. A. Dream. About. Me?"

I decide in an instant I have nothing to lose. I have to be honest. It is my only chance to get through to her, "Yes."

As I speak, Emma turns fully to face me. She walks out of the shadows, into the flickering candle light. In an instant she reveals what she has been hiding, "Did you see this?"

Involuntarily, I step back, shaking my head in horror, as I stumble over my words, "No. No, I saw worse, much worse."

I can clearly see Emma's face, highlighted by the transient light. Her right cheek sports an inch deep cut and is badly bruised. Her right eye is blackened. In fact, the whole right side of her face is badly swollen, giving the impression that she might have sustained a fracture during her bashing. Though she is not showing any signs of discomfort, her injuries are so extensive that I can only imagine that her pain must be incredible.

Emma raises her eyebrows in surprise, "You claim to be some kind of soothsayer yet you didn't foretell that he beats me?"

I correct and expand on my explanation, sensing I am losing her confidence, "Yes, in my premonition he beats you but...., but........."

"But what?" she asks, her deformed face taunting me to explain myself.

Holding my ground, I look Emma straight in the eyes. I don't mince words, "He shoots you."

Emma's reaction is most curious. She laughs with gusto as tears form in her eyes, "He shoots me! Malcolm can have a temper, of that there can be no doubt. However, this is quite simply impossible."

I scowl, confused as to why someone, so badly beaten, would doubt what I have to say, "Why do you think that?"

"He doesn't own a gun!" Emma says simply. She shrugs her shoulders as she tries to explain further. "Look, Malcolm and I have a lot to work out. We have a lot of problems. However, he is not going to kill me. He loves me, even though he sometimes has a strange way of showing it. Our fights have been occurring for a long time. I just have to make sure I'm doing what he wants, all the time. It's mainly my fault. We just need to be left alone to work things out. It will all be good in the end. Just you wait and see."

Fearing I am losing her consideration, I move a step forward, "Please....."

Emma takes two steps backwards, holding up a hand imploring me to come no further forward, "No please. I've heard enough. You need to leave."

"You can't just ignore what I have to say....."

"You have no evidence to show me that Malcolm is going to kill me. It's just a small problem we are having at the moment; nothing that concerns you. I just need to be a better wife."

I stand my ground pleading, "Emma...."

Tears of sadness begin to roll down her face. Her voice quivers as she begs, "Please, you need to leave. If Malcolm knew that I have spoken to you… well, things would get worse. Please, can you leave now?"

I stand frozen for a few seconds, exasperated at my inability to convince Emma of the seriousness of her situation. I can see her distress. However, she is clearly not in a sufficiently stable emotional state; one where she is able to consider the possibility that my words make a whole lot of sense. I feel if I continue, she will think I am insane. If that happens, she will ignore my cautioning words. My only choice is to let her contemplate what I have told her. I must pray that she will want to talk to me further once I arrive back from our anniversary celebrations in Melbourne, in a few days' time.

"Look, I'll go now, though we need to talk later. Can we do that?"

Emma nods, yet I know in my heart she is reluctant, "Go, please."

As I begin to walk out, I stop and turn, leaving one last message for Emma. I desperately hope she listens to what I have to say. Concentrating hard, so my voice is strong and precise, I say, "Whatever you do, look after yourself."

Emma nods, saying nothing. Her battered face a stark reminder of the evil she lives with daily.

I walk out of the house, closing the door behind me. Pulling the door, I hear the deadlock click shut. It sounds so final. I sigh deeply.

I hope she listened. She has to look after herself.

I find myself left with an overwhelming fear that she won't. I have read too many stories in the papers about women who stay too long with abusive partners rather than leaving or seeking help. I am all too aware of how lethal the consequences of deciding to stay and 'work things out' can be. I hope my intuition is wrong in this case.

As I walk along the driveway, past the lawn, I notice a single white dove sitting peacefully, staring directly at Emma's house. To my surprise, the bird fails to react or fly away as I pass close by to it. I have never seen a wild bird behave like this as a person walks within inches of it. I look over my shoulder at the bird. It remains fixated, glaring intently at Emma's house. I shake my head.

That's weird. Everything seems weird these days.

'Plain Truth'

A curious question posed,
When would a murderer,
Not a murderer be?

The day is young,
Maybe with time,
The answer shall be set free.

Chapter 16

March 15th, 1692.
Salem, Massachusetts.

Mary and Thomas arrive on foot at the inconspicuous house. It is a house all too familiar to Mary as it has taken center stage in her disturbing dreams. The house is similar, both in design and construction, to their own. A simple cottage made of cedar logs, sealed with mud. As they approach from the rear, they can see a steady plume of smoke wafting skywards from the stone chimney. They remain silent as they look on, reaching for and finding an obliging hand to hold onto. Both are apprehensive, their fears growing as they near their ultimate destination. Their fingers drift apart as the move closer to their ultimate goal.

Mary is aware the lady at the center of her visions is called Jane, though there are precious few other clues in her possession that she can use to prevent the tragedy that is about to unfold. Alas, the visions only ever provide so much. They always leave so many questions unanswered. Who are these people? How many people are present? What is the actual nature of the predicament unfolding? How on earth is Mary going to help? Unfortunately, both Mary and Thomas are resigned to the fact that these and many other questions will only be answered once they turn the corner, enter the house and see with their own eyes what tragedy lies in wait. They both hold on tenuously to the hope that they will not be too late to make a difference.

As they turn around the corner, through the snowy slush, they come face to face with a small gathering of men and woman that has formed outside the front door. Their weather beaten clothes attest to the fact that they are hardworking farmers, accompanied by their dutiful wives. Most confronting to Mary is their grim, blank expressions. They are testament to the fact that they have not gathered here for a celebration. Their deafening silence reinforces this first impression in Mary's mind. Their ashen faces show the strain they are burdened by and the grave fears they hold in their hearts.

Mary pauses for a second as all are startled. She doesn't care for introductions, choosing instead to barge her way past those assembled and march directly into the single room house. Thomas remains outside. He stands nervous. As a small gesture of good will he nods shyly at the gathered crowd, knowing their gaze is upon him. He can sense they are curious, yet they leave their questions unspoken. They are somber, suffering in shock that proceedings, usually straight forward, are not going to plan today.

Initially, Mary's intrusion into the cottage goes unnoticed. She sees Martha, Jane's mother, sitting on a wicker rocking chair with a multi colored, patchwork quilt draped loosely over her rickety legs. Martha is beside the bed holding Jane's hand while her older daughter Helen is trying desperately to deliver Jane's baby. Jane, lying on top of the bed sheets, is dressed in a light cotton nightie. The sheets and blankets are pulled back neatly and folded at her feet. Her knees bent, she bites down hard on the leather strap in her mouth. Though the temperature in the room can only be considered mild, Jane is dripping wet in sweat, as are the bloodstained sheets. All three women appear anxious and visibly upset. The grimace on Jane's face highlights the fact she is under great duress.

"It won't come. I be unable to move it around. It won't come!" Helen exclaims as she struggles to turn the baby around inside her sister so that it can be delivered safely. Her attempts over the last two days have been sapping for both her body and soul, particularly her soul. Her beliefs are faltering as a thought stealthily creeps into her brain.

Why doth God allow this to be?

Mary watches silently as she slowly stalks around the room, hovering in the background. Nervously she places her crucifix pendant in her mouth, biting down on the woodwork as she strolls unobstructed. Only Jane has noticed Mary is in the room. In an instant Mary's brain begins to sift through the visual images before her, effortlessly blending them with the burning memories of her visions. Suddenly the visions begin to make sense.

Calmness descends upon her.

She knows what must be done.

Mary sighs deeply looking to the heavens as if for guidance and strength.

Two white doves flutter and land on the window sill.

Mary is conscious of Jane's predicament; she has seen snippets of her catastrophe in her waking dreams. She is armed with the knowledge her vision will become reality if she doesn't act quickly and do that which has to be done. She remains haunted by the vision of the two coffins, particularly the smaller one, suitable for a baby. Mary readies herself to take charge as Helen stands up, stretching her tired limbs and wiping her bloodied hands on a piece of equally bloody cloth.

Jane appears to be drifting in and out of consciousness. Her breath is labored as she struggles to breathe regularly. Her labor has been progressing for over forty hours now. Her will to continue is waning as the pain and distress grows and lingers. She turns her head to face Mary. Mary can see the desperation in her eyes. She sees Jane's lips move, silently pleading for help. Jane is putting on a brave face yet she knows, without some sort of miracle, her fate and that of her unborn baby will be certain.

Mary and Jane's eyes lock as Mary lets the crucifix fall from her mouth. For Mary it feels like she is looking deep into Jane's soul, sharing her pain, sharing her dreams as they shatter before her. Most of all, Mary shares Jane's innermost fears.

For Jane sharing this burden provides her with a brief injection of strength. A tonic, maybe an elixir of hope, stands before her. Maybe, just maybe. Jane hopes Mary is an angel, sent by God to either save her or bring forth an everlasting peace from the excruciating pain she endures.

"Leave us," Mary says softly as she closes her eyes.

"What? Who be thou? Thou hath no business here!" Helen shrieks, startled, towel in hand. Up to this point in time she has been too pre-occupied to notice Mary's presence. She is completely dumbfounded as to why a stranger would be intruding into their house at such a pivotal, private moment.

Mary opens her eyes. Without blinking, even for an instant, she says with more urgency, "All shall leave this house now. I must hath room to work."

She stares at Martha and Helen who obstinately refuse to move, confused by Mary's sudden intrusion into their lives. With venom in her voice Mary screams, "Out!"

Mary glides swiftly behind Helen and begins to push her towards the door. Helen thrashes her arms around, protesting vigorously. Once Helen is out, Mary moves towards Martha, taking Jane's mother by the arm and pulling her slowly but forcefully from her chair. Holding her arm, she walks her towards the door. Martha begins to cry uncontrollably as she tries in vain to reach out for her daughter as she is slow lead away..

"It shall be alright," Mary reassures her softly though with uncertainty dancing amongst her nervous words. Martha continues to sob while nodding her vacuous acknowledgement. She is holding onto her belief that God will protect her daughter and unborn grandchild from any harm on this day. It is the only measure of hope she retains. She guards it closely in her heart. She begins to utter the Lord's Prayer almost silently, struggling to enunciate the words.

As Martha and Mary return to the daylight outside the house, Mary is stunned to see all the faces staring in her direction as if she is some sort of mad woman, rudely intruding on their personal business. The air is charged with the volatile scent of growing anger and fear. Undaunted she says confidently, making her position completely unambiguous, "Thou shall not enter. Jane needs my help if it be that she and her baby are to live through this day. I need naught save for silence and thou to heed my words."

With fire burning in her eyes, Helen makes a move to walk back in. Mary plants an outstretched hand in her midriff, pushing her forcefully back. She hisses, "Doth thou want thy sister to perish with child? Heed my words and thinketh wisely!"

Shocked, Helen stumbles a couple of steps backwards without saying a word. She is hugged and shielded from Mary by a grim faced older lady in amongst the throng. Mary pays her look of derision no heed.

Mary turns on the heel of her foot, directing her focus towards Thomas. The nerve above her left eye twitches as she scowls at her husband with a maddening, unflinching stare. Thomas has never seen this side of Mary before. She has changed so much in the past few weeks, not just the two inch wide streak of silver hair which has appeared down the right side of her head. The stark change in her behavior is what most disturbs him. In fact he is beginning to worry that she is on the edge of losing her sanity altogether. However, even as his fears grow, this thought is overridden by the fact he loves her with a passion that can't be denied. He has always trusted her judgment in the past. To this day, she has never let him down.

"Keep them out!" she whispers, her face so close to his that he can feel her warm breath on his skin. He is unsure as to whether this sensation comforts or scares him.

Mary disappears back into the house, closing the door firmly behind her.

Thomas smiles sheepishly at the gathered crowd whose focus has fallen from Mary onto him. His skin crawls as he is aware all eyes are upon him. The crowd remains nervously silent; an awkward silence which Thomas is well aware will not last. Confusion reigns supreme. That is, until it is eventually over thrown, inevitably, by action of some sort. It is Mary's actions he fears most. He knows that the repercussions could be dire if things go wrong.

How doth I keep thirteen people out of a house if they have the mind to enter?

Inside the house, Jane's senses are heightened as a result of the excruciating pain she is experiencing. Jane has heard all of Mary's words. She interprets them as positive, thinking Mary is strong enough in spirit to help her through this troublesome birth. She is beginning to feel confident that this stranger might have a plan, might know what to do. Though she is in great pain, her face and body seem to be a little more relaxed having heard Mary speak about saving both her and her unborn child. As Mary re-enters and walks towards the bed, Jane continues to bite down hard on the leather strap, preparing for what is next. Her eyes sparkling with hope.

Mary sees the relief engulfing Jane's face. She smiles at Jane; a smile like a well-loved friend who has come a long distance to visit someone who is gravely ill. Jane is reassured further by Mary's demeanor. Mary bends forward, gently caressing Jane's hair in a loving manner. Mary leans forward and whispers clearly to her so there can be no misunderstanding, "Thou needth to be calm. I hath seen thy future. I see two coffins if I doth not help. I see a healthy lad if I do that which must be done. I can save thy boy. Alas, I fear I cannot save thee too."

As she stands, Mary notices the change in Jane's face almost immediately. Her facial muscles tense as her brain struggles with confused and fearful thoughts mixed with a yearning to find some shred of hope that her plight is not so dreadful. Her eyes dart to and fro as fear becomes the overriding emotion coursing through her veins. Mary stays calm, fully aware that any outburst from Jane would produce catastrophic results for not only Jane and her unborn baby, but also for herself and Thomas. She slowly brings a finger to her lips, urging Jane to remain silent.

Mary tries to ease Jane's fears by telling her stories of what she has seen in her visions in hushed, soothing tones, "I doth see a descendant of thy son, a grandson no less. He shall be a great leader of men, a wise man. If thy son dies, this man shall never be born. Doth thou want thy son to die? Doth thou want thy descendants to never see the light of day? Doth thou want the world to suffer due to thy vain attempt to cheat death?"

Jane begins to cry. She doesn't know what to make of Mary's visions. She places little credence in Mary's vitriolic words. She fears Mary must be insane, or worse, a witch with unholy insight.

If thou be a witch then thy words may be filled with truth.

Her natural maternal instincts and the agonizing pain send the same message directly to her brain. The message is repeated, over and over again. It is very precise, very blunt. The message is that she has little chance that both her and her baby will live through this horrific birth. She knows in her heart she has little chance of living through this, no matter what. Her strength is waning and she is drifting in and out of consciousness. However, she is still coherent enough to realize that the pool of blood on the sheets around her is growing. She knows Helen cannot save her baby; she has tried valiantly. She wonders if this stranger might have a chance. She wonders if there is still a chance that her baby may live.

Maybe there still be some hope?

"Doth thou want thy boy to live?" Mary asks for a second time, more urgently now. She can see she has little time left to try to help, before both lives are lost.

Reluctantly Jane shakes her head in affirmation as tears roll down her face.

Mary smiles again. Jane is not fooled by this hollow token of good will. She watches, gasping audibly, as Mary walks slowly and deliberately over to the kitchen area and takes a large carving knife from the bench. Mary returns as Jane's eyes bulge, dreading the impending hideous act to be dealt to her and the pain to be inflicted. Sweat pours from her brow as her body tenses every muscle in anticipation of the grievous assault to be perpetrated.

Mary holds the knife up for Jane to see. Its large shiny blade shimmers as it reflects the light from the open fire. Mary's face is expressionless, devoid of any emotion at all. She looks at Jane with a wide eyed manic stare and says strongly, "Thou must stay silent. I cannot save thy baby if thou were to scream. Thy family will prevent what I must do. Doth thou understand my words?"

Jane nods vigorously. She closes her eyes and bites down on the leather strap with all her might and braces herself for the sting of the blade. Her mind drifts to happier times, back when she first met John at a town dance, so many years ago. He was so dashing back then. They danced all night and became inseparable after that. She remembers their courting and of course their wedding day and the lavender that smelled so sweet. Ah, the lavender. A tear escapes her closed eye as she wishes she had one last chance to speak to him, to tell him everything was alright, to tell him how much she loved him.

Her face relaxes a little, as her brain remembers the pleasant aroma of that day. While she drifts away to this pleasant place she begins to recite 'The Lord's Prayer' silently in her head. She hopes God will repay her for the sacrifice she is about to make.

Outside the house, the gathered crowd waits patiently. Everyone is silent, trying desperately to hear any sounds from inside which might provide a clue as to what is happening. With each second of every minute they hear nothing, just silence. This silence goes on and on until finally they hear a joyous sound, the ultimate sound, the sound of life. From within the building a baby's cry resonates loud and healthy. In pleasant disbelief they turn to each other and begin to smile. Helen and her mother are ecstatic. Helen runs to Thomas and kisses him on the check. She smiles and rushes back inside to greet the new arrival, to see Jane and to thank Mary.

Jezebel crouches down in the slush and grass, watching proceedings from higher ground. Her fur is soaked yet, as she shivers, she remains firm in her resolve to stand guard over Mary. She knows more than ever, this is a dangerous time for her lifelong friend. She knows she must be close at hand when she is needed. She knows there is no turning back. A decision has been made. Consequences will follow.

With gaze unflinching, she watches the cabin as the screaming begins.

'Windows of the Soul'

A break from the norm,

To rest you must.

Keep your eyes open,

For clues that go past.

Escape you will try,

Fail you must.

Unable to shut your eyes,

To dreams of the past.

Chapter 17

Saturday 25th February, 2006.
Morning.
Melbourne, Australia.

The major thoroughfares are deserted, as is to be expected at this early hour of the day. After all, it is 9am on a weekend when there are no major sporting events in town. No cricket matches are scheduled for the MCG or Docklands. The city is, for once, devoid of testosterone; a good thing in my book. It is one of those rare weekends where Melbournians either relish a sleep in or clog the roads out of town, heading away from the hustle and bustle that is their normal existence. Today Melbourne is a peaceful ghost town, just the way I like it. This is my own private city, to do with as I please.

As we drive onwards I am optimistic I can leave all this nonsense about my visions back home, at least for a few days. My mind has become addled trying to decipher all that I have been witness to and also what it all means in the bigger scheme of things. I can feel the physical pressure pushing down hard on my brain. The visions seem like one confused, tangled web of images that may or may not be prophecies of the future. I am convinced I had an opportunity to save Dr. Khan though failed to realize this at the time. My continuing visions of Emma have me thinking that something will occur and that I am the only one capable of saving her. I remain confused, however.

My visions of Emma are tangled with images of the woman that I thought I had hit with my car. This vision has not played out in reality. I am beginning to wonder if this is something I have simply made up.

There is the sound of a girl singing a nursery rhyme and another of a baby's muffled cries. The smell of acrid smoke is always present too. All these things I regard as irrelevant. I assume my brain is struggling with what is real and what is not and as such is running with the visions and creating some fictitious dreams to murky the waters. In this way my brain protects itself from being overwhelmed. Does that make any sense? I don't know. Anyway, that is my current theory and will remain so until I can prove or disprove what is actually happening.

I shake my head as I make a conscious effort to focus my frazzled mind on the passing scenery beyond my window. All I need to do is relax a little. That is the only thing I know for certain. I'm sure everything will become clearer after that. I must stop thinking about the strange things I am seeing.

Down Russell Street, then right onto Flinders. We seem to be having an incredible run of luck, catching every green light. We pass the shimmering earthy shards of a nearly deserted Federation Square. A few lovers are staggering home, arm in arm, suffering a little from the long, indulgent night, just savored. The occasional jogger pounds the pavement, proving that a few are primed and ready to 'seize the day'. Traffic is minimal; just a street sweeper picking up carelessly discarded litter. It is accompanied in its plodding journey by several early morning trams which scuttle past, heading along Swanston Street.

The cafes, gymnasium and other assorted shops in the newly converted 'Banana Alley' vaults are completely silent and lifeless. The refurbishments look fantastic. The renovations are even better than the rumors I have heard. Maybe they will be open later. I'd love to explore them with Peter, if I get the chance. I can't wait to become absorbed in shopping and discovering for a few hours, once we are settled. It may help to wash away the problems of the last few days. Lord knows I could do with a distraction at this point in time. I desperately need some 'me' time to recharge the batteries.

I catch my first glimpse of the Crown Towers as we turn the corner and come out from under the railway overpass. They stand like two monoliths, dominating the city skyline. Their windows glisten in the early morning sun, forcing me to lower my sun glasses from the top of my forehead. A fantastic landmark, they are indeed a most impressive sight.

The Crown Towers have become a Melbourne institution now. However, this has not always been the case. Controversy has dogged the whole Crown Casino complex since tenders were first called for under the Fitzgerald Liberal government. The project was heralded as a great opportunity for Melbourne to become recognized as one of the most liveable, cosmopolitan cities of the world, particularly as we edge nervously into the twenty first century. They hoped the whole casino precinct would become a focal point to attract lucrative overseas dollars into Melbourne. These dollars would have a flow on benefit to the traders of Melbourne due to the increased number of visitors to our fair city. Tourism was certain to boom. In fact the entire community was going to benefit from the increased taxes to be levied from the gamblers.

Detractors at the time were plentiful. The pubs and clubs around the border with New South Wales, particularly Echuca-Moama, felt it would deter tourists from travelling North, resulting in less money flowing through the country communities. They felt it would lead to job losses and cause some regional centers to become little more than ghost towns. They were right.

Social workers claimed twenty four hour pokies in Melbourne would lead to kids being abandoned in the car park, increased numbers of people being addicted to gambling, increased bankruptcies, more marriage break-ups and more crime. They were right too. Prostitution, armed theft and all manner of organized crime were drawn to the casino precinct, like moths to a flame.

Of course the Labor opposition screamed long and hard, though lacked the votes required to do anything meaningful to put a stop to the project or restrict the Casino's trading hours. The irony of it all is, once the Labor government came into power, it became a friend and major beneficiary of the casino. Its major works projects could not be undertaken without the voluminous taxes collected from the casino on a daily basis. Of course, these voluminous taxes are just a pittance compared to the wealth that is slipping through the hands of punters with stars in their eyes.

It is now the Liberal opposition which is the champion of the community; condemning the ever growing crime wave that is developing around the casino precinct. The Labor government has taken a different tack. They have rightly claimed that the illegal activity outside the casino's doors has nothing to do with the casino. They have chosen to ignore all crimes occurring in and around Enterprise Park, directly opposite the casino. On a clear night the park is filled with prostitutes, pimps and drug dealers. The only thing missing is the police who seem to be permanently posted elsewhere. As we pass Enterprise Park now, in the relative safety of day, it appears to be empty, devoid of any people altogether. There is some rubbish fluttering across the lawn in the light early morning breeze. It is not at all corresponding with the image of the scary place I had envisaged.

Topiaries, growing in giant Tuscan inspired concrete pots come into view as Peter swings our car around into the loading zone in front of the hotel. The decadent shops are closed till the evening. However, their window displays are amazing none the less. To the left, 'Mischief' is filled with the latest designer clothes, straight from the catwalks of Milan.

To the right is Versace; elegant in the extreme. Its storefront is tastefully uncluttered. Just the odd gilt edged furniture with plenty of cushions made from the highest quality fabrics, sourced from around the world. I wonder if I can walk into these stores or if I need an appointment and credit check!

As we come to a halt, the doorman walks forward, resplendent in his finely tailored uniform. He is immaculately dressed in a black hat with gold trim, a red coat with black cuffs over exquisitely pressed trousers. As he walks briskly towards my car door, his polished and well-practiced smile shines brightly.

"Good morning, Madam," he says with a graceful air as he opens my door, before I have the chance to do so myself.

Stepping out of the car I look at the doorman, then at the Towers and their surrounds. It is magnificent. I twirl on the spot, trying to take in everything. I want to remember every last detail. It is truly breathtaking.

"Good morning," I say meekly, a little dazzled by the display in front of me.

I look over the top of the car and see Peter standing, leaning on the bonnet, looking most smug, "Glad you like it, Angel."

"Like it! I love it. This is just what I need to recuperate a little," I say, making no attempt to contain my enthusiasm.

Peter is suitably impressed by my response. He smiles as he glides behind the car, opening the boot in order to extract our bags. The Bell Hop is racing towards us, pushing his empty three tiered trolley.

"Maybe you should wait until you get inside; the place could be a dive. Never judge a book by its cover, you know," he says with more than a faint hint of sarcasm in his voice.

"I don't think you need worry, sir," the doorman says very seriously. He doesn't seem to get Peter's strange sense of humor. "The Crown Towers are a world class hotel built with meticulous attention to detail. As such they have been the residence of choice for visiting dignitaries such as Bill Clinton, Mick Jagger and the Rolling Stones, Tom Jones....."

"It's fine mate. I'm only joking."

Peter and the doorman's conversation drifts slowly into the background as I walk further towards the entrance. As I enter I become completely absorbed in the brilliant decor which surrounds me. No expense has been spared. As I look around, only one nearly adequate word springs to mind, 'Wow!'

I walk slowly around the foyer, taking in every last detail. The wide marble floor which leads to a huge, grey, spiral staircase is absolutely stunning. Each of the steps is inlaid with a fine gold trim. A massive chandelier dominates the ceiling, illuminating the space to dramatic effect. Water cascades down over a unique water feature encompassing numerous Roman inspired statues. The entire display is breathtaking.

As I wander through the foyer in a trance like state, I remain blissfully unaware that I am lost in a world of my own. I am engrossed in the dazzling architecture in front of me. So much so, I stumble accidentally into another person, knocking them to the floor.

"I'm so sorry," I say quickly as I come crashing back to reality. I look down, face to face with the person in front of me. He is a young lad, around about twelve years of age, dressed simply in a red T shirt, blue baggy jeans and shiny new runners. He gazes in my general direction, somewhat shocked to be knocked off his feet by a total stranger. I feel like such an idiot as I notice the boy is carrying a white cane. He is completely blind.

"I am awfully sorry. I just didn't see you there," I wince as my tactless words come flooding out with little thought of censorship. "Oh God, that's just the most insensitive thing I could possibly say, isn't it? I am so sorry."

I take the young lad by the arm and help him back onto his feet. As he regains his composure, he leans on his cane and laughs, "That's okay. I didn't see you either."

"Are you okay?" I ask, worried about the force of our impact.

"Not sure. I'll have to check with my doctor. I seem to be having some trouble with my vision. Who knows, I may be permanently blind and have to sue you for damages," he jokes.

I begin to smile, charmed by the breezy nature of this young man in front of me. His life must represent such an incredible impediment at times, yet he seems so happy and easy going. I certainly couldn't handle being blind; I don't think I would be able to adjust.

"Nothing seems to bother you, does it?" I ask.

He shakes his head, "No, not really. Why should it? I've been blind all my life so I'm used to the odd, unexpected accident. I just enjoy life, I don't know what I'm missing so, I don't miss it. I have noticed though, that the adults in my life seem to be bothered by the trivial things that life throws at them."

He strikes me as a very perceptive boy. Maybe his blindness has allowed him to read people and their idiosyncrasies better than someone distracted by sight. I understand exactly what he is saying. Adults are stressed by many trivial things. It's what makes us adults, "Tell me about it!"

The boy's face changes in a heartbeat from being bright and alive, morphing towards a more serious complexion. He tilts his head and asks with a little uncertainty, "Can I ask you a strange question?"

"Sure," I say, wondering if I have upset him in some way.

"I don't know how to say this other than to be direct," he says warily.

"Direct is always the best way," I reply, wondering what he wants to ask me, a total stranger.

"Well," he dithers. "I was just wondering why you are scared of your nightmares?"

A chill courses through my body as my brain slowly latches onto the question being asked. Does this blind boy know something about my visions? How on earth could he? I didn't tell him. He is a complete and utter stranger to me. How could he know anything about my visions? I shake my head. This is just madness, completely insane.

"What are you talking about?" I ask, listening with anticipation for his reply.

"I'm sorry. I didn't mean to pry or cause offence. It's just that I'm intrigued by your visions and dreams," he chimes more contentedly now that the awkward subject has been broached. "You know, you shouldn't worry about them, these nightmares. They aren't exactly what they seem. I don't know the word for it, what is it?'

"What do you mean?" I ask, confused and worried as to how a blind child, unfamiliar to me, could possibly know so much about me and the drama which is my life.

"Awe, yeah," he continues casually, seemingly unaware of my dismay. "They're more like opportunities. An opportunity can either be taken or ignored. There is choice involved here. Do you know what I mean?"

"I have no idea what you mean!" I say, my frustration beginning to surface in my voice.

He sighs as he tries to state his thoughts in such a manner that I will grasp his meaning, "Well, as you know. They certainly aren't nightmares. Nightmares are simply a mixture of past experiences combined with unbridled fantasy. These dreams of yours are events yet to occur, events whose outcome remains uncertain. They are events that you and you alone have a special insight into. As such, you have been granted an opportunity to decide how they will play out."

"What on earth are you talking about?" I say as my mind struggles desperately to comprehend the concepts this young boy is trying to explain. My mind aches as if I have just sat through a two hour lecture from a university professor on advanced astrophysics.

"Your nightmares are not from your imagination. They are real, very real. However, they are not necessarily an accurate picture of what is to be. They have a human element which adds much uncertainty. Am I making myself clear?"

"No, not at all. What......?" I try to ask as I am abruptly cut off by a third person.

"I'm terribly sorry that he is bothering you. He likes to talk to strangers. He doesn't have many friends because of his disability. C'mon Frank, we need to get going. Say goodbye to the nice lady.

"Bye," Frank says as his mother grabs his hand and guides him away towards the exit of the hotel.

"But ....." I proclaim as I watch them walking away. They continue on their way, slowly and steadily, disappearing out the door. I am left dumbfounded, my mind racing.

What was all that about? What does it all mean? Why?

I continue to watch them leave, stepping deliberately into a shiny BMW parked just outside the door. Suddenly my ears pick up on the words coming through on a portable radio held by a man to my left. I turn and stare at the man who is seated, listening intently to the news. He looks uncomfortable under my gaze. My stomach begins to tighten. I am filled with a sense of dread and disbelief as I listen to the report.

"......... now back to our breaking news. What appears to be a murder-suicide has rocked the tiny hamlet of Kinglake. Local residents say the unfortunate couple were new to the area, having moved into their cottage sometime in the last few weeks. They were described by locals as 'quiet' and kept largely to themselves. Outwardly, they gave no inkling of being anything other than completely happy. Police say Malcolm Nguyen shot his wife Emma once at close range to the head before turning the gun onto himself......"

Oh my God!

My head spins as nausea rapidly takes control of my body and all its muscles. The marble floor begins to sway and rotate around me. My vision blurs, my eyelids flutter. In my distressed state I can vaguely distinguish Peter coming towards me, dangling a set of keys in his hand.

"Room 12b, river side, view included. How good is that? Julie? Julie!"

My sight becomes simpler in its complexity, just a blur of colors, as I sway a little. I am overcome with the realization I can't breathe. My eyes flutter violently shut, turning everything around me to black. My head becomes light as I faint, crashing like a rag doll to the solid lobby floor. I am out cold.

'Contradictions'

Complex answers you seek,
From logical questions unspoken.

Productive solutions to riddles,
Give rise to no thought at all.

The truth is what matters
No matter how false.

Trust none of your senses,
'Cept the curious visions of course.

Chapter 18

Saturday, 25th February, 2006.
Late Afternoon.
Crown Towers, Melbourne, Australia.

Grrrrrwwww!

I look from one person to the next in quick succession. What I seek, I do not find. Every man, woman and child is staring back at me with dark, fearful eyes. Though I understand that I am perceived as the curious interloper, intruding on their private shindig with the monsters, I am ill at ease at being the center of attention. All I want is there to be a leader of sorts, hiding amongst them. Someone with the will to fight for what is right, someone to stand in the face of pure evil and not give any ground. I realize quickly that I will not find anyone who even vaguely resembles this description without finding a mirror first.

Their faces are scarred and covered in grime. Confidence lies at their feet in tatters. They are certainly a forlorn bunch. Hope has all but disappeared from their hearts. So much so that they choose to stand, staring at me, rather than fleeing the monsters. There is no desire amongst the group to fight for freedom. I wonder how many of their compatriots have been murdered by the monsters. What does it take to steal all sense of hope from a human heart?

A bolt of mauve lightning, far off in the cavern, distorts the normal wavelength of light as it flickers for an instant. I am shocked by the unusual property this modified light exhibits. It causes the skin of the people around me to appear transparent, presenting them like a living x-ray. They are skeletons in motion, shaking with fear. The allusion is only temporary, a curious trick of my senses. As the light changes back to normal, the people resume a more typical form once more. It is unnerving enough to stimulate me into action. I cannot have the blood of these people haunt me forever. I cannot let any more innocents die.

Grrrrwwww!

They draw nearer!

My eyes are drawn to the camp fire. I watch the billowing flames stream high towards the ceiling, waving in the subtle breeze. I watch mesmerized as a message begins to form in amongst the shimmering orange, red and yellow flames.

"Hope is a waking dream."

I smile.

I have no time to lose.

Searching the camp, I look for anything we can use as a weapon to fight. I spy two long spears, carved and sharpened from slender tree trunks. I signal for the others to come forward. Eventually, with much earnest gesturing, they shuffle forward. I line the men up, five to a spear. This is just enough men to enable us to lift the end of each spear and point it in the direction of the oncoming attack.

I walk briskly away from the men. I take the hand of the nearest woman and place it in the hand of a child. I signal for the others to do like wise. Then, I lead them towards the bush, waving my arm around, desperately encouraging them to run and hide. I look into the eyes of the woman next to me; there is a little spark of hope in the center of her eyes. She nods and leads everyone into the relative safety of the beckoning shrubbery. In an instant they are gone, hidden by the luscious undergrowth.

Grrrrwwwww!

They are nearly upon us now. Their footsteps shake the ground we stand upon. I rush back and take the lead position on the right spear. In unison, we lift and angle our poles, ready for the fight. I can smell the fear in the air as I see my new found friends glancing at each other nervously. I pray this feeble plan will work.

Suddenly three monsters appear, the biggest one halting inches before the upraised spear. He looks at us and smiles. Somehow, he must be intelligent enough to realize how close he has come to grief from our unsuccessful trap. He knows he has the upper hand. There is little we can do as the men standing to my left waiver in their resolve. I watch in horror as their grip on the spear falters. As I hear their frantic unintelligible chatter I turn to offer some verbal encouragement.

"Hey!"

Too late! They drop their spear and head in numerous directions, one monster giving chase. With a sweep of its powerful claw, it effortlessly scoops up one of the men. He screams in pain for a brief moment before his back is broken by a swift flick of the monster's powerful hand.

All the other men panic, releasing their grip on their spear as they run into the bush, a second monster giving chase. I am left holding the spear. I struggle valiantly for a moment before releasing my grip, letting it fall in the dust at my feet. It is simply too heavy. I look up as I hear a low murmuring growl.

Mmmmmmm.

I find myself staring face to face with the biggest of the monsters. Pungent saliva slides out of his mouth as his taste buds yearn to savor the taste of my flesh. His foul, sinister breath buffets my face and hair. I can see the obvious pleasure displayed in his eyes. He has no fear of losing. He wouldn't know what that was.

Taking a deep breath I stand my ground. If this is it, I am determined to die with dignity. Straightening my posture I place my hands on my hips. Defiantly I scream at the top of my lungs, "I am not scared of you!"

The monster stands up on its hind legs, throws its head back and roars with tremendous force. His voice echoes throughout the cavern. He falls back onto all fours with a thud and moves slowly closer to my face. I brace for the final attack.

*   *   *

I wake rested and at ease, though a little disorientated. As I yawn quietly to myself, my eyes explore my new surroundings. My new abode is plush and opulent in the extreme. To my left, on the side wall, hangs a large, gold trimmed mirror which dazzles with the reflection of the city lights. Straight ahead, at the foot of my four poster bed, is an enormous watercolor painting. It seems to depict Victoria towards the end of the nineteenth century as numerous two masted schooners sail in and out of the Port of Melbourne.

I feel the bed beneath me. It is quite simply extraordinary. So firm yet so comfortable. I can only imagine this is how it feels to recline on a fluffy white cloud as it slowly drifts towards the horizon. I could sleep peacefully here for a month. The sheets are so silky and soft, in a soft apricot color which blends seamlessly with the cream colored walls. I am at sea in the large bed; I guess it is a king size. Just oh so luxurious.

Tilting my head to the right I see Peter, sound asleep, sitting in the arm chair he has placed close to the bed. His jacket hangs nonchalantly on one corner of the chair while his head is leaning against the other. His feet are crossed and lifted, resting on the edge of the bed. From the intermittent snoring exiting his mouth, I have no doubt he is sound asleep. I suspect he has been in this position for some time now. I smile; what a sweet soul to sit by me while I sleep.

I stretch my arms high above my head then pull them behind my back, trying to loosen my stiff muscles. I feel as if I have been cooped up in a tiny space for days and as a consequence, my body is protesting most vigorously. As I wriggle about, extending my flexibility back to a suitable level, Peter begins to stir. He opens his eyes, blinking without comprehension, as he looks at me.

"Hi Babe," I say as I lean over and kiss him on the lips.

The fog surrounding Peter's head suddenly clears as he wakes with a start. He jumps violently out of his chair, grasping for my right hand with both of his. He reels off his questions in quick succession, like they are being shot from a high powered machine gun. He doesn't pause to wait for my answer, just moves straight into the next thought which cries out from his troubled mind, "Are you alright? How are you feeling? You gave me such a scare, do you know that? What happened? Do you remember what happened?"

I ponder this last question for a few seconds as the events of the morning come flooding back. I nod as I realize what has happened. I remember being in the lobby, taking in the grandeur of the Crown Towers foyer. This was before my curious conversation with the blind boy; a complete stranger who seemed to have some form of insight into my visions and what they actually mean. I remain frustrated that I didn't have the opportunity to pursue his opinions in greater detail. Finally, I remember hearing the tragic news report about the murder-suicide of Emma and Malcolm. I remember being overcome by a sense of hopelessness prior to everything fading to black.

"I guess I must have fainted," I propose not knowing anything that has happened after that time.

"Fainted! That's the biggest understatement of the century. You took a swan dive backwards onto the hard marble floor in the foyer. I'm surprised you didn't crack your skull open. Doesn't it hurt."

"Not really," I say as I reach for the back of my head. As I touch the top of my scalp, I can feel a sizeable lump. A sharp pain registers in my brain. I vent my feelings loudly, "Bloody hell!"

Peter smiles, as I rub my head gingerly, "I thought it must hurt."

"Thanks for your heartfelt sympathy, mate," I say as I grimace in pain.

That floor was hard!

Peter laughs as he moves towards me, his arms open as if to embrace me, "Oh, you poor dear. Here, let me kiss it better for you."

I pull back, instinctively protecting my tender head, "No you don't."

Peter reaches out and rubs my leg in a comforting manner, instead. Smart man. Glancing at his watch he says, "Well I guess I should let you rest. I had plans to take you out tonight before all this excitement. I guess you're not up to it now."

"Not up to it! I'll have you know, mister, I've been resting for.... for.... for however long it is and I feel great. Well, great as long as I don't touch my head but, having said that, I have never felt better. It's like the conversation with Frank has lifted a weight from my shoulders. Maybe it has accidentally answered some of the questions I have labored under since my visions started."

"Wait, wait. Who is Frank?" Peter asks confused, seeking some sort of clarification as to what I am talking about. I suddenly remember that Peter wasn't present at the time I conversed with Frank. Having not met him, he must be thinking that this 'Frank' is yet another figment of my highly vivid imagination.

I grin as I sigh and explain myself, "Yes well, I guess you were busy getting our key or something. Anyhow, Frank is a blind boy I met in the lobby. I knocked him over accidentally. As I helped him to his feet, we began to talk. At first we simply engaged in small talk. Suddenly, out of the blue, he asked me why I was afraid of my nightmares."

Peter is astonished. I can just imagine how incredulous this sounds, "Your nightmares! How exactly did he know that you were seeing things that aren't there?"

"That's the thing," I continue. "I didn't get the opportunity to ask him how he knew what I am going through. His mother appeared from nowhere and promptly marched him away to a waiting car. That was just before I fainted."

"Maybe he was just making it up," Peter suggests. I assume by his quiet tone of voice that even he doesn't give this notion much credence. "Maybe it was just a stupid, childish remark which you misunderstood and took for something more than it actually was."

"No. No, he was very specific. Just like he could see what I could see. However, unlike me, he seemed to know how to interpret what he was seeing. Sorry, that's not right. I mean, he could interpret what 'I' am seeing," I state awkwardly. I listen to my own words, knowing how stupid they must sound.

"Right," Peter says slowly, like he is struggling to grasp the meaning of my explanation. "Let me get this straight. You're saying a blind boy, who has never met you before, is seeing the same things you are and is saying they actually mean something? In essence you are saying that a blind boy has better vision than yourself."

I consider Peter's words carefully for a second then nod in agreement, "In a strange way that is about right. I don't know how he does it. I guess it is his brain which is seeing the images, not his eyes. Maybe that is what is happening to me too, I don't know. The one thing I do know is that he is having visions as well. I am convinced about this fact. He isn't seeing what I am seeing but he knows that I am having similar nightmares. He told me not to be afraid of them, that they are opportunities, not a threat."

"What do you think he meant by that?" Peter asks skeptically.

"I think it's obvious, don't you?" I ask. I can see by the blank expression on Peter's face that he has no idea what I am talking about. "The images I'm seeing in my visions are opportunities, pure and simple, because they are small glimpses of the future. They are catastrophic events that are going to happen."

"Visions of the future, do you believe that?"

I take a deep breath, "I think that must be right. It sounds like madness, particularly if you consider the notion with a rational mind. However, these visions don't meet anybody's definition of what is rational. I think Frank might be right. I don't know. They must be occurring for a reason, not just to torment me. Anyway, if they are images of the future, they might be events that, if I am attentive enough, I might be able to change. I might be able to save some of these people from the horrible calamity to which they are destined."

Peter scratches his head, lost in thought. It is obvious to me that he is struggling to place any faith in the validity of my visions. I am sure he thinks they are just tricks my mind is playing on me, "Look, I don't know. I think it's all a little too far-fetched."

I sigh and reach out for Peter's hand, "I don't know too. All I know is that I need to get some answers and soon. We both need to know what this is all about. The only thing I know for sure, at the moment, is that I am sane and that this bump on my head, though painful, is not affecting my judgment in any way. At least that's a start. The rest I will just have to work out as we move along."

Peter laughs as he bends forward and kisses me on the tip of the nose, "I know that too, never doubted you for a second. Even in simpler situations than this, we all question our sanity at one stage or another. I know you are sane. All I want is for you to get the answers you need, so you can find some sort of peace. I want you to be happy. I'm just worried that these visions or whatever they are will only bring you misery. I hope I am wrong. You know I'll be there for you, no matter what, while we are working this out together. You know that don't you?"

"Thank you," I say gazing into the eyes of the man I love so much. I think I have taken him for granted too often in the past. Finding someone like Peter is something I should learn to appreciate more often.

He pats my hand gently as he suggests, "Let's leave this for the moment; I don't think we are going to solve any riddles tonight. Are you sure you want to go out tonight? We can always just stay in. You might be better off getting some more rest. I'm sure the room service is pretty nice."

I don't give any consideration to Peter's offer, whatsoever. I can feel the energy running through my body like an electric bolt. I feel ready to paint the town red, "Am I sure? Too right! Let's go and light up this town. I need to enjoy life for once. After all I have had to endure in recent weeks, I need to live a little."

I throw back the blankets and swing my feet slowly off the bed. I feel a little queasy as the blood rushes to my head. I try not to let Peter know I am a little shaky as I take my time walking to the bathroom to fix my makeup and hair. I don't want to faint again, not tonight. Within half an hour I am ready, black billowing cotton dress and all. Then it is Peter's turn. He takes about five minutes, slapping on some black jeans, a long sleeve mauve shirt with collar and running some gel through his hair. God I hate how men do that! He looks so great for such little effort. I'm still not sure my outfit is a hundred percent perfect.

Ten minutes later, we are entering a completely different world. Gone is the brightness, the cleanliness and relative safety of the Crown Towers. We cross the bridge, along King Street, to an area shrouded in shadows and innuendo. Who knows what these sinister shadows hide tonight. This is the seedier side of the Yarra, the one place in Melbourne where anything and everything goes. It is a lawless place of ill repute, a reputation that is well earned over many grubby years.

The darkness is broken by the railway underpass which is lit up in its bright fluorescent blue. These lights are meant to be a deterrent to the drug addicts; preventing them in their quest to find a vein in their arms and shoot up. In reality, the lights aren't much of a problem. The prostitutes still congregate here, plying their trade. They wander into the light looking for clients and back into the shadows to service them. Once they have enough money to feed their habit, they then buy the drugs from any of the numerous dealers who move in and out of the park unhindered by the police. The working girls then walk a short distance to reach the normal street lights. They shoot up on the pavement while the busy traffic passes by. The world doesn't seem to care what goes on in this place. It is Melbourne's version of Hell, fuelled by the ignorance of all the relevant authorities.

My hands grip Peter's arm firmly as we walk along the footpath between Kings St and Enterprise Park. So much so that I'm sure there will be bruises on his skin, hidden under his shirt. I don't like this place at all. There are several girls walking around searching for customers. One looks at us and smiles in anticipation as we walk by. She is a bottle blonde, wearing a short leather mini skirt revealing too much cellulite and a white blouse with the top three buttons undone. Her breasts bounce, unrestrained as she walks towards us. Her stomach is bulging slightly suggesting she might be several months pregnant. I watch her closely. She reminds me of someone I know though I can't quite place her.

"Looking for some fun tonight?" she asks as she looks me up and down with a glint in her eye. "I do threesomes too, you know, honey."

I grip Peter's arm even more firmly as I snuggle closer for protection. He looks down at me and laughs. He says politely as we continue to walk on, "No thanks. We'll be fine."

"Suit yourself, honey," the floozy says as she twirls on one of her high heels and flounces back towards the park. With a wave of her hand she says, "If you change your mind, you know where to find me. I'll be here all night."

"Can we please get out of here?" I whisper through gritted teeth, gently pushing Peter more hurriedly under the overpass, towards Flinders Street.

"Sure," Peter says walking at a slightly quicker pace. "We're nearly there."

"Where are we going anyway, or is that some big secret?" I ask as we wait for the lights to change.

"You'll find out soon enough," Peter says as he begins to cross Flinders Street. He guides me gently to the Tram Stop before glancing at his watch.

"Do we need to catch a tram?" I ask, wondering where on earth we are heading. I rack my brain, searching for a restaurant that Peter would know about, somewhere nice and classy. I have heard about a new Italian place on Collins Street that is getting rave reviews. Maybe Peter has booked there? I guess I won't have to wait too long to find out for certain.

"Not just an ordinary tram," he says pointing down the road. I turn in time to see a brown tram coming over the rise. Around its roof is a line of bright fairy lights which twinkle on and off with great excitement.

I smile in disbelief as I turn, jumping straight into Peter's arms. I hug him tight as I share an impulsive, lingering kiss.

"I love this. You know I always wanted to try the Tram Car Restaurant. Thank you, thank you, thank you. This will be great."

"Thought you'd like it," Peter says, looking suitably smug that his idea is so well received. He must have booked the reservation weeks ago, the little devil.

The Tram Car Restaurant is amazing. It is made up of two carriages. Both carriages are modified greatly; the entire interior removed in order to provide enough space to produce the services required. The first carriage contains the kitchen area. There seems to be at least two staff preparing the fine cuisine meals in there. The marvelous smells of fresh food cooking steadily waft into the second cabin as the two waiters move through the swing dividing doors.

The main dining area is set up like a miniature five star restaurant. It contains eight small, yet intimate dining tables. Each table has an ornate gas lamp flickering in the center which, along with the dimly lit interior, adds a touch of romance to the ambience of the restaurant. The lace table cloths and comfortable arm chairs, upholstered in rich red velvet, also assist in providing an unexpected luxurious touch. All in all, you don't feel like you are boarding a tram as you enter the vehicle.

The meals are superb. They take the order for our main course. For entrees they bring out a trolley packed with a range of crackers, freshly made dips and a decadent range of cheeses. I sample many of these as we chat. I particularly like some of the soft cheeses which the waiter informs me are a specialty of the Yarra Valley region.

Our main meals are to die for. I have the sumptuous Tasmanian Salmon presented on a creamy pasta base. This comes with a side serve of salad dressed in a light creamy cheese sauce. Peter has the veal in tartare sauce with a side serve of chips. This comes with a garden fresh salad of capsicum, lettuce, parsley, and tomato with a special combination of spices lightly sprinkled on top. We sample each other's meals to the satisfaction of our enthusiastic palates.

For dessert we both fancy the chocolate sundae. This is assembled in a tall glass with a layer of liquid chocolate at the base. Placed on top of this are sliced bananas mixed with diced apple. Next is a layer of ice cream capped with a large star shaped cone of cream. This is covered by more chocolate. Finally, this masterpiece of culinary delight is sprinkled with peanuts. Absolutely mouth-watering, something everyone should savor at least once in their lifetime.

It is so relaxing, sipping our white sparkling wine, eating our meals and watching the ever changing Melbourne nightlife outside our windows. This is the escape I so desperately needed. As I smile, laugh and talk the night away, I begin to feel just a little normal again. I guess, in the end, this night has helped to take my mind off the tragic circumstances surrounding the death of Emma. A niggling feeling still chews at my soul, though. I guess it always will. An accusing thought that I should have done more. I had an opportunity to save her and I let it slip. I can never get that back. Her death will haunt me forever.

We disembark, having concluded our hour long feast, at the Swanston and Flinders Streets intersection. Hand in hand we walk without saying a word, for no words are needed. Both content and at peace, enjoying a wonderful evening out in each other's company. There could be nothing more perfect than this.

We wait for the lights on Elizabeth Street to change. A white dove lands on the pavement on the opposite side of the road. It stares in our direction. I pay it little heed; Melbourne has lots of birdlife. I pull Peter into my arms. Placing my hands gently around the back of his head, I kiss him passionately for a few seconds.

"Wow, what was that for?" he asks as I release my grasp.

I smile, intoxicated in a blissful state of euphoria as I explain my sudden outburst of affection, "Just for being you."

I continue to smile as a lady walks up to the curb. She pauses, waiting beside us, engrossed in a vigorous conversation with someone on her phone. "No I don't care. The kids are expecting us to put on one heck of a show and that's exactly what we will do. I am not about to disappoint a group of kids with cancer. Now I know you Warren, you're just as passionate as I am in ensuring that everything goes off like a dream tomorrow. You will make it happen, you always do."

"Hope is a waking dream," I hear clearly as it is whispered by a softly spoken, female voice. No one else is present. The voice is carried mysteriously on the wind from some unknown location to my receptive ears.

I glance around, looking for the source of these whispered words yet find none. Almost immediately, I begin to doubt that I actually heard them spoken in the first place. I suppose they are just a remnant thought from my nightmares. Something stuck in my brain, something hard to dislodge. I wonder where I first heard that statement, anyhow.

I become distracted by the lady standing beside me. She turns to me and smiles. She is dressed in a smart white business suit and skirt which is complimented by expensive white leather platform shoes. Carrying a dark briefcase in one hand with the mobile phone held to her ear in the other, she looks the epitome of the high powered business woman.

To my horror, I realize I know her. I have seen her several times before, though not like this. Her image is engrained in my brain. My heart begins to pound as I stare at her. This is the only sound I can hear. All the street noise has faded into the background and is lost to me. I watch her mouth moving; though fail to hear a single word she is saying. I know it is rude, yet I can't avert my gaze, not even for a second.

Oh my God! Oh my God! This is not right. This is different. Why is this different?

My thoughts race as I try to work this out. My emotions jumble up. I can see her so clearly. She is the lady I knocked down with my car a few days ago. That feels like years ago now. She seems so real, so life like. She looks like I could reach out and touch her though I know I can't. She is not real. However, I am experiencing a strange nagging feeling that something is not right, this is not the same. It doesn't feel the same as before.

Quick, why is this different? What is going on?

The images are more organized in this vision. It seems to be very systematic and straight forward. There is something missing here, something important, something obvious, too obvious for me to see. I can't quite put a finger on it.

What the hell is it?

I stand, staring at her, trying desperately to work out what is missing. She seems to be growing wary of my unwelcome curiosity. The lady twists her stance slightly away from me as she keeps a watchful eye on my movements. I understand her unease; this is an unsavory part of town.

"Are you alright Julie?" Peter asks, noticing I am transfixed by the lady beside me. I fail to reply to his question. My mind is busy trying to unravel the truth hidden in this mystery.

Finally it dawns on me. I know what is missing.

Jesus Christ! No pain! I have no phantom pain in my chest. This is real! This must be real!

I reach out just as the lady takes an unexpected step forward, moving out onto the roadway, as the lights change. Grasping her left shoulder, I pull her backwards with all the force I can muster. She staggers, struggling to keep her footing while dropping her briefcase in the process. The locks break and the briefcase opens, scattering documents over a wide area of the pavement.

"What the......?" she yells as the red Mazda, driven at excessive speed, narrowly misses her. The "P" plate driver hurtles through the red light without a care in the world, his car horn blaring vigorously in denial of responsibility as he passes by.

The lady slowly regains her composure as Peter runs after her scattered paperwork. Her breathing is heavy as her mind tries to establish exactly what has just occurred. She looks at me in an odd fashion, mobile phone limp by her side. Someone on the other end is calling out, to no response, "Susan? Susan where are you? Are you okay?"

"Thank you," she says as Peter places the papers back in her briefcase in a haphazard manner. He closes it as best he can before handing it back to her as she tries to catch her breath. "Thank you, I want to thank both of you. The foolishness of the youth of today never fails to astound. What was he thinking? I could have been killed. I just can't thank you enough. I am amazed you had time to react. I didn't see him coming, not in the slightest."

I stand there silently as I shrug my shoulders. The lady reaches out and takes my hand, shaking it vigorously, "Thank you."

Peter and I watch as she walks more cautiously across the road. She turns twice to look at me and smile. My heart begins to slow, coming back to idle at its normal rate. I whisper to Peter, "That was her."

"That was who," he asks completely lost.

I take a deep breath as I continue, "That was the lady I thought I ran down on Valentine's Day. That was the lady I thought I killed."

"Oh," Peter says bluntly. He stands on the pavement, dumbfounded for a few seconds, unable to speak. After a few moments he asks succinctly, "So....?"

I consider my words carefully then turn to face Peter. I say matter of factly, "I didn't see the car coming. I just knew she was going to be hit and probably would die. That's how it happened in my vision."

"So.....?" Peter repeats, his eyes wide open, staring at me. I command his full attention.

"So, I think my visions are premonitions of the future. I think I might have just proved that. If I read them correctly, I can do something to prevent these horrible events from taking place. I know I can. I just changed the future. I have the power to make a difference."

Peter pauses, looking away from me, back towards the lady walking down the road, off into the distance. Finally he says, with more than a little skepticism, "Okay, we probably need to sit down and talk about this a little more."

I nod as I watch the lady disappear around a corner, "Yep, I think we need to do a lot of talking and work out where we go from here."

Peter nods. He averts his gaze as he reaches out and takes my hand, squeezing it tightly. "We'll work this all out Darling. It might just take a little while."

"I'm sure it will," I say as the evening breeze picks up slightly. A flash of lightning hits the ground, somewhere in the far distance in front of us. "I think though, we'd better get back to the hotel before that storm hits."

"I think you're right," Peter says as he guides me back towards the hotel. "I don't need premonitions to know you are right on that score."

As we wander towards the Crown Towers, I feel a deep sense of satisfaction flood through my body. I feel like I have awoken from a deep sleep only to discover a brand new world. It is a world which only I can roam. I feel like I have discovered some sort of hidden super power. No, that's a little ridiculous. That's a bit over the top. Anyway, I'm excited by what has transpired. My world has changed forever.

Tonight, I made a difference!

'The Right Thing'

You do what is right,

No matter how wrong it be,

Seeking approval from others,

Anger and retribution is all you shall see.

Chapter 19

March 15th 1692.
Salem, Massachusetts.

A cold breeze begins to buffet the valley. At first it comes from the South West, not the North East where the storms usually hail from. In an instant it seems to chop and change as if it is coming from a number of different directions, converging finally into one mighty wind. All at once it moves swiftly down the slope, through the tops of the cedars then down into the clearing till it mischievously tosses the leaves around the feet of those gathered outside the homestead. The gust is so strong that it is extraordinary that no one notices its passing. If anyone had, they might have considered it a sign. For those a little more superstitious it may have even been considered foreboding; an omen that something sinister is looming on the horizon.

Dark clouds rapidly descend over the homestead, carried by strong winds at higher altitudes. The temperature starts to dive as the midday sun is shaded by the encroaching storm. A flash of lightning illuminates the distant horizon. It is followed, momentarily, by the dull roar of thunder echoing from valley to valley. This too goes unnoticed by the crowd. Everyone is occupied with a myriad of conflicting thoughts battling for supremacy in their fearful minds.

Another flash of lightning precedes the beginning of the rain. At first the droplets are sparse. Large droplets land in the snow causing tiny craters to form. Everyone moves towards the front wall, preparing for the inevitable downpour. A booming clap of thunder reassures them they are accurately assessing the mood of the weather. The thatched roof protrudes little more than six inches over the edge of the wall. However, with the direction the wind is blowing, it at least gives some protection from the oncoming rain.

The rain begins to fall with a rush as the assembled crowd hears the baby's first lonely cries from inside the homestead. They all begin to smile, exchanging celebratory glances of bewildered astonishment. This is the beautiful sound they had all feared their ears would never have the pleasure of hearing. Relief spreads steadily through their bodies as Helen runs back into the house, narrowly stepping over a dead white dove in the doorway. Her mother staggers slowly yet purposefully behind her. This universal relief, however, is short lived as the in-humane, blood curdling screams of the two women reverberate from within the walls of the house, out into the surrounding bushland. Their chilling screams are relentless, un-dampened even by the rain falling steadily now.

John runs into the house. He strides just a few steps inside before his leg muscles tense, refusing to go any further. He stands frozen to the dirt floor, completely silent. All the blood drains instantly from his face. His pale complexion has a somewhat green tinge to it. His stomach churns as the bile threatens to rise and explode from his throat. With a trembling hand he reaches upwards pulling his fingers roughly through his dark curly locks as his gristly face contorts in pain. Eyes bulging, looking straight at Jane, he shakes his head slowly, unable to accept what is in plain sight before him. Hands on hips he lurches over, dry reaching uncontrollably.

Thomas and three other men enter the house just behind John. Again they all take a few steps forward before halting in horror at the scene laid bare before them. The ability to speak is lost to them. They lack any useful words to explain the emotions they are enduring. To a man they are in agony. They disbelieve what their eyes see as the truth. What their eyes perceive as real. However, as time moves on, their brains refuse to swayed by fact. The men continue to deny the validity of what they see. It is just ludicrous. What they see is simply too horrific to consider, too terrible to contemplate, even for an instant. One of the men suddenly runs from the room, unable to stomach what he has seen. The noise of his vomiting outside makes those left behind just a little more sick to the stomach.

By the flickering light of the fire place, they can see Helen kneeling on the floor repeating the Lord's Prayer over and over again. Her words are hoarse and only semi coherent. She is bowing to the floor as if she has lost her mind. Tears stream freely from her glazed, bloodshot eyes. They roll down her cheeks, falling intermittently into a small though growing pool on the floor in front of her. Her mother is lying sideways on the floor, curled in a ball. Arms folded across her stomach, her face contorted in pain. She is screaming as loud as her lungs will allow.

Mary is holding the baby, wrapped in a blood stained blanket, while sitting on a chair in the corner. Her face is shrouded by a shadow as she sings quietly to the new born, all the time rocking him from side to side. Her demeanor seems completely at odds to the other two women in the room. She appears at peace, relishing the birth of a new child into the world. Her attention fixated on the baby, she laughs briefly as the baby moves one of its tiny hands.

Jane lies motionless on the bed. Her porcelain white skin glistens in sweat. One arm dangles loosely over the edge of the bed. Her hair is drenched, unkempt and plastered to her head. Her eyes are haunting, filled with terror. They are wide open, pleading for mercy or help. It is clear her pleading has been in vain. The bed sheets are covered in blood.

The bloody carving knife rests by her side. She does not move. Most crucial of all, her heart no longer beats.

John stares at his obviously dead wife, the blood, the knife and doesn't say a word. His face is pale, his stomach still contracting periodically. As his heart pounds relentlessly, he draws in deep breaths of oxygen, acting as if his lungs have collapsed and he is struggling to breathe. One of the men places a comforting hand on his shoulder. He shrugs off the gesture of condolence mumbling something unintelligible. In one swift movement John turns and runs from the room, barging his way past the other men.

Thomas moves forward towards Mary and the baby. He is ill at ease, fearing his wife may have completely lost her mind. He is hesitant; worried that she might lash out towards him. Somehow he refuses to believe his wife could be a cold blooded murderer. However, as he reviews the stark evidence laid out before him, the truth appears too damning, too hard to ignore. He asks softly, "What in God's name has thou done?"

Mary sits in the chair silently cradling the baby in her arms, rocking him gently. A flash of lightning illuminates her face for an instant so Thomas can finally get a clear view of his wife. She appears calm, as if in a trance. Even though her cheeks are covered in tears, she looks up at Thomas with pride, showing off the new arrival. She is the only person at ease in the room. One of the men becomes physically sick in the corner while the other stands completely stunned, un-reactive to the situation at all. A clap of thunder echoes through the house. Everybody except Mary jumps.

With a thud John kicks the door open with his heavy right boot. He marches purposefully back into the house, brandishing a pitch fork. With conviction he walks towards Mary.

Thomas, startled by John's dramatic entrance, turns around. He sees the rage engulfing John's face, his expressionless eyes and his movement towards Mary. In a heartbeat he stands bolt upright, places his hands on hips as he defiantly obstructs John's path, "No, thou shan't do this!"

John, hatred burning strongly in his bloodshot eyes, pauses in front of Thomas. His grip on the pitchfork does not falter. A lightning flash illuminates its sharp, shiny prongs as he holds it horizontal, armed and ready to take his revenge for Mary's despicable act of treachery. His voice low and menacing, his words passing through gritted teeth as he spits, "I hath no quarrel with thou, just with thy witch that thou be familiar with. Stand aside!"

Thomas's body shakes with fear, yet he stands firm. There is no way he will let John pass with the pitchfork and his overpowering urge for vengeance. There is no way he will let any harm come to Mary, no matter what she has done. His only indication of frailty is the tears welling in his eyes. The rest of his body remains defiant. He speaks clearly and calmly, enunciating every word in such a manner that John can be under no misapprehension, "Over my cold, lifeless body shall that be done."

John stares at Thomas, undaunted by his obstruction yet also wary of the consequence of proceeding down his vengeful path. He appears conflicted. His right eyebrow begins to twitch uncontrollably. He considers his response carefully. Lowering his eyes to the floor, he shakes his head. Pausing briefly, he raises his head slowly. Biting his upper lip till it begins to bleed, he slowly twists his head around until he is staring directly at Jane, lifeless and bloody.

Taking a deep breath he replenishes his lungs with much needed air as his chest heaves up and down. A vein on his forehead begins to pulse as his face becomes ruddier. Turning back to face Thomas, his hands clasp the handle more tightly. He stares directly at Thomas as he says with confidence, "So be it."

John pulls the pitch fork back as Thomas braces himself for the deadly blow. The other two men, seeing the danger, swiftly clamber to grasp John by his arms. A short scuffle ensues. Eventually the men succeed in preventing John from plunging the fork deep into Thomas's stomach. The vigorous commotion finally begins to dissipate as John is subdued. John bellows, releasing his agony from deep within his heart as he is pushed back to the far wall, away from Thomas and Mary. He tries to break free though he is restrained by the two men once again. Finally he stops fighting, choosing instead to talk his way out of his captors hands.

"I must hath my revenge for this brutal, murderous act!"

One of the men, Adam, looks John in the eyes, hoping to send a message of sanity, deep into his soul. He has always received John's respect in the past. In fact many people in Salem regard Adam Douglass as a wise and thoughtful man and respect him as such. This reputation has been gained over many years by being calm when a crisis is occurring. It is an impression enhanced by his grey hair and long scholarly beard.

Adam speaks quickly in a hushed voice so that only John can hear, "I give thou my solemn word, thou shall see justice done. It shan't be done in this way. Not on this day. This man be innocent and should be treated as such."

John, regains a little rage though he remains restrained. He firmly declares, "An eye for an eye, that be what I say!"

Adam loosens his grip, placing one large hand around the back of his friend's neck in a gesture of comfort. He tries to console John, "This be not retribution, this be murder. It be not God's lore."

"I must hath justice!" John screams unrepentant, as he stretches, trying to see Mary from his obstructed vantage point.

"Thou shall, I promise thee. As God is my witness it shall come to pass," Adam says calmly as John looks into his eyes, trying to gauge what plan he has in mind. "We must take her to Salem where she shall be tried and convicted as the witch she be. Then she shall die. I give thou my word. I shall ensure she forever dwells in her vile master's realm, never to walk in heaven nor on this Earth again."

John relaxes his muscles. Adam and Herbert release their grip on John, taking a step backwards. Herbert looks at Adam for guidance. Adam whispers softly something to his friends who both listen intently. John, placing the fork on the floor, begins to rub his arms, trying to get the blood flow back into his hands. He places a trusting hand on Adam's shoulder, like he is a brother, as he says, "Let it be done. Get this filthy abomination out of my sight."

Adam nods and beckons Herbert to follow him. They walk over to Helen. Adam bends down and whispers something indiscernible in her ear. She stops praying and stands upright, slowly dusting off her cotton dress. Staggering a little, she accompanies the men over to Mary, glaring intently at her during the few steps it takes to cross the room. Mary is sitting in the shadows, cradling the baby like she is its mother.

"Give him to me," Helen says curtly.

Mary ignores Helen's demand, giving no response. She simply continues to rock the baby and sing softly to him. Helen and the others can see from their proximity that Mary's hands and clothes are covered in Jane's blood. The baby's blanket is also stained where Mary has touched it. The baby, however, gives every indication of being in good health. The boy is blowing bubbles as his eyes watch the indistinct shadows moving around him, completely oblivious to the drama his unusual birth has caused.

Helen looks at Adam, nodding towards Mary. He sighs reluctantly as he moves forward, grasping the baby and lifting it gently from Mary's hands. Mary begins to protest, though releases her grip as Adam whispers to her in a soothing manner, "Shhhhh. We mean him no harm."

Adam moves slowly away with the baby, turning and handing him to Helen. Mary continues to sit quietly, arms fully outstretched, watching as the baby moves farther away. Adam walks towards the back of the room to speak to John and Herbert once more. He speaks softly, too softly for Thomas to decipher what they are saying. They huddle together, listening intently to Adam's earnest words while Thomas watches from the other side of the room. Thomas is fearful of the calm that has descended over those gathered in the room. He feels it is a false truce and chooses to stand close by Mary's side. Every now and then John looks up, giving Thomas a dark rage-filled stare. This just serves to reinforce Thomas's feelings of unease. Eventually the three men separate from the huddle and move in different directions around the room.

Adam yells, startling Mary and Thomas, "Now!"

John runs, head-butting Thomas in his stomach, sending him crashing into the wall. Thomas exhales a brief groan as his head hits the solid wall. His face contorts before he slumps, falling unconscious to the floor. A small trail of blood is left dripping down the wall. John stands up and looks down at Thomas, sprawled on the floor and smiles.

Helen jumps backwards, pulling the baby out of harm's way, as the two men scamper past her straight at Mary, knocking her off the chair. Mary begins to scream as she kicks and punches the two attackers. Little by little the men overpower her. Though Mary is only tiny in stature, she puts up a fierce fight against this unexpected assault.

Adam sits on her left leg then successfully grabs her right. Herbert is having more trouble with Mary's arms. She spits in his face twice before carving deeply into his cheek with three razor sharp finger nails. He screams out in pain. However, Mary's act of defiance only strengthens Herbert's resolve to restrain her. Using his shoulder, he pins one of her arms before grabbing the other in a swift, effective movement. Finally Mary is restrained. Though captive she continues to struggle valiantly. Screaming, wriggling and thrashing around as best she can under duress from the two men sitting on her.

Jezebel is feverishly scratching at the outside of the front door. Nobody hears the sound of her futile effort to gain entry to be with her friend in Mary's time of need. The sound of her rescue attempt is lost in amongst the commotion of the attack on Mary. No one takes much notice until a bloodcurdling squeal resonates from the cat, cutting deep into their skin.

"Pass me the rope!" Adam screams at John, ignoring Jezebel's mournful howls. He is fearful that Mary may somehow escape if she is not subdued completely. After all, witches are known to be cunning with many mysterious tricks at their disposal.

A flash of lightning illuminates the room.

John grabs the rope hanging on the wall. He walks calmly over to Mary, watching her intently, clasping the rope in his hand. When he reaches her he looks down and sees Mary, fully incapacitated, yet full of fight. As his hatred bubbles to the surface, from deep within his soul, he speaks directly to her, "This will quieten thou vile witch."

He lifts his leather shod foot and violently kicks her across the side of her face, opening up a deep, wide cut. She falls unconscious as the men loosen their grip. John throws the rope on top of her as his friends look at John, stunned by his brutality.

"Now thou can tie thy demon."

John strolls away and out of the house, kicking the cat out of his way as he passes. Jezebel scurries reluctantly into the scrub. She spins around, watching John's every movement cautiously. She knows her time will come.

John is content, for the moment at least. He has successfully released some of his pent up rage.

Outside the house, the rain begins to slow. There is one last flash of lightning, far off into the distance, as the rain stops completely.

John falls to his knees as the enormity of what has happened suddenly hits him. Tears flow freely as his body begins to shake violently. Hatred and retribution is pushed to the back of his mind as grief engulfs his body.

Jezebel watches on, without any sympathy.

'Satan's Playground'

Darkness hides the filth,

Out to plunder,

The ladies of the night.

Alas, it cannot hide,

The sense of foreboding,

On this God forsaken night.

Satan's deals are done,

Nobody cares,

If it is wrong or right.

For who will shed a tear,

For an angel fallen,

On this God forsaken night.

Chapter 20

Saturday, 25th February, 2006.
Night.
Crown Towers, Melbourne, Victoria.

"Look, I've been thinking, Angel," Peter says hesitantly as I begin to unlock the hotel door.

"Are you alright?" I ask, a little alarmed at the docile tone of his voice. He was very somber on our short walk back to the hotel. Actually, he seemed a little tense; like he has much on his mind.

A little more brightly, Peter continues as he rubs my arm in a reassuring manner, "Yeah, yeah. Everything is okay. I just feel I need to think about what is happening, let it settle overnight."

"You don't want to talk about it tonight?" I ask, wondering what is going through Peter's head. It has been a taxing time for me, dealing with the visions and questioning my own sanity. I can't imagine what Peter is thinking on the subject. It must seem, from his perspective, to be a whole lot of codswallop. I remain eager to talk, even though I know it is getting late. I am drained of energy and in desperate need of a good night's sleep. However, Peter's peace of mind is paramount. I need his understanding and support now, more than ever.

"No, not tonight, I don't think we can work out much tonight. Let's leave it till the morning," he suggests without conviction.

Trying to hide my concern, I reach out and grasp his hand tightly, "Okay, if you think that's best. Let's just sleep on it tonight."

Peter pulls away from my hand, as he avoids eye contact. He says plainly, "I'll be up soon, Sweetheart. I just want to grab a beer or two from the bar. To help me sleep better, you know. It's been a big night."

I look at Peter with skeptical eyes, worried that he is uncomfortable with what has occurred. I guess he has to come to terms with the impossible notion that the imaginary things I see are real. I can't help but wonder if he still loves me. These visions represent a lot of excess baggage to bring to a relationship. I try not to let my fears show, though I can see from his down cast eyes that something is wrong. I choose to do something completely out of character, I lie, "That's fine, Darling. I'll see you when you get back."

"See you soon," he says as he turns and walks briskly down the hall towards the elevators. I watch him leave, wondering to myself just how many beers he will down tonight. I guess I will find out by morning.

Please come back soon, Babe. Please.

I swipe the pass key by the electronic lock and the door clicks open. I experience mixed feelings as I enter the room. I am scared about Peter, though I try to hide these thoughts at the back of my mind.

I also feel like I should crack open a bottle of champagne, strip off and luxuriate in the spa, reveling in the knowledge that tonight is a night to remember. It's the first time I have been able to decipher my visions enough to change the future. I saved a life. It feels good, extremely good.

Thoughts of Peter continue to temper my celebrations. My emotions seem to be on a roller coaster; no sooner do I fear the exhilaration of success then I am gripped by the fears I try to hide from myself. I suddenly feel completely exhausted as my adrenalin begins to wane.

As the door closes behind me I choose the appropriate option. I head straight for the double bed, leaping onto it with my arms outstretched and bouncing face first on the soft surface. I lay there for a second or two, enjoying the comfort beneath me. Before I have a chance to move, sleep comes upon me. I am out cold in an instant.

*   *   *

"Ahhhhh!" I scream as the piercing pain cuts deep into my chest. Placing my hands, one over the other, I clutch at the source of my torment. In great distress, I roll off the bed, landing heavily on the floor. I lay curled up in a fetal position begging for the pain to dissipate. No merciful God answers my prayers for help. Sweat beads on my forehead. My face distorts with agony. I begin to fear that I will succumb to this pain if help doesn't arrive soon.

Peter! Where are you Peter? I need you.

Suddenly, I am distracted from my aguish. I catch a glimpse of a shadow reflected, moving rapidly across the free standing mirror which is located next to the side wall, directly in front of me. The creature moves out of frame too quickly for me to determine what it is. I simply know they shouldn't be here. As my mind races, fearful of what beast has cast the shadow, my irregular breathing grows more desperate. Panic sets in as I search for essential oxygen, in order to prevent my oncoming asthma attack.

For God's sake! Pull yourself together. There's someone in the room here. Control your breathing. Control it now! You need to be strong.

I scold myself with silent thoughts as I see the shadow pass back across the mirror. The intruder is retracing its steps as if they are stalking their prey.

I wonder if they know I am here. Are they stalking me?

I shut my eyes, trying to block out the fact that I am not alone. With much effort, I try to concentrate on the task at hand. Little by little I slow my breath. Little by little my breathing becomes more regular, though my heart still races. After about a minute or so I open my eyes. The stabbing pain in my chest endures, though I have calmed. The pain is familiar to me. I don't know what causes it to flare, though I do know it is not life threatening. I certainly know what the pain brings with it.

I pull myself to my feet using the edge of the bed. Stumbling as I walk, I move in a fairly direct manner towards my handbag. I fumble through its contents in search for my preventative Ventolin. With much relief I pry it free from the bag.

Good!

Breathing in the soothing droplets, I survey, through bleary eyes, the room around me. I can't see nor sense any movement. I keep my fear under control as I take a second puff of the Ventolin, scanning the room for the intruder. The intruder must still be here, there is no easy escape route. I mustn't let my guard down for a second.

Maybe he's hiding.

My gaze falls back on the mirror once more. From where I am hiding on the floor, the mirror is at an angle to me. By moving slightly, I can see the other side of the room where the intruder must be lurking. I should be able to see the intruder, without them spotting me. At least that's my plan at this stage. I hope this gives me an advantage.

Shit!

I scurry back a little, startled by the shadow moving across the mirror once more. I am fortunate to have a clear view of the mirror as the intruder's reflection moves across it. However, though I have an excellent opportunity to establish what or who the intruder is, all I see is an indistinct blackness. My eyes can't distinguish a form or structure. In effect, all I see is a shadow; not a person, not a creature. In short, I see nothing tangible.

Pull yourself together. Do something!

A woman's laughter echoes through the room as I drop nervously to the floor. I search for its owner without success. The laughter eases, and then stops as the mysterious woman scolds me, "Yes, why don't you do something. That would make a change."

In agony, I defiantly push myself off the floor and back onto my feet with barely a groan. Wincing, I look from side to side as I walk towards the mirror, improving my angle with every step. Eventually, I pause, standing directly in front of the reflective surface. I am so close; I can nearly reach out and touch it. My view of its reflection is crystal clear. I am surprised to see a shot of grey hair in amongst my jet black. My bloodshot eyes scare me. I stare into the fear, held deep within my soul.

I continue to scan the room for the intruder. Overwhelmed by confusion, I struggle to decipher what is real and what is imaginary. I know full well that the pain in my chest is somehow linked to my lifelike visions. That means some of the things I see in the room are not real. They are merely visions of the future. I can't be hurt by anything that is not real. At the very least, that is my hope.

Work it out. What is real, what is not? Work it out!

I feel somehow, that the mirror is a key; something that will help me to unlock the mystery of my current vision. I can see my reflection outlined clearly as I stand about three feet in front of it. My reflection and that of the room behind me are the only things visible. I stare intently; watching, waiting for something out of place but there is nothing. Then it happens, a sudden indistinct movement. A large shadow, passes from left to right across the mirror.

I stare unswervingly at the reflection, refusing to take a backward step. As my heart pounds and my chest aches unbearably, I am overcome by a feeling of isolation. I feel very much alone. Even so, one thing is certain; I am not in the least bit scared. I am not about to let this beat me. As the shadow races across the mirror from right to left, I simply shake my head in defiance.

You're not real! I am not scared of you!

A face appears in the mirror, blocking my reflection completely. It is shadowed in darkness, blurring its features. However, it is quite clearly the face of a man. He smiles grotesquely as he watches me, his teeth sparkling in an odd fashion. The light catches the side of his face slightly, making it appear as if he is horribly disfigured. He nods slightly as he moves forward slowly. I walk backwards as he steps out of the mirror. Something is held in his hand. I see it glint in the light for a brief moment. Then it is hidden in the ruffled fabric of his old overcoat.

You're not real! I do not fear you.

I halt as commonsense floods through me. He cannot harm me. He is not real. The intruder stops walking when our faces are no more than a few inches apart. He chuckles a little; a cold, humorless laugh which puts me on edge. My nose is disgusted by the foul stench of cigarettes that he breathes on me. I steadily avert my gaze downwards, trying to avoid eye contact with this loathsome character. I feel a shiver run down my spine as my gaze falls onto my stomach and I witness the infamous deed his hands are perpetrating.

To my surprise, I feel no pain. I can see the intruder holding the long, carved ivory handled knife. Half the blade is out of sight, hidden deep inside my stomach. Blood is oozing steadily, in pulses, down the length of my dress and onto the floor. I watch in stunned disbelief as he twists the knife to increase the already substantial damage to my stomach.

"What you deserve, my Darling. What you deserve," the intruder growls, spraying spittle all over my face.

You're not real!

I raise my head and look him in the eyes as sweat and spittle drip down my face. I retort through gritted teeth, "You're not real, you bastard!"

The intruder simply smiles, unconcerned in regards to my protestations. He appears very confident, too smug for my liking. Maybe he believes he can get away with anything, without repercussions, who knows. All I know is that he is truly evil and highly dangerous.

In a moment of contemplation, I make a decision to try something impossible. I reach down and take hold of the intruder's hand on the knife. To my surprise, my experiment works. I grip his hand with all the force I can summon. I state firmly as I look into his eyes, "You're not going anywhere, mate. I want a good look at you and what's around you."

His grin fades rapidly as he tries to break my hold. In a heartbeat, I realize I am interacting with my vision. His reaction proves that even though I know this situation is unbelievable. His rough hands feel cold, pressed against my skin. I am determined to hold on. I must have a good look at this murderer and note any clues lurking in the background of this vision.

"Eloise you bitch, let go of me," he squeals as he tries desperately to free himself from my grip. I hold fast, my fingers turning white as I refuse yield my grip.

Eloise! Well at least I have a name.

I begin to look for any clues as to where and when Eloise is going to be stabbed. There must be something here. I smile as I notice the watch on the intruder's wrist. The dial is clearly visible. I can read it, even though the digital display is so small.   *11:28.*

I turn my attention to the scene behind the intruder. I study the mirror intently looking for even the most insignificant clue, something which may prove vital later. It is dimly lit, making it extremely hard to discern details.

It must be night time.

The light that is present is strange. Somehow its distinct color suggests that it is man-made. I have a nagging feeling that I know precisely what that lighting is. Yet I just can't quite place it at the moment.

What is that?

My mind registers a sound, a baby crying some distance away. Suddenly there is a blood curdling scream to my right.

Is that connected to the stabbing? It must be, surely.

I sniff the air. I can smell smoke; thick, acrid, polluted smoke. The lights of a car briefly illuminate the scene as they unintentionally scan the area. From what I glimpse breifly, it appears the intruder is in some sort of park, somewhere near a road. There seems to be a bridge with large concrete pylons. I hear a voice scream out in pain. A horrible sound which sends shivers up my spine because, even in distress, it sounds very familiar. Maybe it is someone I know or have met. I have a terrible feeling I should know who that is.

"You're nothing but a worthless whore, now let me go!" the intruder screams as he intensified his attempts to escape my grasp. It appears he is uncomfortable with his victim fighting back.

"Not on your life," I say, refusing to release my hold. "Not until I work out who you are and what you are up to?"

To my surprise the intruder seems to acknowledge my presence and respond to my words. He begins to smile; a cold and dangerous smile. In an emotionless voice he whispers, "You know who I am, little whore. I'm the nightmare that haunts your dreams since childhood. I'm the nightmare that stalks you in the dark and makes you look over your shoulder in fear. I'm the nightmare of your death."

Without flinching a muscle, I say defiantly in a clear, loud, unwavering voice, "Not today, Mister. Not a chance."

"We'll see," he hisses increasing his attempts to free himself with more urgency now. I can feel my grip starting to fail. I know I don't have much time.

I need more information, more clues. This isn't enough!

My eyes flitter as they seek to gleam any additional information from the image in the mirror. The detail of the park is hidden deep amongst the shadows of darkness that dominate the landscape. Suddenly, another car travels down the nearby road, passing us by without slowing. Its lights illuminate and outline a large sculpture at the edge of the park. It is something I know, something I have seen on this very night. It is a giant anchor which I know is at the edge of Enterprise Park, directly opposite the Crown Towers, on the other side of the Yarra.

That wasn't a bridge, that's the railway overpass. A murder is going to take place there. But, oh my God, when?

"Bugger," I say as my grip fails and the intruder escapes my clutches. He laughs as he swings the knife wildly in my direction, missing me by a fraction of an inch. I watch in disbelief as he drifts backwards, disappearing into the shadows of the park. To my horror, the park and the rest of the vision in the mirror start to fade fast as the mirror's true reflection comes to the fore.

I need more clues. Dammit, I need more clues!

As I feel a mist of despondency descend over my body, I am distracted by the sound of a bouncing ball directly behind me. I turn in time to see a tennis ball bounce several times before reaching and passing straight through the wall. The ball leaves neither a mark nor a hole. It simply evaporates into the plaster. I hear the sound of a young boy giggling. It seems to be coming from all around me rather than a specific direction. This laughter fades quickly back into silence as I notice something new on the wall.

I note, with a mixture of excitement and trepidation, that there is a calendar on the wall. A specific day circled heavily in red texta.

Saturday 25th February, that's today!

On this date the letters "XIV" are scrawled roughly. As I study the calendar, searching for more clues, it begins to disappear rapidly.

"Help me please," I hear a young girl plead weakly.

"Who are you? Are you Elouise?" I ask tentatively. I listen for further words but there are none, just the overwhelming sound of silence which envelopes the room.

The pain in my chest has completely evaporated. Looking at my dress I stare in amazement. The cut and all the litres of blood are gone without leaving a residue or trace. I pull at the cloth, searching for a hole somewhere in amongst the folds and find nothing, no damage from the knife to my dress or myself.

I sit on the bed for several minutes, lost in thought, completely silent, gazing at a white dove which has appeared on my window ledge. As he taps his beak on the wood work looking for food, my mind begins to wonder what he is doing so high up. My mind soon returns to the task at hand. After all, there is a life to be saved. I glance at my watch; ten past eleven. I nod, knowing full well I have no choice.

"Well, here we go," I encourage myself. "I guess it's time for a little adventure. What do you say, Miss Mahoney, do you want to go for a walk in the park on a beautiful night like this?"

The rumble of distant thunder rattles the windows of my suite. Through the window I can see numerous lightning strikes, probably out towards Sunbury.

I sigh as I consider who or what I might encounter in Enterprise Park tonight. There is no escaping the danger which lurks outside the safety of these walls. I stand and walk to the window to get a better view of the encroaching storm. Another thunder clap rattles through the room.

"Ah well. It's a perfect night for heroes, I guess," I say as I turn, grab my handbag, keys and head for the door.

*   *   *

As I reach the edge of Enterprise Park, I check my watch under the street light. 11:20pm. I survey the darkness, fearful that there is much I cannot see. I am not confident that I will see danger, even if it is standing directly in front of me. It is just so dark. I can see why this place has attracted so many unsavory people and practices over recent years. It is a place no decent person would consider spending any length of time. With mounting second thoughts I stroll boldly, or many would say stupidly, into the park.

I notice numerous prostitutes as they provocatively saunter under the dim street lights, hawking for business. They look as if they have all used the same instructional manual on how to dress successfully as a tart. Ruby red lips with plenty of makeup are used to hide their pale skin and drawn haggard eyes. Maybe they hope it will hide the emptiness that dwells in their hearts too. From my vantage point that is how they appear; lost and alone, the forsaken existing in a cruel underworld filled to the brim with danger. I suspect this is not the image they are hoping to convey. I think they are hoping to appear strong, feisty and alluring. This seems to be a misguided ambition, in my opinion.

Tight, thigh high skirts, which leave little to the imagination, are common place. They seem to either choose to don the standard slutty T-shirt, two or three sizes too small or opt for a buttoned shirt. Enough buttons are undone to attract the attention of dubious pedestrians. They are drawn, like moths to a flame, to the girl's natural assets as they bounce provocatively while they walk. Thigh high, leather boots are the foot wear of choice though some of the brave, or maybe foolish, have dared to wear ridiculously high heels into the park tonight.

As I watch the streetwalkers, half out of curiosity, half searching for signs of trouble, they seem curious as to why I would be roaming around alone in Enterprise Park at night. I must look completely out of place. My clothing consists of an old grey windcheater over a pair of black jeans and scruffy, serviceable runners. They glance in my direction, yet pay me little attention. I guess they consider that the way I am dressed, I represent no threat to their earning capacity this evening.

I walk along the edge of the road trying to see throughout the park with the aid of the dim blue light from the adjacent overpass. Visibility is poor. I can see several people wandering in the shadows along the grass. I guess these are mainly prostitutes with the odd potential client too. Deeper in the shrubbery there is some static movement. I am more wary of what is occurring in these darkened recesses. Discreet, muffled sounds of pleasure can be heard coming from these areas. I stand at the edge searching, though reluctant to move closer. I am conscious of one thing. There is no sign of police being present in the vicinity, none at all. This is a concern. I am on my own if trouble starts.

I sigh deeply as I shake my head. Being ultra-cautious just isn't working. Time is running out. From where I stand, I can't see any mischief, other than the sexual kind, occurring in the park. I know I only have two choices; turn and walk away or move into the park and get amongst it all. Standing at the edge I can see and do nothing. My mind drifts back to poor Emma as my resolve strengthens.

I can't let that happen again.

After experiencing the horrific vision in my hotel room, I am certain of one thing. There is no way I can walk away and let someone experience that sort of brutal attack for real. I couldn't live with myself if I didn't at least try. I have no choice other than to enter the park and take my chances. For better or worse, my destiny awaits my arrival into the sinister shadows of this park.

I notice the dimly lit sculpture of a large anchor. My pulse begins to race. Squelching onto the dewy grass, I know I am close. I step slowly and lightly, cautious not to make too much of a commotion. I walk with purpose, looking intently for anything out of the ordinary. I pass one of the railway pylons and gasp audibly. A man is standing, legs splayed, hiding behind it. On hearing my footsteps, he looks up and smiles lecherously in my direction. I avert my gaze and continue on as I see he is not alone. A lady, for want of a better word, is kneeling in front of him. Her head bobs up and down in rhythmical motion.

I move on a little more quickly now. My sense of unease about my surroundings and the people hidden in the shadows is overwhelming. This feeling grows stronger, the deeper I move into the park. I wonder if it is wise to attempt this rescue on my own. I shake my head. It is too late to get Peter. I do not know where he is anyway. I must remain resolute. I must get this done.

I hear murmuring behind some bushes to my left. Bracing myself for what I might see, I walk as quietly as possible around the edge of the shrub obstructing my view. Rounding the tree, I find myself in a dimly lit clearing. I peer around slowly and carefully, surveying the scene I have stumbled across. I can see a short man walking to and fro, cigarette in hand, burning bright in the somber light. He takes four or five steps to the left, then move the same distance back to the right. At first I can't see anyone else. Though, as I move closer, I can see her, cowering against the wall. Her eyes are intoxicating, held wide open, unflinching, tear filled and bloodshot. To me, she looks completely frightened out of her wits.

The man halts unexpectedly, suspending the callous stalking of his prey. Instead he simply stands still, quiet and imposing, directly in front of her. It is as if he is waiting for something, but what? I hear a soft, high pitch murmur from the girl. From this distance, her words are indiscernible. However, one thing is certain. There is much agitation in her quivering voice. She is aware that she is in diabolical trouble. I know that much is true.

Suddenly the man yells, as his pent up emotion comes to the fore, "Do you think that matters. In the end you're nothing but a stupid whore."

The man's shoulders soften, losing their tension steadily as he controls his obvious anger. His voice drifts back into a lower, indiscernible mumble as he begins to pace to and fro. He continues to state his thoughts to his captive. In the dim light I see the streaks on her face where her tears have caused her makeup to run. Curled into a ball, she watches his every movement as she shivers on this balmy night.

Something draws my sight from the miserable waif back to the smoking man. As he paces, I suddenly catch a glimpse of something large as he nonchalantly slides it down his sleeve and into the vice like grip of his right hand. He holds it firmly in his glove as its blade glints in the dim light. To my horror, I can see that the girl has not noticed this development. Her eyes are fully focused on the man's face as she desperately pleads for forgiveness for whatever perceived crime she has committed.

He's got a knife. It's him. He must be the murderous villain from my dreams.

I begin to sweat nervously as I struggle to develop a plan. I am wary of the sting of his blade, though eager not to stand idle as he carries out his murderous intent. My response needs to be swift and well executed, that is for sure. Time is fast running out.

I decide in an instant that I have to move forward; I have to discover the nature of their conversation. Proximity is the key here. If anything begins to happen, I must be close enough to react and react swiftly. I have to try and help in some way. I have no idea how I am going to achieve this, particularly considering the lack of police. I doubt the people who lurk throughout the park will be distracted by the shrill screams of a woman under threat. They are so sick they would probably just smile, imagining the pleasure someone is receiving from the grief of another. My body tenses as it opposes my notion to move towards the danger before me.

I walk slowly forward, cautiously touching the ground with each and every step. I try to make as little noise as possible as I squelch across the grass. I dare not look down. My eyes stay peeled on the villain before me. I know he is my only real danger here. I must not alert him to my presence.

CRUNCH!

Instinctively I freeze, as fear spreads through my entire body. I close my eyes and pray silently that my presence has gone unnoticed. Stepping on and breaking a crisp twig is simply the worst thing I could have done. It made such a heavy sound in the stillness that I am sure it must have been heard. I open my eyes with the knowledge that my fate lies in the hands of this villain. I pray he remains in blissful ignorance of my watchful gaze.

I can see the man has stopped pacing. He tilts his head around slightly as a burst of lightning illuminates the night sky. I catch a glimpse of the right side of his stubble clad face. A cigarette hangs loosely between his pursed lips. His blue eyes shimmer with perverse delight as he is hidden in the darkened shadows once more.

"I see we have a spectator to our little tête-à-tête," he says loudly, making sure I can hear every word with the utmost clarity. His voice is calm and confident, just like in my vision. His words send a message of underling malevolence which tingles at my nerves. "If they are clever enough they will know that the best thing to do is to just walk away and forget what they have seen. This is a private dispute between two individuals. It would be unfortunate if an innocent third party was to become an unwitting participant in proceedings."

Damn!

A thunder clap booms loudly, making me jump slightly.

I find myself haunted by the look on the lady's face, revealed by the lighting, as she cowers against the wall. I have never seen such a look of fear before on someone's face. It is an expression which can only be described as that of 'pure hopelessness'. A look of someone who is aware of the dire nature of their predicament and knows for certain that they are about to die a horrible, painful, gruesome death. A death no one will care about.

Even though we are shrouded in darkness, I can tell the man continues to watch me, looking over his shoulder as he draws deep on his cigarette once more. I feel weak in the face of danger. I know the only safe option I have at my disposal is to turn and walk away. As I see his knife glint once more, in a stray beam of light, I know it is the only rational thing to do.

I sigh as I shake my head. My life has been anything other than rational in recent times. The visions are certainly not rational. To stand idle and let someone murder another does not feel rational either. I know what is right and what is wrong. This is wrong by anyone's definition. All I can do is put up a fight on behalf of this fragile angel who shelters, scared to death, in the dim blue light by the bluestone wall.

I consider my options. I decide to try to bluff my way out of this situation. I must provide the allusion of being strong in the face of a bully. I take a deep breath before stating in a controlled manner, "I can't do that."

The man turns stiffly to face me now as the rain slowly begins to fall. I wonder if he is curious as to who might be foolish enough to question his authority in the middle of his fortified domain. Maybe he is a little nervous that someone is willing to take him on. Maybe he is just preparing to attack. Maybe he is just steadying himself for the kill. Maybe he wants to see the face of the fool who is about to die. I hope not.

I notice the woman fails to take her opportunity to run. The focus has been drawn from her to me, yet she doesn't move to scamper off into the safety of the darkness. I guess she is simply too fearful to move or to think. I can only wonder if she is suffering from the side effects of the illegal drugs which, I suspect, course through her veins. After all, aren't all the sex workers in Enterprise Park drug addicts? That is why they have to risk a life on the streets rather than the relative safety of the massage parlors.

The man smiles, his teeth reflected in the dim light. He throws the knife skilfully from hand to hand. Coldly, in a calm voice he says, "Never let it be said that Mad Dog Maddock is nothing, if not a fair man. This is not your problem, my Darling. You don't have to die too in this God forsaken place on this, the most terrible of nights. Think of your family, think of your friends. Do you really want to have them go to the Coroners to identify your badly mutilated body? You would have to be truly heartless to want that."

The words I am about to offer rattle through my brain. All sorts of alarm bells are ringing, though I choose to ignore their perceptive warning. I say boldly, trying to stop my voice from quivering, "If you want to kill her, you'll have to kill me first."

A bolt of lightning illuminates the park. I am shocked to see Mad Dog's face, deeply scarred from a knife attack many years ago, I guess. His eyes are wide open and threatening. His manic stare sends a message; he is seeking blood to be spilled in retaliation for my unwarranted insolence. The knife shimmers with anticipation of action. As he falls back into darkness, I see him shake his head and slowly begin to walk in my direction, "There is no accounting for the stupidity of some people."

"Stay back!" I say defiantly, though with noticeable uncertainty as I begin to walk backwards.

"Don't be frightened, Darling," Mad Dog says, continuing to walk towards me at a slow, considered pace like a panther that has cornered its prey and knows it is only a matter of time for nature to take its course. The knife glints in the dim light, twisting in his hand, as he tries to hide it by his side. "Maybe we can come to some sort of arrangement. After all I have no quarrel with you."

My mind struggles with the concept of 'an arrangement' with a devil like this. I shudder to think what he might seek as fair compensation for sparing my life. I try to summon extra courage and stand my ground. I stop backing away, standing firm on the dew soaked ground, looking directly at the villain moving towards me with sinister intent. I say clearly, "I don't make deals with thugs and murderers."

Mad Dog laughs as he lowers his head and shakes it vigorously. He continues to move towards me as he speaks, "My Darling, you have it all wrong, I haven't murdered anyone. This is all just a curious misunderstanding. I'm sure we can work it all out if you simply stroll a little closer. Maybe we can find a solution in the shadows over there."

I glance over his shoulder as he continues to approach me. The girl has slumped into a ball at the base of the pylon. She is shuddering as she cries uncontrollably. She appears completely distraught with fear. I know she is unable to help herself. She will die tonight if I choose to forsake her. I cannot do that.

For God's sake run!

Taking advantage of my distraction, Mad Dog moves forward, seeking to plunge the knife deep into my stomach. I fail to see the assault coming. However, at the exact same moment Mad Dog lunges, a black cat appears out of the bushes, leaping straight for the arm holding the knife. The cat digs its claws into his flesh producing three long scratch marks along the length of his arm.

"Ahhhh!" Mad Dog screams as he waves his arm, flicking the cat solidly into the nearest pylon. The cat groans mournfully before regaining its feet and slinking off into the scrub. Waving his arm about has caused him to momentarily lose his grip on the knife. It flies up into the air, landing point down into the grass that lies between us. I rush forward, crouching to pick it up. However, Mad Dog is too quick. He reaches the knife before I can grasp it. I take several hurried steps backwards as he slowly stands upright, knife in hand, pointing it towards me once more.

"So you think you are faster than me. Maybe you think you are smarter than me too. Maybe you're just a stupid whore who doesn't know any better," he says shedding his shroud of pretenses that he is my friend.

"I'm just me and that's more than enough to deal with the likes of you," I retort meekly. My stomach squirms as I think of how feeble and weak I must sound. What else can I do? Somehow I have to keep this mongrel's attention and drag him out into a less isolated location. I need to drag him out of his comfort zone, out into the real world where there might be people. Then maybe, just maybe, someone will come to my aid. That might allow the girl to get away, if I am lucky. Not much of a plan, yet it is all I have. All I can do is run with it and hope that it works. At the very least it might buy me some much needed time to think of something better.

I wish there was another way. I wish I wasn't here.

A crack of lightning briefly lights up the shadowy park and illuminates my attacker. He is little more than a few feet away from me now. I can see the cold grin on his face, his wide open, unblinking eyes and the deep scar that dominates his cheek. I can also see the blood dribbling down his arm from where the cat has scratched him.

"Such a pretty one," he says as he continues to walk towards me in a most menacing fashion. I decide to back away at the same pace, trying to keep him in clear sight always. I fear the prospect of falling over something, hidden in the darkness behind me, though I dare not avert my gaze for a second. That is just what this devil wants, an opportunity to strike. "Such a shame you have to die."

"Not today," I say taking a quick glance over my shoulder. I find myself in a fairly open, grassy area. Good, less chance of tripping over something. I also catch a glimpse of the anchor sculpture a short distance away. This is my goal. That sculpture is near the road and bound to be close to people; people who can help. I must draw him to this area if I am to have any chance of surviving this night.

The rain begins to fall heavily now. Mad Dog raises his arms in the air, yelling at the top of his lungs, though barely audible over the raucous noise of the pelting droplets, "See, you can yell as loud as you like, my Darling. No one will hear your cries."

I am about to respond when suddenly he lowers his arms, looks at me with an evil glint in his eye and moves towards me at marching pace. I turn my back, deciding my only chance is to run. I run for all it is worth, slipping every now and then on the damp grassy surface. I turn slightly, not knowing how far my attacker is behind me. I reach the anchor safely and turn around, searching for Mad Dog. He has stopped, only a few feet from me. His position boxes me in. There is no path to escape other than directly past him. My heart pounds as I reach for my back pocket.

"Any last words you'd care to share with me, my Darling?" Mad Dog asks as he lifts the knife high in the air for my benefit. "Do you want to beg for my benevolence?"

I shake my head calmly, "Not really. Actually I would just like to mention that I am not your Darling!."

"Ahhhhh!" Mad Dog screams as he claws desperately at his eyes. He writhes in agony as my hair spray bites deep into his corneas. He stumbles about me, one hand on his eyes, the other swinging the blade wildly, searching for vengeance. I move deftly, avoiding each lunge with ease. My confidence soars as I see Mad Dog floundering. I decide to become more proactive. I lift my leg and let fly with a raised kick to his stomach, sending him staggering backwards. He lands awkwardly on the anchor monument. His form is hidden in the shadows that pervade; so much so that, at first, I cannot determine if I have injured him or not.

"Oh my God!" I scream as another lightning flash illuminates Mad Dog's body, sprawled on the solid metal anchor. Finally I can determine that he is indeed badly injured. His left arm is at an odd angle; an unnatural angle. He stands up, highlighted by the dim light which emanates from the smoldering street lights. He examines his misshapen arm with bewildering calmness. I can see a bone protruding through the broken skin about two inches or so.

To my surprise he laughs raucously, "Pain is nothing to me, my Darling. I wouldn't be cracking open the champagne and breaking out the fondue set just yet."

Mad Dog grasps the wrist of his broken arm and, through gritted teeth, pulls it straight again with a short vicious movement. I cringe at the sound as his bones are roughly aligned back into place.

"Hey, what's going on there?" a man calls out from the bridge. He is one of five blokes running towards us at a frantic pace. I smile knowing help is not far away.

The cavalry is coming!

Mad Dog sees the mob getting closer and decides to conclude our tête-à-tête, at least for now. He leaves me with a parting shot, "I have a memory like an elephant. You had better hope our paths don't cross again, my Darling. I never lose you know. Never!"

With that simple threat, he disappears into the darkness of the park.

"Are you okay?" the first man enquires as my white knights finally arrive. A young man in his twenty's looks me squarely in the eyes, patiently awaiting my response. His friends dash into the park, trying to track Mad Dog in the darkness. I know they will not find him. He is too cunning to be caught so easily. After all, he must know this park like the back of his hand.

"I'm fine but....., but the girl?" I turn and rush back into the bushes, the young man close behind. Within a few seconds we reach the girl. She remains cowering on the ground by the pylon. After some coaxing and reassuring, two of the men help her to her feet, placing a jacket around her shoulders to stave off the cold, unrelenting rain. She looks at me with glazed eyes, her makeup streaming down her face. Somehow she seems to recognize me and gain some comfort from my presence. To my surprise, I recognize her too. She is the pregnant prostitute I encountered earlier in the evening, while walking with Peter.

"Thanks," she murmurs feebly as she smiles with genuine warmth.

"Why did he.....?" I ask as I take her hands in mine.

She places my hands on her stomach as she explains, "I can't earn as much now that I'm carrying his child. It's all my stupid fault, I guess. I should have been more careful."

I pull away, horrified. I shake my head as I back away in the pelting rain. I am astonished by the inhumanity of man. How could some low life try to kill the woman who carries his unborn baby? I stare blankly as the men escort the woman towards the edge of the park. One calls for an ambulance on his mobile phone as I slowly slip away under the cover of chaos. I don't want to answer all the unasked questions that are multiplying in the dark.

Elouise is a forlorn sight, bedraggled and sorrowful, barely able to stay awake now. I shake my head in disbelief at the desperate depths a life can reach. I turn my back on her and head back towards the Crown Towers, knowing in my heart, she should be safe now, at least for tonight. Though sick to the stomach, I walk away content.

*　　　　　*　　　　　*

The door buzzes open as I swipe my electronic key. It swings wide open to reveal Peter standing in front of me, fear engulfing his face.

"Where the hell .....?"

Adrenalin pulses through my body as my mind races, trying to digest what has happened and more importantly what is to occur. I wonder about the smoke, the little girl singing nursery rhymes, the boy with the bouncing ball. Are these all just visions of a future yet to happen? What about the pain in my chest? What is that all about? And the doves, there seems to be a lot of doves behaving strangely or is that just my mind running wild? So many questions; so few answers.

I watch as Peter slowly changes. His image slowly morphs into that of a lady in a ragged, old world dress. She is carrying a baby in her arms. The babies blanket and her dress are covered in blood.

The woman's face glows with excitement even though she is bleeding from a deep cut to her cheek. She says clearly, in a calm voice, as she holds the baby outwards so that I can see, "Hope is a waking dream."

Peter's voice falters as he sees me standing there, hair drenched, clothes soaking wet and clinging to my body. Eyes bloodshot, tears streaming down my face, staring into the distance; I must look quite a sight. I do not see him. I am focused on the strange, though somehow familiar, lady. Instinctively I say softly, "Mary?"

The woman smiles as she slowly disappears in a shower of falling stars. A new question rattles through my overloaded brain.

How do I know your name when we have never met before?

My eyes flutter as I contemplate all the unanswered questions in my life. I need time. I need to work this all out. I need to analyze and decipher. I need to understand everything now. I need to.......

I take two awkward steps forward and faint into Peter's arms.

The world stops spinning.

I am finally relaxed.

Exhausted, though safe at last!

Everything is swallowed by black.

Epilogue

The monster stands up on its hind legs, throws its head back and roars with tremendous force. His voice echoes throughout the cavern. He falls back onto all fours and moves slowly closer to my face. I brace for the final attack.

Suddenly, it dawns on me. I stare into the eyes of the beast as drool oozes from his mouth onto the dust below. I scream at the top of my lungs, "I do not fear you. You cannot harm me. I have vanquished pure evil before, it can be done again. You pose no threat to me."

The beast steps back, blinking his eyes as his feeble brain tries to fathom the meaning of my words. After a few seconds he opens his mouth wide, ready to unleash another earth shaking roar.

I stand my ground. With hands on hips I yell, "Be gone foul beast!"

In a puff of smoke the beast before me disappears. The other beasts look at each other before they too disappear, one after the other. Finally, I am alone in the deserted campsite.

There is a rustle in the bushes as the humans tentatively make their way out from their hiding spots. Eventually all the natives are gathered, looking surprised that the monsters have gone. Flying elves flitter here and there, savouring their new found freedom from tyranny.

Suddenly the earth begins to shake. Part of the roof of the cavern is dislodged, falling as a shower of dust and pebbles. The earth under our feet begins to crack into a fissure. Slowly, from this opening, a mountain like structure begins to emerge. As the rumbling begins to ease, a curious light catches my eyes. Sunlight streams through the settling dust. As my vision clears, I can see the newly formed mountain leads up to a gap in the ceiling, leading out into the world above.

I smile as I think to myself, "There is always hope."

*   *

I wake with a start, expecting to see Mary. I am relieved to see she has gone. Instead, Peter is sound asleep in the bed beside me. I have no idea what time it is other than it is late and still dark outside. There are no monsters. They are all gone now. I shake my head as I think how foolish my nightmares have been. Maybe the monsters were simply the manifestation of my concerns about my strange visions. Maybe the monster disappearing in a cloud of smoke symbolizes that I no longer fear that which I am yet to fully understand. I'm sure that is it, well mostly, anyway. These strange visions no longer worry me.

I changed the future tonight.

I changed people's lives for the better.

I can surely do it again.

Nothing could possibly go wrong now that my eyes are finally awake to this new realm of reality.

Nothing could surely go wrong………… could it?

I smile as I believe that I am now safe. Carefully I lay back down so as not to disturb Peter. Sleep comes to me easily. I am nothing other than exhausted.

For the first time in days, I am at peace.

Grave Misgivings

Book 2

Phoenix

By C. E. Sundstrom

"Hope Is An Illusion"

Julie Mahoney

Prologue

Autumn 2001.
Tuesday Morning.
Salem, New Jersey.

A crisp bronze leaf drifts slowly to the ground. Its movements are uncertain, almost hesitant, as if it has a clear premonition of its fate and is trying desperately to prevent what is about to occur. Swaying, turning, pausing then continuing on its lonely journey. Finally it reaches its inevitable destiny, falling gently on top of the hundreds of similar leaves which cover the meandering curves of Oak Street on this fresh Tuesday morning. The leaf lies silent, without movement, seemingly resigned to the fact that there is no hope. Its journey has concluded. It is simply the natural cycle of life. Born, live, die. No living creature can expect to cheat death. No living creature ever does.

A sound reverberates, drifting in and out, as it is carried on the gentle breeze. At first it is indiscernible, an indistinct mish mash of voices. As the breeze grows steadily stronger, the sound becomes clearer. It is the joyful sounds of children playing, running, riding and getting up to limited mischief. This sound is the reason why properties in this particular suburb are so highly sought. Demand always far exceeds supply. This is a street where neighbors smile, wave and stop to chat; a rare thing in this day and age. Oak Street is a prime example of why people move to Salem, New Jersey. Close enough to commute to offices in New York but safe, predictable and serene. It is America's best kept secret. A place where kids can grow and live safely and their parents can sleep, fully at ease, at night.

Joe Hawkins lives in one of the older buildings in Oak Street. Though he has spent several thousand dollars having the house re-clad in aluminum about six years ago, the basic structure of the building remains the same. It is nearing one hundred and fifty years old.

During the re-cladding, he insisted that the basic structure of his house remain untouched. In fact, he was so concerned about his precious house that he positioned his rocking chair on his front lawn every morning at 7.05am precisely, waiting for when the builders arrived. He would sit there silently, glaring over the top of his newspaper, as the workers went about their business. In his own distinctive words, he was making, "Damn sure" no damage was done to his precious home.

Joe's one great love in life is the preservation of useful old things from by-gone eras. On a good day, he will joke that he aptly meets that description too. On most days he certainly feels like a relic from another time. He gains a sense of strength, of defiance, whenever he encounters old relics. It is like they have found some sort of magical way to endure the ravages of time and thus should be applauded and respected for their unintended longevity. He spends his free time scouring through markets, rummaging through yard sales and the like, searching for his next treasure to acquire and reclaim from the now disinterested world. It is a hobby that he finds very liberating, helping to keep his mind from dwelling on past problems for which he has lost the opportunity to remedy. Though resigned to the fact that he cannot change the past, his mind can't help but revisit and replay situations over and over again, situations which could have had more favorable outcomes if only he had been more diligent, more pro-active. At the end of the day, rehashing the past simply leaves Joe drained and hollow. Sadness overwhelms him as he relives each tragedy which has befallen his life. Collecting distracts his mind, grants him a little peace from a chaotic and often spiteful world.

Joe has another strange quirk of which none of his acquaintances are particularly aware. However, over the years, he has made no attempt to hide it. He just doesn't talk about it. He is a very private individual. One who feels he will be wildly misunderstood by anyone he meets and converses with at length. For this reason, he keeps to himself. His determination to remain completely anti-social is the reason he has no friends to speak of. Life is easier that way, less complicated, less messy. However, his quirk remains undeniable.

When choosing a place to live, Joe searches for various characteristics. He likes quiet, peaceful and pleasant surroundings. He also prefers a reasonable climate, without the extremes in temperature. Overriding everything is one essential requirement, 'Joe's quirk'. For you see, Joe will only settle in a town with a name that appears to be compatible with his unique, warped view on life. The name of the place has to reflect who he is and what he is about, if it is to appeal to him. 'Salem' seems to be just perfect, at least for his present stage in life. After all, where else would someone who regards themselves as little more than a warlock reside? By any definition, those few who know him well, regard him as some sort of warlock. He even has the obligatory black cat as a constant companion, though that is not through choice. It is more 'meant to be'; preordained by the greater universe. Oscar was never invited into his household, he simply arrived one day, taking advantage of an open window and making himself comfortable on a sitting room chair. Joe never had the heart to turf him out. Oscar was just another stray, just the same as Joe.

His house is square. A simple yet sturdy and serviceable design; seven rooms, including a kitchen, sitting room, dining room, laundry and three bedrooms. Joe's bedroom overlooks the glorious view of colorful, century old oak trees which were planted along the road by forward thinking town planners, now long deceased. The facade of the building is brilliant white. Window ledges are painted olive green as a stylish contrast. The shutters remain locked permanently open, no matter what the season or how cold the weather turns. Joe can't be bothered with such mundane tasks as opening and closing shutters. It would send him mad. That is, of course, considering that he may already be insane, by any thinking person's definition of that term.

Joe's house is not huge. Cozy and comfortable would be a more apt description. The two bedrooms upstairs are no longer used, other than for storage. If the truth be known, for several years now, they have steadily been filled to the brim with an eclectic collection of nick-nacks, papers, newspapers and notes scrawled on anything even remotely resembling a piece of paper. These rooms are kept locked at all times even though there appears to be no one desperately seeking admission. It is simply the case that Joe feels that the information housed in these rooms for future reference is too important and, most of all, private. Everything relates to the past in some way. Everything links him to the past. There are too many secrets here. Secrets Joe is determined to keep hidden.

Joe spends most of his time living in the lower half of the house. It certainly shows. Rubbish is strewn everywhere. Pizza boxes are mainly piled up in one corner of the sitting room in a vain attempt at tidiness. Clothes are strewn everywhere; over chairs, on the kitchen table, on the floor, even hanging awkwardly over a reading lamp which stands precariously on a stained, pine side table. There is no way of distinguishing which clothes are clean and which ones are due to be laundered. In fact, the scene presents any unsuspecting visitor with the impression that most of the clothes need to be washed.

Empty beer cans are scattered in a chaotic manner throughout all of the lower floor rooms. The black garbage bag, set aside for them in the kitchen, is empty save for three cans correctly stowed in a brief moment of house cleaning four months ago. Six month supplies of empty bottles of 'Jack' are partially visible from under disheveled cushions on the sofa. They also sit on the mantle in the sitting room and on several of the window sills. There is even a large collection which completely covers the top of the television. Recent newspapers are thrown onto a hap hazard stack in the corner of the sitting room. It is an understatement to say that any stranger who has the misfortune to enter into Joe's slum would quickly and correctly comment that 'it lacked a woman's touch'.

From amongst the sheets and blankets, thrown carelessly in a heap on the bed, something indiscernible begins to stir. After a brief struggle, a bleary eyed, grey balding head appears. Joe frowns as he slowly comes to terms with the pain undissipated from the night before. Scratching his scalp vigorously, he ruffles his long, sparse hair into a wiry mess. Moaning, still groggy as a result of the sedatives and alcohol consumed earlier, he rises awkwardly from amongst his refuge of blankets. Dangling his scrawny legs over the side of the bed, he takes a moment to gather some breath and elusive energy. He pauses, breathing deliberately, as he waits for his stomach to settle a little and the threat of a cataclysmic eruption to abate. Slowly reaching down, he pulls on some shoes; one a brown slipper, the other a fluffy purple moccasin. Joe is completely unconcerned with his appearance. When you live alone there is no one passing judgment on your fashion sense. Practicality is of greater importance. Both shoes are comfortable and available, that is all that matters.

Eventually Joe rises successfully with an audible 'creak' caused by straightening his arthritic legs. He busily rubs his half-closed eyes back to life with one hand while scratching his backside, through his baggy black and white polka dot shorts, with the other. Staggering through his self-created minefield of obstacles, he moves towards the sitting room as he searches desperately for his 'salvation'.

The bottle of pain killers is easy, still in his shorts pocket from the night before. Still containing a few more days respite. A source of liquid is harder to find. Tap water is out of the question. The mere suggestion of drinking that 'piss' would be enough to offend his sensibilities and incur the full force of his ill-tempered, unbridled wrath. Something strong which warms and clears the throat is what his heart desires. He tries several bottles of Jack Daniels, dispatching each losing candidate to a different spot on the floor with a casual, hate filled throw. Finally, he finds a bottle behind a cushion on the couch. Holding it by the neck, he sways dangerously as he raises it above his head. Catching a narrow beam of light seeping through a crack between the curtains, he illuminates its contents. He smiles as he discovers it still contains one more mouthful of precious elixir. Taking an inexact handful of tablets, followed by a Whiskey chaser, he completes his goal of trying to self-medicate some relief.

Joe's pain is constant and relentless. However, he is well aware it is not life threatening, not for him at least. It is an all too familiar pain which stabs viciously at his chest, causing him great discomfort. He has experienced this pain many times over the years though, in the past, it has been far less severe than its current inflammation. Joe is well aware of its cause, well aware that there is no doctor in the world who can cure what ails him. He has become an expert, untrained practitioner, who has become adept at self-treatment without doing self-harm. However, he is unsure of how to alleviate the pain this time. Though he won't admit it, this more ferocious pain scares him greatly. He is well aware the pain will pass, just not quite sure when. It has never lasted for weeks before; usually only minutes, maybe hours at most.

"So what are you planning to do, just ignore your pain? You know what it means, why don't you do something?" asks the familiar voice of the man seated in the only comfortable arm chair, located on the other side of the sitting room. The man is young, probably in his early twenty's. He is dressed in a stylish leather jacket over a white T shirt. Grey trousers fail to hide his expertly polished leather shoes. His dark brown hair is slicked back with grease. His deep brown eyes glow with smugness. If, by chance, his eyes were filled with anger and self-loathing instead, their similarity would be unmistakable, they would be identical to Joe's.

Joe holds the bottle by the neck as he shakes his head, trying to ignore his brother. His vision remains cloudy; a major concern. Joe has developed, over the years, an ability to view situations clearly. To walk his way through what he can see in order to identify problems and try his best to alleviate any adverse situations. His inability to see the current situation with clarity prevents him from being able to promptly rectify his problems. He knows if he can't overcome his problems, then other people will suffer too. Many people will suffer. Many people will die. The painkillers and alcohol, though deadening the pain a little, are certainly not helping his situation at all.

"You can't ignore what is going on," Stanley implores as he stands lithely, brushing the creases out of his trousers. "You must act and act now!"

"Shut up!" Joe says as he stares into his brother's eyes. "What do you expect me to do? This is too big. This is just too damn big for me, for anyone."

Joe's brother returns the stare with pleading eyes. He wonders how Joe's sanity and strength are holding up. He has grave fears for his younger brother's mental state. After all, Joe has been through an awful lot since this all began. He has seen more tragedy than most during his lifetime. Stanley decides to change tack, "Hey, brother. Never forget. There is always hope. You must not......"

Joe fumes, all his emotions bubbling to the surface at once, "There is no damn hope! There is no such word. That emotion, that God damn sensation is lost to me. All that remains is pain, misery, death and ..... and ....."

"And what?," Stanley enquires partly through interest and partly to see if he can generate some measure of fight in this tired old man staggering awkwardly in front of him.

Joe looks at Stanley as rage courses through every cell of his body. Coolly he talks in a calm, clear, yet strangely manic voice. He leaves his brother with little doubt as to his state of sanity. His voice rises in intensity with each word uttered, "And with any luck there is another God damn bottle of this fine beverage to help deaden the pain. All I seek is a blissful stupor of ignorance so that I don't need to continue to listen to your pitiful drivel and meaningless piffle!"

Taking careful aim, Joe throws the empty bottle at his brother. His accuracy is exceptional considering his intoxicated state. The bottle somersaults and flies straight at his brother's head, causing a curious reaction. Instead of hitting him squarely, causing considerable injury, the bottle travels straight through him. His body changes, becoming a shower of sparkling dust particles. This metamorphosis occurs from head to toe until all the star dust falls steadily to the carpeted floor and disappears without a trace. Nothing is left of his brother. The bottle hits the back of the armchair and bounces harmlessly onto the floor. Laughter echoes through the room as Stanley taunts his brother still, in Joe's empty yet crowded mind.

Joe turns away. His shoulders slump with a sensation of melancholy which slowly spreads through his body. The noise resonating in his ears is something he has never experienced before, something inhumane. It is a screeching, buzzing sound growing steadily in intensity. It is unrelenting as it builds to its ultimate crescendo.

Throughout the house, near every open window, Joe has placed dozens of different wind chimes in order to help dampen any imaginary sounds his mind might normally hear. There are ones with metal cylinders, another with glass butterflies. Several are ceramic. One is made from discarded cutlery. Joe's wind chimes are installed in such a way that they operate effectively, even in the absence of a gentle breeze. If there is no wind, he simply switches on strategically placed fans to activate the chimes. This process is normally extremely effective and fulfils Joe's yearning for a noise interrupted environment. The detailed process he has implemented at least dampens the noise from which he seeks sanctuary. It is his way of making the most of a bad hand which life has dealt him.

Moving swiftly around the room, he switches on fan after fan until all ten are activated, creating a mini whirlpool of wind and a terrible racket.

He stands with hands on hips, frustrated, head bowed, drained of meaningful ideas. This new sound is impossible to block out. It is a powerful, droning sound, filled with fear and horror. It is a sound that will not be denied, a sound which refuses to identify itself. It is a foreboding sound which Joe both respects and dreads greatly. It is the sound of an approaching 'shit storm', the likes of which the world has never seen.

Joe's epic staggering leads him back to the faded curtains drawn tight at his bedroom window. With a quick movement he opens the curtains, revealing a bright, sunny, autumn morning. He becomes aware of his mistake instantly as his eyes scream out in pain. He squints and moans loudly as he closes them with a flourish. Suddenly, a little clarity appears in his mind. He begins to realize that some of the noises rattling through his tormented brain might be coming from his surroundings, rather than being figments of his furtive imagination. He focuses momentarily, trying to locate the source of the sound. Finally his brain deciphers the direction and cause of the unnecessary disturbance. There is someone pounding on his front door. He shakes his head as he wonders what more this day can bring.

Changing direction, he slowly shuffles towards the bedroom door. Joe grabs at his eyes in obvious distress as he yells, "Okay, okay already. I'm coming for God sake!"

The pounding continues unabated as Joe stumbles across the sitting room floor once more, lacking any sign of genuine coordination. Successfully negotiating the one step to the front door, he reaches for the handle. Looking down he sees Oscar sitting, staring at the door. Oscar turns and stares at Joe with his bloodshot eyes as a tuft of fur drops quietly from his mangy skin, onto the floor.

"Don't you start," Joe says quietly to his only friend, the twelve year old scruffy, black cat. Lashing out in Oscar's direction, he flicks his slipper at the cat. Oscar quickly scurries away, out of sight, emitting a disgusted squeal. After all, all he was trying to do was help.

In an instant everything is gone. There is nothing; not a sound, a shape, an object or a smell. Joe is simply weightless, surrounded by a dark vacuous void. It is like he is floating in the center of a black hole. Only darkness, silence and Joe exist in this realm. Everything else, that ever was, has simply vanished. For a moment Joe is content. He is at peace. Drifting slowly in his private universe, he remains calm. He is not frightened in the slightest by the darkness that abounds. Instead he rejoices in its tranquility of emptiness. In his heart he prays that this is what death will be like, once his name is finally elevated in italics to the top of the Grim Reapers scroll of doom. An eternity of nothing would be heaven; no one wanting help, no one accusing him of inaction. No problems, no voices, just nothing, just heavenly peace.

Through the depthless black, Joe sees a small creature walking towards him. Instantly he recognizes his friend and loyal companion. Oscar walks slowly up to Joe, purring as he rubs affectionately against his leg. Joe nods resigned somewhat, "I know, I know old fella. I have to face what burdens me so. I know. It is not right to hide here. It's not right to lash out at you too when the problem is with me. I'm sorry for treating you wrong."

Joe sighs and belts the side of his head several times with the open palm of his hand. His action is primitive and painful though has been effective before in correcting the short circuit malfunction in his brain. Slowly his eyes become foggy then readjust as normality begins to re-appear like a billowing mirage in front of his eyes. Within a few seconds, everything has returned. He reclaims his world, reluctantly tolerating the normality returning in all its familiar glory. He glances around the room quickly, taking in his surroundings, satisfying himself that everything is right with his world. Ensuring nothing has changed is important. His vulnerability is at its greatest when he has these episodes. Sometimes they last for seconds, sometimes for days. Thankfully this episode seems to be seconds or maybe minutes at most. Joe nods, satisfied nothing has changed, before continuing to move towards the door.

Hobbling on one clothed foot, he takes a step forward. Clenching his eyes shut in preparation for the light, Joe grasps the handle and yanks the door open as he yells, "What?"

A thin, blonde haired, well groomed man in a smart, navy blue business suit is standing on the doorstep. He is carrying a clip board looking very officious and slightly startled. The man takes a step backwards as he regains his composure and assesses the situation before him. He was not expecting to be greeted by an aggressive, old, derelict of a man scratching his crotch in a pair of polka dot boxer shorts while wearing one fluffy purple moccasin. Straightening his suit, brushing back his already immaculately moussed hair, composure restored, he moves his arm forward in anticipation to shake Joe's hand. He says politely, "Good morning, Sir. I'm Horatio Sparks, President of the West Salem residents group and I'd like to speak......"

Joe frowns, eyes locked firmly closed. He says angrily, "I couldn't give a damn who you are; I'm still not buying any raffle tickets or inedible cookies made in a Korean sweat shop three years ago by some peasant who doesn't even have clean water to wash their filthy hands with. That is why you are here aren't you? To be annoying, invading my privacy and the like? There is only one thing you can do for me today. You can go and piss off!"

With all the force he can muster, Joe tries to shut the front door.

Horatio, places his shiny, size 11, business shoe in the doorway, preventing its closure. He draws a deep breath before stating his case succinctly, in a completely unambiguous manner for Joe, "Sir, you misunderstand the purpose of my visit. My conversation with you is of the utmost importance and cannot be left to another day. I implore you to at least allow me the opportunity to come inside and discuss the problem at hand, like mature gentlemen. I'm sure once we've discussed the issue thoroughly, we will be able to develop some form of resolution, to your satisfaction, that will satisfy all aggrieved parties in this instance."

With anger brewing from deep in his soul, Joe slowly opens his eyes and glares down at the insolent foot blocking his door. He pulls the door open once again, moving forward as he confronts his trespasser. He asks abrasively, "What the hell are you talking about? What problem? What's your problem?"

"This problem," Horatio says as he takes a step backwards. He turns and motions with his arm in a wide arc. The area he highlights encompasses the entire region directly beyond the front step, out into the front yard and beyond.

For the first time, Joe looks around and surveys the situation outside the walls of his house. Blinking, he steps forward. Brushing Horatio aside as, gob smacked, he strives for a better look. Every muscle in his body begins to tense as he realizes the time has come. He gazes in disbelief at the sight in front of him. His brain tries to reason with the enormity of what his eyes are witnessing. However it is too bizarre, even for Joe. During his life he has seen many unusual events, which few would believe. The scale and nature of this event leaves Joe numb.

A breeze rustles Joe's wispy hair as a voice whispers in his ear, "Hope is......."

"Shut up!" Joe screams.

"I'm sure we can fix the problem. Maybe if you stopped feeding them," Horatio says, more as a token gesture than anything else. He can clearly see Joe is not listening. Joe is wandering around, mouth gaping open, silent, in thoughtful contemplation. He knows the ramifications of this 'sign', though he refuses to admit to himself that there is a problem here. It is a problem too large for Joe to have any hope of fixing at this late stage, in his current state of mental and physical health.

On his lawn, his car, his fences, every branch of his oak tree, the road in front of his property and on all the adjourning properties they sit. All of them are behaving exactly the same way. There are too many to count. At a guess there must be thousands of pure, snow white doves cooing, all staring directly at Joe's house as if they are waiting for him, begging with their sorrowfully eyes to do something, anything that might help avert a catastrophe.

Residents have gathered en-mass to look at this extraordinary, once in a life time event. They are climbing on the fences, standing on the lawn pointing, in the middle of the road taking photos. Some are smiling; some are more cautious and a little fearful. All in all everyone is looking dumbfounded, wondering what has transpired to bring about this strange gathering of doves around a single house in a quiet non-descript street. The only person not wondering is Joe. He knows exactly why they are here and what their large numbers imply.

"Oh my God, oh my God!' Joe begins to call out repeatedly. At first his words are nearly inaudible, drowned out by the incessant cooing of the birds and the dull murmur coming from the crowd. His words increase their intensity rapidly and, within a matter of seconds, Joe has the full attention of the assembled masses. It is at this moment that he turns sharply and starts to run in an awkward, slow, arthritic manner back towards the sanctity of his house. His body cannons into Horatio's shoulder leaving him sprawled, bruised and shaken on the ground. Joe, inconsiderately, runs past him without offering an apology or a sideways glance. Grabbing the door handle, he slams the door shut behind him, bolting it firmly as he disappears from inquisitive eyes.

Everyone continues to stand around nervously, watching the masses of seemingly friendly doves gathered in front of them. Conflicting theories abound as to what they are waiting for. However, one thing is certain; they don't want to miss what happens next. Maybe, at the very least, someone will explain what is happening. Everyone feels it is more important to be watching this curious sight, first hand, rather than leaving for school or work. Something extraordinary is happening in their own neighborhood and they all want to be part of it.

Police and fire crews assemble. Though coordinated, they are unprepared to deal with this strange situation. They gather to one side in a huddle. Chatting, shaking their heads, while their faces remain emotionless as they try to assess the impossible situation in front of them. The camera crews, with their media vans, begin to arrive, setting up for their first live broadcasts of the 'Amazing Dove Incident'. Two reporters are preparing for a live cross as the whole scene changes unexpectedly for the worst.

One dove in the middle of the lawn suddenly spontaneously combusts in a ball of orange flames, causing an audible hush in the crowd. In a fraction of a second the unbelievable begins to occur. Several hundred of the doves die, raining down onto the lawn from out of the oak tree and along the line of the fence. Others catch fire, for no apparent reason, as they walk around or fly by. The fiery airborne doves begin to rain down like a barrage of flaming missiles, landing amongst the spectators, hitting some of their cars. Still more doves seem to disintegrate into balls of flame, disappearing in clouds of dust and ash. About three quarters of the birds appear unaffected and continue to sit calmly amongst the chaos that abounds. They stare unflinching at Joe's house. It is as if they are waiting for his return, seeking his blessed gift of salvation.

Children and adults alike begin to run in a frenzied, traumatized fashion. They try desperately to escape the carnage that is unfolding before their disbelieving eyes. Many are horrified, their brains in neutral, thoughts going blank. All they can think of is self-preservation. They clamber over each other as they run towards the perceived safety of their homes. Considering the apocalyptic nature of the drama unfolding before them, some fear their nearby homes are in jeopardy too. These people run down the street trying to get as far away as possible from the danger at hand. Some just run, knowing instinctively they should run, yet not knowing when or where it is safe to stop.

The camera crews are nearly ready to start their coverage when the reporters pause. They hold onto their earpieces as they receive some form of message from a faceless person manning a control room some distance away. They appear distracted by the message, disregarding the incredible story unfolding right in front of them. They signal earnestly to the bewildered cameramen. Suddenly the crews begin to pack the equipment back into the vans at a brisk pace. The faces of the film crews are ashen, devoid of blood, as if they have all simultaneously seen a ghost. Their actions seem peculiar considering they have all independently made a collective decision to halt coverage of the biggest story of the century unfolding before their eyes. This is the most bizarre situation they would ever have the opportunity to cover, yet somehow, they are simply not interested.

Frantic announcements resound loud and clear over the emergency radios. There appears to be a larger story beginning to unfold; something which overshadows the bizarre events in front of the emergency services. The police and fire brigades all begin to pack up and leave. Visibly shaken, they clamber onto their vehicles. Flicking on lights, engaging sirens, they race to leave in a frenzied tangle of appliances. All are fearful. All are confused.

Though their minds refuse to acknowledge what is occurring, they all know that it is something big; something at the World Trade Center in New York. The initial reports are saying there is some kind of major fire or bomb blast in one of the towers. Within minutes they are all hurrying as they hear the first frantic eye witness reports that a plane may have hit one of the towers. The story about the doves is over shadowed and lost from its rightful place as the lead story on every channel of the world's media. From this moment on there is only one story of significance, only one story that will be covered today and in the weeks to come. From this point on, nobody will remember the strange exploding doves.

Inside the house Joe is distraught. With tears running down his face he slumps into his old, comfortable armchair as he stares in disbelief at the scenes unfolding on the television in front of him. The pain in his chest is excruciating, though he knows all too well it is not life threatening. Death will not be a source of peaceful release from the misery that he endures. The screams are loud and long, inside his head. He shuts his eyes, though this doesn't help. He can still see them in pain, burning, moving around him in a disorientated manner, screaming for help, their arms outstretched, pleading. He says softly, repeatedly as the words catch in his throat as if they are barbed, "I couldn't...., they wouldn't listen....., I couldn't......"

Oscar walks slowly over to the foot of the chair. He looks up at the only human companion he has ever known. He surveys the pain visible in his tense facial muscles and the tears rolling steadily down Joe's face. Oscar stretches up to rub his head against his master's limp hand as a sign of respect and comfort in a time of grief. With a deft leap he lands on his master's lap, moving through a turn and a half before finally curling into a ball and settling. He purrs with vigor, trying to help in the best way he can, to alleviate some of the pain his friend is feeling. He has always been there for Joe in his hour of need.

Outside the house, calmness has descended. All the voyeurs have disappeared. The remaining live doves sit calmly next to the recently deceased. All the doves remain staring at Joe's house, cooing sweetly. They all seem to be waiting for something. There is nothing Joe can do for them now. It is all too late. Their pleading eyes continue to haunt him in the darkness behind his closed eyes.

From one of the Oak trees a single leaf is shed. Carried on the prevailing wind its movements are hesitant, almost uncertain, as if it has a clear premonition of its fate. Swaying, turning, pausing then continuing on its lonely journey, it moves towards Joe's front door. Gently it lands on the welcome mat. It lays silent, immobile, apparently resigned to its fate. It appears to realize its life has finished. It seems to know there is no hope.

www.ingramcontent.com/pod-product-compliance
Lightning Source LLC
Chambersburg PA
CBHW061311170626
46817CB00001B/138